Praise for *New York Times* and *USA TODAY* bestselling author Jayne Ann Krentz

"One of the hottest writers of romance today."
—*USA TODAY*

"Krentz's storytelling shines with
authenticity and dramatic intensity."
—*Publishers Weekly*

"Krentz's flair for creating intriguing, inventive plots;
crafting clever dialogue between two perfectly matched
protagonists; and subtly infusing her writing with a deliciously
tart sense of humor are, as always, simply irresistible."
—*Booklist*

Praise for *New York Times* and *USA TODAY* bestselling author Lindsay McKenna

"Talented Lindsay McKenna delivers
excitement and romance in equal measure."
—*RT Book Reviews*

"Another masterpiece."
—*Affaire de Coeur* on *Enemy Mine*

"Buckle in for the ride of your life."
—*Writers Unlimited* on *Morgan's Mercenaries: Heart of Stone*

Praise for *USA TODAY* bestselling author B.J. Daniels

"Daniels has a knack with small towns,
bigger-than-life characters and twisted situations."
—*RT Book Reviews*

"Daniels knows how to write a mystery
and a strong family drama."
—*RT Book Reviews*

Tough Enough

NEW YORK TIMES BESTSELLING AUTHORS

JAYNE ANN KRENTZ

& LINDSAY MCKENNA

USA TODAY BESTSELLING AUTHOR

B.J. DANIELS

HQN™

ISBN-13: 978-0-373-77660-3

TOUGH ENOUGH

Recycling programs
for this product may
not exist in your area.

PLEASE RECYCLE
THIS PRODUCT IS RECYCLABLE

THE COWBOY

CONTENTS

THE COWBOY   7

THE COUGAR   215

MURDER AT LAST CHANCE RANCH   427

PROLOGUE

"Margaret, promise me you'll be careful." Sarah Fleetwood Trace, struggling to get out of her frothy wedding gown with the help of her two best friends, paused
and frowned. For an instant the joyous glow that had
infused her all day vanished. She looked at Margaret
Lark, her fey hazel eyes clouded with sudden concern.

Margaret smiled reassuringly as she carefully
lifted Sarah's veil and set it aside. "Don't worry about
me, Sarah, I'll be fine. I promise to look both ways
before crossing the street, count calories and not talk
to strange men."

Katherine Inskip Hawthorne, concentrating on the
row of tiny buttons that followed Sarah's spine, flashed
a brief grin. "Don't get carried away, Margaret. You're
allowed to talk to a few strange men. Just exercise some
discretion."

Sarah groaned, her golden-brown hair moving in
a heavy wave. Diamonds set in an old-fashioned gold
design glittered in her ears. "This isn't a joke, you two.
Margaret, I have a feeling…" She nibbled her lip in con-
centration. "I just want you to be careful for a while, all
right?"

"Careful?" Margaret arched her brows in amusement. "Sarah, you know I'm always careful. What could
possibly happen to me while you're on your honeymoon?"

"I don't know, that's the whole problem," Sarah said in exasperation. "I told you, I just have this feeling."

"Forget your feeling. This is your wedding day." Kate undid the last of the buttons, green eyes sparkling with laughter. "Your famous intuition probably isn't functioning normally at the moment. All the excitement, champagne and rampaging hormones have undoubtedly gotten it temporarily off track."

Margaret grinned as she hung up the wedding gown. "I don't know about Sarah's hormones, but I think it's a good bet Gideon's are rampaging. The last time I saw him, he was looking very impatient. We'd better get you changed and on your way, Sarah, before your husband comes looking for you. He's very good at finding things."

Sarah hesitated, her worried gaze still on Margaret, and then she relaxed back into the glorious smile she had worn for the past few hours. "Having a big wedding was Gideon's idea. He'll just have to put up with the necessary delays."

"Gideon doesn't strike me as the type to put up with anything he doesn't want to put up with." Margaret handed a quince-colored shirt to Sarah along with a pair of jeans.

Kate chuckled as she reached for a brush. "I had the same impression. He's a lot like Jared in that respect. Are you really going to spend your honeymoon on a treasure hunt, Sarah? I can think of better things to do."

"I can't," Sarah said blithely as she slipped into the jeans. She leaned toward the mirror to touch up her lipstick.

Margaret met her eyes in the mirror, warmed by her friend's evident happiness. "Hoping to find another treasure like the Fleetwood Flowers?"

Sarah touched the diamond earrings she was still wearing. "There will never be another treasure like the Flowers. After all, when I went looking for them, I found Gideon."

"What did you do with the other four sets of earrings?" Kate asked.

"Gideon has them safely hidden. He chose this pair for me to wear today." Sarah turned away from the mirror and buttoned the bright-colored shirt. "Okay, I'm ready." She hugged Kate and then Margaret. "Thank you both so much. I don't know what I would do without either of you. You're more important to me than I can ever say."

Margaret felt herself grow a little misty. She quickly blinked away the moisture. "You don't have to say it. We all understand."

Kate smiled tremulously. "That's right. You don't have to say it. Friends for life, right?"

"Right. Nothing will ever change that." Sarah pulled back, her expressive face full of emotion. "There's something very special about a woman's friends, isn't there?"

"Very special," Margaret agreed. She picked up Sarah's shoulder bag and handed it to her. "Something very special about a husband like Gideon Trace, too. Don't keep him waiting any longer."

Sarah's eyes danced. "Don't worry, I won't."

Margaret followed her friends into the elevator and across the hotel lobby to the large room where the wedding reception was still in full swing. A crowd composed chiefly of other writers, bookstore people and their families milled about inside, sipping champagne and dancing to the music of a small band.

As the three women stepped through the open doorway, two big, lean men moved into their path. One of them reached for Sarah's hand, a look of proud satisfaction on his face. The other flashed a wicked pirate's grin and took Kate's arm.

Margaret stood quietly to the side, studying the two males who had claimed her best friends as brides. On the surface there was no great similarity between Gideon Trace and Jared Hawthorne, other than the fact that they were both large and both moved with the kind of fluid grace that came from strength.

But although they looked nothing alike there was something about them that stamped them both as being of the same mold. They were men in the old-fashioned sense of the word—men with an inner core of steel, a bit arrogant, perhaps, a bit larger than life, but the kind of men who could be relied upon when the chips were down. They were men who lived by their own codes.

Margaret had met only one other man who was in the same league. That momentous event had occurred last year and the fallout from the explosive encounter had destroyed her career in the business world and left her bruised emotionally for a very long while. A part of her would never completely recover.

Dressed in black and white formal attire, both Jared and Gideon were devastating although neither was particularly handsome. There was an edge to them, Margaret realized—a hardness that commanded an unconscious respect.

Jared was the more outgoing of the two. He had an easy, assured manner that bordered on the sardonic. Gideon, on the other hand, had a dour, almost grim look about him that altered only when he looked at Sarah.

"About time you got down here," Gideon said to his

new wife. "I've had enough wedding party to last me a lifetime."

"This was all your idea," Sarah reminded him, standing on tiptoe to brush her lips against the hard line of his jaw. "I would have been happy to run off to Las Vegas."

"I wanted to do it right," he told her. "But now it's been done right. So let's get going."

"Fine with me. When are you going to tell me where, exactly, we're going to?"

Gideon smiled faintly. "As soon as we're in the car. You've already said goodbye to your family?"

"Yes."

"Right." Gideon looked at Jared. "We're going to slide out of here. Thanks for playing best man."

"No problem." Jared held out his hand. His eyes met Gideon's in a man-to-man exchange. "See you on Amethyst Island one of these days. We'll go looking for that cache of gold coins I told you about."

Gideon nodded as he shook hands. "Sounds good. Let's go, Sarah."

"Yes, Gideon," Sarah spoke with mock demureness, her love as bright in her eyes as the diamonds in her ears. Gideon took her hand and led her swiftly out the door and into the Seattle night.

Margaret, Kate and Jared watched them go and then Kate rounded on her husband. "What cache of gold coins?"

"Didn't I ever tell you about that chest of gold my ancestor is supposed to have buried somewhere on the island?" Jared looked surprised by his own oversight.

"No, you did not."

Jared shrugged. "Must have slipped my mind. But unfortunately that old pirate didn't leave any solid clues behind so I've never bothered trying to find his treasure. Trace said he might be able to help. I took him up on the offer."

Kate smiled, pleased. "Well, at least it's a good excuse to get Gideon and Sarah out to the island soon. You'll come, too, won't you, Margaret?"

"Of course," Margaret agreed. "Wouldn't miss it for the world. Now, if you'll excuse me, I promised one more dance to a certain gentleman."

Kate's eyes widened. "You mean, an *interesting* gentleman?"

"Very interesting," Margaret said, laughing. "But unfortunately, a bit young for me." She waved at Jared's son, David, as the boy zigzagged toward them through the crowd. The youngster, who was ten years old, was an attractive miniature of his father, right down to the slashing grin. He even wore his formal clothes with the same confident ease.

"You ready to dance yet, Ms. Lark?" David asked as he came to a halt in front of her.

"I'm ready, Mr. Hawthorne."

THREE HOURS LATER, MARGARET got out of the cab in front of her First Avenue apartment building and walked briskly toward the entrance. The cool Seattle summer evening closed in around her bringing with it the scent of Elliott Bay.

A middle-aged woman with a small dog bouncing at her heels came through the plate-glass doors. She smiled benignly at Margaret.

"Lovely evening, isn't it, Ms. Lark?"

"Very lovely, Mrs. Walters. Have a nice walk with Gretchen." The little dog yapped and hopped about even more energetically at the sound of her name. Margaret smiled briefly and found it something of an effort. She realized that she was suddenly feeling tired and curiously let down.

There was more to it than that, she acknowledged as she crossed the well-appointed lobby and stepped into the elevator. An unusual sense of loneliness had descended on her after the wedding reception had ended. The excitement of planning the event and the fun of seeing her two best friends again was over.

Her friends were both gone now, Sarah on her mysterious honeymoon, Kate back to Amethyst Island. It would be a long time before Margaret saw either of them again and when she did things would be a little different.

In the past they had all shared the freedom of their singlehood together. Late evening calls suggesting a stroll to the Pike Place Market for ice cream, Saturday morning coffee together at an espresso bar downtown while they bounced plot ideas off each other, the feeling of being able to telephone one another at any hour of the day or night; all that had been changed in the twinkling of two wedding rings. Sarah had found her adventurer and Kate had found her pirate.

Sarah and Kate were still her closest friends in the world, Margaret told herself. Nothing, not even marriage, could ever change that. The bond between them that had been built initially on the fact that they all wrote romance novels had grown too strong and solid to ever be fractured by time or distance. But the practicalities of the friendship had definitely been altered.

Marriage had a way of doing that, Margaret reflected wryly. A year ago she herself had come very close to being snared in the bonds of matrimony. A part of her still wondered what her life would be like now if she had married Rafe Cassidy.

The answer to that question was easy. She would have been miserable. The only way she would have been happy with Rafe was by changing him and no woman could ever change Rafe Cassidy. Everyone who knew him recognized that Cassidy was a law unto himself.

Now what on earth had brought back the painful memories of Rafe?

She was getting maudlin. Probably a symptom of post-wedding party letdown. She thought she had successfully exorcised that damned cowboy from her mind.

Margaret stepped out of the elevator into the hushed, gray-carpeted hall. Near her door a soft light glowed from a glass fixture set above a small wooden table that held an elegant bouquet of flowers. The flowers were shades of palest mauve and pink.

Margaret halted to fish her key out of her small gilded purse. Then she slid the key into the lock and turned the handle. She thought fleetingly of bed and knew that, tired though she was, she was not yet ready to sleep. Perhaps she would go over the last chapter of her current manuscript. There were a few changes she wanted to make.

It was as she pushed open the door and stepped into the small foyer that she realized something was wrong. Margaret froze and peered into the shadows of her living room. For a moment she saw nothing but deeper shadow and then her vision adjusted to the darkness and she saw the long legs clad in gray trousers.

They ended in hand-tooled Western boots that were arrogantly propped on her coffee table. The boots were fashioned of very supple, very expensive, pearl-gray leather into which had been worked an intricate design of desert flowers beautifully detailed in rich tones of gold and blue.

A pearl-gray Stetson had been carelessly tossed onto the table beside the boots.

The hair on the back of Margaret's neck suddenly lifted as a sense of impending danger washed over her.

Sarah's words came back in a searing flash. *Promise me you'll be careful.*

She should have heeded her friend's intuitive warning, Margaret thought. Instinctively she took a step back toward the safety of the hall.

"Don't run from me, Maggie. This time I'll come after you."

Margaret stopped, riveted at the sound of the deep, rough-textured voice. It was a terrifyingly familiar voice—a voice that a year ago had been capable of sending chills of anticipation through her—a voice that had ultimately driven her away from the man she loved with words so cruel they still scalded her heart.

For one wild moment Margaret wondered if her thoughts had somehow managed to conjure reality out of thin air. Then again, perhaps she was hallucinating.

But the boots and the hat did not disappear when she briefly closed her eyes and reopened them.

"What on earth are you doing here?" Margaret whispered.

Rafe Cassidy's faint smile was cold in the pale gleam of the city lights that shone through the windows. "You know the answer to that, Maggie. There's only one reason I would be here, isn't there? I've come for you."

CHAPTER ONE

"HOW DID YOU GET IN HERE, Rafe?" Not the brightest of questions under the circumstances, but the only coherent one Margaret could come up with in that moment. She was so stunned, she could barely think at all.

"Your neighbor across the hall took pity on me when she found out I'd come all this way just to see you and you weren't here. It seems the two of you exchanged keys in case one of you got locked out. She let me in."

"It looks like I'd better start leaving my spare key with one of the other neighbors. Someone who has a little more common sense."

"Come on in and close the door, Maggie. We have a lot to talk about."

"You're wrong, Rafe. We have nothing to talk about." She stood where she was, refusing to leave the uncertain safety of the lighted hall.

"Are you afraid of me, Maggie?" Rafe's voice was cut glass and black velvet in the darkness. There was a soft, Southwestern drawl in it that only served to heighten the sense of danger. It was the voice of a gunfighter inviting some hapless soul to his doom in front of the saloon at high noon.

Margaret said nothing. She'd already been involved in one showdown with Rafe and she'd lost.

Rafe's smile grew slightly more menacing as he reached out and flicked on the light beside his chair. It gleamed off his dark brown hair and threw the harsh, aggressive lines of his face into stark relief. His gray, Western-cut jacket was slung over a convenient chair and his long-sleeved white shirt was open at the throat. Silver and turquoise gleamed in the elaborate buckle of the leather belt that circled his lean waist.

"There's no need to be afraid of me, Maggie. Not now."

The not so subtle taunt had the effect Margaret knew Rafe intended it to have. She moved slowly into the foyer and closed the door behind her. For an instant she was angry with herself for obeying him. Then she reminded herself that this was her apartment.

"I suppose there's not much point in telling you I don't want you here?" she asked as she tossed her small golden purse down onto a white lacquer table.

"You can kick me out later. After we've talked. Why don't you pour yourself a brandy for your nerves and we'll continue this conversation in a civilized manner."

She glanced at the glass he held in one hand and realized he'd found her Scotch. The bottle had been left over from last year. No one she knew drank Scotch except Rafe Cassidy and her father. "You were never particularly civilized."

"I've changed."

"I doubt it."

"Pour the brandy, Maggie, love," he advised a little too gently.

She thought about refusing and knew it wouldn't do much good. Short of calling the police there was no way to get Rafe out of her apartment until he was ready to leave. Pouring brandy would at least give her something to do with her hands. Perhaps the liquor would stop the tiny shivers that seemed to be coursing through her.

Rafe's hard mouth twisted with faint satisfaction as he realized she was going to follow orders. With laconic grace he took his booted feet off the coffee table, got up and followed her into the gray and white kitchen.

"I never did like this picture," he said idly as he passed the framed painting on the wall. "Always looked like recycled junk stuck in paint to me."

"Our taste in art was one of several areas in which we had no common ground, wasn't it, Rafe?"

"Oh, we had a lot in common, Maggie. Especially in the middle of the night." He stood lounging in the doorway as she rummaged in the cupboard for a glass. She could feel his golden-brown eyes on her, the eyes that had always made her think of one of the larger species of hunting cat.

"Then again, the middle of the night was about the only time you had available to devote to our relationship," she reminded him bitterly. "And I recall a lot of nights when I didn't even get that much time. There were plenty of nights when I awoke and discovered you were out in the living room going through more papers, working on more ways to take some poor unsuspecting company by surprise."

"So maybe I worked a little too much in those days."

"That's putting it mildly, Rafe. You're obsessed with Cassidy and Company. A mere woman never stood a chance of competing."

"Things are different now. You look good, Maggie. Real good."

Her hand shook a little at the controlled hunger in his voice. The brandy bottle clinked awkwardly on the rim of the glass. "You look very much the same, Rafe." *Overwhelming, fierce, dangerous. Still a cowboy.*

He shrugged. "It's only been a little over a year."

"Not nearly long enough."

"You're wrong. It's been too damn long. But we'll get to that in a minute." He picked up her brandy glass as soon as she finished pouring and handed it to her with mock gallantry. His big hand brushed against her fingers in a deliberate movement designed to force physical contact.

Margaret snatched her glass out of his hand and turned her back on him. She led the way into the living room. Beyond the wide expanse of windows the lights of Seattle glimmered in the night. Normally she found the view relaxing but tonight it offered no comfort.

She sat down in one of the white leather chairs. It was something of a relief not to have to support her own weight any longer. She felt weak. "Don't play games with me, Rafe. You played enough of them a year ago. Just say whatever it is you feel you have to say and then get out."

Rafe's eyes raked her face as he sat down across from her. He gave her his thin smile. It was the only sort of smile he had. "Let's not get into the subject of who was playing games a year ago. It's a matter of opinion."

"Not *opinion*. Fact. And as far as I'm concerned, the facts are very clear."

He shook his head, refusing to be drawn. "We can sort it all out some other time, if ever. Personally, I think it's best to just forget most of what happened a year ago."

"Easy for you to say. It wasn't your career and your professional reputation that were ruined."

Rafe's eyes darkened. "You could have weathered the storm. You chose to walk away from your career and take up writing full-time."

Margaret allowed herself a small, negligent shrug. "You may be right. As it happens I had a better career to walk to. Best professional move I could have made. I love my writing and I can assure you I don't miss the business jungle one bit. I wouldn't go back for anything." Her writing, which had been part-time until last year, had become full-time after the disaster and she didn't regret it for a moment.

"You dropped out of sight. Found a new apartment. Took your listing out of the phone book." Rafe leaned back in his chair and crossed his ankles once more on the coffee table. He sipped reflectively at his Scotch. "Took me a while to find you when I started looking. Your publisher refused to give out your address and your father was not what you'd call cooperative."

"I should hope not. I told him I never wanted to see you again as long as I lived. I assumed the feeling was mutual."

"It was. For a while."

"When did you start looking for me?"

"A few months ago."

"Why?" she demanded bluntly.

"I thought I made that clear. I want you back."

Her stomach tightened and her pulse thrummed as it went into a primitive fight-or-flight rhythm. "No. Never. You don't want me, Rafe. You never wanted me. You just used me."

His fingers clenched the glass but his face betrayed no change of expression. "That's a lie, Maggie, love. Our relationship had nothing to do with what happened between Cassidy and Company and Moorcroft's firm."

"The hell it didn't. You used me to get inside information. Worse, you wanted to taunt Jack Moorcroft with the news that you were sleeping with his trusted manager, didn't you? Don't bother to deny it, Rafe, because we both know it's the truth. You told me so yourself, remember?"

Rafe's jaw tightened. "I was mad as hell that morning when I found you warning Moorcroft about my plans. As far as I was concerned, you'd betrayed me."

The injustice of that seared her soul. "I worked for Jack Moorcroft and I discovered you were after the company he was trying to buy out; that you'd used me to help you try to outmaneuver him. What did you expect me to do?"

"I expected you to stay out of it. It had nothing to do with you."

"I was just your pawn in the game, is that it? Did you think I'd be content with that kind of role?"

Rafe drew a deep breath, obviously fighting for his self-control. "I've thought about it a lot during the past year. Every damn day, as a matter of fact, although I told myself at the time that I wasn't going to waste a minute looking for excuses for you. It took me months to calm down enough to start assessing the mess from your point of view."

"Since when did you ever bother to examine anything from my point of view?"

"Take it easy, Maggie, love. I realize now that you felt you had some legitimate reason to do what you did. Yes, sir, I've given it a lot of thought and the way I see it, the whole thing was basically a problem of confused loyalties. You were mixed up, that's all." His mouth curved ruefully. "And a multimillion-dollar deal went down the drain because of it, but I'm willing to let bygones be bygones."

"Oh, gee, thanks. Very magnanimous of you. Rafe, let's get one thing straight. I never asked you to make excuses for me. I don't want you making excuses for me. I don't need your forgiveness because I didn't do anything wrong."

"I'm trying to explain that I don't feel the same way about what happened as I did last year," he said, his voice edged with impatience.

"If you're feeling a twinge or two of guilt about the way you used me and the way you treated me afterward, I hereby absolve you. Believe me, if I were in the same situation again, I'd act exactly the same way. I'd still warn Moorcroft. There. Does that make you feel justified in treating me the way you did?"

He stared at her, his leonine eyes brilliant with some undefined emotion. "You weren't his mistress, were you? Not before or afterward."

She wanted to strike him. It took everything she had to maintain her self-control. "Why should I confirm or deny that?"

"Moorcroft said you'd been sleeping with him up until he realized I was interested in you. He saw a golden opportunity and decided to take advantage of it. He told you to go to me, let me seduce you, see what you could learn."

Margaret shuddered. "You and Moorcroft are both outright bastards."

"He lied to me that morning, didn't he? You were never his."

"I was never any man's."

"You were mine for a while." Rafe took another swallow of his Scotch. "And you're going to be mine again."

"Not a chance. Never in a million years. Not if you were the last man on earth."

Rafe ignored each carefully enunciated word. He

frowned thoughtfully as he stared into the darkness. "From what I can tell, you never even saw Moorcroft again after you handed in your resignation. Why was that, Maggie? Did he kick you out because you'd become a liability? Was that it? He didn't want you working for him once the scandal broke? Did he force you to resign?"

"Wouldn't you have asked for my resignation in the same circumstances? If you found out one of your top management people was sleeping with your chief competitor, wouldn't you have demanded she leave?"

"Hell, yes. Everyone who works for me knows that in exchange for a paycheck the one thing I demand is loyalty."

Margaret sighed. "Well, at least you're honest about it. As it happens, Jack didn't have to ask me to turn in my resignation. I was very anxious to go by then. I'd been planning to quit my job in another couple of years to pursue my writing full-time, anyway. The scandal last year just speeded up the process a bit."

Rafe swore softly. "I didn't come here to argue with you. I've told you, as far as I'm concerned, the past is behind us and it's going to stay there."

"Why did you come here? You still haven't made your reasons clear. I'm out of the business world these days, Rafe. I have no secrets to spill that might help you force some company into an unwilling merger or enable you to buy out some poor firm that's gotten itself into a financial mess. I can't help you in any way."

"Stop making it sound as if I only used you for inside information," Rafe said through gritted teeth.

"You knew who I was before you approached me at that charity function where we met, didn't you?"

"So what? That doesn't mean I plotted to use you."

"Oh, come on, now, Rafe. I'm not a complete fool. Do you swear it never crossed your mind that it might be useful to talk to someone who was as close to Jack Moorcroft as I was? Wasn't that why you introduced yourself in the first place?"

"What the hell does it matter why I approached you that first time? Within five minutes of meeting you I knew that what we were going to have together had nothing to do with business. I asked you to marry me, damn it."

She nearly choked on her brandy. "Yes, you did, didn't you? The first week I met you. And I was actually considering it even though every instinct I possessed was screaming at me to run." That was not quite the truth. A few of her more primitive instincts had shouted at her to stay and take the risk.

"I'm going to ask you again, Maggie."

She was suddenly so light-headed she thought she might faint. "What did you say?"

"You heard me." Rafe got to his feet and paced soundlessly across the white carpet to the window. He stood looking out into the night. "I'm prepared to give you a little time to get accustomed to the notion again. I know this is coming out of the blue for you. But I want you, Maggie. I've never stopped wanting you."

"Is that right? I distinctly recall you telling me you never wanted to see me again."

"I lied. To myself and to you."

She shook her head in disbelief. "I saw the rage in you that morning. You hated me."

"No. Never that. But I was in a rage. I admit it. I couldn't believe you'd gone straight to Moorcroft to warn him about my plans. When you didn't even bother to defend yourself, I decided I'd been had. Moorcroft was more than willing to reinforce the idea."

"I did go straight to Moorcroft," Margaret agreed grimly. "But I was the one who'd been had. As far as I'm concerned you and Moorcroft both took advantage of me. It's one of the reasons I left the business world, Rafe. I realized I didn't have the guts for it. I couldn't handle the level of warfare. It made me sick."

"You were too soft for that world, Maggie, love. I knew that from the first day I met you. If you'd married me, you would have been out of it."

"Let's be honest with each other, Rafe. If I'd married you a year ago, we'd have been divorced by now."

"No."

"It's the truth, whether you want to admit it or not. I couldn't have tolerated your idea of marriage for long. I knew that at the time. That's why I put off giving you my answer during those two months we were together." She also knew that if the blowup hadn't occurred, she probably would have succumbed to Rafe's pressure tactics and married him. She would have found a proposal from Rafe impossible to resist. She had been in love with him.

Rafe glanced over his shoulder, his mouth gentling. "It might have been a little rough at times but it would have worked. I'd have made it work. This time it will work."

Margaret squeezed her eyes shut on hot tears. Determinedly she blinked them back. When she looked at Rafe again, she saw him through a damp mist but she was fairly certain she wouldn't actually break down and cry. She must not do that. This man homed in on weakness the way a predator homed in on prey.

"I'm surprised at you, Rafe. If you felt this strongly

about the matter, why did you wait an entire year to come after me?" Margaret thought with fleeting anguish of the months she had spent hoping he would do just that before she had finally accepted reality and gotten on with her life. "It's not like you to be so slow about going after what you want."

"I know. But in this case things were different." His shoulders moved in an uneasy, uncharacteristic gesture. "I'd never been in a situation like that before." He turned toward her and swirled the Scotch in his glass. His eyes were thoughtful when he finally raised them to meet hers. "For the first few months I couldn't even think clearly. I was a menace to everyone during the day and stayed up most of the nights trying to work myself into a state of exhaustion so I could get a couple of hours' sleep. Ask Hatcher or my mother if you want to know what I was like during that period. They all refer to it as the Dark Ages."

"I can imagine you were a little upset at having your business plans ruined," Margaret said ironically. "There was a lot of money on the line and Moorcroft's firm cleaned up thanks to my advance warning. You lost that time around and we all know how you feel about losing."

Rafe's gaze sparked dangerously but the flare of anger was quickly dampened. "I can handle losing. It happens. Occasionally. But I couldn't handle the fact that you'd turned traitor and I couldn't deal with the way you'd walked out without a backward glance."

"What did you expect me to do after you told me to get out of your sight?"

Rafe smiled bleakly. "I know. You were hardly the type to cry and tell me you were sorry or to grovel on your knees and beg me to forgive you and take you back, were you?"

"Not bloody likely," Margaret muttered. "Not when I was the innocent victim in that mess."

"I used to fantasize about it, you know."

"Fantasize about what? Me pleading for your forgiveness?"

He nodded. "I was going to let you suffer for a while; let you show me how truly sorry you were for what you'd done and then I was going to be real generous and take you back."

"On your terms, of course."

"Naturally."

"It's a good thing you didn't hold your breath, isn't it?"

"Yeah, I'd have passed out real quick because you sure as hell never came running back to me. At first I assumed that was because you'd gone back to your affair with Moorcroft."

"Damn you, there never was any affair with Moorcroft."

"I know, I know." He held up a hand to cut off her angry protest. "But I couldn't be certain at the time and I could hardly call up Moorcroft and ask, could I? He'd have laughed himself sick."

"It would have served you right."

"My pride was already in shreds. I wasn't about to let Jack Moorcroft stomp all over it."

"Of course not. Your pride had been a lot more important than whatever it was we had together, hadn't it?"

He turned to face her. "I'm here tonight, aren't I? Doesn't that say something about my priorities?"

She eyed him warily. "It says you're up to something. That's all it says. And I don't want any part of it. I learned my lesson a year ago, Rafe. Only a fool gets burned twice."

"Give me a chance to win you back, Maggie. That's all I'm asking."

"No," she said, not even pausing to think about her response. There was only one safe answer.

He watched her for a moment and Margaret didn't like the look in his eyes. She'd seen it before and she knew what it meant. Rafe was running through his options, picking and choosing his weapons, analyzing the best way to stage his next assault. When he moved casually back to the white chair and sat down, Margaret instinctively tensed.

"You really are afraid of me, aren't you, Maggie, love?"

"Yes," she admitted starkly. "You can be an extremely ruthless man and I don't know what you've got up your sleeve."

"Well, it's true there are a few things you don't know yet," Rafe said softly.

"I don't want to know them."

"You will."

"All I want is for you to leave."

"I told you when you opened the door tonight that you don't have to be afraid of me."

"I'm not afraid of you. But I have some common sense and I will admit I'm extremely cautious around you. I definitely do not intend to get involved with you again, Rafe."

He turned the glass in his hands. "What I had in mind was a little vacation for you."

That alarmed her. "A *vacation?* I don't need or want a vacation."

"At the ranch," he continued, just as if she hadn't spoken.

"Your ranch in Arizona?"

"You never had a chance to see it. You'll like it, Maggie."

"No, absolutely not. I don't want to go to any ranch. I hate ranches. If I wanted to go on a vacation, I'd choose a luxury resort on a South Sea island, not a ranch."

"You'll like this one." Rafe swallowed the last of the Scotch. "It's just outside of Tucson. I grew up there. Inherited it when Dad died."

"No."

"You don't have to worry," Rafe said gently. "You won't be alone with me. My mother will be there."

"I thought she lived in Scottsdale."

"She does. But she's paying me a visit. My sister, Julie, is going to drop in on us, too. She lives in Tucson, you know. I thought you'd feel more comfortable about going down there if you knew you weren't going to be completely alone with me."

"Look, I don't care who's going to be down there. Rafe, stop stalking me like this. I mean it."

"There'll be someone else there, too, honey."

"I just told you, I don't care who's there. In case you didn't realize it, knowing your mother will be around is not much of an incentive for me to go to Tucson. She undoubtedly hates my guts. She thinks the sun rises and sets on you. She made her opinion of me clear that one time I met her last year, and I'm sure she thinks even less of me after what happened between us. I'm sure she blames me for your losing Spencer Homes to Moorcroft. I wouldn't be surprised if your sister feels exactly the same."

"Now, Maggie, love, you've got to allow for the fact

that people change. My mother is looking forward to seeing you again."

"I don't believe that for a minute and even if it's true, I'm not particularly anxious to see her."

"You'd better get used to the idea of seeing her," Rafe said. "She's going to marry your father."

"She's *what?*" Margaret felt as if the world had just fallen away beneath her feet. She clutched at her brandy glass.

"You heard me."

"I don't believe you. You're lying. My father would have said something."

"He hasn't said anything because I asked him not to. I wanted to handle this my own way. He's the other person who will be at the ranch while you're there, by the way."

"Oh, my God." She felt physically sick as she put the untouched brandy down on the table.

"Are you all right?" Rafe frowned in concern.

"No."

"It's not as bad as all that. They make a great couple, as a matter of fact."

"When...where...how did they meet?"

"I introduced them about four months ago."

"For God's sake, why?"

"Because I had a hunch they'd hit it off. Your father wasn't too keen on the idea at first, I'll admit. He was more inclined to string me up from the nearest tree. Seems he was under the impression I was the bad guy in that mess last year. When I straightened him out on a few details, including the fact that I still wanted to marry you, he settled down and saw the light of sweet reason. Then he met Mom and fell like a ton of bricks."

Margaret stared at Rafe in bewildered horror. "I

don't understand any of this. What's behind it? You never do anything unless the bottom line is worth it. *What is going on here?*"

He smiled his thin smile. "If you want to find out you'll have to take a couple of weeks off and come down to the ranch." He reached inside the jacket he'd slung over the back of the chair and removed an airline ticket folder. "I've made the reservations for you. You're scheduled on the eight-o'clock flight to Tucson next Monday."

"You're out of your mind if you think you can just walk in here and take control of my life like this. I'm not going anywhere."

"Suit yourself, but I think you'll want to find out what's happening and the only way to do it is to come down to Arizona."

"If my father is crazy enough to get involved with your mother, that's his affair. I'll give him my opinion when he asks for it, but until then, I'm staying out of it."

"It isn't just their relationship that's at stake," Rafe said calmly.

Margaret dug her fuchsia-colored nails into the white leather upholstery. "I knew it," she bit out. "With you there's always a business reason. Tell me the rest, damn you."

"Well, it's true your father and I are thinking of doing a little business together."

"Good Lord. What kind of business?"

"I'm going to buy Lark Engineering."

It was the final bombshell as far as Margaret was concerned. She leaped to her feet. She wanted to call him a liar again, but even as the words crossed her mind, she was terribly, coldly afraid. "My father would never sell the firm to you. He built it from the ground up. It's his whole life. If he's thinking of selling out, it's because you're forcing his hand. What have you done, Rafe? What kind of leverage are you using against him?"

Rafe rose slowly to his feet, looming over her. He dominated the elegant room—a dark, dangerous intruder who threatened Margaret's hard-won peace of mind as nothing else ever had. She looked up at him, feeling small and very vulnerable. But she refused to step back out of reach. She would not give him the satisfaction.

"You really don't think very much of me, do you?" Rafe's mouth was taut with his rigidly controlled anger. "It's a good thing I learned something about handling my own pride this past year because the look in your eyes right now is enough to make a man feel about two inches tall."

"Really?" Her voice was scathing. "And do you feel two inches tall?"

"No, ma'am," he admitted. "But I probably would if I were guilty of whatever it is you think I'm doing to your father. Lucky for me I'm as innocent as a new foal."

"Are you saying you're not forcing him to sell out to you?"

"Nope. Ask him."

"I will, damn you."

"You'll have to come down to the ranch to do that," Rafe said. "Because that's where he is and he won't reassure you on the phone."

"Why not?"

"Because he knows I want some time with you down there and he's agreed to act as the bait. You'll have to fly to Arizona if you want to convince yourself that I'm not pulling a fast one."

"And if I don't go?"

"Then I reckon you'll sit here in Seattle and worry a lot."

She shook her head, dazed. "I don't believe any of this. Why are you doing it?"

"I've told you why I'm doing it. I want another chance with you. This is the only way I know to get it."

"Even if that disaster last year didn't stand between us, we have no business thinking about getting involved again. I've told you that. I could never marry you, Rafe. Not for long, at any rate."

"I'll make you change your mind."

"Impossible. I know you too well now. The truth is, I knew you too well last year. That's the reason I didn't give you an answer the first time you asked. Or the second or the third. Your first love is business and your overriding passion in life is for making money, not making love."

Rafe contrived to look hurt. "I don't recall you complaining too loud in bed."

Margaret clenched her fists. "On the rare occasions you managed to find time to take me to bed you performed just fine."

"Why, thank you, honey. It's real sweet of you to remember."

"You're missing the point," she hissed.

"Yeah?"

"The point is, you don't have a lot of time in your life for a relationship of any kind. During the two months we were dating you were always flying into Seattle for a weekend and then flying out again Monday morning. Or you would show up on my doorstep at midnight on a Wednesday, take me to bed and then disappear at six the next day to get to a business conference in L.A."

"I admit I used to do a fair amount of traveling, but I've cut back lately."

"And when you weren't traveling, you were tied up at the office. Remember all those times you called from Tucson and told me you wouldn't be able to make it up here to Seattle? I was expected to rearrange all my plans to accommodate you. Or else you'd arrive with a briefcase full of work and Doug Hatcher in tow and the two of you would take over my living room for a full day."

"Now, honey, there was a lot going on at the time."

"With you there always will be a lot going on. It's your nature. Your mother was kind enough to point that out to me. Said you were just like your father. You thrive on your work. Beating the competition to the draw is the most important thing in your life."

"You're getting carried away now, Maggie, love. Just take it easy, honey. I'm dead serious about this. I want to get married."

"Oh, I believe you. You'd find a wife useful. You want a wife who will be a convenience for you—someone to handle your entertaining, your home, your social life. Someone who will warm your bed when you want it warmed and stay out of your way when you've got other things to do. Someone who knows how to live in your world and who will accommodate her entire life to yours. In short, you want the perfect corporate wife."

"Give me the next couple of weeks to prove that I'm willing to make a few accommodations of my own."

Margaret's head came up sharply. "You're hardly starting out on a promising foot, are you? You're trying to blackmail me into going down to your ranch."

He sighed. "Only because I know it's a surefire way to get you there. Maggie, listen to me…"

She glared at him. "Don't call me Maggie. I never did like the way you called me that. No one else ever calls me Maggie."

Rafe's brows rose. "Your dad does."

"That changes nothing. I dislike being called Maggie."

"You never said anything about it before."

"It didn't seem worth arguing about last year. Good grief, there wasn't time to argue about it. This year is different, however. I'm not putting up with anything from you this year."

"I see. That's too bad. I always kind'a liked Maggie."

"I don't."

"All right," he said soothingly, "I'll try to remember to call you Margaret."

"You don't have to try to remember anything. You won't be around long enough to make the mistake very often."

"You're not going to give an inch, are you?"

"No." Margaret eyed him defiantly.

Rafe's mouth curved faintly. "I had a feeling you were going to be like that. Which is why I went to so much effort to set this whole thing up the way I did. I need you to give me a chance to prove that I've changed. I'm only asking for two weeks."

"You're not asking, you're demanding. That's the way you always did things, Rafe. You haven't changed at all."

Temper flashed briefly in his eyes and was almost immediately overlaid with something far more dangerous: frustrated desire. Rafe lifted a hand to slide around the nape of Margaret's neck beneath the neat chignon of her hair. She froze.

"How much have you changed, Maggie?" he asked softly, his mouth only inches from hers. "Do you still remember this?" He brushed his lips across hers in the lightest of caresses. "Do you still go all hot and trembly when I do this?" He caught her lower lip gently between his teeth and then released it.

Margaret flinched from the jolt of deep longing that knifed through her. She did not move. She was not sure she could have moved if she'd tried. She was paralyzed—a rabbit confronted by a mountain lion.

Rafe's mouth slanted across hers again and she was thoroughly confused by the unexpected tenderness of his kiss. His fingers stroked her nape, featherlight against her sensitive skin. A tremor sizzled along her nerve endings. She shivered.

"Yeah, you still do, don't you? I've been thinking about this for the past year," Rafe muttered. "One whole year, damn you. Every night and every day. There were times when I thought I'd go clear out of my mind with wanting you. How could you do that to me, Maggie?"

She was shaken by the bleak depths in his voice. "If it was the sex you missed, I'm sure there must have been someone around to give you what you wanted."

"No," he stated harshly. "There was no one. There hasn't been anyone since you, Maggie."

She stared up at him in shock. When he finally had found time for bed, Rafe had proved himself to be a deeply sensual man. She remembered that much quite vividly. "I don't believe you."

"Believe it," he growled as his mouth grazed hers one more time. "God knows I do. I had to live through every night alone and it nearly drove me crazy."

"Rafe, you can't walk back in here after a whole year and do this to me," Margaret said desperately. "I won't let you."

"Let me stay tonight."

"No."

He drew back slightly, releasing her. "I had a hunch you'd say that but I had to ask. Don't worry about it, I've waited this long, I can wait a little longer."

"You'll wait until hell freezes over," she said crisply. "You've said what you had to say, Rafe. Now leave."

He hesitated briefly. Then he nodded and picked up his hat. He jammed it down low over his glittering eyes. As he reached for his jacket, he glanced at the airline ticket he'd left on the table. "Next Monday. The eight-o'clock flight."

"I won't be on it."

"Please."

Margaret's mouth fell open in amazement. "What did you say?"

"I said *please*. Please be on the eight-o'clock flight. Come to Arizona to talk to the woman who will probably be marrying your father. Come to Arizona to find out what kind of evil deal I've cooked up to get your dad to sell his company to me. Come to Arizona to see if I really have changed. Come to Arizona to give us both a second chance."

"I'd be a fool to do it."

"There hasn't been anyone else for either of us for the past year, Maggie. That should tell us both something." He hooked the jacket over his shoulder and strode to the door.

"Rafe, wait, I'm not going to do it, do you hear me? I won't be on that plane." Margaret managed to unstick herself from the carpet and go after him, but she was too late.

The door closed softly behind him before she could ask him how he knew there had been no one else for her during the past year.

CHAPTER TWO

IT HAD BEEN THE LONGEST YEAR of his life, Rafe thought savagely, and Maggie looked as if she'd spent it sleeping on rose petals and sipping tea. It was almost more than he could take to see her looking so serene and untouched by the past twelve months.

He clung to the knowledge that she had been as celibate as he had. It was the only thing that gave him any real hope. On some level she had been waiting for him, he told himself. On some level she was still his and knew it.

Outside on the street in front of her apartment building he managed to find a cab for the ride back to his hotel. Knowing he was heading toward a lonely hotel room when he should have been spending the night in Maggie's bed did nothing for Rafe's temper. Still, the players in the game were finally in position at last and the first moves had all been made. The action was ready to start.

She was as striking as ever, he admitted to himself as he sprawled back against the seat in the cab. More so. She was a little more sure of herself now than she had been a year ago. And a hell of a lot less willing to accommodate herself to his schedule, he thought with grim humor.

The sight of her tonight had nearly shattered his carefully honed self-control. He had promised himself he would remain in command of the situation, but when she had walked through the door his first instinct had been to pull her down onto the carpet of her elegant living room and make love to her until she was wild. He needed desperately to feel her respond to him the way she had the last time on that memorable night before everything had gone up in smoke. Lord, he was starving for her.

He had never been so hungry in his life and he had to be patient. He stared moodily at the cheerfully garish lights of the public market as the cabdriver turned east on Pike Street. It had been a year since he had seen Seattle at night.

The cab halted in front of the lobby of the expensive hotel and Rafe got out. He reached for his wallet.

"Nice boots," the cabbie remarked as he pocketed the excessive tip.

"Thanks." Rafe turned toward the lobby.

"Hey, if you've got nothin' else to do this evenin'," the cabbie called after him, "I can give you a couple of suggestions. I know where the action is here in town. No sense spendin' the night alone."

"Why not? It's the way I spend all of my nights lately."

Rafe went on into the marble and wood-paneled lobby. He couldn't stop picturing Maggie as she had looked tonight standing framed in the doorway of her apartment. Her sleek black hair had been pulled back to accent the delicate lines of her face. Her aquamarine eyes were even larger and more compelling than they had been in his dreams.

The sophisticated silk dress she wore glided over subtle, alluring curves. She looked as if she'd put on a couple of pounds but they had gone to the right places. She still moved with the grace of a queen.

Maggie had obviously found her footing in her new career as a writer. In fact, she looked depressingly content. Rafe felt like chewing nails. It seemed only fair that she should have suffered as much as he had. But apparently she hadn't.

He reminded himself once more of the report from the discreet investigative agency he had employed. Maggie dated only rarely and never seriously. Until recently she had spent a lot of her free time with two other women who had been friends of hers for the past couple of years.

Rafe had never met Sarah Fleetwood and Katherine Inskip, but their names showed up so often in the reports that he had come to think of the unknown women as duennas for his lady. Somewhere along the line he had unconsciously started depending on them to keep Maggie out of trouble.

Trouble meant another man in Maggie's life, as far as Rafe was concerned. But as luck would have it, Sarah and Katherine had been the ones who had found the other men. He wasn't making his move any too soon, Rafe told himself. No sense leaving a woman like Maggie at loose ends for very long.

Rafe went into the hotel bar and found a secluded booth. He ordered a Scotch and sat brooding over it, analyzing the scene in Maggie's living room, searching for flaws in the way he'd handled the delicate negotiations, wondering if he'd applied just the right amount of pressure.

He'd spent months putting the plan together and he'd used every lever he could find. He would have bargained with the devil himself to get Maggie back.

But tonight he'd played the last cards in his hand. Now he could only pray Maggie would be on that Monday morning flight to Tucson. His whole future was hanging in the balance and Rafe knew it. The knowledge made his insides grow cold.

THE BOOK SIGNING SESSION on Saturday morning went well. Margaret thoroughly enjoyed talking to the readers and other writers in the area who had made their way by car, bus and monorail into downtown Seattle to meet the author of *Ruthless*. She was especially grateful for the enthusiastic crowd this morning because it took her mind off the difficult decision that had to be made by Monday. For a while, at least, she did not have to think about Rafe Cassidy.

"I just loved *Ruthless*." A happily pregnant woman with a toddler clinging to her skirts handed her copy of the book to Margaret to sign. "I always feel good after I've read one of your books. I really love your heroes. They're great. Oh, Christine is the name, by the way."

"Thanks, Christine. I'm glad you liked the book. I appreciate your coming downtown today." Margaret wrote Christine's name on the title page, a brief message and then signed her own name with a flourish.

"No problem. Wouldn't have missed it for the world. I was an account executive at a brokerage house here in Seattle before I quit to raise kids for a while. I really identify with the business settings in your stories. When's your next book due out?"

"In about six months."

"Can't wait. Another hero like Roarke, I hope?"

Margaret smiled. "Of course." Roarke was the name of the hero in *Ruthless*, but the truth was all her heroes were similar. They all bore a striking resemblance to

Rafe Cassidy. That had been true from her first book, which had been written long before she had ever met Rafe. It was probably why she had fallen so hard and so fast for him when he'd exploded into her life last year, she thought.

At first sight she had been certain Rafe was the man of her dreams.

Except for the boots, of course. Looking back on the disaster Margaret knew she ought to have been warned when her dream man showed up in a Stetson, fancy boots and a silver belt buckle. In her books her heroes always wore European-styled suits and Italian leather shoes.

Hard, savvy and successful businessmen for the most part, her male characters always had a ruthless edge that made them a real challenge for the heroines. But in the end, unlike Rafe, they all succumbed to love.

A stylish-looking woman in a crisp suit who was standing directly behind Christine extended her copy of *Ruthless.* "Christine's right. Give us another hero like Roarke. He was great. I love the tough-guy-who-can-be-taught-to-love type. I think of them as cowboys in business suits."

Margaret stared at her. "Cowboys? Good heavens, what makes you call them that? I like the sophisticated urban type. That's the kind I always write about."

The woman shook her head with a knowing look in her eye. "But your heroes are all cowboys in disguise, didn't you know that?"

Margaret eyed her thoughtfully. She had long ago learned to appreciate some of the insights her readers had into her books but this one took her aback. "You really think so?"

"Trust me. I know cowboys when I see them, even if they are wearing two-hundred-dollar silk shirts."

"She's right, you know," another woman in line announced with a grin. "When I'm reading one of your books, I always visualize a cowboy."

"What on earth makes you do that?" Margaret asked in utter amazement.

The woman paused, considering her answer. "I think it's got something to do with their basic philosophies of life—the way they think and act. They've got a lot of old-fashioned attitudes about women and honor and that kind of thing. The sort of attitudes we all associate with the Old West."

"It's true," someone else in line agreed. "The shootouts take place in corporate boardrooms instead of in front of the saloon, but the feeling is the same." She leaned forward to extend her copy of *Ruthless*. "The name is Rachel."

"Rachel." Margaret hurriedly signed the book and handed it back. "Thank you."

"Thank you." Rachel winked mischievously. "Speaking of cowboys," she said, exchanging a smile with the other woman, "maybe one of these days you can give us the real thing, horse and all."

"We'll look forward to it," the first woman declared as she collected her signed book.

Margaret managed a laugh and shook her head, feeling slightly dazed. "We'll see," she temporized, not wanting to offend the readers by telling them she'd once run into a real corporate gunslinger who was very much a cowboy and the result had been something other than a happy ending.

She turned, smiling, to greet the next person in line and nearly dropped her pen when she caught sight of the familiar figure standing in front of her. It never rained but it poured, she thought ironically.

"Hello, Jack. What are you doing here? I didn't know you read romance."

Jack Moorcroft smiled down at her, his light hazel eyes full of genuine curiosity. "So you really made it work, did you?"

"Made what work? My writing? Yes, I've been fortunate."

"I didn't think you could turn it into a full-fledged career."

"Neither did anyone else."

"Can I buy you a coffee or a drink when you're finished here? I'd like to talk to you."

"Let me guess what this is all about. I haven't seen you since the day I resigned. You moved the headquarters of Moorcroft Industries to San Diego nearly a year ago, according to the papers. And now, out of a clear blue sky you suddenly show up again in Seattle two days after Rafe Cassidy magically reappears. Can I assume there's a connection or is this one of those incredible coincidences that makes life so interesting?"

"You always were one smart lady. That's why I hired you in the first place."

"Forget the flattery, Jack. I'm immune."

"I get the feeling you're not enjoying old ties with your former business associates?"

"You're very perceptive for a businessman."

Jack nodded, accepting the rebuff. "I think I can understand. You got a little mauled there at the end, didn't you? Cassidy can play rough. But I do have to talk to you. It's important, Margaret. Coffee? For old times' sake?"

She sighed, wishing she could think of a polite way

out of the invitation. But the truth was Jack had been a reasonably good boss. And he'd never actually asked for her resignation. It had been her idea to leave the firm. "All right. Coffee. I'll be finished here in another fifteen minutes or so."

"I'll wait."

Twenty minutes later Margaret bid goodbye to the bookstore manager and the last of the readers who had dropped by the store to say hello. Slinging her stylish leather shoulder bag over her arm, she went to join Jack Moorcroft who was waiting patiently at the entrance of the store near the magazine racks.

He smiled when he saw her and put back the copy of *Forbes* he had been perusing. She studied him objectively as he held the door for her. Moorcroft was five years older than Rafe, which made him forty-three. On the surface he fit her mental image of a hero better than Rafe ever did. For one thing, there wasn't a trace of the cowboy in Moorcroft's attire or his accent. He was pure corporate polish.

Moorcroft was also a genuinely good-looking man. He kept himself trim by daily workouts at an exclusive health club and he dressed with impeccable finesse. His light brown hair was streaked with silver and thinning a bit, but that only served to give him a distinguished look. His suit was European in cut and the tie was silk.

By right Moorcroft should have been a living, breathing replica of one of her heroes, but Margaret had never once thought of him that way.

In addition to his beautifully cut suits, Jack Moorcroft also wore a wedding ring. He was married and that fact had made him off-limits from the day she had met him.

But even if he had not been married Margaret knew

deep down she could never have fallen for him the way she had fallen for Rafe. What she couldn't quite explain was why Moorcroft could never have been the man of her dreams.

"All right, Jack, let's get the cards on the table." Margaret sat down across from her former boss at a small espresso bar table. "We both know you're not in Seattle to rehash old times."

Jack toyed with the plastic stir stick that had come with his latte. He eyed Margaret thoughtfully for a long moment. "You've changed," he said finally.

She cocked a brow, amused. "Everyone does."

"I suppose. You like the writing business?"

"Love it. But that's not what you're here to talk about, is it?"

"No." Moorcroft took a sip of the latte and set the cup down on the small table. "My information says Cassidy came to see you this week."

Margaret shrugged. "Your information is good. He was here Thursday night. What does that matter to you?"

"He wants revenge, Margaret. You know him as well, if not better than I do. You know he always gets even."

"He's already had his revenge against me. You were there that morning. You heard him tell me to get out of his life."

"But now he's back, isn't he?" Jack's mouth twisted. "Because he never got his revenge against me. He kicked you out of his bed but there wasn't much he could do to me."

Margaret felt her cheeks burn at the blunt reference to her relationship with Rafe. "Why should he want revenge against you? I was the one he thought betrayed him."

Moorcroft's eyes narrowed. "Ah, but you betrayed him to me, remember?"

"Damn it, I didn't betray anyone. I was caught in the middle and I did what I had to do."

"The way he saw it, when the chips were down, I was the one who owned your loyalty. He was right in a way, wasn't he? But he didn't like that one bit, Margaret. I think he saw me as the other man in your life."

"You were my employer, nothing more. Rafe knew that. Tell me something, Jack, did you really lie to him about us?"

Moorcroft shrugged apologetically. "Cassidy was out of control that morning. He thought what he wanted to think, which was that you felt loyal to me not only because you worked for me but because we'd been involved in an affair."

Margaret shook her head in sheer disgust. "You did lie to him."

"Does it matter if I let him think what he was already thinking? The damage had been done. He'd already thrown you out and he knew he'd lost Spencer to me."

"So you decided to take advantage of the situation and gloat over your victory."

Moorcroft smiled cryptically. "I'll admit I couldn't resist the chance to sink the knife in a little deeper. Two years ago Cassidy cost me a bundle when he wrecked a merger I had set up. I owed him."

"And I just happened to get caught in the middle this time."

"You probably don't believe this, but I'm sorry about what happened, Margaret."

"Sure. Look, let's just forget this, all right? I've got better things to do than talk over old times."

"Unfortunately I can't forget it." Moorcroft leaned forward intently. "I can't forget it because Cassidy hasn't forgotten it. He's after me."

"What are you talking about?"

"This isn't just a business rivalry between that damned cowboy and me any longer. Because of you it's turned into some kind of personal vendetta for him. A hundred years ago he would have challenged me to a showdown at high noon or some such nonsense. But we live in a civilized age now, don't we? Cassidy's going to be a bit more subtle about his vengeance."

Margaret stared at him. "What in the world are you talking about, Jack?"

Moorcroft sat hunched over his latte, his hazel eyes intent. "He's up to something, Margaret. My sources tell me he's got a deal going, a deal that could directly affect Moorcroft Industries. I need to find out what's going on before it's too late. I need inside information."

"Sounds like you've already got information."

"Some. I don't know how much I can trust it."

"That's your problem, Jack."

"Look, Cassidy always plays his cards close to his chest but after what happened with you last year, he's more cautious than ever. Whatever he's working on is being kept under very tight security. I have to find out what he's up to, Margaret, before it's too late."

"Why are you coming to me about this? I don't work for you any longer, remember? I don't work for anyone except myself now. And I like it that way, Jack. I like it very much."

Moorcroft smiled. "Yes, I can see that. You look good, Margaret. Very good. I know you're out of the scene and you want to keep it that way, but I'm desperate and I need help. That business between me and Cassidy last year?"

"What about it?"

"That's all it was until you got involved. Business as usual. Cassidy and I have tangled before. Bound to happen. We're natural competitors. But after you came into the picture all that changed. Cassidy's out for blood now. Lately I've had the feeling I'm being hunted and I don't like it. I'm asking you to help me."

"You're out of your mind. I can't help you. I wouldn't even if I were in a position to do so. As you said, I'm out of this."

Moorcroft shook his head. "It's not your fault, Margaret, but the truth is, unwittingly or not, you started it. And now Cassidy is involving you again."

Margaret sat very still in her chair. "What makes you say that?"

"He's invited you down to that spread of his in Arizona, hasn't he?"

"How do you know that?"

Moorcroft sighed. "I told you, I don't have totally reliable inside information, but I have some. I've also heard your father has been seeing Beverly Cassidy."

Margaret grimaced. "Your information is better than mine, Jack. I didn't know that myself until Thursday night. My own father. I didn't even believe it at first. How could Dad…" She bit her lip. "Never mind."

She had spent most of Thursday night trying to convince herself that Rafe had lied to her. But several phone calls on Friday had failed to elicit any response from her father's home in California. His housekeeper had told her he had gone to Arizona.

When Margaret had angrily dialed the Cassidy

ranch she had been told by another housekeeper that her father was unable to come to the phone but was looking forward to seeing her on Monday.

The unfortunate reality was that Rafe Cassidy rarely bluffed—so rarely, in fact, that when he did, he usually got away with it. Connor Lark probably was involved with Mrs. Cassidy and if that much was true, the part about selling Lark Engineering to Rafe was probably also true.

That knowledge gave Margaret a sick feeling. What was Rafe up to? she wondered.

"We're on the same side this time, Margaret." Jack's tone was soft and cajoling. "We're natural allies. Last time you were caught in the crunch. You were in love with Cassidy but you felt loyal to me. A real mess. But that's not true this time, is it? You don't owe Cassidy anything. It's payback time."

"What are you talking about? I don't want revenge, I just want out of the whole thing."

"You can't get out of it. Your father is involved. If he marries Beverly Cassidy, you're going to spend the rest of your life connected by family ties to Rafe Cassidy."

"That notion is certainly enough to kill what's left of my appetite," Margaret said morosely. The thought of being related by marriage to Rafe was mind-boggling.

Moorcroft picked up his latte and took a swallow. "You'll be going to Arizona, won't you?"

She groaned. "Probably." She had been facing that reality since Rafe had walked out the door on Thursday night. She had to find out what, exactly, was going on.

"All I'm asking is that you keep your eyes and ears open while you're down there. You may pick up something interesting, something we can both use. Maybe something that could save my hide. I'd make it worth your while, Margaret."

She looked up sharply. "Forget it, Jack. If I go down there, it won't be as your spy. I have my own reasons."

He exhaled slowly. "I understand. It was worth a shot. I'm a desperate man, Margaret. There's an outlaw on my trail and I'll do anything to survive."

"You're that afraid of Rafe?" she asked in genuine surprise.

"Like I said—before we were just business rivals. Win some, lose some. No problem. That's the name of the game. But this time things are different. This time I have a feeling I may be fighting for my life."

"Good luck."

Moorcroft turned his cup of latte carefully in his hands. He studied Margaret's face for a long moment. "You're not going to help me, are you?"

"No."

"Because you love him?"

"How I feel about Rafe has nothing to do with it. I just don't want any part of this mess, whatever it is."

"I guess I can understand that."

"Terrific," she murmured. "I'm so glad."

"Margaret, there's something I want to ask you."

She waited uneasily. "Yes?"

"If Cassidy hadn't ridden up when he did and swept you off your feet, do you think you could ever have been interested in what I had to offer?"

"You didn't have anything to offer, Jack. You're a married man, remember?"

"But if I hadn't been married?"

"My best guess is no."

"Mind telling me why not?"

"First, when I was in the business world I had a

policy of never getting involved with my employers, even if they did happen to be single. From what I saw, it's almost always a bad career move for a woman to sleep with her boss. Sooner or later, she finds herself looking for another job."

"And second?"

"Let's just say you're not exactly the man of my dreams," she said dryly.

RAFE WAS WAITING AT THE airport gate. Margaret didn't see him at first. She was struggling with her carry-on luggage and scanning the crowd for her father. She was annoyed when she couldn't spot him. The least Connor Lark could do after causing all this commotion in her life was meet her at the airport, she told herself. When someone moved up behind her and took the travel bag from her arm, she spun around in shock.

"I'll take that for you, Maggie, love. Car's out front."

She glared up at Rafe, who was smiling down at her, a look of pure satisfaction in his gaze. He was dressed in jeans and boots and a white shirt that had the sleeves rolled up on his forearms. His hat was pulled down low over his eyes. The boots were truly spectacular—maroon leather with a beautiful turquoise and black design worked into them.

"I thought my father would have had the courtesy to meet me," she muttered.

"Don't blame Connor. I told him I'd take care of it." Rafe wrapped his hand around the nape of her neck, bent his head briefly and kissed her soundly. He did it hard and fast and allowed her no time in which to resist.

Margaret had barely registered his intentions before the whole thing was over. Scowling more furiously than ever, she stepped back quickly. She longed to slap the expression of triumph off his hard face. But at the last instant she reminded herself it would be dangerous to show any sign of a loss of self-control.

"I would appreciate it if you would not do that again," she bit out in a tight voice.

"Have a good flight?" Rafe smiled his thin, faint smile as he started down the corridor.

Margaret recalled belatedly that Rafe was very good at ignoring things he didn't care to deal with at the moment. He was already several feet away, moving in a long, rangy, ground-eating stride. She swore silently as she hurried to catch up with him. Following him was not an easy task dressed as she was in high heels and a turquoise silk suit that had an extremely narrow skirt.

"Good Lord, it's like an oven out here." Margaret gasped as she stepped through the doors of the Tucson airport terminal and into the full, humid warmth of a July day. She pulled a pair of sunglasses from her purse and glanced around at her surroundings.

The unrelenting blue of a vast desert sky arched overhead. There wasn't a cloud in sight to offer any relief from the blazing sun. Heat welled up off the pavement and poured down from above. Around her the desert stretched out in all directions, meeting the purple mountains in the distance.

"It's summer in the desert," Rafe pointed out. "What did you expect? You'll get used to it."

"Never in a million years."

"I know it's not Seattle." Rafe led the way to a silver-gray Mercedes parked in the short-term parking lot. "Gets a little warm down here in the summer. But as I said, you get used to it."

"You might be able to get accustomed to it, but I certainly never would." It was a challenge and she knew it.

"Try, Maggie," he advised laconically. "Try real hard. You're going to be here awhile. Might as well learn to enjoy it."

"Threats already, Rafe?"

"No, ma'am. Just a little good advice." He unlocked the passenger door of the Mercedes and held it open for her.

She glared up at him as she slid into the seat. The glare turned to a wince of pain as the sun-heated leather burned through her thin silk suit.

"I'll have the air conditioner going in a minute," Rafe promised. He tossed her bags into the trunk and then got in beside her to start the Mercedes. When the car purred to life he paused for a moment with his big, capable hands on the wheel and looked at Margaret. There was a dark hunger in his eyes but it was overlaid with a cold self-control.

Margaret was grateful for the protection of her sunglasses. "How far is it to your ranch?"

"It's a few miles out of town," he said carelessly, his attention clearly on other things. "You know something? It's hard to believe you're really here. It's about time, lady."

She didn't like the way he said that. "You didn't give me much choice, did you?"

"No."

"I should have known I wasn't going to get an apology out of you."

"For what?"

"For your high-handed, arrogant, overbearing tactics," she snapped, goaded.

"Oh, those. No, you shouldn't expect an apology. I did what I had to do." He put the Mercedes in gear and pulled smoothly out of the lot. "I had to get you down here, Maggie. There wasn't any other way to do it."

"You're wasting your time, Rafe. And please stop calling me Maggie. You gave me your word you'd remember to call me Margaret."

"I said I'd try to remember."

"Try, Rafe," she murmured, mimicking his earlier words. "Try real hard."

Rafe gave her an amused look as he stopped to hand some cash to the gate attendant. "But I've got a lot on my mind these days and the small stuff tends to slip through the cracks."

Her hands clenched in her lap. "That's all I ever was to you, wasn't it, Rafe? Small stuff. Unimportant stuff."

"You're small, all right." His voice had an affectionate, teasing edge to it now as he pulled away from the gate. "But no way are you going to slip through the cracks. Not this time."

"You don't want me back, Rafe."

"No? Why would I go to all the bother of blackmail to get you here if I didn't want you back?"

She frowned. "I've been thinking about that. The only conclusion I can come up with is that in your mind I'm the one who got away. It's true you kicked me out of your life, but when I went without a backward glance and stayed out, your ego took a beating, didn't it?"

"You did a number on my ego, all right," he agreed dryly. "It hasn't been the same since."

"Is that what this is all about? Revenge?" She shivered, remembering what Jack Moorcroft had said. *Cassidy is out for blood.*

"I would do a lot of things for revenge under certain circumstances," Rafe said, "but getting married isn't one of them. I'm not masochistic. Don't make any mistake about it, Maggie. I brought you down here to give myself some time to undo the damage that got done last year."

"The damage is irreparable."

"No, it's not. We're going to put that mess behind us and get on with our lives."

"I have been getting on with my life," she pointed out. "Very nicely, thank you. I've been quite happy this past year."

"Lucky you. I've been to hell and back."

She sucked in her breath. "Rafe, please, don't say things like that. We both know you're not the type to pine for a woman, especially one you think betrayed you. You're far more likely to look for a way to reap some vengeance against her. And I suspect that's exactly what you're doing by going after my father's firm."

"I'm not going after it. Your dad wants to sell to me. It's a profitable operation that will fit in well with the other businesses Cassidy and Company runs, so I'm taking a serious look at it. That's all there is to it."

"I don't believe that."

"I know. That's why you're here, isn't it? To rescue Connor from my clutches. You might be able to do that, Maggie, but I doubt you'll get him out of my mother's hands. Wait until you see them together. They're made for each other."

"It's all part of some plot you've cooked up, Rafe. Why don't you tell me what you're really after?"

"You're beginning to sound paranoid, honey."

"I'm not paranoid, I'm careful."

He smiled fleetingly at that. "No, Maggie, you're not careful. If you were careful, you wouldn't be here."

Margaret took refuge in silence for the next several miles. She folded her arms beneath her breasts and stared out the window at the arid landscape as she tried desperately to think. She had been struggling to put together some sort of battle plan ever since she had accepted the inevitability of this trip. But she was still very uncertain of what to do now that she was here. Part of the problem was that she could not be sure of what Rafe was really up to.

She did not believe for a moment that he wanted to marry her. But it was entirely possible he wanted to seduce her so that he could have the satisfaction of punishing her for her so-called betrayal.

Then, too, there was Moorcroft to consider. She didn't care what happened to Jack or his firm but she had to wonder if Rafe intended to use her in some scheme to get even with his rival.

Finally there was the business of her father getting involved with Beverly Cassidy and planning to sell Lark Engineering to Rafe.

No doubt about it, the situation was complicated and potentially dangerous.

A typical Rafe Cassidy operation, Margaret thought.

CHAPTER THREE

"THIS IS YOUR HOME, RAFE?" Margaret watched in amazement as the main buildings of the Cassidy Ranch came into view.

Set in the foothills with a sweeping view of Tucson in the distance, the ranch was an impressive sight. At the end of a long, winding drive was a graceful house done in the classic Spanish Colonial style. The walls had the look of warm, earth-toned adobe and the roof was red tile. Lush greenery surrounded the place, a welcome antidote to the rugged desert landscape. Low, white, modern-looking barns, white fences and green pastures spread out from the house. Margaret could see horses in the fields.

"Things were a little rushed during that two-month period after we met," Rafe reminded her coolly. "There wasn't time to get you down here to see the place before you…left me."

"You mean before you threw me out of your life."

Rafe drew a breath. "It was an argument, Maggie. A bad one. I lost my temper and said a lot of things I didn't mean."

"Oh, you meant them, all right. Where are the cows?" Margaret added in mild curiosity. "Shouldn't there be cows on a ranch like this?"

"This time of year the cattle are scattered all to hell and gone up in the foothills," Rafe said impatiently.

"Why so many horses? They don't look like quarter horses."

"They aren't. They're Arabians. We breed them. Some of the best in the world. The profit margin is a lot more reliable than cattle. In fact, I'm thinking of getting out of the cattle business altogether."

"Well, that figures. I don't see you getting involved in anything that doesn't show an excellent profit margin. Have you considered chickens?"

"*Chickens?*" His expression was a mask of outrage, the sort of outrage only a true cattleman could manage.

"Sure. Red meat is out, Rafe. Haven't you been following the latest health advice? Chicken, fish and vegetables are in. Oh, and turkeys. You might try raising turkeys. I understand they're not real bright so you should be able to figure out a way to round them up and brand them if you feel you must maintain the old traditions."

"Forget chickens and forget turkeys," he growled.

"All right. I imagine the real basis for the family fortune is Cassidy and Company anyway, isn't it? You rustle companies now instead of cattle."

Rafe slanted her a brief, annoyed glance as he parked the Mercedes. "You're determined to make this difficult, aren't you?"

"As difficult as I can," she assured him as she opened her own car door and got out. "Where is my father?"

"Probably out by the pool. That's where I left him when I went to get you." Rafe got out of the Mercedes just as a young man wearing a striped shirt and black jeans came around the corner of the house. "Tom, this is Maggie Lark. Maggie, this is Tom. He takes care of the house gardens and a lot of other odds and ends around here. Tom, grab the lady's luggage, will you? It goes into the south guest bedroom."

"Sure thing, Rafe. Afternoon, Miss Lark. We've been expecting you. Have a good trip?"

"Fine, thank you, Tom." Margaret smiled coolly at him. "Where is the pool?"

Tom looked surprised. "The pool? Out in the patio. Straight through the house. But don't you want to settle into your room first? Maybe change your clothes?" He eyed her silk suit dubiously.

"I want to see my father first. This is a business trip as far as I'm concerned."

"Oh, yeah. Sure. Business." Tom was obviously baffled by that statement. "Like I said, right through the middle of the house."

Margaret did not wait for Rafe to do the honors. She felt his sardonic gaze on her as she turned and strode straight toward the wide, dark wooden door of the Spanish-style home. She opened it and found herself in a cool, tiled hall. The air-conditioning felt wonderful. She took off her sunglasses and glanced around with unwilling curiosity.

This was Rafe's hideaway, she knew, the Cassidy family ranch. He had mentioned it once or twice during the brief time she had been dating him. It was the place he came to when the pressure of his fast-track lifestyle occasionally caught up with him. That wasn't often. Rafe's stamina was legendary.

The Southwestern style of the outside of Rafe's home had been carried on inside. Soft earth tones, terra cotta, peach and pale turquoise dominated. Here and there was a shot of black in the form of a vase or a lamp. Heavily beamed ceilings and rugs with geometric

Indian designs woven into them gave a rustic effect that was also surprisingly gracious.

Through the floor-to-ceiling windows that lined one entire wall of the long living room Margaret could see the pool. It occupied the center of a beautifully landscaped courtyard that was enclosed by the four wings of the house. Two figures were seated under an umbrella, a pitcher of tea on the table between them. Connor Lark and Beverly Cassidy were laughing in delight over some private joke.

Margaret watched the couple for a moment, uncertainty seizing her insides. Her father looked happy—happier than she had ever seen him since her mother died several years ago. She sensed suddenly that her mission to rescue him was going to be difficult to carry out.

"What's the matter, Maggie? Afraid it's not going to be so simple after all?" Rafe asked as he walked into the hall behind her. "I told you they were made for each other."

She glanced back at him, her eyes narrowing. "Hard to imagine you as a matchmaker, Rafe."

"You think I arranged for them to fall for each other just to make it easier to get my hands on Lark Engineering?" He sounded amused. "I'm good, Maggie, but I'm not that good. I take full responsibility for introducing them. After that, they did it all by themselves."

"You think you're very clever, don't you?"

"If I were really clever, we wouldn't have wasted a year of our lives apart. Look, Maggie, do everyone a favor and don't take your father's relationship with my mother as a personal threat, okay? The fact that he fell in love with her doesn't translate directly into a betrayal of you. It's not like your father has gone over to the enemy camp."

Her fingers tightened on the strap of her purse as the shot went home. A part of her had been viewing the situation in exactly that light, she acknowledged privately. It was irrational but the feeling was there on some level. "My father was already halfway into the enemy camp before he met your mother. He took to you right from the start, didn't he?"

"He thought I'd make you a good husband. He was right."

"Oh, yes, he thought you were the ideal husband for me. A genuine cowboy. The son he'd never had, or something along those lines I imagine. I swear, if he'd had the power to arrange the marriage, I think he would have done it. Lark Engineering would have been my dowry."

"There is something to be said for arranged marriages, isn't there?"

"This is not a joke, Rafe."

"So Connor and I get along." Rafe leaned against the wall and folded his arms. "So what?"

Margaret smiled grimly. "Well, at least I've got one person on my side."

"Who?" His eyes were taunting.

"Your mother. She must have been enormously relieved when you threw me out of your life last year."

The lines of his face hardened. "Don't count on it. And stop saying I threw you out."

"That's what happened."

"It was your damn pride that screwed everything up, and you know it. If you'd had the grace to admit you were wrong a year ago, we could have worked things out."

"I wasn't wrong. I did what I had to do. If you'd had the decency not to use me in your campaign to beat Moorcroft to Spencer in the first place, the entire situation would never have developed."

Rafe swore softly and then straightened away from the wall as Tom approached with the luggage. "Go say hello to your father, Maggie."

Feeling a little more cheerful because it seemed like she'd just won that round, Maggie crossed the living room and opened one of the glass doors. Her father looked up as she stepped onto the patio.

"Maggie, my girl, you're here. It's about time. Come on over and have some tea. Bev and I've been waitin' for you to come rescue me from Cassidy's clutches. Good to see you, girl, good to see you. Been a while since we talked."

"We could have had a nice long talk if you'd bothered to answer the phone when I called down here to see what was going on."

"Now, Maggie, girl, don't go gettin' on your high horse. I only did what I thought was best. You know that."

It was impossible to hold on to her anger when her father looked at her with such delight. Margaret saw the relaxed good humor in his eyes and she sighed inwardly. No question about it, her father was here of his own free will.

Connor Lark was a big man, almost as big as Rafe, and he was built like a mountain. There was a hint of a belly cantilevered out over the waistband of his swimming trunks, but he still looked very solid. His black hair had long since turned silver and his aqua eyes, so like her own, were as lively as ever.

Margaret's mother had always claimed he was a diamond in the rough whom she'd had to spend a great deal of time polishing. Connor always claimed she'd enjoyed every minute of the task and Margaret knew she had. From a desperately poor background as a rancher, Connor had risen to become a self-made entrepreneur who had built Lark Engineering into a thriving modern business.

"Well, Dad. Looks like you're enjoying the process of selling out." Margaret smiled affectionately at her father and then turned a slightly wary smile on the attractive woman who sat on the other side of the table. "Hello, Bev. Nice to see you again."

Rafe's mother was a trim, energetic-looking woman who was approximately the same age as Connor, although she looked younger. Her short, well-styled hair was the color of fine champagne. She was wearing a black-and-white swimsuit cover-up and a pair of leather sandals that projected an image of subtle elegance, even though they constituted sportswear. Bev's expression was gracious but her pale gray eyes held the same hint of wariness Margaret knew were in her own.

"Hello, Margaret. I'm pleased to see you again."

Margaret leaned down to kiss her father's cheek, thinking that she and Bev were both good at social lies. She was well aware she had not made a particularly good impression on Beverly Cassidy on the one occasion they had met last year. There was an excellent reason for that. Bev Cassidy had not considered Margaret a good candidate as a wife for her one and only son. Margaret tended to agree with her.

"Do sit down, Margaret," Bev said, reaching for the pitcher of iced tea and pouring her guest a glass. "You must be exhausted from your trip. Your father and I just finished a swim. After you've said hello you must go and put on your suit. I'm sure a dip in the pool will feel good." She turned her welcoming smile on her son as Rafe came through the glass doors and followed Margaret to the shaded loungers. "Oh, there you are, Rafe. Iced tea?"

"Thanks."

He held out his hand for the glass as he sat down beside Margaret on one of the loungers. His powerfully muscled thigh brushed her leg and Margaret promptly shifted to put a few more inches between them. He ignored the small retreat.

Margaret took a long, fortifying sip of iced tea and studied the three people who surrounded her. Her father and Bev appeared to be waiting for her to make the next move. Rafe didn't look particularly concerned one way or the other. To look at him one would have thought this was a perfectly normal family gathering. Margaret frowned over her glass.

"Why don't we all stop playing games," she suggested in a voice that she hoped hid her own inner tension. "We all know this isn't a happy little poolside party."

"Speak for yourself," Connor suggested easily. "I'm happy." He reached across the table and caught Bev's hand, smiling at the older woman. "And I think Bev is, too. Did Rafe tell you the good news?"

"That you and Bev are involved? Yes, he did."

Connor scowled slightly. "I don't know about *involved*. I'm not up on all the new terminology. Is that what they call plannin' to get married nowadays?"

Margaret swallowed. Rafe had been right. This was serious. "You're planning marriage?"

"Yes, we are." Bev looked at Margaret with a faint air of challenge. "I hope you approve."

"I wish you both the best," Margaret made herself say politely. "You'll understand that the news has come as something of a shock. I had no idea you two had even met until Rafe mentioned it."

"Take it easy, Maggie, girl," Connor said gently. "There were reasons I didn't want to talk about it until now."

"Reasons?" She pinned him with her gaze.

"Now, Maggie, lass, you know what I'm talkin' about. The situation 'tween you and Rafe here has been a mite tense for some time."

Margaret arched her brows and slid a long, assessing glance at Rafe. "Tense? I wouldn't say that. I wasn't particularly tense at all during the past year. Were you tense, Rafe?"

"I had my moments," he muttered.

She nodded. "Well, I did try to warn you about stress, didn't I? As I recall, I gave you several pithy little lectures about your long hours, nonexistent vacations and general tendency to put your work first."

"I believe you did mention the subject. Several times, in fact."

Margaret smiled coldly. "Come now, Rafe, you can be honest in front of Dad and your mother. Admit the full truth. Toward the end there I was starting to turn into a full-blown nag when it came to the matter of your total devotion to work, wasn't I? I think I was even beginning to threaten you that if our relationship didn't get equal time there wouldn't be a relationship."

Bev shifted uneasily in her chair, her eyes swinging to Connor.

Margaret's father whistled soundlessly. "Oh, ho. So that's the way of it, is it?"

Rafe gave Margaret a repressive stare. "I had my

hands full last year when we met, if you'll recall. I was juggling a couple of companies that were valued in the millions. Things are different now. I'm making some changes in my life."

"Such as?"

"I've cut way back on the juggling, for one thing." He flashed her a quick grin.

Margaret was not amused. "I find that hard to believe."

"Hey, I'm down here in Arizona with you, aren't I?" He smiled again. "Two full weeks, maybe three if I get lucky. You have my full attention, Maggie, love."

"Not quite. You're in the middle of negotiating a deal with my father, remember?"

Connor chuckled. "She's got you there, Rafe. We are supposed to be talking business off and on, aren't we?"

"Speaking of this little matter of selling the company you built with the sweat of your brow, Dad, just what is going on?" Margaret pinned her father with a quelling glare.

"What can I tell you?" Connor shrugged massively. "It's the truth. If I can get a decent offer out of Cassidy, here, Lark Engineering is his."

"But, Dad, you never told me you were thinking of selling."

"The time has come to enjoy some of the money I made with all that brow sweat. Bev and I plan to do a lot of traveling and a fair amount of just plain fooling around. I'm even looking at a nifty little yacht. Can't you just see me in that fancy yachting getup?"

"But the company has always been so important to you, Dad."

"It's still important. Maggie, girl, I'll be perfectly truthful with you. If you'd stayed in the business world, shown a real interest in it, I'd probably have turned it over to you one of these days. But let's face it, girl, you aren't cut out for that world. And now you've got yourself a fine new career, one you've taken to like a duck to water. I'm glad for you, but it leaves me with a problem. I've got to do something with the firm."

"So you're just going to hand it over to Rafe?"

"He's not exactly handing it over," Rafe muttered. "Your father is holding me at gunpoint. You ought to hear what he's asking for Lark."

"I see." Margaret felt some of the righteous determination seep out of her. Everything was already beyond her control. Rafe was in command, as usual. Things would go his way. A curious sense of inevitability began to come over her. Determinedly she fought back. "Where's the ubiquitous Hatcher?" Margaret asked, glancing meaningfully around the pool. "Surely you haven't dismissed your faithful, loyal, ever-present assistant for two solid weeks?"

Rafe took a swallow of tea. "Hatcher is going to drop by occasionally to brief me on how things are going at the main office. But that's all. I've delegated almost everything else. I'm only available for world-class emergencies. Satisfied?"

"You don't have to worry about my feelings on the subject," Margaret said. "Not anymore. You're free to run your life any way you choose."

"Ouch." Connor winced.

"I know what you mean," Rafe remarked. "She's been sniping at me like that every chance she gets. But I've promised myself I'll be tolerant, patient and understanding. She can't keep it up forever."

"Don't bet on it." Margaret got to her feet. "I believe I will have that swim now. If you'll excuse me, Bev?"

"Of course, dear. The water is lovely."

Bev looked relieved to see her go. But there was an unexpected trace of unhappiness in her gaze, too, Margaret noticed. She wondered about that as she turned to walk back into the house. Surely after the things Bev Cassidy had said to her last year, she couldn't be hoping for a reconciliation between her son and his errant mistress.

Mistress. The old-fashioned word still burned in Margaret's ears whenever she remembered Bev's last words to her. *You'd make him a better mistress than you would a wife.*

"Cocktails at six out here by the pool, dear," Bev called after her. "We'll be eating around seven-thirty. Connor and Rafe have promised to grill us some steaks."

"Right," Connor said cheerfully. "Got us some of the biggest, juiciest, thickest steaks on the face of the planet."

Margaret laughed for the first time since Thursday night. She looked back at the small group gathered under the umbrella. "I almost forgot to mention that I've made a few lifestyle changes myself during the past year."

"Such as?" Rafe asked, lion's eyes watchful.

"I never touch red meat." Margaret walked on into the cool house, paying no attention to her father's bellow of astonishment.

SHORTLY AFTER ONE O'CLOCK in the morning, Margaret eased open the patio door of her bedroom and slipped out into the silent courtyard. She had changed into her bathing suit a few minutes earlier, finally admitting that she was not going to be able to sleep.

The balmy desert air was still amazingly warm. It carried a myriad of soft scents from the gardens. Overhead, the star-studded sky stretched into a dark infinity. Margaret had the feeling that if she listened closely she might actually be able to hear a coyote howl from some nearby hilltop.

The underwater lights of the swimming pool glowed invitingly. Margaret slipped off her sandals and slid into the water. She hovered weightlessly for a long moment and then began to swim the length of the pool. The tension in her muscles slowly dissolved.

It had been a difficult evening.

If she had any sense she would leave tomorrow, she told herself as she reached the far end of the pool and started back. It was the only thing to do. Her father was happy. It was obvious he was not being bamboozled out of Lark Engineering. He truly wanted to sell out to Rafe so there was nothing she could say or do. It was his business, after all.

Yes, she should definitely leave tomorrow. But every time she felt Rafe's eyes on her she found herself looking for an excuse to stay. The excuse of doing battle with him was the only one she had.

There was no sound behind her on the flagstone, but something made Margaret pause in the water and look back toward the far side of the pool. Rafe stood there in the shadows clad in only a snug-fitting pair of swim trunks. Moonlight gleamed on his broad shoulders and in the darkness his eyes were watchful and mysterious.

"Couldn't sleep?" he asked softly.

"No." She treaded water wondering if she should flee back to the safety of her bedroom. But she seemed to lack the strength of will to get out of the pool.

"Neither could I. I've been lying in bed wondering

what kind of reception I'd get if I went to your bedroom."

"A very cold reception."

"You think so? I'm not so sure. That's what was keeping me awake, you know. The uncertainty." He lowered himself silently into the water and stroked quietly toward her.

Margaret instinctively edged back until her shoulders were against the side of the pool. She gripped the tiled edge with one hand as Rafe came to a halt in front of her. "Rafe, I don't think this is a good idea. I came out here to swim alone."

"You're not alone any longer." He put his hands on either side of her, gripping the tile and effectively caging her against the side of the pool. But he made no move to bring his body against hers.

"Are you trying to intimidate me?" Margaret asked, shockingly aware of the brush of his leg against hers under water. Old memories, never far from the surface, welled up swiftly, bringing with them the jolt of desire.

"My goal isn't to intimidate you, honey, it's to remind you of a few things," Rafe said gently. "A few very good things." He came closer, causing the water to lap softly at her throat and shoulders. "Maggie, I've wanted you back in my bed every night since you left. Every damned night. Doesn't that mean anything to you?"

She shivered, although the water was warm. "Did you mean what you said last Thursday? There hasn't been anyone else since you and I...since we've been apart?"

"I meant it. The only thing that kept me sane was knowing you weren't sleeping with anyone else, either."

She scowled. "How did you know that, anyway?"

His mouth thinned. "It's not important."

"You aren't just guessing about my love life during the past year, are you? You know for a fact I haven't been serious about anyone else. Damn it, Rafe, there's only one way you could be so certain. You hired someone to spy on me, didn't you?"

"Maggie, honey, I told you, it's not important."

"Well, it's very important to me. Rafe, how could you?"

"Hush, love." His hand wrapped around her nape and he kissed her lightly. "I said it's not important. Not any longer."

"You should be ashamed of yourself."

"Have pity on me, love. I was a desperate man."

"Rafe, the last thing I will ever have for you is pity. Just what did you think you were going to do if I got involved with someone else?" she demanded.

"Could we discuss something else? Your voice is rising. If you're not careful, you'll wake Mom and Connor. Their bedrooms open onto this courtyard, too."

The last thing she wanted was for anyone to overhear this particular conversation. Margaret reluctantly lowered her tone to a fierce whisper. "What did you think you were going to do, Rafe?"

"Move our thrilling reconciliation up a few months," he told her wryly.

"You're impossible." She didn't believe for a moment that was all he would have done. It was becoming very clear that Rafe had never stopped thinking of her as belonging to him during the past year. Only the knowledge that he'd been celibate during that entire time himself kept her from going up in flames over the matter.

"Tell me you missed me, Maggie. Just a little?"

She shook her head mutely.

"Admit it," Rafe urged, moving a little closer in the water. "Give me that much, honey."

"No." The single word was a soft gasp of dismay. He was only inches from her now. His hands were on either side of her, trapping her.

"You remember how good it was, don't you, love?" He kissed her fleetingly again, closing the distance between them until there wasn't any at all. "I didn't go looking for anyone else because I knew it would be useless. You knew there wasn't anyone else for you, either, didn't you?"

"Oh, Rafe." She muttered his name in a soft cry that was part protest, part acceptance of a truth that could not be denied.

"Yeah, Maggie, love. You do remember, don't you? A whole year, sweetheart. A year of pure hell."

Margaret felt his leg slide between hers as his mouth came down to claim her lips. She felt her breasts being softly crushed against his chest. The hot, sweet rain of passion too long denied swept through her, pooling just below her stomach. Rafe was the only man who had ever been able to do this to her, the only one who could bring her to such shockingly intense arousal with only a look and a kiss and a touch.

Nothing had changed.

"Maggie, love, this time we'll make things work between us." Rafe's mouth moved on hers, gliding along the line of her jaw up to the lobe of her ear. He bit gently, tantalizing her with a pleasure that was not quite pain. "Just give me a chance, sweetheart. I'm going to prove it. Everything is going to be different this time around. Except for this part. No need to fix this, is there?"

He was right about one thing, Margaret thought. This part was still very, very good. Slowly, with a growing sense of inevitability, she felt herself sliding back into the magic world of sensuality that she had shared all too briefly with Rafe.

"Let me love you, Maggie. Let me hold you the way I used to hold you."

"Back when I was your mistress?"

He shook his head, his gaze suddenly fierce. "I never thought of you as a mistress. You were the woman I was going to marry. I knew that from the first day I met you."

"Your mother said I would make a better mistress for you than I would a wife and I think she may have been right."

Rafe's head came up abruptly. "What the devil are you talking about?"

"Never mind. As you said a minute ago, it's not important."

"Maggie, stop talking in riddles."

"I've got a better idea," she suggested softly. "Let's not talk at all." She put her arms around his neck as she made her decision. Heaven help her, she did not have the power to deny herself a night in Rafe's arms. "You were right, Rafe. This part was always very good." She brushed her lips lightly across his and felt his shudder of response.

"Maggie, love." Rafe's voice was a husky groan. "Are you telling me the waiting is over?"

"I want you, Rafe. I never stopped wanting you."

Rafe's mouth closed over hers once more, hard and passionate and filled with a year's worth of pent-up need. Margaret felt his hands moving on her under the water, relearning the shape and feel of her.

His tongue surged between her lips as his fingers slipped under the edge of her swimming suit bra. She gasped as she felt his thumbs slide over her nipples.

"Rafe?"

"Not here," he muttered. "Too much chance of an audience. I'm taking you back to my room."

He hauled himself up onto the tiled edge of the pool with easy strength, then reached down and lifted her up beside him. Margaret looked up into his dark eyes and saw the undiluted hunger there. She felt the answering ache of desire within herself and knew she was still in love with Rafe Cassidy.

You'd make him a better mistress than a wife.

Bev Cassidy's words rang in Margaret's ears once more as Rafe swept her up into his arms and started toward the open door of his bedroom.

CHAPTER FOUR

THE BEDROOM WAS FILLED WITH the inviting mysteries of the night. The woman in Rafe's arms was intoxicating and seemed a part of that glittering darkness.

He was only half-conscious of the dark, cool shadows and the pooling white sheets on the wide bed. All Rafe could think of now was the warm, sensual weight of the woman he held. *His woman.* She was finally back where she belonged.

"It's been so long," he muttered thickly as he set her down beside the bed and reached for a towel. "Too damn long."

He used the towel carefully, tenderly, lovingly. He squeezed the moisture out of her hair and then combed the damp strands back from her forehead with his fingers. She had a misty look on her face. She smiled at him and kissed him gently.

He stroked the water droplets off her arms and knelt to sleek it from her long, curving legs. As he worked he touched her, aware of a surging sense of pure delight as he trailed his fingers along her smooth skin.

When he was finished he quickly dried himself and tossed the towel aside. Then he reached for her.

"Maggie, love. My sweet, sexy Maggie." He pulled her against his chest until her head was resting on his shoulder and then he undid the fastening of her swimsuit bra. Carefully he pulled it free, sliding the straps off her shoulders. He looked down and saw the hardened tips of her breasts and for an instant he thought the desire would overcome him then and there.

It took all his self-control not to rush. He stroked her the way he would one of his beautiful, sensitive mares—gently and slowly. She responded at once, vividly, the way she always had to his touch. Her reaction only served to enhance his own. When her lips moved against his bare skin and her arms went around his waist, he shuddered.

"I missed you so, Rafe."

The soft admission nearly sent him over the edge. "Oh, babe." His fingers trembled as he slid them under the edge of her bikini and pushed the scrap of material down over her hips. It fell to the floor and she stepped daintily away from the damp fabric.

Rafe took a deep breath as he looked down at her. "You're more lovely than you were even in my dreams. And believe me I had a few that were so hot I'm amazed you didn't feel the flames all the way up there in Seattle."

"I had a few of my own." Her eyes were luminous in the shadows as she slid her fingers through the hair on his chest. She traced the shape of his shoulders and then her palm shaped the muscles of his upper arms.

Rafe couldn't wait any longer. He picked her up and set her down on the bed. He felt heavy, his body taut with arousal. His mind whirled with it. He stripped off his swim trunks and lowered himself down beside her. Then he flattened his palm on her stomach and moved his fingers into the triangle of curls at the junction of her thighs. Suddenly his hand was still.

"Rafe, what's wrong?" Margaret asked softly.

"Nothing. Nothing's wrong." He bent his head and

tasted one full nipple. The sensation was exquisite. "I'm just half out of my mind with wanting you now that I've finally got you back in my bed. But I want to do this right. I intended to take it slow. I've waited this long to make it perfect for you."

She laughed, a soft, throaty sound that made him want to hug her. "Rafe, it was always so good, no matter how we did it—fast, slow or in between. You don't have to worry about how we do it tonight."

He groaned and kissed her throat. "Touch me, baby. Feel how much I want you."

Her gentle fingers closed around him and Rafe sucked in his breath, his eyes slitting in reaction to the caress. "You're right. It was good any way we did it and there's no way I can take it slow tonight." He reached over and yanked open the drawer in the nightstand, groping for the small box he had optimistically put there earlier. He used one hand and his teeth to open the packet so he could keep the other hand on Maggie's thigh. He didn't want to let go of her for a second.

A moment later he moved again, rolling on top of Maggie with the wild eagerness of a stallion. He tried to control himself but she was reaching up to clasp him to her and her willingness was his undoing. He parted her legs with his own.

"Yes, Rafe. Please."

He felt her silken thighs alongside his hips and a near-violent wave of desire surged through him. When he probed her carefully he met the damp, welcoming heat and that was all he could stand. He guided himself into her, driving forward into her core. She was so tight. He wondered if he should stop and give her time to adjust to him. After all, it had been a whole year.

But he couldn't stop. Not now. He needed to bury

himself within her. Rafe moaned as he slid fully into her depths. He heard her soft cry in his ear and her nails dug into his shoulders.

"Am I hurting you?" he asked, his breathing turning ragged.

"No. No, it feels wonderful. It's just…been a while, that's all."

"Too damn long for both of us."

"Yes." She lifted her hips against him, telling him she was ready now, urging him into the ancient rhythm.

Rafe needed no additional coaxing. He held her so tightly he was half afraid of crushing her. But she clung to him just as fiercely. He sank himself again and again into her heat until he felt her tightening around him in the old, familiar way.

"*Rafe.*"

"That's it, Maggie, love," he muttered against her mouth. "Come on, honey. Go wild for me."

She shivered and cried out again. He opened his mouth over hers and swallowed the soft, sweet sound. She bucked beneath him and he groaned heavily. Nothing had ever been as shatteringly sexy to Rafe as the feel of Maggie climaxing beneath him.

He waited until the last of the tremors were fading and then he slammed into her one more time and felt himself explode.

Rafe rode the storm for what seemed like forever, the passion in him apparently limitless. And then it was over. He relaxed heavily on top of Maggie, squashing her into the damp sheets.

His last coherent thought was that the waiting and planning were finally finished. He had his Maggie back. No one had ever made him feel the way Maggie did.

It was a long time before Rafe reluctantly stirred. He

only did so because he felt Maggie pushing experimentally against his shoulder.

"What's wrong?" he mumbled, half asleep.

"You're getting very heavy."

"Nag, nag, nag." He levered himself slowly away from her and rolled onto his back. He cradled her close to his side and yawned. "Better?"

"Umm-hmm." She kissed his jaw and then his shoulder, her lips incredibly soft against his skin. "I'd better get back to my own room before I fall asleep."

"No," he muttered instantly. He opened one eye to glare at her. "You sleep here."

She smiled. "I think it would be better if I went back to my own room."

"Why?" He was beginning to feel belligerent.

"Because we aren't alone in the house, remember?"

"My mother and your father both know we've had an affair in the not so distant past and they both know why you're here now. They're not going to ask any questions about why you spent the night in my room. They've taken more than one weekend trip together, you know. Hell, I wouldn't be surprised if your father is paying a late night visit to my mother even as we speak."

"Even if he is, you can bet he'll be back in his own room by dawn. That's the way their generation does things. It's a matter of propriety."

"Yeah? Well, our generation is different."

She chuckled softly. "I'm not so sure about that." Her eyes sobered. "Please, Rafe. I think it would be better if I go back to my own room. It would be embarrassing for me in the morning if…" Her voice trailed off abruptly.

Rafe grinned knowingly and ran his fingers through her hair. "You mean if everyone in the house finds out you surrendered after only one night back under my roof? Yeah, I can see where that would be a little embarrassing for you."

She poked him in the ribs and scowled. "I did not surrender."

Her eyes searched his face. She looked as if she was about to say something and changed her mind. "Good night, Rafe."

He didn't like it but he didn't want to argue with her. Not now that things were finally all right again. "You always were a little shy about this kind of thing, weren't you?"

"I prefer to think of it as circumspect."

"Downright prudish if you ask me. You know what? You're just an old-fashioned girl at heart. But I guess I can put up with your modesty until we make things official." He dragged her head down for another slow, deep kiss and then he forced himself to his feet. He stretched broadly, flexing his muscles for the sheer physical pleasure of it. He hadn't felt this good in a long, long time. A year, to be exact.

"You don't have to walk me back to my room. It's just across the patio. Won't take me ten seconds to get there." Margaret was already reaching for her swimsuit and a towel. He watched her fasten the bra of the suit and wrap the towel around her waist.

"Hey, you're not the only old-fashioned one around here. I'm a little old-fashioned myself. I always walk my dates home, if I can't persuade them to stay until morning." He spoke lightly but when she gave him a strange, searching glance, he frowned. "Something wrong?"

She shook her head quickly, her still-damp hair clinging beguilingly to her throat. "No. I was just remembering something someone had said to me a couple of days ago at a book signing session. Something about cowboys being old-fashioned when it came to things like women."

"Yeah, well, that's what I am when you come right down to it, Maggie, love. A cowboy."

"But you're a very modern sort of cowboy," she said, as if trying to convince herself of something. "You run a large corporation and you routinely make multimillion-dollar deals."

"I can also work cattle and break a horse."

"You can order good wine when the occasion calls for it."

"Yeah, but I don't drink it unless somebody's holding a gun to my head."

"You know the best hotels to stay in when you travel."

"I can also build a fire and skin a rabbit."

"Rafe, I'm trying to make a point here."

"So? What's the fact that I can move in two different worlds got to do with anything? Once a cowboy, always a cowboy. Take a look at your father. He was born and raised on a ranch. He may have gotten an engineering degree but that doesn't change what he is deep down inside. That's one of the reasons he and I get along. We understand each other."

"Oh, what's the use. You may be right. I have to tell you the truth, Rafe. I never wanted to get involved with a cowboy, modern or otherwise."

"Too bad, Maggie, love, because you are involved with one. For your own sake, don't go trying to convince yourself you've gotten hooked up with one of those new, sensitive, right-thinking males you read about in ladies' magazines."

Margaret wrinkled her nose. "What would you know

about the new, sensitive, right-thinking man? You don't read women's magazines."

"I heard all about 'em from Julie once when she was trying to convince me to approve of some damned psychologist she was dating."

"Rafe, did you ruin that relationship for her?"

"I didn't have to. The guy ruined it for himself. She found out he was seeing someone else on the side and when she confronted him he told her he needed a relationship in which he could be free to explore his full potential as a human being."

Margaret eyed him curiously. "What happened?"

"What do you think happened? Julie's a Cassidy, too. Cassidys don't believe in open relationships. She gave him a swift kick in his new, sensitive, right-thinking rear."

"Good for her," Margaret said automatically and then frowned darkly. "Still, you shouldn't judge the new, sensitive, right-thinking man by one bad apple, Rafe."

"I'm not going to judge the new, sensitive, right-thinking man at all. I'm going to ignore him and so are you." He bent his head and brushed her lips with his own.

Her mouth was still full and soft from the after-effects of their recent lovemaking. The scent of her hung in the room and would be clinging to his sheets. Rafe felt himself getting hard all over again just thinking about what was going to happen to him when he climbed back into those sheets.

"Rafe?"

"You're sure you want to go?"

"Yes."

"As I said, I can wait. I'm one hell of a patient man,

Maggie, love." He pulled on his trunks, took her hand and led her out onto the starlit patio.

MARGARET ROSE VERY EARLY the next morning after a restless night's sleep. Her thoughts, confused and chaotic, had tumbled about in her head after Rafe had left her to return to his own room. She could not regret their lovemaking or the resumption of their precarious relationship, but she knew there was trouble on the horizon.

There were too many unresolved issues, too many things from the past that had not changed. Rafe was still Rafe. And that meant there would be problems.

Still, this morning she could allow herself to think more positively about the possibilities of an affair with the man she loved. She would never find anyone else like him, Margaret knew.

She chose a pair of designer jeans that were cut to show off her small waist and emphasize the flare of her hips. She added a rakish red shirt and sandals and went out onto the patio to savor the short cool hours of early morning in the desert. Soon the temperature would start climbing rapidly.

"Good morning, Margaret. Come and join me in a cup of coffee."

Margaret glanced in surprise at Bev Cassidy who was sitting alone under the umbrella. A stout-looking woman in her fifties had just finished putting a silver pot of coffee and a tray of fresh breakfast pastries and fruit down on the table. The woman smiled at Margaret and nodded a greeting. Margaret smiled back.

"Margaret, this is Ellen. Ellen comes in during the days to take care of the house for Rafe."

"Ellen."

"Nice to meet you, Miss Lark. Hope you enjoy your stay. By the way, I love your books."

"Thank you very much."

"Sit down," Bev urged as the housekeeper disappeared.

"You're up bright and early, Bev." Margaret summoned up a smile and walked over to take a seat opposite her hostess. She had known when she had boarded the plane that there would be no way to avoid Rafe's mother. She braced herself for this first one-on-one confrontation.

"I love the early hours in the desert." Bev poured a cup of coffee and handed it to Margaret. "Did you sleep well, dear?"

Margaret took refuge in a social white lie. "Very well, thank you."

Bev smiled gently. "I'm sorry you had to learn about your father's engagement the way you did. Rafe was very insistent on keeping the full truth from you until…" She let the words slide away into nothingness.

"Until he was ready to close his trap?" Margaret nodded as she sipped her coffee. "That's Rafe, all right. Sneaky." She reached for a slice of melon.

Bev let out a small sigh. "He cares very deeply about you, Margaret. I hadn't fully realized just how much until you left him last year."

"I would like to clear up a major misconception around here, Bev. I didn't leave Rafe. He told me to get out of his life."

"And you went."

"Yes."

Bev slowly shook her head. "I won't deny that at the time I thought it was for the best."

"I can imagine your feelings on the matter. I know

exactly how you felt about me as a wife for your son."
Margaret smiled to cancel any bitterness that might
have tinged the words. "If it makes you feel any better,
I've come to agree with you."

Bev's eyes widened with sudden shock. "What are
you saying?"

"That you were right when you told me I would
make a lousy wife for Rafe."

"I only said that because I was afraid you would try
to change him—make him into something he was not.
Margaret, please believe me when I tell you that I never
had anything at all against you personally. The truth is,
I like you very much. I admire you." Bev smiled. "I've
even started reading your books. I'm enjoying *Ruthless*
enormously."

Margaret grinned. "As any author will tell you, flattery will get you anywhere. We're suckers for people
who say they like our books."

"Good. Then perhaps you'll forgive me for some of
the things I said to you last year?"

"We both know they were true, Bev. I would probably make Rafe very unhappy, frustrated and eventually blazingly angry if I were to marry him."

"I used to think so but I'm not so sure about that
anymore, Margaret."

"I am. For starters, I would insist on our relationship
getting equal billing with his business interests. Truth
be known, I'd go farther than that. If the chips were
down, I'd insist that our marriage come first. I would
make every effort to force him to live a more balanced
life. I would make him work regular hours and take vacations. And I would not play the role of the self-sacrificing executive's wife who always puts her husband's
career first."

Bev sighed. "I sensed that when I met you. I think I reacted so strongly to you because I had played exactly that role for Rafe's father. I was certain Rafe needed a wife who would do the same."

"I think you're right. He does need a wife like that. But I couldn't live that life, Bev. It would turn me bitter and unhappy within a very short period of time. I want a husband who loves me more than he loves his corporation. I want a man who puts me first. I want to be the most important thing in his life. And we both know that for Rafe, business is the most important thing in the world. For him, a wife will be only a convenience."

"Margaret, listen to me. Last year I believed that every bit as much as you did. But now I no longer think that's true. Rafe has changed during the past year. Your walking out on him did that."

"I did not walk out on him."

"All right, all right, I didn't mean to put it that way." Bev held up one hand in a placating fashion. "Losing you did change him, though. I wouldn't have believed it possible if I hadn't seen it with my own eyes. Until you were gone, he was as driven to succeed as his father had been—more so because the stakes were higher after John died."

Margaret frowned. "Rafe was trying to show that he could be as successful as his father?"

"No, he was trying to rescue us from the financial disaster in which John left us." Bev's mouth tightened. "My husband was a good man in many respects, but his business was everything to him. He ate, slept and breathed Cassidy and Company. But shortly before he was killed in a plane accident, he suffered some enormous financial losses. You'll have to ask Rafe for the details. It had to do with some risky investments that went bad."

"Was Rafe involved?"

Bev shook her head. "No. Rafe had gone off on his own. He was too much like John in many ways and he knew it. He realized from the time he was in high school that he could never work for his father. They would have been constantly at each other's throats. They were both stubborn, both smart and both insisted on being in charge. An impossible working situation."

"Did your husband accept that?"

"To his credit, John did understand. He wished Rafe well when Rafe started his own business. But John always assumed that when he retired, Rafe would take over Cassidy and Company and then John was killed."

Margaret watched Bev toy with her coffee cup. "Rafe did come back to take over Cassidy and Company, then, didn't he? Just as your husband would have wanted."

"Oh, yes. Rafe took the reins. And that's when we discovered that John had been on the brink of bankruptcy. Rafe worked night and day to save the business and he did save it. Against all odds. You can be certain the financial community had already written off Cassidy and Company. We survived and the company is flourishing now, but the experience did something to Rafe."

"What do you mean?"

Bev poured more coffee. "Watching Rafe work to salvage Cassidy and Company was like watching steel being forged in fire. He went into the whole thing as a strong man or he wouldn't have survived. But he came out of it much harder, more ruthless and a lot stronger than he'd been before his experience. Too hard, too ruthless and too strong in some ways. His sister, Julie, calls him a gunslinger because he's made a habit of taking on all challengers."

Margaret had never met Julie. There had been no opportunity. But it sounded as if the woman had her brother pegged. She looked down into the depths of her coffee. "He didn't like losing to Moorcroft's firm last year."

"No, he did not." Bev smiled briefly. "And you can be certain that one of these days he'll find a way to even the score."

Margaret felt a frisson of uneasiness go down her spine. She thought about her conversation with Jack Moorcroft shortly before leaving Seattle. "I'm glad I'm out of it."

"What Rafe does about Moorcroft is neither here nor there. It's your relationship with my son that concerns me. Rafe put a lot of his life on hold while he worked to save Cassidy and Company. One of the things he avoided was marriage. Now he's nearly forty years old and time is running out. I think he realizes that. I want him to be happy, Margaret. I have come to realize during the past year that you are probably the one woman who can make him happy."

Margaret stared at her helplessly. "But that's just it, Bev. I can't make him happy. Not as his wife, at any rate. I simply can't be the kind of wife he wants or needs. So I'm going to take your advice."

Bev looked at her with worried eyes. "What advice?"

"I'm going to try having an affair with him."

"You mean you're not going to marry him?" Bev looked stunned.

Before Margaret could respond, her father's voice bellowed over the patio. "What the hell do you mean, you're not marrying him? Cassidy swore he was offering marriage. That's the only reason I agreed to get involved in this tomfool plan to get you down here. What the blazes does he think he's trying to pull around here?"

"Dad, hang on a minute." Margaret turned in her chair to see her father bearing down on her. "Let me explain."

"What's to explain? I'll have Cassidy's hide, by God. I'll take a horse whip to that boy if he thinks he can lead my little girl down the garden path."

"Sit down, Dad."

Bev tried a pacifying smile. "Yes, Connor. Do sit down and let your daughter explain. You didn't hear the whole story."

"I don't need to hear anything more than the fact that Cassidy isn't proposing. That's enough for me." Connor glowered at both women, but accepted the cup Bev pushed toward him. "Don't you worry, Maggie. I'll set him straight fast enough. He'll do the right thing by you if I have to tie him up and use a branding iron on him."

Rafe came out of his bedroom at that moment, striding across the patio with his usual unconscious arrogance. Margaret watched him, memories of the night flaring again in her mind. He looked so lithe, sensual and supremely confident in a pair of jeans and a shirt that was unbuttoned at the throat. His dark hair was still damp from a shower and his eyes told her he, too, was remembering what had happened out here between them last night. When he saw he had her full attention, a slight smile edged his mouth and his left eye narrowed in a small, sexy wink.

"Morning, everyone," he said as he came to a halt

beside the table. He bent his head to kiss Margaret full on the mouth and then he reached for the coffeepot. He seemed unaware of the fact that his mother was looking uneasy and that Connor was glowering at him. "Beautiful day, isn't it? When we're finished here, Maggie, love, I'll take you out to the barns and show you some of the most spectacular horseflesh you've seen in your entire life."

"Hold on there, Cassidy." Connor's bushy brows formed a solid line above his narrowed eyes. "You aren't going anywhere with my girl until we sort out a few details."

Rafe lounged back in his chair, cup in hand. "What's with you this morning, Connor? Got a problem?"

"You're the one with the problem. A big one."

"Yeah? What would that be?"

"You told me you intended to marry my Maggie. That's the only reason I overlooked the way you treated her last year and agreed to help you get her down here."

Rafe shrugged, munching on a breakfast pastry. "So?"

"So she just said you two weren't gettin' married after all."

Rafe stopped munching. His eyes slammed into Margaret's. A great deal of the indulgent good humor he had been exhibiting a minute ago had vanished from the depths of his gaze.

"The hell she did," Rafe said, his eyes still locked with Margaret's.

"Heard her myself, Cassidy, and I want some answers. Now." Connor's fist struck the table to emphasize his demand.

"You're not the only one." Rafe was still staring grimly at Margaret.

Margaret groaned and traded glances with a sympathetic-looking Bev. "You shouldn't have eavesdropped, Dad. You got it all wrong."

"I did?" Connor stared at her in confusion. "But I heard you tell Bev you and Cassidy weren't going to get married. You said something about settling for a damned affair."

"Is that right?" Rafe asked darkly. "Is that what you said, Maggie?"

Margaret got to her feet, aware of the other three watching her with unrelenting intensity. She felt cornered. "I said that I would not make a good wife for Rafe. That does not mean, however, that he and I can't enjoy an affair. I've decided to pick up where we left off last year."

"We were engaged last year," Rafe reminded her coldly.

"No, Rafe. You might have felt you were engaged because you had asked me to marry you several times, but the truth is I was still considering your proposal when everything blew up in my face. I had doubts about the wisdom of marrying you then and after having had a full year to think about it, I have even more doubts about it now. Therefore, I'm only willing to go as far as having an affair with you. Take it or leave it."

"The hell I will."

"Rafe, your mother was right. I'll make you a much better mistress than I would a wife." Without waiting for a response, Margaret turned and started toward the sanctuary of her bedroom.

She never made it. Rafe came silently up out of his chair and swooped across the patio in a few long strides. He caught her up in his arms and tossed her over his shoulder before she knew quite what had happened.

Rafe didn't pause. He didn't say a word. He simply carried her through one of the open glass doors, across the living room and out into the hot sunshine.

CHAPTER FIVE

"WHAT DO YOU THINK you're doing, Rafe? This is inexcusable behavior, absolutely inexcusable. I will not tolerate it."

"It's cowboy behavior and I'm just a cowboy at heart, remember?" He strode swiftly toward one of the long, low white barns.

"You're an arrogant, high-handed bastard at heart, that's what you are." Margaret was suddenly acutely aware of an audience. Tom and another man in work clothes and boots glanced toward Rafe and grinned broadly. "Rafe, people are watching. For heaven's sake, put me down."

"I don't take orders from a mistress."

"Damn it, Rafe."

"Now, I might listen to an engaged lady or a wife, maybe, but not a mistress. No, ma'am."

"*Put me down.*"

"In a minute. I want to find us some privacy first."

"Privacy. Rafe, you're creating an embarrassing public spectacle. And you have the nerve to wonder why I never came crawling back to you on my hands and knees this past year begging you to forgive me. This sort of behavior is exactly why I considered I'd had a very lucky escape."

"Let's not bring up past history. We're supposed to

be making a fresh start, remember? If I can let bygones be bygones, so can you."

"You are unbelievably arrogant."

"Yeah, but even better, I usually get what I want."

He carried her into the soft shadows of a long barn. Hanging upside down as she was, Margaret had an excellent view of a straw-littered floor. The earthy scents of horses and hay wafted up around her. A row of equine heads with pricked ears appeared above the open stall doors.

Margaret gasped as Rafe swung her off his shoulder and onto her feet. As she regained her balance she glared at her tormentor and fumbled to readjust the clip that held her hair at her nape.

"Honestly, Rafe, that was an absolutely outrageous thing to do. I'd demand an apology but I know I won't get one. I doubt if you've ever apologized in your entire life."

"Maggie, love, we'd better have a long talk. There appears to be a slight misunderstanding here."

"Stop calling me Maggie. I've told you a hundred times I don't like it. That's another thing. You never really listen to me, do you? You think everything has to be done your way and the rest of us should just learn to like it that way, no matter what. Your mother tried to tell me this morning that you'd changed during the past year but I knew better and I was right, wasn't I? You just proved it. You're still a thickheaded, domineering, bossy, overbearing cowboy who rides roughshod over everyone else."

"*That's enough.*" Rafe stood with his booted feet braced, his hands on his hips, his eyes narrowed dangerously.

"Good Lord, you are a real cowboy, aren't you?" Her

voice was scathing. "You look right at home here in this barn with that…that *stuff* on your boots."

He glanced down automatically and saw the stuff to which she referred with such disdain. There was a small pile of it near his left boot. Prudently he moved the elaborately tooled black leather boot with its red and yellow star design a few inches to the right.

"Goes with the territory," Rafe said. He looked up again. "And you can quit playing the sophisticated city girl who's never seen the inside of a barn. I know the truth about you, lady. Connor and I have had a few long talks."

"Is that right'?" she sniffed.

"Damned right. I know for a fact you were born on your dad's ranch in California and you were raised on it until you were thirteen. You didn't start picking up your fancy airs until Connor sold the place and your family went to live in San Francisco."

"I prefer to forget my rustic background," she retorted. "And for your information, my standards have changed since I was thirteen. For all intents and purposes, I'm very much a city girl now and I expect a certain level of appropriate behavior from the male of the species."

"You'll take the behavior you get. Furthermore, I think I've had all the squawking I want to hear from you, *city girl*. You're not the only one who expects a certain level of appropriate social behavior. You're acting like a sharp-tongued, temperamental prima donna who thinks she can play games with me."

"That's not true."

"Yeah? Then what was all that nonsense by the pool a few minutes ago? What do you think you're doing telling our folks you don't intend to marry me?"

"It's the truth. I don't intend to marry you. I've never said I would marry you. Marrying you would be an extremely dumb thing for me to do."

The glittering outrage in his eyes was unnerving. Rafe took a single step closer. Margaret took a prudent step backward. A horse in a nearby stall wickered inquiringly.

"I didn't bring you down here to set you up as a mistress and you know it," Rafe said between his teeth.

"Don't use that word."

"What word? Mistress? That's what you're suggesting we call you, isn't it?"

"No, it's not." Margaret scowled angrily. "That's your mother's word. I explained to you last night, people like her and my father come from another generation."

"You also said that deep down you didn't think we were all that different from them," Rafe shot back. "What the hell did you think you were doing last night if you weren't agreeing to come back to me?"

She lifted her chin. "Last night I decided that we might try resuming our affair."

"That's real generous of you. The only problem is that we don't happen to have an affair to resume."

She glared at him in open challenge. "Is that right? What do you call us sleeping together for nearly two months last year?"

"Anticipating our wedding vows."

Margaret stared at him, openmouthed. She did not know whether to laugh or cry. Rafe looked perfectly serious, totally self-righteous. "You're joking. That's what you called our affair? How quaint. But there never was a wedding, so what does that make the whole business? Besides a big mistake, I mean?"

"There's damn well going to be a wedding."

"Why?" she asked bluntly.

"Because you and I belong together, that's why. And you know it, Maggie. Or have you forgotten last night already?"

"No, I haven't forgotten it, but just because we're good together in bed does not mean we should get married. Rafe, listen to me. I've tried to explain to everyone that I would make you a lousy wife. Why won't anyone pay any attention to what I'm saying?"

"Because you're talking garbage, that's why."

Margaret sighed heavily. "This is impossible. We're getting nowhere. Talk about a communication problem. I'd better leave—the sooner the better."

Rafe reached out and caught her arm as she would have turned away. A fierce determination blazed in his eyes and his voice had a raw edge to it. "You can't leave. Not now. I spent six months in hell trying to pretend you didn't exist and another six months figuring out ways to get you back. I'm not going to let you go this time."

"You can't stop me, Rafe. Oh, I know I let you coerce me into coming down here. But we both know you can't make me stay against my will. And the truth is, there's nothing I can do here, anyway. I've seen for myself that my father is happy with your mother. I would hurt him by trying to interfere. And if he wants to sell Lark Engineering to you, that's his business. It's clear you're not trying to cheat him out of the firm."

"I didn't bring you down here so that you could protect your father. We both know he can take care of himself. I got you down here so that we could start over again, Maggie, and you know it. Furthermore, if you're honest with yourself for once, you'll admit that's why you used that ticket so damn fast once I'd given you a good enough excuse."

He was right and that jolted her. She had known all along that her father could take care of himself, even against the likes of Rafe Cassidy. Everyone involved had politely let her pretend that she had rushed down here to rescue Connor but everyone knew the truth.

"This is extremely humiliating," Margaret said.

"If it makes you feel any better, take it from me you don't know what I was going through yesterday morning at the airport waiting to see if you were on that flight. I was afraid to even call your apartment in Seattle in case you answered the phone. How's that for proof that you have an equal ability to make me feel like an idiot?"

The intensity of his words shook her. She bit her lip and then reached out hesitantly to touch his hand. When he glanced down she withdrew her fingers immediately. "Rafe, it won't work. We might have managed a long-distance affair. For a while. But we'll never manage a marriage. Your mother was right all along."

"Stop saying that, damn it. She was wrong and she admits it. Why do you keep quoting something she said a year ago as if it were carved in stone?"

"Because she was right a year ago. You're a driven man when it comes to business or anything else you decide you want. This morning she told me more about why you're driven but that doesn't change anything. It just helps explain why you are the way you are."

Rafe swore in disgust. "She gave you some tripe about me being somewhat, uh, aggressive in business because I had to work so hard to rescue Cassidy and Company, didn't she? Julie says that's her current theory on my behavior."

"Well, yes. And you're not *somewhat* aggressive, Rafe, you're a real predator. What's more, you get downright hostile when someone steals your prey the way you think I helped Moorcroft do last year."

"Look, maybe I'd better make one thing clear here. My mother likes to think I'm the way I am—I mean, was—because of what happened after Dad was killed. But the truth is, I was like that long before I took over Cassidy and Company. Dad knew it. Hell, I was born that way, according to my father. Same as he was."

Margaret nodded sadly. "You didn't change so that you could salvage the company, you managed to salvage the company because you were already strong enough and aggressive enough to do it."

"But things are different now. I've changed. I keep telling you that. Give me a chance, Maggie."

"Last night I thought I could."

"You call having an affair with me giving me a chance?" he demanded incredulously.

She nodded. "It was a way to try again. A way that left us both free to change our minds without breaking any promises. It would have given us time to observe each other and reassess the situation."

"Hell." He ran his hand through his hair in a gesture of pure frustration. "I don't need any more time, Maggie. I've been reassessing this damned situation for months."

"Well, I do need time."

"This isn't just a question of my work habits, is it?" he asked shrewdly. "The truth is you aren't going to forgive me for what happened between us last year, are you?"

"You've never asked me to forgive you, Rafe." She smiled bleakly. "You're much too proud for that, aren't you? Oh, you very generously forgave me, but you don't think you need to be forgiven. It's all black and white to you. You were right and I was clearly in the wrong."

"You made a mistake. Conflicting sets of loyalties, as I said. You were under a lot of pressure at the time and you got confused."

"So confused I'd do it again if I had to. I didn't like being used, Rafe."

His jaw tightened. "I did not use you."

"That's not the way I saw it. You knew I was working for Jack Moorcroft when you started dating me, didn't you?"

"Yeah, but damn it…"

"I, on the other hand, did not have the advantage of knowing you were a business rival of his. I didn't even realize you two knew each other, let alone were fierce competitors. You kept that information from me, Rafe."

"Only because I knew you'd have a problem dating me in the beginning if you knew the whole truth. I didn't want to lose you by telling you Moorcroft and I were after the same prize. You'd have felt guilty going out with me. And if you'll recall, I never tried to pump you for inside information."

"You let me talk about my job," she accused. "You let me tell you about the projects I was working on. You showed so much interest in me. I was so terribly flattered by that interest. It makes me sick to think how flattered I was."

"What was I supposed to do? Tell you not to talk about your work?"

"Yes. That's exactly what you should have told me."

"Be reasonable, Maggie. If I had tried to explain just why you shouldn't talk to me about your job, you'd have very quickly figured out who I was. I couldn't let that happen."

"Because you needed the inside information in order to beat Moorcroft to Spencer."

"That's a lot of horse manure," he told her roughly. "I didn't tell you to shut up about your work because I'd have lost you if I had. If it makes you feel any better, you can rest assured I had all the information I needed to beat Moorcroft to the punch from other sources. Nothing you told me made any difference in my plans."

"Oh, Rafe."

"You want the flat honest truth? Moorcroft's the one who got the advantage out of our relationship. You ran to him that morning and warned him I was after Spencer. Thanks to you, he was able to move his timetable ahead fast enough to knock me out of the running. I was the one who lost out because I was sleeping with a woman who felt her first loyalty belonged to another man."

Margaret looked up at him appealingly, longing to believe him and knowing she should not. "Rafe, is that the full truth? Really? You didn't use any of the information I accidently gave you?"

His mouth twisted ruefully. "It's the truth, all right. If you'd known everything in the beginning, you'd have assumed I'd started dating you because of your connection to Moorcroft and you'd have backed right off. Don't try to deny it. I know you. That's exactly how your brain would have worked—exactly how it did work when you finally discovered who I was."

Margaret felt cornered again. He was right. She would have been instantly suspicious of his motives if she'd known who he was back at the beginning. "And you really didn't need inside information from me?"

"I already had most of it. Nothing you told me was particularly crucial one way or the other. In fact, if you'll stop and think about it, you'll recall that you didn't talk all that much about your job. You mostly talked about the career in writing that you were working on. I heard all your big plans to work two more years in the business world and then quit to write full-time."

"I wish I could believe that." She clasped her hands in front of her, remembering her terrible feeling of guilt at the time. "I felt like such a fool. I felt so used. I went over and over every conversation we'd had, trying to recall exactly what I'd told you. I knew I had to go straight to Moorcroft, of course. He had trusted me. I had to make up for what I'd done to him."

"You didn't do one blasted thing to him," Rafe roared. "I was the one you screwed."

She frowned in annoyance. "You don't have to be quite so crude about it."

He spread his hands in a disgusted movement and made an obvious grab for his self-control. "Forget it. I'm sorry I mentioned my side of the story. I know you aren't particularly interested in it. You're only concerned with your side."

Tears welled in Margaret's eyes. She blinked them back as she sank down onto a bale of hay and tried to think. "It was such an awful mess at the time," she whispered. "And when I tried to do the right thing by warning Moorcroft about you, you turned on me like a…a lion or something. All teeth and claws. The things you said to me… You ripped me to shreds, Rafe. I wasn't certain for a while if I was ever going to recover."

"You weren't the only one who felt ripped up." Rafe

sat down beside her, elbows resting on his knees, his big hands loosely clasped. He stared straight ahead at a pretty little gray mare who was watching the proceedings with grave curiosity. "I wasn't sure I was going to make it, either." He paused for a moment. "My mother says it was probably the best thing that ever happened to me."

"She said *what*?"

"She said I needed a jolt like that to make me pay attention to something else in life besides business." His smile was ironic. "Believe me, after what happened last year, you had my full attention. I couldn't stop thinking about you no matter how hard I tried. I've put more energy into getting you back than I've ever put into a merger or a buyout."

Margaret thought she really would cry now. "Rafe, I don't know what to say."

He turned his head, his eyes glittering with intensity. "Say you'll give me a chance, a real chance. Let's start over, Maggie. For good this time. Give me the next two weeks and be honest about it. Don't spend the time looking for excuses and a way out."

The love for him that she had been forced to acknowledge to herself last night made Margaret lightheaded. She looked into his tawny eyes and felt herself falling back into the whirlpool in which she had nearly drowned last year. "You are a very dangerous man for me, Rafe. I can't go through what I went through last time. I can't."

He caught her chin on the edge of his hand. "You're not the only one who wouldn't survive it a second time. So there won't be a second time."

She searched his eyes. "How can you be so certain?"

"Two reasons. The first is that we learned something

from that fiasco. We've both changed. We aren't quite the same people we were last year."

"And the second reason?"

He smiled faintly. "You aren't working for Moorcroft or anyone else, so the pressures you had on you last time don't exist."

"But if they did exist?"

Rafe's smile hardened briefly. "This time around your commitments are clearer, aren't they? This time around you'd know your first loyalty belongs to me."

"What about *your* loyalty?" she challenged softly, knowing she was sliding deeper into the whirlpool. In another moment she would be caught and trapped.

Rafe cradled her face between two rough palms. "You are the most important person in my life, Maggie, love. My first loyalty is to you."

"Business has absolutely nothing to do with this?"

"Hell, no."

"If there were to be a conflict between our relationship and your business interests, would our relationship win?"

"Hands down."

Her fingers tightened around his wrists. Everything in her wanted to believe him. Margaret knew her future was at stake. If she had any sense she would get out while she still could.

"Rafe…"

"Say it, Maggie. Say you'll stay here and give me a real chance."

She closed her eyes and took a deep breath. "All right."

He groaned and pulled her close against him, his arms locking around her. His mouth moved against her sleekly knotted hair. "You won't regret it, Maggie. This time it will work. You'll see. I'll make it work. I've missed you so much, sweetheart. Last night…"

"What about last night?" she asked softly.

"Last night was like taking the first glass of cool water after walking out of the desert. Except that you're never cool in bed. You're hotter than the sun in August. Lord, Maggie, last night was good."

She hugged him, her head resting on his chest. "Yes."

"Maggie?"

"Um?"

"You said a few minutes ago that I'd never asked for forgiveness because I was too arrogant to think I needed it. But I'm asking for it now. I'm sorry I was so rough with you last year."

She took a breath. It was probably as much of an apology as she was likely to get. "All right, Rafe. And I'm sorry I assumed you'd been using me to beat Moorcroft. I should have known better."

"Hush, love. It's all right." His hands stroked her back soothingly. "We'll make this a fresh start. No more talk about the past."

"Agreed."

For a long while they sat on the bale of hay, saying nothing. If anyone came or went in the barn, Margaret didn't notice. She was conscious only of the feel of Rafe's hands moving gently on her. With a deep sigh of newly found peace, she gave herself up to the luxury of once more being able to nestle in Rafe's strong arms. *A fresh start.*

For the first time in a year something that had felt twisted and broken deep inside her relaxed and became whole again.

"Boss?" Tom's shout from the far end of the barn

had a trace of embarrassed hesitation in it. "Hatcher's here. Says he needs to talk to you."

Rafe slowly released Margaret. "Tell him I'll be there in a minute."

"Right."

Rafe looked down at Margaret, his expression rueful. "Sorry about this. Hatcher's timing isn't always the best. Want to come say hello to him?"

"Okay. But he probably doesn't want to say hello to me."

"Maggie, love, you're getting paranoid. You thought my mother wouldn't want to see you again, either, but she could hardly wait for you to get down here, right? Don't worry about Hatcher's opinion. He works for me and he does what I say."

Shaking her head, Margaret let Rafe tug her to her feet. He draped an arm possessively around her shoulders and guided her out of the barn. She blinked as she stepped out into the hot sunlight. There was an unfamiliar car in the drive.

Doug Hatcher was already standing in the doorway of Rafe's home, a briefcase in one hand. Rafe's chief executive assistant looked very much as Margaret remembered him from the occasions he had accompanied his fast-moving boss to Seattle.

Hatcher was in his early thirties, a thin, sharp-faced man with pale eyes. He was dressed in a light-colored business suit, his tie knotted crisply in defiance of the heat. He did not seem surprised to see Margaret coming out of the barn with his boss.

"Good morning, Miss Lark." Hatcher inclined his head politely. "Nice to see you again."

"Thank you, Doug." She knew he was lying through his teeth. The poor man was no doubt struggling might-

ily to maintain a polite facade. There was little chance
he was actually glad to see her. Hatcher was fiercely
loyal to Rafe and he probably blamed her for the collapse of the Spencer deal last year. She was not at all
certain his opinion of her would have changed just because Rafe ordered him to change it.

Then again, when Rafe gave orders, people tended
to obey.

"What's up, Hatcher?" Rafe asked easily. "I'm on
vacation, remember?"

"Yes, sir." Hatcher indicated the briefcase. "I just
need to update you on a couple of things. You said you
wanted to keep close track of the Ellington deal. There
have been a couple of recent developments I felt you
should know about. I also have some figures to show
you."

Rafe released Maggie abruptly. His good mood
seemed to have suddenly evaporated. She recognized
the signs instantly. She could almost feel him shifting
gears into what she always thought of as his "business
alert" mode. He was fully capable of remaining in it
for hours, even days, on end. When he was caught up
in it nothing else mattered to him. He brooked no dis-
tractions, not even from the woman he was currently
bedding.

"Right," Rafe said. "Let's go inside and take care of
it. Maggie, why don't you take a swim or something?"

Her first reaction was a rush of anger. Same old
Rafe. As soon as business reared its ugly head, he was
like a hunter who had caught the scent of prey. He was
already dismissing her while he took care of more important things.

Then she looked at his face and saw the tension in
him. He knew what she was thinking. The fact that her

incipient disapproval had gotten through to him was something, she told herself. Last year he wouldn't have even noticed.

"I don't really feel like a swim, Rafe."

"Honey, this won't take long, I swear it. I guarantee I've developed some new ways of working lately, but I can't just let go of everything, you know that. I'm still responsible for my family, the ranch and a heck of a lot of jobs at Cassidy and Company. Be reasonable."

She relaxed slightly as she saw the expression in his eyes. "I know, Rafe. It's all right. I understand. I think I will have that swim, after all." Of course he couldn't let go of everything. She didn't expect him to abandon his business altogether. She just wanted him to learn to put things in perspective. He was trying, she realized. And that was the first step.

Rafe nodded once, looking vastly relieved. "Thanks. Let's go, Hatcher. I want to get this over with as fast as possible. I've got other things to do today. More interesting things."

"Yes, sir."

Margaret preceded both men into the house and was turning to go down the hall to her bedroom when Bev Cassidy came through the patio doors. Connor Lark was right behind her. They both looked anxiously first at Margaret and then at Rafe.

"You two get this marriage business settled?" Connor demanded aggressively. "Bev and I aren't takin' off for Sedona day after tomorrow the way we planned if you two haven't worked this out."

"Don't worry, Connor. Everything's under control," Rafe said mildly.

"You sure?"

"I'm sure," Rafe said.

"About time."

"Yeah. You can say that again." Rafe started toward the study he used as an office. "I need to spend a few minutes with Hatcher. Maggie's going swimming, aren't you, Maggie?"

"Looks like it," said Maggie.

Bev brightened. "I've got another idea, if you're interested, Margaret?"

"What's that?" Margaret smiled.

"How would you like to go shopping? I thought you might want to buy something to wear to the engagement party tomorrow evening."

Margaret reeled. Her eyes widened in shock as she whirled to glare at Rafe. "*Engagement party.* Now, just hold on one minute, here, I've never said anything about getting officially engaged. Don't you dare try to rush me like this, Rafe. Do you hear me? I won't stand for it."

Hatcher, Conner and Bev looked at each other in obvious embarrassment. But there was a suspiciously humorous glint in Rafe's eyes when he said very gently, "Mom is talking about the engagement party she and Connor are giving tomorrow night to celebrate their engagement. Not ours."

"I'm so sorry, dear," Bev said quickly. "In all the excitement of your arrival yesterday, I forgot to mention it. We're having a few friends over to celebrate tomorrow evening. The next day Connor and I are going to take a little trip."

Margaret learned the meaning of wishing the floor would open up and swallow her whole. "Oh," she said, flushing a bright pink. She turned to Bev. "Shopping sounds like a wonderful idea. I haven't a thing to wear."

CHAPTER SIX

MARGARET PAUSED AT THE EDGE of the pool, glanced around quickly at the patio full of well-dressed guests and realized she was alone at last. When she spotted her father disappearing into the house by himself she decided to take advantage of the situation. She put down her empty hors d'oeuvres plate and hurried after him.

"Caught you, Dad." She grinned triumphantly at a startled Connor as he headed toward the kitchen.

"Maggie, my girl." Connor made an effort to look genuinely pleased to see her. "I was wonderin' how you were gettin' along. Enjoyin' yourself, girl? Bev sure knows how to throw a mighty fine party, doesn't she? One of the things I love about her. She knows how to have a good time. Wouldn't think it to look at her, but she's not a bit stuffy or prissy. Great sense of humor."

Margaret folded her arms and regarded her father with a sense of amusement mixed with exasperation. "Bev Cassidy appears to be an all-around wonderful person and I'm delighted the two of you are so happy together, but I didn't corner you in here to listen to a glowing litany of her attributes. You've been avoiding me since I got here, Dad. Admit it."

Connor appeared shocked and horrified at the accusation. "Avoidin' you? Not a chance, girl. How could you think such a thing? You're my own little Maggie, my only child, the fruit of my loins."

"Hold it, Dad."

"It's nothin' less than the truth. Hell's bells, girl, why would I want to avoid you? I'm delighted you got down here for my engagement shindig. A man's one and only child should definitely be present when he takes the great leap into marriage."

"That's arguable, depending on when the leap is made," Margaret said dryly. "But your impending nuptials, exciting as they may be, are not what I wanted to discuss."

"Maggie, girl, you know I'm always available to you. I'm your father. Your own flesh and blood. You can talk to me about anything."

"Terrific. That's just what I'd like to do. I have a little matter I've been wanting to discuss with you ever since I got here."

Connor brightened. "Wonderful. We'll have us a nice father-daughter chat one of these days just as soon as we both have a spare minute."

"I've got a spare minute right now."

"Well, shoot, too bad I don't." Connor's face twisted into a parody of sincere regret. "Promised Bev I'd get on the kitchen staff's tails. We're runnin' out of ice. Maybe sometime in the mornin'?"

"Rafe is going to take me riding in the morning, if you'll recall."

"Hey, that's right. I remember him sayin' somethin' about that earlier today. You haven't been ridin' for quite a while, have you? You used to be darn good at it. Don't worry about bein' out of practice. It's like bicyclin'. Once you get the hang of it, you never forget. Rafe's got some fine horses, doesn't he?"

"I'm sure Rafe's horses are all first class. They're a business investment and Rafe has excellent instincts when it comes to business investments. Dad, stop trying to sidetrack me. I want to talk to you."

Connor exhaled heavily, surrendering to the inevitable. He eyed Margaret warily. "More likely you want to chew me out for my part in Rafe's little plot. You still mad about that? I thought you and Rafe had settled things."

"Rafe and I have an ongoing dialogue about certain matters."

Conner wrinkled his nose. "Is that a fancy way of sayin' everything's settled?"

"It's a way of saying we're both reevaluating the situation and waiting to see how things develop."

"You know, Maggie, girl, for a woman who's made a career out of writin' romance novels, you sure do have an unexcitin' turn of phrase when it comes to describin' your own love life. *Reevaluatin' the situation*?"

Margaret smiled ruefully. "I guess it does sound a little tame. But the truth is, Dad, after last year I'm inclined to be cautious."

Connor nodded, his eyes hardening slightly. "Yeah, I can understand that. Hell, I was inclined toward a few things, myself, after I got wind of what happened."

"Like what?"

"Like murder. Damn near killed Cassidy at our first meetin' a few months back. Raked that boy over the coals somethin' fierce, I can tell you that."

"You did?" Margaret was startled. But, then, no one had seen fit to inform her of that meeting.

"Sure. You hadn't told me all that much about what had happened, remember? You just said it was over and Cassidy had said some nasty things there at the end. But I was mad as hell because I knew how much he'd hurt my girl."

Margaret drummed her fingers thoughtfully on her forearms. "Just what did Rafe say at that first meeting?"

Connor shrugged. "Not much to start. Just let me rant and rave at him and call him every name in the book. Then, when I'd calmed down, he poured me a glass of Scotch and gave me his side of the story."

"And you instantly forgave him? Figured he was the innocent party, after all?"

"Hell, no." Connor glowered at her. "You're still my daughter, Maggie. You know I'd defend you to the last ditch, no matter what."

"Thanks, Dad."

"But," Connor continued deliberately, "I was extremely interested in the other side of the story. I'd taken to Cassidy right off when you introduced us last year. You know that. Figured he was just the man for you. Don't mind sayin' I was real upset with myself to think I'd misjudged the man that badly. I was relieved to find out the situation wasn't exactly what you'd call black and white. There was a lot of gray area and after a couple of Scotches and some rational conversation I could sort of see Cassidy's point of view."

"Rafe can be very persuasive," Margaret murmured.

"And you, Maggie, girl, can be a bit high in the instep when it suits you."

"So it was all my fault, after all? Is that what you decided?"

"No, it wasn't. Don't put words in my mouth, girl. All I'm sayin' is that when I heard Cassidy's side of the tale, I did some thinkin'."

Margaret couldn't help but grin. "You mean you reevaluated the situation?"

Connor chuckled. "Somethin' like that. At any rate, when I realized Cassidy was dead serious about gettin' you back, I figured I might lend him a hand." Connor's smile broadened conspiratorially. "Then he introduced me to Bev and I knew for certain I'd help him out."

"Your father," Rafe announced from the open doorway behind Margaret, "is a man who has his priorities straight. He just wanted you and me to get ours straightened out, too."

Margaret jumped and turned her head to glance over her shoulder. Rafe sauntered into the room, a drink in his hand. He was dressed for the party in a pair of gray, Western-cut trousers, a black shirt and a bolo tie made of white leather. His boots were also made of white leather with an elaborate floral design picked out in silver and black.

"How long have you been standing there?" Margaret asked, thinking that there were times when she felt distinctly underdressed around Rafe.

"Not long." He put his arm around her waist and grinned at Connor. "I wondered when she'd cut you out of the herd and demand a few private explanations, Connor. Need any help?"

"Nope. Maggie and I got it all sorted out, didn't we, girl?"

"If you say so, Dad."

Rafe grinned. "Good. Now that you two have that settled maybe you can give me some advice on what to do about Julie's artist friend. Did you meet him yet?" He shook his head. "I knew when she went to work managing that art supply store she'd be mixing with a bad crowd."

Margaret glared at him. "I met Sean Winters earlier this evening when I was first introduced to your sister. I like him. He seems very nice and he treats Julie like a queen. Where's the problem?"

Rafe gave her a sidelong glance as he took a swallow out of his glass. "Weren't you listening? The problem is that the guy's an artist."

"So?" Margaret arched her brows. "I'm a writer. You got something against people who make their living in the creative fields, Cassidy?"

Rafe winced. "Now, Maggie, love, don't take what I said as a personal comment, okay? I just can't see my sister marrying some guy who makes a living painting pictures."

"Why not?"

"Well, for one thing, it's not exactly a stable profession, is it? No regular salary, no benefits, no pension plan, no telling how long the career will last."

"Same with writing," Margaret assured him cheerfully. "And what's so all-fired safe about other professions? A person is always at risk of getting fired or being laid off or of being forced to resign. Look at my situation last year."

"Let's not get into that," Rafe said tersely.

"Nevertheless, you have to admit no job is really guaranteed for life. How many times have you seen a so-called friendly merger result in a purge of management that cost dozens of jobs?"

"Yeah, but..."

"I wouldn't be surprised if some of the mergers and buyouts you've instigated have resulted in exactly that kind of purge."

"We're not talking about me, here, remember? We're discussing Julie's artist friend. Hell, he's from a whole different world. They've got nothing in common. Julie's got a degree in business administration, although she has yet to do much with it. She's not the artsy-craftsy type. What does she see in Winters?"

"You're just looking for excuses, Rafe. You've got a typical redneck macho male's built-in prejudice against men in the creative arts, and you're using the insecurity of the business as a reason to disapprove of Sean as a boyfriend for your sister."

"Damn." Rafe looked appealingly at Connor. "Wish I'd kept my mouth shut."

"Don't look to me for backup on this one." Connor gave his host a wide grin. "I learned my lesson a few years back when Maggie here was dating an artist. I tried to give her the same lecture. Couldn't see my girl getting involved with some weirdo who hung out with the art crowd. You should have seen his stuff, Cassidy. Little bits of aluminum cans stuck all over his canvases."

That got a quick scowl out of Rafe. He glanced at Maggie. "How long did you date the weirdo?"

"Jon was not a weirdo. He was a very successful multimedia artist who has since gone on to make more from a single painting than I make from a single book. I've got one of his early works hanging in my living room, if you will recall."

Rafe's eyes narrowed. "That thing on your wall that looks like a collection of recycled junk?"

"I'll have you know that if I ever get desperate financially I'll be able to hock that collection of recycled junk for enough money to live on for a couple of years. It was a terrific investment."

"How long did you date him?" Rafe demanded again.

"Jealous?"

"Damn right."

Margaret grinned. "Don't be. Jon was a wonderful

man in many respects but it was obvious from the start we weren't meant for each other."

"Yeah? How was it so obvious?"

"He was a night person. I'm a morning person. And never the twain shall meet. At least not for long."

"Glad to hear it."

"The point is, our incompatibility had nothing to do with his profession. And you shouldn't judge your sister's boyfriend on his choice of careers. Besides, Julie's old enough to make her own decisions when it comes to men."

"That's another point. He's too old for her."

"He is not. He's thirty-five. The difference between their ages isn't much more than the difference between our ages, Rafe."

"Okay, okay, let's drop this discussion. We're supposed to be celebrating an engagement here tonight." Rafe looked at Connor with a hint of desperation. "Need some help with the ice?"

"Appreciate it," Connor said.

Rafe gave Margaret a quick, hard kiss. "See you outside in a few minutes, honey."

"Go ahead. Make your escape. But keep in mind what I said about giving Sean Winters a chance." Margaret fixed both men with a meaningful glance before she turned and headed for the door.

"Whew." Rafe exhaled on a sigh of relief as he watched her leave the room. He stared after her departing figure for a moment, enjoying the sight of her neatly rounded derriere moving gently under her elegant cream silk skirt.

"I know what you mean," Connor said. "Women get funny notions sometimes. Maggie tends to be real opinionated."

Rafe took another sip of his Scotch. "Was she really torn up after she stopped seeing the artist?"

Connor laughed and started for the kitchen. "Let me put it this way. One week after she'd stopped dating him she was dating a banker. One week after you and she broke up, she went into hibernation."

Rafe nodded, satisfied. "Yeah, I know. If it makes you feel any better, Connor, my social life followed roughly the same pattern during the past year."

"That's one of the reasons I agreed to help you get her back," Connor said. "Couldn't stand to see the two of you sufferin' like a couple of stranded calves. It was pitiful, just pitiful."

"Thanks, Lark. You're one of nature's noblemen."

OUTSIDE ON THE PATIO MARGARET helped herself to another round of salad while she chatted easily with several of the guests. She was answering a barrage of questions concerning publishing when Rafe's sister materialized with her friend the artist in tow.

Margaret had met Julie and Sean earlier in the evening and had liked them both although she had sensed a certain reserve in Julie. Rafe's sister was a pretty creature with light brown hair, her mother's delicate bone structure and dark, intelligent eyes.

Sean Winters was a tall, thin man who had an easygoing smile and quick, expressive features. He greeted Margaret with a smile.

"How's it going, Margaret? Cassidy find you? He was looking for you a few minutes ago," Sean said.

"He found me. He's inside helping my father with the ice. It's a lovely party, isn't it?"

"Well, hardly the sort of bash we weird, bohemian

types usually enjoy. No kinky sex, funny cigarettes or heavy metal music, but I'm adjusting," Sean said.

Margaret laughed but Julie looked stricken.

"Don't say that," Julie whispered tightly.

Sean shrugged. "Honey, it's no secret your brother isn't all that enthusiastic about having an artist in the family."

Julie bit her lip. "Well, he's going to have one in the family, so he better get used to the idea. I won't have him insulting you."

"He didn't insult me. He just doesn't think I'm good enough for you."

"He's tried to play the role of father for me ever since Dad died," Julie explained apologetically. "I know he means well, but the trouble with Rafe is that he doesn't know when to step back and let someone make their own decisions. He's been giving orders around here so long, he assumes that's the way the world works. Rafe Cassidy says jump and everyone asks how high. He's totally astounded when someone doesn't." Julie glanced at Margaret. "The way Margaret didn't last year."

"I don't know what you mean," Margaret said calmly. "I followed orders last year. Rafe said to get out and I went."

Julie sighed. "Yes, but you were supposed to come back."

"So I've been told. On my hands and knees."

"Would that have been so hard?"

"Impossible," Margaret assured her, aware of the sudden tightness in her voice. Her pride was all she'd had left last year. She'd clung to it as if it had been a lifeline.

"My brother was in bad shape for a long time after you left. I've never seen him the way he was this past year and I admit I blamed you for it. I think I hated you myself for a while, even though I'd never met you. I couldn't stand what you'd done to him." Julie's dark eyes were very intent and serious.

Margaret understood the reserve she'd sensed in Rafe's sister. "It's natural that you'd feel protective of your brother."

"It was a battle of wills as far as Rafe was concerned. And he lost. He doesn't like to lose, Margaret."

Margaret blinked. "He lost? How on earth do you figure that?"

"He finally realized that the only way you were going to come back was for him to lower his pride and go and get you. It was probably one of the hardest things he's ever done. Mom says now that it was good for him, but I'm not so sure."

"Lower his pride?" Margaret was flabbergasted by that interpretation of events. "You think that's what Rafe did when he went to Seattle to fetch me down here?"

"Of course."

"Julie, it wasn't anything like that at all. Not that it's anyone else's business, but the truth is, I was virtually blackmailed and kidnapped. I didn't notice Rafe having to surrender one square inch of his pride."

"Then you don't know my brother very well," Julie said. She put her hand on Sean's arm. "But I shouldn't say anything. It's between you and Rafe. Mom may have been right, maybe Rafe did need the jolt you gave him. He's accustomed to having things his way and it's no secret that people cater to him. But that doesn't change the fact that he's human and he can be hurt. And he's got a thing about loyalty."

"I don't think you need to worry about protecting

your big brother," Sean murmured. "Something tells me he can take care of himself."

Julie groaned. "You're right. Besides, right now I've got my own problems with him. To tell you the truth, Margaret, I'm inclined to sympathize with you at the moment. Rafe can be extremely bullheaded when it comes to his own opinions. I haven't dared tell him yet just how serious Sean and I are. He thinks we're just dating casually, but the truth is Sean and I are going to get married whether Rafe approves or not."

"Give Rafe a chance to know Sean." Margaret smiled at the artist. "He's really fairly reasonable about most things, once you get his full attention."

"If you say so."

"I'm sure you know as well as I do that folks in the business world have a hard time understanding people in the art world."

"True." Sean's eyes gleamed with amusement. "And the situation isn't improved any by the fact that Cassidy is basically a cowboy who happens to be a genius when it comes to business. Maybe I should invite him to a showing of some of my work. Then he could at least judge me on the basis of my art. If he's going to criticize me, he might as well know what he's talking about."

"But Rafe hates modern art," Julie exclaimed.

"He's fully capable of appreciating it if he puts his mind to it," Margaret said. She remembered the discussion she'd had with Rafe on good wine and good hotels. "He may be a cowboy at heart, but he's very good at moving in different worlds when he feels like it."

Julie eyed her thoughtfully. "You've got a point. My brother likes to play the redneck when it suits him, but I've heard him talk European politics with businessmen from England and Germany and I've even seen him eat sushi with some Japanese distributors."

Margaret looked up at Sean. "Letting him see your work is not a bad idea at all, Sean. When's the next scheduled exhibition of your work?"

Julie interrupted before Sean could reply. "There's one on Monday evening at the gallery here in town that handles Sean's work. Do you think you could convince Rafe to come?"

"I'll talk to him," Margaret promised.

"Don't get your hopes up, Julie." Sean's voice was gentle. "Even if Margaret gets him there we can't expect him to instantly change his mind about me."

"No," Julie agreed, "but it would at least be a sign that he's willing to give you a chance. Margaret, if you can pull this off, I will definitely owe you one."

Margaret laughed, feeling completely relaxed around Julie for the first time since she had met her. "I'll keep that in mind."

Julie turned to Sean. "Look, the band is starting up again. Let's dance."

"All right. I could use a few more lessons in Western swing. If I'm going to marry a ranch girl, I'd better learn a few of the ropes." Sean put down his glass. He nodded at Margaret. "Thanks," he said as he took Julie's arm.

"No problem. Us nonbusiness types sometimes have to stick together."

"You've got a point."

Margaret watched the handsome couple disappear into the throng of people dancing on the patio. She was idly tapping her foot and wondering where Rafe was when she suddenly became aware of Doug Hatcher standing behind her. She turned to smile brightly at him, thinking that he was about to ask her to dance. But his first remark dispelled that illusion.

"You're settling in very quickly around here, aren't you?" Doug's words were carefully enunciated, as if he was afraid of slurring them.

Margaret felt a frisson of uneasiness. "Hello, Doug. I didn't see you there. Enjoying the party?" She eyed the half-empty glass in his hand and the careful way he was holding himself and wondered if he was a little drunk. She realized she had never before seen him drink anything at all.

"You've definitely moved in on the Cassidy clan." Doug took a long pull on his drink. "You're changing things around here."

"I am?"

"Don't be so modest, Miss Lark." Doug stared at her and nodded, as if at some private understanding. "Yeah. You've changed him all right."

"Are we talking about Rafe?"

"He's different now."

"In what way, Doug?"

"Getting soft."

"*Soft?* Rafe?" She was genuinely startled by that comment.

"It's true." Doug nodded again, frowning. "When I first went to work for him he was like a knife. He'd just cut through everything in his path. But a year ago things changed. Oh, we put together a couple of good deals this past year, but it's not like the old days. I thought it was going to be all right for the first few months but then he decided he wanted you back."

"He talked about me to you?"

Doug shook his head, the gesture slightly exaggerated. "He didn't have to. I know him. I knew what he was thinking about and it wasn't about business. Like I said, he's gone soft, lost his edge. When he does think about business, he only thinks about one thing these days." He turned abruptly, caught himself as he nearly lost his balance and then vanished into the crowd.

Margaret took a deep breath as she dared to hope that the one thing Rafe thought about most these days was her. She didn't expect him to spend the rest of his life focusing entirely on her, she told herself. She fully understood that he had a major corporation to run and a ranch to manage. She had no intention of being unreasonable.

But it was comforting to know that there was growing evidence that she was finally important enough to him to make him alter his normal way of doing business. A year ago she had not been at all certain she held that much significance in his life.

"You look like you're enjoying yourself, Maggie, love." Rafe materialized out of the crowd and took her hand to lead her onto the dance floor. "Can I conclude that the thought of engagement parties in general no longer is enough to send you running for cover?"

She smiled up at him, aware of the sheer pleasure of being in his arms. His beautifully controlled physical strength was one of the most compelling qualities he possessed. She loved being wrapped up in it. "I'm having a great time at this one," she admitted.

"One of these days we'll start planning another one."

His certainty always left her feeling breathless. "Will we?"

"Yeah, Maggie, love. We will."

"I thought I was going to get plenty of time to make up my mind."

"I promised you a little time to get used to the idea

of marrying me, but don't expect me to give you an unlimited amount of rope. Knowing you, you'd just get yourself all tangled up in it."

She shook her head in wry wonder. "You are always so sure of yourself, aren't you?"

"I am when I know what I want." Rafe came to a halt in the middle of the dance floor. "And now, if you'll excuse me, it's time to make the big announcement. I've been assigned to do the honors."

"Doesn't it seem a little odd that you're announcing your own mother's engagement?"

"We live in interesting times." He kissed her forehead. "Be back in a few minutes."

The crowd broke into loud applause and cheers as Rafe grabbed a bottle of champagne, vaulted up onto the diving board and strode out to the far end. He held up the bottle in his hand to get the crowd's attention.

"You all know why you're here tonight, but I've been told to make it official," he began with a grin. "I would therefore like to say that it gives me great pleasure to do as my Mama tells me and announce her engagement to one smooth-talking cowboy named Connor Lark."

A roar of approval went up. Rafe gave the crowd a couple of minutes to grow quiet once more before he continued.

"I'm here to tell you folks that I've got no choice but to approve of this match. It's not just because I've had Lark checked out and decided he can take care of my mama in the style to which she has become accustomed—"

The crowd interrupted with a burst of applause.

"And it's not just because she seems to actually like the guy or the fact that he's crazy about her. No, folks, I am giving my heartfelt approval to this match because

Lark has informed me that if I do not, he will personally drag me out into the desert and stake me out over an anthill. Folks, I am a reasonable man. I want you to know I can hardly wait for Connor Lark to marry my mother."

Laughter filled the air as Rafe let the cork out of the champagne bottle with a suitable explosion. Again the crowd yelled approval. Connor, standing at the side of the pool next to Bev, grinned broadly at Rafe as he held a glass up to be filled with bubbling champagne.

Rafe filled the glass with a flourish and then a second one for his mother and everyone toasted the guests of honor. Connor finished his drink in one swallow and kissed his fiancée. Then he gave a whoop and grabbed her hand.

"Honey, let's dance," Connor crowed, sweeping Bev into a waltz. She laughed up at him with undisguised delight.

"They make a great couple, don't they?" Rafe leaped lightly down from the diving board and went to stand beside Margaret. He put an arm around her shoulders and drew her close to his side.

"Yes," Margaret said, her eyes on her father's face. "They do. I think they're going to be very happy."

"No happier than you and me, Maggie, love, you'll see." Rafe kissed her soundly and then dragged her over to the section of the patio that was being used for dancing. He smiled down into her eyes as he whirled her into the Western waltz.

A moment later the patio was filled with dancing couples and Margaret gave herself up to the joy of the music that flowed around her like champagne. *Yes,* she allowed herself to think for the first time in a year, *yes, she could be very happy with Rafe*. She could be the happiest woman in the world.

RAFE SAW HATCHER HANGING BACK as the last of the guests took their leave. He scowled at his assistant, wondering if Doug had followed orders two hours ago and laid off the booze.

"You sober enough to get behind the wheel, Hatcher?" he asked bluntly as the two men stood isolated on one side of the front drive.

"I'm fine," Hatcher muttered. "Haven't had anything but soda for the past couple of hours. Just wanted to tell you I left the Ellington file in your study. You'd better take a look at it as soon as possible."

Rafe eyed him. "Something new come up?"

Hatcher nodded, his eyes sliding away to follow the last car out of the drive. "Today. I've updated the file so you can take a look for yourself. I didn't want to say anything before the party. Seemed a shame to ruin it for you."

"Since when have I ever asked you to shield me from bad news? That's not what I pay you to do and you know it."

Hatcher's jaw tightened. "I know, but this is different, Rafe."

"What am I going to be looking at when I open the file?"

Hatcher hesitated. "The possibility that we've got a leak."

"Damn it to hell. You sure?"

"No, not entirely. Could be a coincidence that Moorcroft came up with the numbers he did today, but we've got to look at the other possibility."

"Someone gave him the information."

"Maybe."

"Yeah, maybe." Rafe watched the last set of taillights disappear down his long drive. "I thought we had this airtight, Hatcher."

"I thought we did, too."

"When I find out who's selling me out, I'll do a little bloodletting. Hope whoever it is realizes what he's risking."

"We don't know for sure yet, Rafe," Hatcher said quickly. "It really could be a genuine coincidence. But regardless of how it happened, there's no getting around the fact that we've got to counter Moorcroft's last move and fast. Thought you'd want to run the numbers yourself."

"I'll do it tonight and have an answer in the morning. Nothing gets in the way of this Ellington thing, understand? It has to go through on schedule."

"Right, well, guess I'd better be off." Hatcher nodded once more and dug his keys out of his pocket. "I'll talk to you tomorrow."

Rafe stood for a while in the balmy darkness watching Hatcher's car vanish in the distance.

Vengeance was a curious thing, he acknowledged. It had the same ability to obsess a man's soul as love did.

"Rafe?"

He turned toward the sound of Maggie's soft, questioning voice. She looked so beautiful standing there in the doorway with the lights of the house behind her. His beautiful, proud Maggie. He needed her more than the desert needed the fierce storms of late summer. Without her, he was an empty man.

And if she ever realized what he was going to do to Moorcroft, she'd be furious. There was even a possibility she'd try to run from him again. He had to be careful, Rafe told himself. This was between him and Moorcroft, anyway. A little matter of vengeance and honor that had to be settled properly.

"I'm coming, Maggie, love." He started toward the doorway. "Mom and Dad still out waltzing by the pool?"

Margaret laughed. "Without a band? No, I think they gave up the waltzing in favor of getting some sleep before leaving for Sedona in the morning."

"Not a bad idea," Rafe said.

"What?"

"Sleep. I could use some myself and so could you. Good night, Maggie, love." He pulled her into his arms and kissed her.

Forty minutes later he watched from the other side of the patio as Margaret's light went out. For a short time he toyed with the idea of going to her room.

But the file waiting in his office was too important to ignore. He'd told Hatcher he'd have an answer by tomorrow morning.

CHAPTER SEVEN

MARGARET FOUND SLEEP impossible. She tossed and turned, listening to the small night sounds that drifted through her window. Her mind was not cluttered with the bright images of the successful party or thoughts of her father and his new love. She wasn't thinking about any of the many things that could have been keeping her awake.

All she could think about was Julie Cassidy's remark concerning Rafe having overcome his hawklike pride in order to find a way to get Margaret back.

The notion of Rafe Cassidy lowering his pride for a woman was literally stunning.

Margaret stared up at the ceiling and realized she had never considered the events of the past few days in those terms. She had felt manipulated at first and there was no denying that to a great extent she had been.

But what had it cost Rafe to admit to himself and everyone else that he wanted her back?

She thought of all the times during those first few months after the disaster when she had almost picked up the phone and called him. Her own pride had stood in her way every time. She had nothing for which to apologize, she kept telling herself. She had done nothing wrong. She had tried to explain her side of the situation to Rafe and he had flatly refused to listen.

And then he had said terrible things to her, things

that still had the power to make her weep if she summoned them to the surface of her consciousness.

No, she could never have made the call begging him to take her back and give her another chance. It would have meant sacrificing all of her pride and her sense of self-worth. Any man who required such an act of contrition was not worth having.

But it was a novelty to think that in some fashion Rafe's apparently high-handed actions lately bespoke a lowering of his own pride. Margaret realized she had never thought of it in that light.

It was true he had not actually admitted that he had been wrong last year. Other than to apologize grudgingly for his rough treatment of her, he had basically stuck to his belief that she was the one who was guilty of betrayal; the one who required forgiveness.

But there was also no denying that he was the one who had finally found a way to get them back together.

Of course, Margaret told herself, somewhat amused, being Rafe, he had found a way to do it that had not required an abject plea from him. Nevertheless, he had done it. They were back together, at least for now, and Rafe was talking about marriage as seriously as ever.

What's more, he really did seem to have changed. He was definitely making an effort to limit his attention to business. The Rafe she had seen so far this week was a different man than the one she had known last year in that respect. The old Rafe would never have taken the time to get so completely involved in organizing his mother's engagement party. Nor would he have spent as much time entertaining a recalcitrant lover.

Lover.

The word hovered in Margaret's mind. Whatever

else he was, Rafe was indisputably the lover of her dreams.

She had missed being with him last night. She and Bev had sat up talking until very late and then retired. Margaret had toyed with the notion of waiting until the lights were out and then gliding across the patio to Rafe's room. But when she had finally glanced out into the darkness she had seen the two familiar figures splashing softly in the pool and quickly changed her mind. Her father and Bev had already commandeered the patio for a late-night tryst.

But tonight the patio was empty. Margaret pushed back the sheet and got out of bed. A glance across the patio showed that Rafe's room was dark. She smiled to herself as she imagined Rafe's reaction if she were to go to his bedroom and awaken him.

In her mind she visualized him sleeping nude in the snowy sheets. He would be on his stomach, his strong, broad shoulders beautifully contoured with moonlight. When he became aware of her presence he would roll onto his back, reach up and pull her down on top of him. He would become hard with arousal almost instantly, the way he always did when he sensed she wanted him. And she would ache with the familiar longing.

Margaret hesitated no longer. She put on the new gauzy cotton dress she had purchased while shopping with Bev and slid her feet into a pair of sandals. Then she went out into the night.

When she reached the other side of the patio it took her a few seconds to realize that Rafe was not in his room. She let herself inside and saw that the bed had never been turned down. Curious, she walked through into the hall.

The eerie glow under the study door caught her eye at once. An odd sense of guilt shafted through her. The poor man, she thought suddenly. Was this how he was accomplishing the job of proving he could love her and run a business at the same time? Had he been working nights ever since she got here?

She crossed the hall on silent feet and opened the door. The otherworldly light of the computer screen was the only illumination in the room. Rafe was bathed in it as he lounged in his chair, his booted feet propped on his desk. He had not changed since the party but his shirt was unbuttoned and his sleeves rolled up to his elbows. His dark hair was tousled.

There was a file lying on the desk in front of him and a spreadsheet on the computer screen. He turned his head as he heard the door open softly. In the electronic glow the hard lines of his face seemed grimmer than usual.

Margaret lounged in the doorway and smiled. "I know you think I'm a demanding woman, but I'm not this demanding. Honest."

"What's that supposed to mean?" Rafe casually closed the file in front of him and dropped it into a drawer.

"Just that when I said I wanted our relationship to get a little more attention than your work, I didn't mean you had to resort to sneaking around in the middle of the night in order to spend some time on the job. I do understand the realities of normal business, Rafe. I worked in that world for several years, remember?"

Rafe's mouth curved faintly. "Believe me, Maggie, love, our relationship has had my full attention lately. This—" he gestured at the computer screen "—was just something Hatcher wanted me to look at. I didn't feel

like sleeping yet so I thought I'd take care of it tonight."
He swung his feet to the floor and punched a couple of
keys on the computer. He stood up as the screen went
blank. "How did you find me?"

Margaret smiled into the shadows as he walked
toward her. "I refuse to answer that on the grounds
that you'll think I'm fast."

His laugh was soft and sexy in the darkness. "As far
as I'm concerned, you could never be too fast for me,
lady, not as long as I'm the one you're chasing." He
stopped in front of her and drew a finger down the side
of her throat to the curve of her shoulder. He smiled
knowingly as he felt her answering shiver of aware-
ness. "You went to my bedroom, didn't you?"

"Uh-huh. You weren't there."

"So you went looking. Good. That's the way it
should be." He kissed her lightly on the tip of her nose
and then brushed his mouth across hers. His voice
deepened abruptly. "Promise me you'll always come
looking for me. No matter what happens. Don't run
away from me again, Maggie, love."

She touched the side of his cheek. "Not even if you
send me away?"

"I was a fool. I won't make that mistake again. I
learned my lesson the hard way. Promise me, Maggie.
Swear it. Say you won't leave even if things get rough
between us again. Fight with me, yell at me, slam a few
doors, kick me in the rear, but don't leave."

She caught her breath and then, in a soft, reckless
little rush she gave him the words he wanted to hear.
"I won't leave."

He groaned thickly and gathered her so tightly
against him that Maggie could hardly breathe. She
didn't mind. She felt his lips in her hair and then his

fingers were moving up her back to the nape of her neck and into her loosened hair.

She wrapped her arms around his waist and inhaled the sensual, masculine scent of him. She kissed his chest where the black shirt was open and felt him shudder.

"Maggie, love, you feel so good."

Rafe moved backward a couple of steps and sank down into his chair. He eased Maggie up against the desk in front of him until she could feel the wooden edge along the backs of her thighs. His hands went to her legs.

"Rafe, wait, we can't. Not here, like this." She stifled a tiny laugh that was part anxiety at the thought of getting caught making love in his study and part joyous arousal.

"Why not here?"

"What if someone hears us?"

"What if they do?" He pushed the gauzy cotton hem of the dress up above her knees. Then he deliberately parted her legs with his hands and kissed the sensitive skin of her upper thigh. "Anyone with half a brain who might happen to overhear us should have enough sense to ignore us."

"Yes, but." Maggie shivered delicately as she felt his mouth on the inside of her leg. His hands had lifted the skirt of the dress up to her waist. She heard him laugh softly as he realized she was naked under the cotton shift.

"Ah, Maggie, love, I see you dressed for the occasion."

"You're a lecherous rake, Rafe Cassidy."

"No, ma'am, just a simple cowboy with simple tastes.

There's nothing I like better than taking a moonlight ride with you."

"A moonlight ride? Is that what you call it?"

"Yeah. You know something? I like you best when you're stark naked." He leaned forward again in the chair and dipped his tongue into the small depression in her stomach. Then his lips worked their way downward into the tight curls below her waist.

"Rafe. *Rafe.*" Maggie's hands clenched his shoulders. She felt unbelievably wanton and gloriously sexy as she stood there in front of him, legs braced apart by his strong hands. Her head was tipped back, her hair cascading behind her. She closed her eyes as his kisses became overwhelmingly intimate.

"So good. Sweet and sexy and so hot already." Rafe eased a finger into her.

Margaret tightened instantly and cried out softly. She could hardly stand now. She leaned back against the desk, letting it support her weight. Rafe's fingers stretched her gently and she dug her nails into his shoulders.

"That's it, Maggie, love. Let me know how it feels. Tell me, sweetheart."

"You already know what you can do to me," she whispered in between gasps of pleasure.

"Yeah, but I like to hear about it." His eyes gleamed in the darkness as he looked up into her face.

"Why?"

"You know why. It makes me crazy."

She half laughed and half groaned and tangled her fingers in his hair. "You make *me* go crazy, Rafe. Absolutely wild. I don't even feel like myself when you touch me like this."

"Good." He stood up slowly, his hands gliding along

her hips and then her waist and above her breasts. He carried the cotton dress along with the movement, lifting it up over her head. When it was free, he tossed it heedlessly onto the floor.

Margaret had one last burst of sanity. "Your room. Just across the hall. We can…"

"No. I like you just fine where you are." He stood between her legs and lifted her up so that she was sitting on the desk. She reached back to brace herself with her hands as his mouth moved on her shoulders and traveled down to her swollen breasts.

Rafe's fingers went to the waistband of his pants. A moment later Margaret heard the rasp of his zipper.

"Aren't you going to at least take off your boots?" Margaret demanded in a husky whisper.

"No need. This'll work just fine."

She look down and saw that it would work just fine. "But what about…about the protection you always use?"

"Got it right here." He reached into his back pocket.

Margaret heard the soft sound of the little packet being opened. "You carry that on you?" she gasped.

"Every minute since the day you arrived. I want to be able to make love to you anywhere, anytime."

"Good heavens, Rafe." She giggled, feeling more daring and wanton than ever. "Isn't there something a bit scandalous about doing it like this—on top of a desk? With your boots on?"

"This is my office, let me run the show, okay?" He caught one nipple lightly between his teeth.

Margaret inhaled sharply. "Yes. By all means, go ahead. Run the show. Please." She sighed in surrender and ceased worrying about decorum.

Rafe eased her down until she lay across the desk in

a blatantly sensual pose. Her legs hung over the edge, open and inviting. She shuddered as he moved closer.

Margaret looked up through slitted eyes as Rafe probed her tenderly with his thumbs and then slowly fitted himself to her. She felt the excitement pounding in her veins and wondered at the magic between them. It was always like this. When Rafe made love to her he took her into a different world, one where she was wild and free and deliciously uninhibited—one where she knew she was temporarily, at least, the center of his universe.

Margaret clutched at Rafe as he surged slowly, deeply into her. She tightened her legs around him as he braced himself above her, his hands planted flat on either side of her.

"Maggie, love. *Maggie*. You're so sweet and tight and, oh, sweetheart, I do love the feel of you. Incredible."

She watched the hard, impassioned lines of his face as he drove into her until she could no longer concentrate on anything except the tide of excitement pooling deep within her. She closed her eyes again, lifting herself against the driving thrusts and then she felt Rafe ease one hand between their bodies.

He touched her with exquisite care and Margaret lost her breath. Her body tightened in a deep spasm and then relaxed in slow shivers that brought an intense pleasure to every nerve ending.

"*Rafe.*"

"Yes, love. Yes." And then he imbedded himself to the hilt within her. His lips drew back across his teeth as he fought to control a shout of sensual triumph and release. A moment later he dropped back into the chair behind him and dragged Margaret down onto his lap.

Margaret huddled against him, aware of his open zipper scratching her bare thigh. Rafe's hand slid slowly, absently along her leg and up to her waist. His head was pillowed against the back of his chair, his eyes closed.

"You are one wild and wicked lady," Rafe said without opening his eyes. "Imagine just walking in here bold as you please in the middle of the night when I'm trying to work and seducing me on my office desk."

Margaret smiled to herself as a thought struck her. "You know something, Rafe?"

"What?" He still seemed disinclined to move.

"I couldn't have done that last year when we were together."

He opened one eye. "Couldn't have done what? Walked into my office and seduced me? You're wrong. I'm a sucker for you. I always was."

She shook her head. "No you weren't. We always made love on your schedule and when you were in the middle of some business matter I always had to wait until you were finished. I could never have interrupted you the way I did tonight and expected you to shut down the computer so that we could make love in the middle of your office. Last year if I'd tried anything like that you'd have patted me on the head and told me to go wait in the bedroom until you finished working."

"Are you sure?"

Margaret lifted her head and glared at him. She saw the laughter in his eyes. "Of course, I'm sure. I have an excellent memory."

"I must have been a complete idiot last year. I can't imagine ignoring you if you'd traipsed into my office wearing that light little cotton thing with nothing on underneath. You know what I think?"

"What?"

"I don't think you'd have even tried it last year. You'd have waited very politely until I was finished. Maybe a little too politely. You were a very self-controlled, very restrained little executive lady last year. Cool, sleek and quite proper. I think the career in romance writing has been good for you. It's made you more inclined to make demands on me."

"You think that's good?" Margaret was startled.

Rafe sighed, his eyes turning serious in the shadows. "I think it's probably necessary. You're right when you called me arrogant and bossy and tyrannical."

"You admit it?"

"I admit it. I'm used to running things, honey. I've been giving orders so long it comes naturally. I'm also used to putting work first. My father always did and there's no denying I was following in his footsteps. Mom let him get away with doing that. But somehow, I don't think you'll let me get away with it."

"And you don't mind?"

Rafe smiled slowly. "Let's just say I'm capable of adapting."

"It's not that I'm completely insensitive to the demands you face, Rafe, you must know that," Margaret assured him earnestly. "I spent enough time in the business world to know that certain things have to be done and certain deadlines have to be met. But I don't want your work to rule our lives totally the way it did last year."

He drew his fingers through her tangled hair. In the shadows his eyes were very dark and deep. "It won't, Maggie. And if it ever threatens to, you know what you can do about it."

She grinned in delight. "Walk into your office and seduce you?"

"My door is always open to you, Maggie, love." Rafe kissed her lightly on the mouth and gave her a small nudge.

"I'm being kicked out already?" Margaret reluctantly got to her feet and reached for her cotton shift.

"Nope. We're both going to retire for the night. It's late and you and I are going to get up early to see Mom and Connor off to Sedona, remember?"

Margaret yawned. "Vaguely. Going to walk me back to my room?"

"You're the one whose sense of propriety insists that you wake up alone as long as the parents are around. If I had my way, I'd just walk you back across the hall to my room."

"Going to sneak back here and work on the computer after you've tucked me in?"

Rafe shook his head as he led her back across the hall, through his bedroom and out into the moonlit patio. "No, I saw all I needed to see. I've got an answer for Hatcher."

"It's very sweet of you to not make a fuss about letting me spend the night in my own bed, Rafe."

"Anything for you, Maggie, love. Besides, things will be different when we have the house to ourselves, won't they? I'm a patient man."

Much later Margaret awakened briefly. She automatically glanced through the glass door and followed the shaft of moonlight that struck full into Rafe's bedroom. She couldn't be positive, but it looked as if his bed was still empty.

CONNOR AND BEV TOOK THEIR leave immediately after breakfast the next morning. Margaret stood with Bev in the driveway as the last of the luggage was loaded into the car.

"We'll be gone about a week, dear," Bev said cheerfully. "We're going to stop in Scottsdale first. That's where I live most of the time now. This ranch is a little too isolated for my tastes. At any rate, I have some friends I want Connor to meet. And then we'll drive on to Sedona. It makes a nice break this time of year. Much cooler up there in the mountains. There are several galleries I always like to visit when I'm there."

"Have a wonderful time, Bev."

Bev searched her face. "You'll be staying on here with Rafe?"

"Do you mind?"

Bev smiled. "Not at all. I'm delighted. I was afraid you might head straight back to Seattle. In fact I told Connor that perhaps we should cancel our plans in order to encourage you to stay here with us a little longer."

"I told her, forget it," Connor said as he walked past with a suitcase under each arm. He was followed by Tom who was carrying two more bags. "I was willing to help Cassidy get you down here but he's on his own now. I refuse to help him with any more of his courting work. I'm too busy tending to my own woman."

Bev's eyes lifted briefly toward the heavens. "Listen to the man."

Connor chuckled hugely as he put the suitcases into the trunk. He looked over at Rafe who was coming through the door with one last bag. "Hey, Cassidy. Tell your mother you can handle my daughter on your own from here on in. She's afraid Maggie's going to take off the minute our backs are turned."

Rafe's eyes met Margaret's. "Maggie's not going anywhere, are you, Maggie?"

Under the combined scrutiny of Bev, Tom, her father and her lover, Margaret felt herself turning pink. "Well, I had thought I might stay a few more days but that decision is subject to change if the pressure gets to be too much," she informed them all in dry tones.

"Pressure?" Rafe assumed an innocent, injured air. "What pressure? There's no pressure being applied, Maggie, love. Just bear in mind that if you take off this time, I'll be no more than fifteen minutes behind you and I won't be real happy."

"In that case, I suppose I might as well stay. As it happens, I have a social engagement here on Monday evening."

That succeeded in getting everyone's attention.

"What social engagement?" Rafe demanded. "You don't know anyone here in Tucson except me."

"That's not quite true, Rafe. I also know your sister and her friend Sean Winters. I've been invited to a showing of Sean's work."

"You're going to some damned art show?"

Margaret smiled serenely. "I thought you might like to escort me."

Rafe's brows came together in one solid, unyielding line. He slammed the trunk shut. "Like hell. We'll discuss this later."

Connor Lark turned to his fiancée. "Something tells me the children won't be bored while we're gone, dear. I think they're going to be able to entertain themselves just fine without us."

Bev glanced curiously from Margaret's cool, deliberate smile to Rafe's thunderous scowl. "Something tells me you're right, Connor."

Rafe stood beside Margaret as Connor drove away from the house. When the car was out of sight he took Margaret's arm and turned her firmly back into the foyer.

"Now tell me what the hell this business is about attending an exhibition of Winters's work."

"It's very simple. Julie and Sean invited me last night before they left. I accepted." She took a deep breath. "On behalf of both of us."

Rafe propped one shoulder against the wall in the negligent, dangerous pose he did so well. He folded his arms across his chest. "Is that right?"

Margaret cleared her throat delicately. "Yes. Right."

"What the devil do you think you're doing, Maggie?"

"Manipulating you into giving your sister's choice of a husband a fair chance?" She tried a smile to lighten the atmosphere.

"Trying to manipulate me is right. At least you're honest about it. But you should know me well enough by now to know I don't like being manipulated, not even by you. And what the hell do you mean my sister's choice of a *husband*? She told you she's actually thinking of marrying that damned artist?"

"They told me their plans last night. I think they have every intention of following through, Rafe, with or without your approval. You'd better learn to accept the situation graciously or risk alienating your sister."

"Damnation." Rafe came away from the wall and plowed his fingers through his hair. "Marry him? I didn't know they were that serious. I thought Winters was just another boyfriend. Julie's always got one or two trailing around behind her."

Margaret eyed him with a feeling of sympathy. "You've been looking after her for so long you may not have noticed she's grown up, Rafe. Julie's an adult woman. She makes her own choices."

"Some choices. She hasn't even been able to choose a job she can stay with for six months at a time. The guy's an artist, Maggie. Why couldn't she have found herself a nice, respectable..." His voice trailed off abruptly and he slid a quick glance at Margaret.

"A nice, respectable businessman? Someone who wears three-piece suits and ties and travels two weeks out of every month? Someone who needs an attractive, self-sacrificing hostess of a wife to entertain his guests while he closes big deals?"

Rafe winced. "Is that what you thought I'd turn you into? The boss's wife?"

"It's one of the things I was afraid of, yes."

"You should have said something."

"I tried. You never listened."

"I'm listening now," Rafe said evenly. His gaze locked with hers. "Believe me?"

Margaret nodded slowly. "Yes," she said, "I think I do."

Rafe nodded once. "Okay, that's settled. But that doesn't mean I'm going to approve of Winters."

"Rafe, they don't need your approval. They're quite capable of getting married without it."

"You think so?" Rafe's mouth twisted. "What if Winters finds out Julie doesn't come equipped with an unlimited checking account and a handful of charge cards?"

"I don't think he's marrying her for her money."

"How do you know? You only met him once last night."

"I liked him. And even if he is marrying her for her money, there's still not much you can do about it. Your best bet is to stay on good terms with your sister regardless of whether her decision is right or wrong."

"I could always try buying Winters off," Rafe said thoughtfully.

"I don't think that would be a very smart thing to do, Rafe. Julie would hate you for it. Give Sean a chance first before you try anything drastic. Come to the gallery show with me."

"Why? What will that prove?"

"It will give you an opportunity to meet him on his turf, instead of yours. If you're going to have him in the family you should make an effort to learn something about his world."

"Stop talking as if the marriage is an accomplished fact."

"Rafe, you're being deliberately stubborn and bull-headed about this. Give the man a chance. You know you should."

"Yeah? Why should I?" he challenged.

"I thought giving the other guy a fair chance was one of those fundamental tenets of the Code of the West."

He scowled ferociously at her. "What the devil are you talking about now? What's this nonsense about a code?"

She smiled again. "You know that basic creed you probably learned at your father's knee. The one he undoubtedly got from his father and so on. The one that's supposed to cover little things like vengeance, honor, justice and fair play among the male of the species."

Rafe swore again in disgust and paced the length of the foyer. He stopped at the far end, swung around and eyed her for a short, tense moment. "You want to play by the Code of the West? All right, I'll go along with that. We'll start with a little simple frontier justice. If you want to manipulate me into going to that damn gallery, you've got to pay the price."

Margaret watched him with sudden wariness. "What price?"

Rafe smiled dangerously. "In exchange for my agreement to go to the showing, you agree to let me announce our engagement. I want it official, Maggie. No more fooling around."

Margaret took a deep breath. "All right."

Rafe stared at her in open astonishment. "You agree?"

"You've got yourself a deal, cowboy."

Rafe gave a shout of triumph. "Well, it's about time, lady."

He took one long stride forward, scooped Margaret up in his arms and carried her down the hall to the nearest bedroom.

This time he took off his boots.

CHAPTER EIGHT

RAFE SADDLED HIS BEST chestnut stallion the next morning at dawn. Out of the corner of his eye he watched with satisfaction as Maggie adjusted her own saddle on the gray mare. He took a quiet pleasure in the competent manner in which she handled the tack and the horse. Connor had been right. His daughter knew her way around a barn.

Rafe wondered how he could have spent two whole months with Maggie last year and never learned that single, salient fact about her.

Then again, those two months had passed in a tangled web of sudden, consuming passion mixed with an explosive game of corporate brinksmanship that had involved millions. There had been very little time for getting to know the small, intimate details of his new lover's past. He had been far too anxious to spend what little free time he had with her in bed.

Money and love were a dangerous combination, Rafe had discovered. A pity he hadn't learned to separate the two before. But, then, in all fairness to himself, he'd never come across the two combined in such a lethal fashion until last year.

He knew what he was doing this time around. He could handle both.

"All set?" he asked as he finished checking the cinch on his saddle.

"I'm ready." Margaret picked up the reins and led her mare toward the barn door.

"We'll ride out over the east foothills. I want to show you some land I'm thinking of selling." Rafe walked the chestnut out into the early-morning light and vaulted lightly into the saddle. He turned his head to enjoy the sight of Maggie's sexy jeans-clad bottom as she mounted her mare. The woman looked good on horseback. Almost as good as she looked in bed. Rafe nudged the stallion with his knee and the chestnut moved forward with brisk eagerness.

The day was going to be hot, Rafe thought. They all were this time of year. But at this hour the desert was an unbelievably beautiful place—still cool enough to allow a man to enjoy the wide-open, primitive landscape. It was a landscape that had always appealed strongly to something deep within him. They had never talked about it, but he'd always sensed the land had affected his father and his grandfather in the same way.

They rode in companionable silence until they came to the point where a wide sweep of the ranch could be seen. Only a handful of cattle were visible. Here in the desert livestock needed vast stretches on which to graze. The cattle tended to scatter widely.

Rafe halted the chestnut and waited for Margaret to bring her mare alongside. She did so, surveying the rolling foothills spread out in front of her.

"How much of this is Cassidy land?" she asked.

"Just about all of what you can see," Rafe admitted. "It goes up into the mountains. My great-grandfather acquired most of it. My grandfather and father added to it. They all ran cattle on it and did some mining in the hills. The land's been good to the Cassidys."

"But now you're thinking of selling it?"

Rafe nodded. "Some of it. It would be the smart thing to do. The truth is, the cattle business isn't what it used to be and probably won't ever be again. The mines are all played out. If I had any sense I would have gotten rid of the stock five years ago and sold the acreage to a developer who wants to put in a golf course and a subdivision."

"Why didn't you?"

"I don't know," he admitted. "Lord knows I don't need several thousand acres of desert. I've made my money buying and selling businesses, not in running cattle. Compared to my other investments, running live-stock is more of a hobby than anything else. But for some reason I haven't been able to bring myself to put the land on the market."

"Maybe that's because part of you doesn't really think it's yours to sell. You inherited it so maybe you think deep down that you're supposed to hold it in trust for the next generation of Cassidys."

Rafe was startled by that observation. She was right, he thought. Absolutely right. "Sounds kind of feudal, doesn't it?"

"A bit old-fashioned in some ways," Margaret agreed. "But I can see the pull of that kind of philoso-phy. When you look at land like this you tend to start thinking in more fundamental terms, don't you?"

"Yeah. When I was younger I used to ride out here and do a lot of that kind of thinking. Then I got away from it for a while. I got back in the habit this past year."

"Because of me?"

"Yeah."

Margaret looked down at the reins running through

her fingers. "I did a lot of thinking, too. It nearly drove me crazy for a while."

"I know what you mean." Rafe was silent for a moment, satisfied that they had both suffered during the past year. "You know, I really should sell this chunk of desert. There are plenty of developers who would pay me a fortune for it."

"Do you need another fortune?"

Rafe shrugged. "No. Not really."

"Then don't sell. At least not now." Maggie smiled her glowing smile, the one that always made him want to grab her and kiss her breathless. "Who knows, maybe the next generation of Cassidys won't be as good at wheeling and dealing in the business world as this generation is. Your descendants might need the land far more than you need more money. No one can predict the future and land is the one certain long-term investment. Hold on to it and let the next batch of Cassidys sell it if they need to do so."

"You mean, tell myself I really am holding it in trust for the family?"

"Yes."

Rafe looked out over the vastness in front of him. Maggie's simple logic suddenly made great sense. It was a relief somehow to be able to tell himself that there was no overwhelming need to sell for business reasons. "I think that's exactly what I'll do. I wonder why I didn't think of it that way before now."

"You've been thinking in terms of good business, as usual. But there are other things just as important. A family's heritage is one of them. My father sold his land because he had no choice. He turned out to be a much better engineer and businessman than he was a rancher. But a part of him has always regretted giving up the land. You're not forced to make the choice, so why do it?"

Rafe reached across the short distance between them and wrapped his hand around the nape of her neck. He leaned forward and kissed her soundly. He had to release her abruptly as the chestnut tossed his head and pranced to one side. Quickly Rafe brought the stallion back under control and then he grinned at Maggie.

"Remind me to bounce the occasional business problem off you in the future, Maggie, love. I like the way you think."

"Praise from Caesar." Her laugh was soft and somehow indulgent. "You do realize this is the first and only time you've ever asked my opinion on a business matter?"

"I'll obviously have to do it more often." Rafe hesitated a few seconds, not sure how to say what he intended to say next. Hell, he wasn't even certain he wanted to say it at all. But for some irrational reason he needed to do it. "Maggie, about our bargain."

She glanced at him in surprise. "What bargain?"

He was annoyed that she had forgotten already. "Don't give me that blank look, woman. I'm talking about the bargain we made the other day. The one in which I agreed to go to Winters's gallery show in exchange for your agreement to let me announce our engagement. Or has that little matter slipped your mind?"

She blinked, taken aback by his vehemence. "Hardly. I guess I just hadn't thought of it as a bargain."

"Yeah, well, that's what it was, wasn't it?"

"I suppose so. In a way. What's bothering you about it, Rafe?"

He exhaled heavily, willing himself to shut his mouth while there was still time. But the words came of their own accord. "I don't want you agreeing to get engaged because we've made a deal, Maggie. I don't like having you feel you've got to do it to defend Julie from my bullheaded stubbornness."

"Oh, Rafe, I really didn't think of it quite like that."

"All the same, I thought I'd tell you that I'll go to that damned art show with no strings attached. I'll give Winters a fair chance. As for us, you don't have to make any promises to me until you're ready. I'm willing to give you all the time you need to make certain you want to marry me."

"You surprise me, Rafe."

"I can see that." He was still irritated. "You don't have to look so stunned. You think I can't be open-minded when I want to be?"

"Well—"

"You think I can't give a guy a fair chance?"

"Well—"

"You think the only way I work is by applying pressure whenever I see an opportunity to do so?"

"Well, to be perfectly honest, Rafe…"

He held up a hand. "Forget it. I don't think I need a truthful answer to that one. But I am doing my best to back off a little here, so let me do it, okay?"

"Okay." She smiled gently.

Saddle leather creaked as he studied her face in the morning light. "I want you to marry me. But I want you to come to me willingly, Maggie, love. Not because I've pushed you into it." Rafe drew a deep breath and got the rash words out before he could rethink them. "Take all the time you need to make your decision."

"So long as I come up with the right one?" Her eyes danced mischievously.

He grinned slowly, relaxing inside. "You've got it. So

long as it's the right one." The sun was getting higher in the morning sky and the heat was setting in already. Rafe crammed the brim of his hat down low over his eyes and turned the chestnut back toward the ranch.

IT WAS OBVIOUS FROM THE MOMENT Margaret and Rafe entered the thronged gallery that the showing of Sean Winters's work was a resounding success. The large, prestigious showroom was filled with well-dressed people sipping champagne and commenting learnedly on contemporary art. Margaret saw Rafe's cool-eyed appraisal of the gathering and smiled.

"Not quite what you expected, hmm, cowboy?"

"All right, I'll admit the man apparently has a market. The place is packed. That must be his stuff on the walls. Let's take a look at it before Julie discovers we're here."

Sean Winters's work was clearly of the Southwestern school, full of the rich, sun-drenched tones of the desert. His paintings for the most part tended toward the abstract with an odd hint of surrealism. There was a curiously hard edge to them that made them stand out from the work of other artists dealing with similar subject matter. Margaret was instantly enthralled.

"These are wonderful," she exclaimed, a bit in awe in spite of herself. "Look at that canyon, Rafe. And that evening sky above it."

Rafe peered more closely at the painting she indicated. "Are you sure it's a canyon? Looks like lots of little wavy lines of paint to me."

"It's titled *Canyon*, you twit. And don't you dare play the uncultured, uncouth redneck cowboy with me, Rafe. This work is good and you know it. Admit it."

"It's interesting. I'll give it that much." Rafe frowned

at the price on the tag stuck next to the painting. "Also expensive. If Winters can really sell this stuff for this kind of money, he's got quite a racket going."

"Almost as good a racket as buying and selling companies."

Rafe gave her a threatening scowl just as Julie came hurrying up to greet them.

"You made it. I'm so glad. I was hoping you'd get him here, Margaret." Julie turned hopeful eyes on her brother. "Thanks for coming, Rafe. I really appreciate it."

"Thank Margaret. She practically hog-tied me and dragged me here. You know I'm not into the artsy-craftsy stuff."

Julie's sudden glowering expression bore a startling resemblance to the one Rafe could produce so quickly. "I'm not going to let you dismiss Sean's work as artsy-craftsy stuff, Rafe. Do you hear me? He is a very talented artist and the least you can do is show some respect."

"Okay, okay, calm down. I'm here, aren't I? I'm willing to give the guy a chance."

Julie glanced uncertainly from her brother to Margaret and back again. "You are?"

"Sure. Code of the West and all that."

"What are you talking about, Rafe?"

Rafe flashed a quick grin at Margaret, who beetled her brows at him. "Never mind."

Julie relaxed and gestured at the art that surrounded them. "Tell me the truth, Rafe. Now that you've had a chance to see it, what do you really think of Sean's work? Isn't it wonderful?"

Margaret didn't trust the response she saw forming in Rafe's eyes. She stepped in quickly to answer Julie's query. "Rafe was just saying how impressed he was, weren't you, Rafe?"

Rafe started to comment on that, caught Margaret's eye again and apparently changed his mind. "Uh, yeah. That's just what I was saying." He looked around as if seeking further inspiration. "Big crowd here tonight."

"Oh, there always is for a new showing of Sean's work. He's had a steady market for some time but lately he's been getting a lot of attention in reviews and articles. His career is definitely taking off."

Rafe nodded. "Things blow hot and cold in the art world, don't they? Not a reliable line of work. An artist can be in big demand one year and dead in the water the next."

Margaret saw Julie's mouth tighten and she turned to pounce on Rafe. But the attack proved unnecessary. Sean Winters had come up in time to hear the remark. He smiled coolly at Rafe.

"Nothing's for sure in the art world or any other. That's why I've paid a fair amount of attention to my investments since I made my first sale."

"Is that right?" Rafe swiped a glass of champagne from a passing tray and gave Sean a challenging look. "What do you put your money into, Winters, paint?"

"I guess you could say that. I own that artists' supply house Julie manages. We grossed a quarter of a million last year and this quarter's sales are already overtaking last quarter's. Or so I'm told. I just read the financial statements. I don't actively manage things. Julie handles everything."

Rafe nearly choked on his champagne. Margaret obligingly pounded him on the back. He gave her a sharp look.

"Sorry. Did I hit you too hard?" She smiled at him with brilliant innocence.

Rafe turned back to Winters. "Julie works for you? You own that place she's been managing for the past few months?"

"Best manager I've got."

"How many have you got?"

"Two. New store just opened in Phoenix last month. Julie's going to be overseeing the management of both branches. I don't like having to worry about the business side of things so I've turned it all over to your sister. She seems to have inherited her fair share of the family talent."

"I see," said Rafe. He took another swallow of champagne and glared around the room. "We've been looking at the paintings. Maggie likes your stuff."

Sean grinned. "Thanks, Margaret."

"It's stunning. I love it. If I could afford it, I'd buy *Canyon* in a red-hot second. Unfortunately it's a little out of my range."

Sean winced in chagrin. "I know. Ridiculous, isn't it? For a long time I couldn't even afford to buy my own stuff. I leave the pricing of my work up to Cecil."

"Who's Cecil?"

"He owns this gallery and one in Scottsdale and let me tell you, Cecil is one ruthless son of a gun." Sean grinned at Rafe. "Come to think of it, you'd probably like him, Cassidy. The two of you undoubtedly have a lot in common. Want to meet him?"

"Why not? I'd like to hear a little more about the inside workings of this art business." Rafe handed his empty glass to Margaret and strode off with Sean.

Margaret and Julie watched the two men make their way across the room for a moment and then Julie looked anxiously at Margaret. "Rafe's going to grill Sean. I just know it."

"I wouldn't worry. I have a feeling Sean can take care of himself."

Julie looked briefly surprised and then she relaxed slightly. "You're right. It's just that I've been defending and protecting my dates from Rafe for so long, it's become a habit. I get nervous whenever he gets near one. He tends to stampede them toward the nearest exit. And now that I've actually decided to marry Sean a part of me is terrified Rafe will scare him off."

"No chance of that," Margaret said cheerfully. "Sean won't scare easily." She turned back to study *Canyon*. "Why didn't you tell Rafe you were actually working for Sean?"

"I wanted to make sure I could make a success of the job before I told either Rafe or my mother. This is the first position I've gotten on my own, you know. Rafe has always taken it upon himself to line up something for me. He had a job waiting the day I graduated college. Said it was my graduation present. Every time I quit one he used his business contacts to line up another one."

"That's Rafe, all right. Tends to take over and run things if you let him."

Julie sighed. "The problem is he's good at running business things. You can't deny he's got a natural talent for it. But when he gets involved in people things he's dangerous."

Margaret laughed. "I know what you mean."

"How are you two doing up there at the ranch without Mom or Connor to referee?"

"We're slowly but surely reaching a negotiated peace."

Julie smiled. "I'm glad. Difficult as my brother is, I want him to be happy. And he definitely has not been happy this past year. Margaret, I want to thank you again for what you've done tonight. You didn't have to go out of your way to help. It was very kind of you."

"No problem. Rafe is basically a good man. He just needs a little applied management theory now and then. When it comes right down to it, he did it for you, Julie. You are his sister, after all."

"No," Julie said with a smile. "He didn't do it for me. He did it for you."

RAFE SHUDDERED HEAVILY and muffled his shout of sensual satisfaction against the pillow under Maggie's head. The echo of her own soft cries still hovered in the air along with the scent of their lovemaking. A moment earlier he had felt the tiny, delicate ripples of her release and he had been pulled beyond the limits of his self-control.

She always had this effect on him, Rafe thought as he relaxed slowly. She had the power to unleash this raging torrent of physical and emotional response within him. When their lovemaking was over he was always left with an incredible sense of well-being. There was nothing else on earth quite like it.

Rafe rolled off Maggie's slick, nude body and settled on his back, one hand under his head. He left his other hand lying possessively on one of Maggie's sweetly rounded thighs.

For a long while they were silent together, just as they always were when they rode into the hills at dawn. In some ways making love with Maggie was a lot like taking her riding, Rafe told himself. He grinned suddenly into the moonlit shadows.

"What's so funny?" Maggie stretched luxuriously and turned onto her side. She put her hand on his chest.

"Nothing. I was just thinking that being with you like this is a little like riding with you."

"I don't want to hear any crude cracks about midnight rodeos."

"All right, ma'am. No crude cracks." He smiled again. "Midnight rodeo? Where'd you get a phrase like that? You've been sneaking around listening to country-western music stations, haven't you?"

"I refuse to answer that." She snuggled closer. "But for the record, I will tell you that you're terrific in the saddle."

"I was born to ride," Rafe said with patently false modesty. "And you're the only little filly I ever want to get on top of."

"Uh-huh. Keep it that way. Tell me what you talked about with Sean Winters tonight at the gallery."

"It was men's talk," Rafe said loftily and was promptly punished by having his chest hair yanked quite severely. "Sheesh, okay, okay, lay off the torture. I'll talk."

"Yes?"

"We discussed business."

"Business?"

"Yeah. The business of the art world. It's real dog-eat-dog, did you know that? Bad as the corporate world. We also talked about the fact that he fully intends to marry Julie. With or without my approval."

"And?"

Rafe shifted slightly on the pillow. "And what?"

"And did you try to buy him off?"

"That's none of your business."

"You did, didn't you?" Maggie sat up abruptly, glaring down at him. "Rafe, I warned you not to try that."

He studied her breasts in the moonlight. She had beautiful breasts he told himself, trying to be objective about it. They fit perfectly into his palms. "Don't worry, we got the issue settled."

"What issue?"

"Winters's paintings are for sale, but he isn't," Rafe explained succinctly.

Maggie flopped back down onto the pillow. "I told you so."

"Yeah, you did, didn't you? Has anyone ever told you that's a nasty habit?" Rafe asked conversationally.

"Saying 'I told you so'?" She turned her head and gave him a sassy grin. "But I'm good at it."

He gave her an affectionate slap on her sleek hip and yawned. "You're good at it, all right. I'll have to admit it looks like the Cassidys are going to have an artist in their ranks."

"You're beginning to like Sean, aren't you?"

"He's okay."

"And you're going to tell Julie you like him and approve of him, aren't you?"

"Probably," Rafe admitted. He was feeling too complacent and sensually replete to argue about anything right now.

Maggie giggled delightfully in the darkness. "I love you when you're like this."

"Like what?"

"So reasonable."

Rafe felt a cold chill go through him. The satisfaction he had been feeling a few seconds ago vanished. He thought of the file in his study and the moves he had instructed Hatcher to make that morning. He levered himself up onto one elbow and looked down at the woman beside him.

She sensed the change in him instantly. "Rafe? What's wrong?"

"What about when I'm not reasonable by your standards, Maggie?" he asked. "Will you still love me?"

She searched his face, her eyes soft and shadowed. "Yes."

Rafe inhaled deeply and told himself she meant it. "Say it straight out for me. I need to hear the words."

"I love you, Rafe." She touched his shoulder, her fingers gliding down his arm in a gentle caress. "I never stopped loving you although I will admit I tried very hard."

Rafe fell back onto the pillow and pulled her down across his chest. He drove his fingers through her tangled hair and held her head clasped in his hands. "I love you, Maggie. I want you to always remember that."

"I will, Rafe."

He lay there looking up at her for a while and then the tension went out of him. His good mood restored itself. "Does this mean we're finally engaged?"

She smiled slowly. "Why, yes, I guess it does."

"You're sure?" he pressed. "You're willing to set a date?"

Maggie nodded. "Yes. If you're very sure you want to marry me."

"I've never been more certain of anything in my life." He used the grip in her hair to pull her mouth closer to his own. When he kissed her, she parted her lips for him, letting him deep inside where he could stake his intimate claim. Rafe growled softly as he felt himself start to grow hard again.

Maggie giggled.

"What are you laughing at, lady?"

"You sound like a big cat when you do that."

He rolled to the edge of the bed, taking her with him. Then he stood up with her in his arms. Maggie laughed up at him as she clung to his neck. "What are you doing? Where are we going?"

"Swimming."

"But it's two in the morning."

"We can sleep late."

"We're both stark naked."

He grinned and eyed her body appreciatively. "That's true."

"You're impossible, you know that?"

"But you love me anyway, right?"

"Right." Maggie looked down as he reached the pool. She glanced up again in alarm as she realized his intentions. "I don't mind a late night swim, but don't you dare drop me into that water, Rafe."

"It's not cold."

She gave him a quelling look. "All the same, I do not like entering swimming pools by being dropped into them."

"Think of this as just another little example of simple frontier justice."

"Rafe, don't you dare. What justice are you talking about, anyway?"

"This is for trying to set me up at that gallery this evening."

Her eyes widened innocently. "But you agreed to go to the show with no strings attached. You said you liked Sean after you got to know him."

Rafe shook his head deliberately. "That's not the point. The point is you tried to set me up. Tried to manipulate me into doing exactly what you wanted.

If you're going to play games like that, Maggie, love, you have to be prepared to pay the price." He opened his arms and let her fall.

She yelled very nicely as she went into the water. When she surfaced she promptly splashed him, laughing exuberantly as he tried to dodge.

Rafe grinned back at her and then dove into the pool thinking that this was probably one of the best nights of his entire life.

CHAPTER NINE

RAFE WAITED UNTIL MARGARET'S back was turned in the large mall bookstore before he strolled casually over to the romance section. He stood there for a moment, lost in a sea of lushly illustrated paperbacks. Then he spotted a familiar-looking name. Fuchsia foil spelled out Margaret Lark. The title of the book was *Ruthless*.

After another quick glance to make certain that Margaret was still busy browsing through mysteries, Rafe examined the cover of her latest book. It showed a man and a woman locked in a passionate embrace. The man had removed the charcoal-gray jacket of his suit and his tie hung rakishly around his neck. His formal white shirt was open to the waist and his hand was behind the lady's back, deftly lowering the zipper of her elegant designer gown.

The couple was obviously standing in the living room of a sophisticated penthouse. In the backdrop high-rise buildings rose into a dark sky and the sparkling lights of a big city glittered.

Rafe opened *Ruthless* to the first page and started to read.

"It's no secret, Anne. The man's a shark. Just ask anyone who worked for any of the companies Roarke Cody is supposed to have salvaged in the past five years. He may have saved the firms but he did it by firing most of the management and supervisory level people. We're all going to be on the street in a week, you mark my words."

Anne Jamison picked up the stack of files on her desk and glanced at her worried assistant. "Calm down, Brad. Cody's been hired to straighten out this company, not decimate the staff. He must be good to have acquired the reputation he's got. Now, if you'll excuse me, I've got to get going. I've got a meeting in his office in five minutes."

"Anne, you're not listening. The guy's ruthless. Don't you understand?" Brad trailed after her to the door. "He's probably called you into his office to fire you. And after he lets you go, I'm next. You'll see."

Anne pretended to ignore her frantic assistant as she made her way down the hall, but the truth was, she was not nearly as confident as she looked. She was as aware of Cody's reputation as Brad was—more so, in fact, because she'd done some checking.

"Ruthless" was, indeed, the right word to describe the turnaround specialist who had been installed here at the corporate headquarters of Seaco Industries. Roarke Cody had left a trail of fired personnel in his wake wherever he had gone to work. He was nothing less than a professional hit man whose gun was for hire by any company that could afford him.

Three minutes later Anne was shown into the new gunslinger's office. She held her breath as the tall, lean, dark-haired man standing at the window turned slowly to face her. One look and her heart sank. She had been putting up a brave, professional front but the fact was, she had known the full truth about this man the first day she'd met him. There was no mercy in those tawny-gold eyes—no compassion in that hard, grim face.

"Good morning, Mr. Cody," she said with the sort of gallant good cheer one adopted in front of a firing squad. "I understand you're on the hunt and you'll be having most of management for dinner."

"Not most of management." Roarke's deep voice was tinged with a hint of a Western drawl. "Just you, Miss Jamison. Seven o'clock tonight." He smiled without any humor. "I thought we might discuss your immediate future."

Anne's mouth fell open in shock. "Mr. Cody, I couldn't possibly..."

"Perhaps I should clarify that. It's not just your future we will discuss," he said smoothly. "But that of your staff, as well."

And suddenly Anne knew exactly how it felt to be singled out as prey.

"For heaven's sake, what are you doing?" Margaret hissed in Rafe's ear.

"Reading one of your books." Rafe closed *Ruthless* and smiled blandly. "Something sort of familiar about this Roarke guy."

To his surprise, Margaret blushed a vivid pink. "You're imagining things. Put that back and let's go get that coffee you promised me."

"Hang on a second, I want to buy this." Rafe reached for his wallet as he started toward the counter.

Margaret hurried after him. "You're going to buy *Ruthless?* But, Rafe, it's not exactly your kind of book."

"I'm not so sure about that."

She stifled a groan and retreated to wait near the door as Rafe paid for the book. A moment later, his package in one hand, Rafe ambled out into the air-conditioned mall. "Okay, let's get the coffee."

Margaret marched determinedly toward a small café near a fountain and sat down. "Are you really going to read that?"

"Uh-huh. Why don't you have your coffee and go shop for a while? I'll just sit here and read."

"Why this sudden interest in my writing?"

"Maggie, love, I want to know everything there is to know about you. Besides, I'm curious to see whether or not I save Seaco Industries."

"Whether or not *you* save it," she gasped in outrage. "Rafe, don't get any ideas about my having used you as a model for the hero in my book."

Rafe paid no attention to that as he dug *Ruthless* out of the sack and put it down on the table in front of him. "Come on, Maggie, love. Light brown eyes, dark brown hair and a Western drawl? Who do you think you're kidding?"

"I have news for you, Rafe. There are millions of men around who fit that description."

"Yeah, but I'm the one you know," he said complacently as he ordered two cups of coffee from a hovering waitress.

Margaret gave him an exasperated glare. "You want to know something? Most of my heroes look like Roarke Cody. And I wrote at least three of them long before I ever met you."

"Is that right? No wonder you fell straight into my

hands the day I met you. I was your favorite hero come to life. The man of your dreams."

"Why you arrogant cowboy. Of all the…"

"Give me a hint," Rafe said, interrupting her casually. "Does the heroine sleep with this Roarke guy in the hope that she can persuade him not to fire her and her staff?"

"Of course not." Margaret was obviously scandalized at the suggestion. "That would be highly unethical. None of my heroines would do such a thing."

"Hmm. But he tries to get her to do that, right?"

Margaret lifted her chin. "Roarke Cody is quite ruthless in the beginning. He tries all sorts of underhanded, sneaky maneuvers to get the heroine."

"And?"

"And what?"

"Do any of those underhanded, sneaky maneuvers work as well as the underhanded, sneaky maneuver I used to get you down here to Tucson?"

Margaret folded her arms on the table and leaned forward with a belligerent glare. "I am not going to tell you the plot."

"Go shopping, Maggie, love. I'll wait right here for you." Rafe propped one booted heel on a conveniently empty chair, leaned back and picked up *Ruthless*.

MARGARET SPENT OVER AN HOUR in the colorful, Southwestern-style shops. The air-conditioned shopping mall was crowded with people seeking to escape the midday heat.

The clothes featured in the windows tended to be brighter and more casual in style than what she was accustomed to seeing in Seattle. It made for an interesting shopping experience that she deliberately lengthened in the hope of causing Rafe to grow bored and restless.

But when she returned to the indoor sidewalk café, several packages in hand, she saw to her dismay that he was still deep into *Ruthless*.

She told herself she ought to find his interest in her book gratifying or at the very least somewhat amusing. But the fact was, it made her uncomfortable. He had guessed the truth immediately. He was the hero of *Ruthless* and of every book she had ever written.

Margaret had been in the middle of writing Roarke and Anne's story when she had met Rafe. She had finished it shortly after Rafe had turned on her and accused her of betraying him. It had not been easy to write a happy ending when her own love life was in shambles.

But a part of her had sought to work out in *Ruthless* the ending that had been denied to her in real life. Her own relationship might have gone on the rocks but she'd still had her dreams of what a good relationship could be. A woman had to have faith in the future.

"Not finished yet?" Margaret came to a halt in front of Rafe.

He looked up slowly. "Gettin' there. Ready to go?"

She nodded. "I could use a swim."

"Good idea." Rafe got to his feet and dropped *Ruthless* back into the paper bag. "You know this Roarke guy started out okay in the beginning. He had the right idea about how to save Seaco. You've got to cut a lot of dead wood when you go into a situation like that. But I get the feeling he's being set up for a fall."

"He's being set up for a happy ending," Margaret muttered.

Rafe shook his head, looking surprisingly serious.

"The problem is, he's starting to let his hormones make his decisions. He's getting soft." Rafe chuckled. "Not in bed, I'll grant you, he's holding up just fine there. But when it comes to business, he's falling apart. Going to shoot himself in the foot if he doesn't get back on track."

"He's falling in love with the heroine and that love is causing him to change," Margaret snapped.

"It's causing him to act stupid."

"Rafe, for pity's sake, it's just a story. Don't take it so seriously."

"Real-life business doesn't work like that."

"It's a story, Rafe. A romance."

"You know," Rafe said, looking thoughtful as they walked out of the mall into the furnace of the parking lot, "your dad was right. It's a good thing you got out of the business world, Maggie. You're not tough enough for it."

"My father said that? I'll strangle him."

"He said it during one of our early conversations and I agree."

"You're both a couple of turkeys."

"Maybe women in general just aren't hard enough to make it in the business world," Rafe continued philosophically. "You've got to be willing to be ruthless, really ruthless or you'll get eaten by the bigger sharks. Women, especially women like you, just don't have that extra sharp edge, know what I mean?"

Margaret came to a full halt right in the middle of the blazing parking lot and planted herself squarely in front of a startled Rafe. She was hotter than the blacktop on which she stood, her anger suddenly lashed into a firestorm.

"Why you chauvinistic, pigheaded, redneck cowboy.

I always had a feeling that deep down inside you didn't approve of women in the business world and now at last the truth comes out. So you don't think women can handle it, do you? You don't think we'll ever make it in big business? That we aren't ruthless enough?"

"Now, honey, it was just an observation."

"It's a biased, prejudiced, masculine observation. I've got news for you, Rafe Cassidy, one of these days women are going to not only make it big in the business world, but we're going to change the way it operates."

Rafe blinked and reached up to pull the brim of his Stetson lower over his eyes. "Is that right?"

"Darn right. You men have been running it long enough and women are getting tired of playing by your rules. We're getting tired of cutthroat business practices and vicious competition—tired of playing the game for the sake of some man's ego."

Rafe shrugged. "That's the way it works, Maggie, love. It's a jungle out there."

"Only because men have made it into one. I suppose that after you got civilized and no longer had the thrill of the hunt for real, you had to create a new way to get your kicks. So you turned all your aggressive instincts into the way you do business. But that's going to change as women take over."

"Uh, Maggie, love, it's kind of hot out here. What do you say we go back to the ranch and continue this fascinating discussion in the swimming pool?"

"Your sister is a good example of the new breed of female businessperson. And Sean Winters has shown the good sense to turn his stores over to her to manage. You could take a lesson from him."

A small smile edged Rafe's mouth. His eyes gleamed

in the shadow of his hat. "You want me to turn Cassidy and Company over to you?"

"Of course not. I don't want anything to do with that company. I've got my own career in writing and I like it. But I swear to God, Rafe, if we have a daughter and if she shows an interest in the family business, you'd darn well better let her have a hand in it."

Rafe grinned slowly. "It's a deal. Let's go home and work on it."

Margaret stared at him in frowning confusion as he took her arm and steered her toward the Mercedes. "What are you talking about?"

"Our daughter. Let's go home and get busy making one. I want to see this brave new world of business once the women take over. The sooner we get started producing the new female executive, the sooner we'll see if it's going to work."

Margaret felt as if the wind had been knocked out of her. She struggled for air. "A daughter? Rafe, are you talking about a baby?"

"Yeah. Any objections?"

She cleared her throat, still dazed by the abrupt change of topic. A baby—Rafe's baby. A little girl to inherit his empire. Margaret recovered from her initial shock and began to smile gloriously.

"Why, no, Rafe. I don't have any objections at all."

RAFE WAS FEELING EXCEPTIONALLY good two days later when he walked down the hall to his study. He had no premonition of disaster at all.

But, then, he'd been feeling very good every day since Margaret had arrived. Now that they had the house to themselves he was indulging himself in the luxury of waking up beside her in the mornings. He loved that time at dawn when they lay together in tangled white sheets and watched the morning light pour over the mountains.

One of these days he really was going to have to start going back into the office on a regular basis, he told himself. But all in all, if the truth be known, he was slightly amazed at how well things were going with him on vacation.

He chuckled to himself at the thought that he might not be as indispensable at Cassidy and Company headquarters as he'd always assumed. Maggie wouldn't hesitate to point that out to him if he gave her the chance.

He rounded the corner, glancing at his watch. Hatcher had gone back out to his car to get another file. They had been working for the past two hours before taking a break and now they were going to finish the business. Rafe was looking forward to joining Margaret out by the pool.

Rafe walked through the door of his study, frowning slightly as he realized he must have left it open. Perhaps Hatcher had already returned from the car.

But it wasn't Doug Hatcher standing beside the desk staring at the open file and the computer printout lying alongside. It was Margaret. One look at her face and Rafe knew she had seen too much.

He sighed inwardly. He would much rather she hadn't found out what was going on, but it wasn't the end of the world, either. She loved him and this time around she was firmly in his camp.

"What are you doing in here, Maggie? I thought you were going swimming."

She was staring at him with wide eyes. A storm was brewing rapidly in their aqua depths. "Doug said you were in here. I wanted to talk to you. But I found this instead." She gestured angrily at the open file. "What in the world is going on, Rafe? What are you up to with this Ellington takeover? Why all these references to Moorcroft?"

"It's just business, Maggie, love. I'll be finished in another half hour or so. You told me you were willing to be reasonable about the amount of time I spent on work. Why don't you go on out to the pool?"

"This is what you were working on that night I found you in here after the engagement party, isn't it? This is why Hatcher comes here to see you every day. I demand to know what is going on."

"Why?"

"Why? Because it's clear Moorcroft is involved in some way and I know you have no liking for him." Her eyes narrowed. "I also know that you're quite capable of plotting revenge. Tell me the truth, Rafe. Are you in competition with Jack to take over Ellington?"

He shrugged and sat down behind the desk. "You could say that."

"What do you mean by that? Are you or aren't you?"

Rafe closed the damning file and regarded her consideringly. She was getting mad but she wasn't going up in flames. "As I said, Maggie, this is just business. It doesn't concern you."

"Are you sure? If this really is just business as usual, you're right. It doesn't concern me. But if this is some sort of vengeance against Jack, I won't have it."

Rafe rested his elbows on the arms of his chair and steepled his fingers. His initial uneasiness was over and he was starting to get annoyed by her attitude. "You think you have to protect Moorcroft? The way you did last year?"

She flinched at that. "No, of course not. I don't

work for him any longer and I don't owe him anything, but—"

"You're right. You don't owe him anything, especially not your loyalty. That should be crystal clear this time around. So let him take his chances out there in the jungle, Maggie. He's been doing it a long time, same as me."

"Rafe, I don't like this. If you're up to something, I think I should be told."

"You're a romance writer these days, not a business executive. You don't need to know anything about this."

"Damn you, Rafe, don't you dare patronize me. I don't trust you to treat Moorcroft the way you would any other business competitor. Not after what happened last year. I want to know—" She broke off abruptly, glancing at the open door.

Rafe followed her gaze and saw Hatcher standing on the threshold. He looked uncertain of what he should do next. "I'll, uh, come back later, Rafe."

"No," Rafe said. "Maggie was just leaving. Come on in, Hatcher. I want to get this Ellington thing finished today. Sit down."

Margaret hesitated a moment and then apparently thought better of making a scene in front of Hatcher. "We'll discuss this later, Rafe." She turned and stalked out the door, the elegant line of her spine rigidly straight with anger.

Hatcher stared after her, looking more uneasy than ever. "She knows about the Ellington deal?"

"She walked in here and saw the damned file lying on the desk."

Hatcher paled. "Sorry. I know you didn't want her to find out about it."

Rafe bit off a curse. "It wasn't your fault. Never

mind, I'll deal with Maggie later. I can sugarcoat the facts and calm her down. Let's get back to work."

Hatcher drew a deep breath. "Rafe, I think there's something you should know."

"What?" Rafe jabbed at a key on the computer console and narrowed his eyes as a familiar spreadsheet popped onto the screen.

"There's been another leak of information."

That caught Rafe's attention. He swung his gaze back to his assistant. "Bad?"

"The latest set of offer figures. The ones we drew up this week. My inside information tells me Moorcroft has them."

"This time around we were very, very careful, Hatcher," Rafe said softly. "Only you and I knew those numbers and they existed only in this file. We wiped them out of the computer after we ran the calculations."

Hatcher studied the desktop for a long moment before he looked up. There was a desperate expression in his eyes. "You're going to have my head if I say what I have to say next, Rafe."

Rafe looked at the man he had trusted for the past three years. "Just say it and get it over with."

"There's been someone else here in your house with access to these figures for over a week. I hate to be the one to point this out to you, but the fact is the really bad leaks began after she got here."

Rafe was so stunned he couldn't even think for a moment. The accusation against Margaret was the last thing he'd been expecting to hear. He had prepared himself for something else entirely.

For an instant he simply stared at Hatcher and then he came up out of the chair, grabbed his startled assistant by the collar of his immaculate shirt and yanked him halfway across the desk. "What the hell are you trying to tell me?"

Fear flashed in Hatcher's eyes. "Rafe, I'm sorry. I shouldn't have said anything. But someone has to point it out to you. And as long as it's gone this far, there's more you should know."

"More?" Rafe's hand tightened.

Hatcher looked down at the corded muscles of Rafe's forearms and then up again. "My sources tell me she saw him shortly before leaving Seattle to come down here."

"Hatcher, I swear, I'll break your neck if you're lying to me."

"It's true," Hatcher gasped. "I've known about the meeting for a couple of days but I've been afraid to tell you. But now you're practically accusing me of being the leak and I've got my own reputation to consider. Ask her. Go on, ask her if she didn't talk to Moorcroft before she flew to Tucson."

"There's no way she would have talked to that bastard."

"Is that right? Ask her if Jack Moorcroft didn't offer her a nice chunk of change to find out what she could about what we're up to. You want to pinpoint the leak? Don't look at me. I've been your man since the day I came to work for you. I've proven my loyalty a hundred times over. Try looking close to home, Rafe."

"Damn it, Hatcher, you don't know what you're saying."

"Yes, I do. I've just been afraid to say it out loud for several days because I knew you didn't want to hear it. But you've never paid me to be a yes man, Rafe. You've always said you wanted me to speak my mind and tell you the facts as I saw them. All right, I'm doing just that. She betrayed you once and she's betraying you again."

Rafe felt himself hovering on the brink of his self-control. He hadn't been this close to going over the edge since the day he'd found Margaret with Moorcroft.

He made himself release his grip on Hatcher. Doug inhaled deeply and stepped quickly back out of reach, smoothing his clothing.

"Get out of here, Hatcher."

Hatcher glanced nervously at the file. "What about the Ellington deal? We need another set of numbers and we need them fast. We've got to make the final move within the next forty-eight hours."

"*I said, get out of here.*"

Hatcher nodded quickly, picked up his briefcase and went to the door. There he paused briefly, his expression anguished. "Rafe, I'm sorry it turned out this way."

"Just go, will you?"

Hatcher nodded and went out the door without a backward glance.

Rafe stared for a long while at the far wall before he yanked open the bottom desk drawer and pulled out a glass and a bottle of Scotch.

Very carefully he poured the liquor into the glass and then he propped his feet on the desktop and leaned back in the chair. He took a long swallow of the potent Scotch and forced his mind to go blank for a full minute.

When he felt the icy calm close in on him he knew he had himself back under control.

"Rafe?"

He didn't turn his head. "Come in, Maggie."

"I heard Doug leave." She walked into the room and sat down on the other side of the desk. Her beautiful, clear eyes met his. "I want to have that discussion now, Rafe. I want to know what's going on and what you're planning to do to Moorcroft. Because if you're bent on getting vengeance on him for what happened last year—"

"Maggie."

Her brows drew together sharply as he interrupted her. "What?"

"Maggie, I have a couple of simple questions to ask you and I don't want any long, involved lectures or explanations. Just a simple yes or no."

"Rafe, are you all right? Is something wrong?"

"Something is wrong, but we'll get to that later. Just answer the questions."

"Very well, what are the questions?"

"Did you have a meeting with Jack Moorcroft in Seattle before you caught the plane to Tucson? Did he ask you to spy on me?"

The shock in her lovely eyes was all the answer he needed. Rafe swore softly and took another long pull on the Scotch.

"How did you know about that?" Margaret whispered in disbelief.

"Does it matter?"

"Yes, it bloody well matters," she shouted, slamming her fist on the desk. "I'd like to know what's going on around here and who's spying on me. I'd also like to know exactly what I stand accused of."

"Someone's been leaking information on the Ellington deal to Moorcroft. You, me and Doug Hatcher are the only ones who've had access to the file in the past few days. Just how badly did you hate my guts after what happened last year, Maggie, love? Bad enough to come back so that you could get a little revenge?"

"How dare you?" Margaret was on her feet. *"How dare you?"*

"Sit down, Maggie."

"I will not sit down, you deceitful, distrusting, son of a…" She gulped air. "I will not go through this a second time. Do you hear me? I won't let you tear me apart into little pieces again the way you did last time. You don't have to throw me out, Rafe. Not this time. I'm already gone."

She whirled and ran from the room.

Rafe finished the last swallow of Scotch and threw the glass against the wall. It shattered into a hundred glittering pieces and cascaded to the floor.

CHAPTER TEN

RAGE, A FIERCE, BURNING RAGE that was an agony to endure drove Margaret from the study. Behind her she thought she heard the crash of breaking glass but she paid no attention. She fled down the hall to her bedroom, dashed inside and slammed the door.

She was gasping for breath, the hot tears burning behind her eyes as she sank down onto the bed. An instant later she leaped up again, hugging herself in despair as she paced the room.

How could he do this to her a second time? she asked herself wildly. How could he doubt her now?

She had to get out of here. She could not bear to stay here under Rafe's roof another minute. Margaret ran to the mirrored chest and threw open the doors. She found her suitcase, dragged it out and tossed it onto the bed. Spinning around, she grabbed her clothes and began throwing them into the open suitcase.

He didn't trust her. That was what it came down to. After all they'd each been through separated this past year and after finally rediscovering their love for each other, Rafe still didn't trust her. He was prepared to believe she'd come here as a spy.

Damn Moorcroft, anyway. If only he hadn't looked her up that day in Seattle. If only she hadn't agreed to have coffee with him.

But if it hadn't been that unfortunate incident, it

probably would have been something else sooner or later. Rafe was obviously ready to believe the worst.

And apparently he had a reason to worry about a Moorcroft spy, Margaret thought vengefully. He was plotting some form of revenge against his old rival. She just knew it. She was caught in the middle again between the two men and she was furious. They had no right to do this to her.

She would take the Mercedes, Margaret told herself. The keys were on the hall table. Rafe could damn well make arrangements to get his car out of the airport lot.

It was intolerable that he had dared to question her reason for being here in Tucson. He was the one who had forced her to come down here in the first place.

Margaret tossed one sandal into the suitcase and looked around for the other. She dropped to her knees to peer under the bed and to her horror, the tears started to fall.

It was too much.

She cried there on the floor until the rage finally burned itself out. Then, wearily, she climbed to her feet and went into the bathroom to wash her face.

She grimaced at the sight of herself in the mirror and reached for a brush. She wondered if Rafe was still in the study.

It flashed through her mind that he probably wouldn't come after her a second time. No, not a chance. In his own way he had sacrificed his pride once before to get her back and that was all anyone could reasonably expect. He was, when all was said and done, a tough, arrogant cowboy who was as hard and unforgiving as the desert itself.

And she loved him.

Heaven help her, she loved him. Margaret stared at

herself in the mirror knowing that if she walked out this time, he would not come after her.

There was only one chance to salvage the situation. She was woman enough to know that this time she would have to be the one who rose above her own pride.

She forced herself to think back on the past few days. She clung to the knowledge that Rafe had changed since last year. He had tried hard to modify his work habits and to realign some of his priorities. He had worked hard to please her, to make her fall in love with him.

In his own way, he had tried to prove that he loved her.

Slowly Margaret put the brush back down on the counter. Turning on her heel, she went back through the bedroom and into the hall. The first few steps took all the willpower she had. Her instinct was to turn and run again but she kept going.

She rounded the corner and saw Rafe leaning in the open doorway of the study, thumb hooked onto his belt. In his other hand he coolly tossed the keys to the Mercedes. He watched her with an unreadable expression. Margaret halted. For a moment they just stared at each other and then Rafe broke the charged silence.

"Looking for these?" he asked, giving the keys another toss.

"No," Margaret said, starting forward deliberately. "No, I do not want the keys to the Mercedes."

"How are you going to get to the airport? You expect me to drive you?"

"That won't be necessary. I am not going to the airport."

"Sure you are. You're going to run, just like you did last time."

"Damn you, Rafe, I did not run away from you last year, I was *kicked out*."

"Depends on your point of view, I guess."

"It is not a point of view, it's a fact." Margaret came to a halt right in front of him and lifted both hands to grab him by the open collar of his shirt. She stood on tiptoe and brought her face very close to his. "Listen up, cowboy. I have a few more facts to tell you. And you, by heaven, are going to pay attention this time."

"Yeah?"

"Yeah." She pushed him backward into the study, too incensed and too determined to pursue her mission to notice just how easily he went. She forced him all the way back to his chair and then she put her hands on his shoulders and pushed downward. Rafe sat.

Margaret released him and stalked around to the other side of the desk. She planted her hands on the polished wood surface and leaned forward.

"If this were a romance novel instead of the real world, this little scene would not be necessary. Because of our great love for each other, you would trust me implicitly, you see. You would know without being told that I would never go to bed with you and then turn around and spy on you so that I could report to Moorcroft."

"Is that right? Your heroes can read minds?"

"The bonds of love make them intuitive, sensitive and insightful and don't you dare mock me, Cassidy."

"I thought I made it clear I'm not one of those modern, sensitive types."

"All right, all right, I accept the fact that this is not a romance novel and you are not exactly the most perceptive, intuitive man I've ever met."

"I'm no romance hero, that's for sure."

She ignored that. "I also accept the fact that I cannot expect you to come after me if I leave here today. You gave us both a second chance, Rafe. It's my turn to give us a third. I only hope this does not indicate a pattern for the future. Now then, let's get one thing straight. I did not make any deal with Jack Moorcroft."

Rafe waited in stony silence.

This was going to be hard, Margaret thought. Resolutely she gathered her courage. "I had not seen or heard from Jack Moorcroft since that debacle last year until he showed up out of the clear blue sky on the Saturday before I was due to come down here."

"Just a friendly visit, right?"

"No, you know very well it was not a friendly visit. He said he thought you might be plotting against him. He told me that since last year he's had the impression you were gunning for him. He thinks you're out to get him."

"I never said Moorcroft was a stupid man. He's right."

"He also said that he would give a great deal to know exactly what you were planning."

"Why didn't you mention the little fact that you'd seen him before you came down here?"

"Are you kidding? The last thing I wanted to do was mention Moorcroft to you. Keeping quiet was an act of pure self-defense. The last time I got between the two of you I got crushed, if you will recall."

"Damn it, Maggie…"

"Besides, I told him to take a flying leap. I made it clear I considered myself out of it. I did not work for him any longer. I owed him nothing this time around. I told him I was going to Tucson for my own personal reasons and that was that."

"And he accepted your answer?"

"Rafe, I swear I haven't communicated with him since that Saturday and I certainly have not handed over any of your precious secrets to him. I don't even know any of your secrets."

"You saw the Ellington file."

"I saw it for the first time this afternoon." Margaret closed her eyes and then opened them to pin him with a desperate gaze. "Rafe, I can't prove any of this. I am begging you to believe me. If Moorcroft has numbers he shouldn't have, then you must believe he got them from someone else. Please, Rafe. I love you too much to betray you."

"Revenge is a powerful motivator, Maggie," Rafe finally said quietly.

"More powerful for you than for me, Rafe."

"Are you sure of that?"

"I love you. When you came back into my life you opened up a wound I had hoped was healed. I was angry at first and frightened. And I didn't know if I could trust you. But I knew for certain the first night I was here that I still loved you."

"Maggie..."

"Wait, let me finish. Julie said something about what it had cost you in pride to find a way to get me back. She was right. I realize that now that I'm standing here trampling all over my own pride in an effort to get you to trust me enough to believe in me. Please, Rafe, don't ruin what we've got. It's too precious and too rare. Please trust me. I didn't betray you."

"You love me?"

"I love you."

"Okay, then it must have been Hatcher, after all." Margaret blinked. "I beg your pardon?"

"I said it must have been Hatcher who gave Moorcroft the numbers. He's been acting weird for the past six months or so, but I wasn't sure he would have the guts to actually sell me out. Hatcher's not what you'd call a real gutsy guy. Still, you never can tell, so I put some garbled preliminary information into the Ellington file to see what would happen."

"Rafe, will you please be quiet for a moment. I am having trouble following this conversation."

His brows rose. "Why? You started it."

She eyed him cautiously, uncertain of his mood. For one horrible second she thought he was actually laughing at her. But that made no sense. "Are you saying you believe me?"

"Maggie, love, I'd probably believe you if you told me you could get me a great deal on snowballs in hell."

She was dumbfounded. Slowly she sank into the nearest chair. "I don't understand. If you believe me now, why didn't you believe me a while ago when you asked if I'd seen Moorcroft?"

"Maggie, I did believe you," he reminded her patiently. "I asked you if you'd seen him before you left Seattle and you, with your usual straightforward style, told me you *had* seen Moorcroft, remember? You didn't deny it."

"But you didn't let me explain. You told me I had to answer yes or no."

"All right, I'm guilty of wanting a simple answer. I should have known that with you the explanation would be anything but simple. There are always complications around you, aren't there, Maggie? And you ran out the door without bothering to try to explain. What was I supposed to think?"

"That I would never have come down here for revenge," Maggie declared in ringing tones. "You should know me well enough to know that."

"Maggie, I know for a fact to what lengths a person will go for revenge. I also know how much I wanted you. It was entirely possible I'd deluded myself into thinking I'd really succeeded in convincing you to come back to me. God knows I want you back bad enough to tell myself all sorts of lies. But when you didn't deny the meeting with Moorcroft..."

"Never mind," Margaret said urgently. "Don't say it. I'm sorry. I should have stood my ground and yelled at you until you believed I was innocent."

Rafe's mouth curved gently. "You don't even have to yell. I'm always ready to listen."

"Hah. What a bunch of bull. You didn't listen last year."

"Yes, I did." Rafe sighed. "Maggie, last year you told me the truth, too. I listened to every damn word. When I caught you in Moorcroft's office you admitted immediately you'd just told him I was after Spencer, remember? You said you'd had to tell him—that it was your duty as a loyal employee of Moorcroft."

"Oh. Yes, I did say that, didn't I?"

"Our problem last year had nothing to do with your lying to me. You were too damned honest, if you want to know the truth. I'll tell you something. I would have sold my soul for a few sweet lies from you last year. More than anything else in this world I wanted to believe you hadn't felt your first loyalty was to Jack Moorcroft instead of me."

Margaret closed her eyes, feeling utterly wretched. "Are you ever going to be able to forgive me for that, Rafe? I don't know if we can go on together if you aren't able to understand why I did what I did."

"Hell, yes, I forgive you." Rafe pulled two more glasses out of his desk drawer and splashed Scotch into each. He handed one glass to Margaret who clutched it in both hands. "I hate to admit it, Maggie, love, but I was the idiot last year. You want to know something?"

"What?" she asked warily.

"I didn't think I'd ever say this, but I admire you for what you did. You were right. In that situation your business loyalties belonged to Moorcroft. You were his employee, drawing a salary from him and you believed you'd betrayed his interests by talking too freely to me. You did the right thing by going to him and telling him everything. I only wish I could count on all of my employees having a similar set of ethics."

Margaret couldn't believe what she was hearing. A surge of euphoric relief went through her. "Thank you, Rafe. That's very generous of you."

Rafe took a swallow of Scotch. "Mind you, I could have throttled you at the time and it took me months to calm down, but that doesn't change the facts. You did what you thought was right, even when the chips were down. You've got guts, Maggie."

She grinned slowly. "And out here in the Wild West you admire guts in a woman, right?"

"Hell, yes. No place for wimpy females around here."

"I thought you said I was soft. Too soft for the business world."

"That's different. You're a woman. Being soft doesn't mean you don't have guts."

Margaret got up, put her glass of Scotch down on the desk and walked around to sit on Rafe's knee. She put her arms around his neck and leaned her forehead down to rest against his. "You are a hopelessly chauvinistic, anachronistic, retrograde cowboy, but I love you, anyway."

"I know," he said, his voice dropping into the deep husky register that always sent shivers down Maggie's spine. "I've been fairly certain of it all along but I knew it for sure when you grabbed me by the shirt a minute ago, shoved me into this chair and begged me to listen to you."

"I did not exactly beg."

He smiled. "Pleaded?"

"Never. Well, maybe a little."

His smile widened into a grin. "It's okay, Maggie. I love you, too. More than anything else on God's earth. And just to prove how insightful, sensitive and intuitive I can be, I'll tell you that I understand what you went through a while ago when you came in here and pinned me down."

"You do?"

"Honey, I know firsthand what it's like to stomp all over your own pride."

"Actually, it's not quite as bad an exercise as I thought it would be."

"I don't know about that. Personally I wouldn't want to have to repeat it too many times. Once was enough for me."

She relaxed against him. "What about Hatcher?"

Rafe tipped her head back against his shoulder and kissed her exposed throat. "Don't worry about him. There's no real harm done. I told you I've been letting him see bad information. The Ellington deal is safe."

"Yes, but, Rafe, don't you think you should try to understand why he did it?"

"I do understand. He's a yellow-bellied snake."

"But, Rafe…"

"I said, don't worry about it." He kissed her full on the mouth, a long, slow kiss that made her tremble in his arms. "That's better," Rafe said. "Now you're paying full attention."

He got up with her in his arms and carried her out of the study and down the hall to her bedroom.

A LONG WHILE LATER MARGARET stirred amid the sheets, opened her eyes and blinked at the hot, lazy sunlight that dappled the patio outside the glass door. She knew without lifting her head to see his face that Rafe was wide-awake. His arm was around her, holding her close against his side but his gaze was on the bright light bouncing off the pool water.

"You're thinking about Hatcher, aren't you?" Margaret asked.

"Yeah."

"What are you going to do, Rafe?"

"Fire him."

She didn't move. "And the Ellington deal?"

"It'll go through."

"This isn't just a case of beating Moorcroft to the punch, is it?"

"No."

"Rafe, tell me what you're planning. I have to know why this Ellington thing is so special to you."

"It doesn't concern you, Maggie, love. Let it be."

She sat up, holding the sheet to her breasts, and searched his face. "It does concern me. I can feel it. Please tell me the truth, Rafe. I have to know what you're going to do."

He regarded her in silence for a long moment. "You won't like it, Maggie. You're too gentle to understand why I'm doing it."

"I've got guts, remember? *Tell me.*"

He shrugged in resignation. "All right, I'll spell it out. But don't say I didn't warn you. The Ellington deal is the first falling domino in a long line that's going to end with Moorcroft Industries."

Margaret froze. "What are you talking about?"

"I've lured Moorcroft way out on a limb. He's mortgaged to the hilt. Going after Ellington will weaken him still further. There's no way he'll be able to fend off a takeover when I get ready to do it."

"You're going to put him out of business? Destroy Moorcroft Industries?" Margaret was appalled. "Rafe, you can't do that."

"Watch me."

Horrified, Margaret grabbed his bare shoulder. "It's because of me, isn't it? You're going to ruin Jack Moorcroft because of what happened last year. He was right. The business rivalry between the two of you has escalated into something else, something ugly."

"This is between Moorcroft and me. Don't concern yourself."

"Are you nuts? How can I help but concern myself? I'm the cause of this mess."

"No."

Margaret shook her head. "That's not true. Answer one question for me, Rafe. Would you be plotting now to take over Moorcroft Industries if that fiasco last year hadn't occurred?"

He eyed her consideringly. "No."

"So you're doing this on account of me."

"Maggie, love, don't get upset. I told you you wouldn't understand."

"I do understand. I understand only too well. You're bent on revenge. You have been all along."

"He's got to pay, Maggie. One way or another."

She could have cut herself on the sharp edges of his voice. "You can't blame him because I felt loyal to him. Rafe, that's not fair. I'm the one you should punish."

"It wasn't your fault you felt loyal to him," Rafe said impatiently. "I told you that. If it makes you feel any better, I don't blame Moorcroft, either. At least not for your sense of loyalty."

"Then why are you plotting to destroy him?" Margaret asked wildly.

"Because of the things he said and implied about you after you left his office that morning."

Margaret was truly shaken now. "Oh, my God. You mean that stuff about me having been his mistress? But, Rafe, he was lying."

"I know. I'm going to see he pays for the insults and the lies he told about you."

"You're doing all this to avenge my honor or something?" she gasped as it finally sank in.

"If you want to put it that way, yes. He shouldn't have said what he did about you, Maggie."

Dazed, Margaret got out of bed and picked up the nearest garment to cover herself. It was Rafe's shirt. She thrust her arms into the long sleeves, sat down on the edge of the bed and clasped her hands. The enormity of what he was planning in the name of vengeance nearly swamped her.

"Rafe, you can't do it," she finally whispered.

"Sure I can. Code of the West and all that, remember?"

"This is not funny. Don't try to make a joke out of it. Rafe, I can't have this on my conscience." She shook her head. "An entire company in ruins because of a few nasty remarks made by some male flaunting his latest victory. I can't bear to be the cause of so much destruction. I fully agree Moorcroft shouldn't have said those things to you."

"Damn right."

"Look, he was deliberately taunting you because he knew he'd won on the Spencer deal. You know how men are, always pushing, jostling, shouldering each other around. They see everything in terms of victory and defeat and when they see themselves as winners, they like to rub it in."

"Thank you for giving me the benefit of your deep, psychological insights into the male sex, ma'am. I think I like the Code of the West approach better, though. It's simpler."

"That's because you like to think in terms of black and white. Rafe, my father himself said that whole mess last year was one big area of gray and he's a great one for preferring things in black and white. If he can let it go, you can, too. We have each other now. That's all that really counts."

"Moorcroft has to pay, Maggie, and that's all there is to it. Stay out of it."

"I can't stay out of it. I caused it. You've said so yourself, often enough. Think about what you're doing. Granted Moorcroft was out of line in the things he said, but he doesn't deserve to be destroyed because of it. He's put his whole life into Moorcroft Industries, just as you've put yours into Cassidy and Company. Furthermore, there will be dozens of jobs on the line. You know that. These things always cost a lot of jobs. Innocent people will get hurt."

"For God's sake, don't try to make me feel sorry for the man or his company."

"Then try feeling sorry for me," she snapped. "I'm

going to have to bear this burden on my conscience for the rest of my life."

"Hell. I was afraid you'd feel that way. I told you, you're too soft when it comes to things like this, Maggie. This is the way the business world functions and that's all there is to it."

"You mean this is the way men function."

"Amounts to the same thing. We still run the business world."

Margaret leaped to her feet in frustration. "I can't stand it. I have never met such a stubborn, thickheaded, unreasonable creature in my whole life. Rafe, you are being impossible. Utterly impossible."

"What the hell do you expect me to do? Act like that dim-witted Roarke Cody in *Ruthless* and let a multi-million-dollar deal go down the toilet just to please a woman?"

Margaret faced him from the foot of the bed, her hands on her hips. "Yes, damn it, that's exactly what I expect."

Rafe watched her with hooded eyes. "And if I don't agree to do what you want?"

"I will be furious."

"I don't care if you get mad. The question is, are you going to walk out on me?"

"No, I am not going to walk out on you, but I am going to be very, very angry and I will not hesitate to let you know it," she shouted.

"Prove it."

"Prove what? That I'm mad? What do you want me to do? Take a swing at you? Break a lamp over your head? Believe me, I'm tempted."

"No. Prove you won't walk out on me."

"The only way to prove it is to let you go through

with this crazy revenge plan. And I won't agree to do that. I'm going to fight you every inch of the way, Rafe, I promise you."

Rafe laced his fingers behind his head and leaned back against the pillows. "You still don't understand. I want you to marry me. Now. Tonight. We can take a plane to Vegas."

Margaret took a step backward, shocked. "Marry you? Tonight? Why? What will that prove? You already know I love you. What's the rush?"

Rafe's smile was dangerous. "Maybe I still feel a little uncertain of you. Maybe I want to know you won't threaten to postpone the marriage as a means of manipulating me into doing what you want. Maybe I want to know that this time you love me enough to marry me even though you're madder than hell at me."

Margaret exploded. "You sneaky son of a... You weren't satisfied with the way I bloodied my knees in that little scene down the hall a while ago, were you? You want me to trample my pride right into the dust, don't you?"

Rafe shook his head. "No. I just want to know that you'll marry me even knowing you can't change me and that you aren't always going to like the way I operate."

Margaret threw up her hands in a gesture of exasperated surrender. "All right, I'll marry you."

"Now? Tonight?"

"If that's what you want. But I promise you I am going to argue this thing about crushing Moorcroft with you all the way to Vegas and back."

Rafe grinned. "It's a deal. Get dressed while I phone the airlines and see how soon we can get out of here."

CHAPTER ELEVEN

TWO DAYS AFTER HIS MARRIAGE, Rafe strode past two startled secretaries and straight into Moorcroft's office. Moorcroft looked up at the intrusion, his expression at first annoyed and then immediately cautious.

"Well, hello, Cassidy. What brings you to San Diego?"

Rafe tossed the Ellington file onto the desk in front of the other man. Then he removed his pearl-gray Stetson and hung it on the end of the sleek Italian-style desk lamp.

"Unfinished business," Rafe explained, dropping into a black leather chair.

Moorcroft hesitated and then opened the file. He scanned the contents, absorbing the implications quickly. When he looked up again, his mouth was tight. "So you knew about my pipeline into your office all along? Knew Hatcher was keeping me informed?"

"I figured something was going on. He used to be a good man. One of the best. But he's changed recently."

"Probably because you've changed." Moorcroft leaned back in his chair. "And he didn't like the change."

"Is that right?" Rafe casually put his silver-and-turquoise-trimmed boots on Moorcroft's richly polished desk. "What didn't he like?"

Moorcroft sighed mockingly. "Don't you understand? You were his idol, Cassidy. The fastest gun in the West. Hatcher thought he was working for the best and he liked being on the winning side. But during the past year he decided you'd lost your edge."

"No kidding."

"Afraid so. In his opinion you'd become obsessed with a certain woman and that obsession had weakened you. A young man on the way up does not like discovering his idol has an Achilles' heel. You were no longer the hotshot gunslinger he'd gone to work for three years ago. No longer the toughest, meanest, fastest desperado on the coast."

Rafe nodded. "I think I get the picture."

"Apparently for the past six months all you've done is plot revenge against me and worked on ways of getting Miss Lark back into your bed. Revenge he could understand, but not your single-minded desire to bed one specific lady."

"Looks like I failed as a role model."

"Something like that. It bothered him, Cassidy. When I contacted him on the off chance I could buy him, I discovered he was ripe for the picking."

"And you offered him a way to prove his newfound loyalty to you."

"What did you expect me to do?"

"Exactly what you did do, I suppose."

Moorcroft shrugged. "You'd have done the same. We live and die on the basis of inside information in this business, Cassidy. You know that. We take it where we can get it."

"True. Going to give him a job when he comes looking for one?"

"Hell, no. The guy's proven he's the type who will sell out his own boss. What do I want with him?"

"Figured you say that."

Moorcroft glanced at the Ellington file. "But in this case it looks like Hatcher may have been a little premature in writing you off. He's been feeding me false information almost from the start, hasn't he?"

"Yeah."

"And especially for the past week or so. It's too late for me to counter now, isn't it? Congratulations, Cassidy. Looks like you win this one." Moorcroft reached behind his chair and opened a small, discreet liquor cabinet. "You drink Scotch, according to Hatcher. Can I offer you a glass?"

"Sure."

Moorcroft poured Scotch into two glasses and pushed one across the desk to Rafe. Then he raised his own glass in a small salute. "Here's to the thrill of victory. I guess this makes us even, doesn't it? I got Spencer last year. You get Ellington this year."

"It's not quite that simple, Moorcroft. Check the printout at the end of that file."

Moorcroft hesitated and then reopened the Ellington file. He flipped to the last page and scanned the detailed financial forecast and spreadsheet he found there. Then he looked up again. "So?"

"So Ellington was merely the first."

"I can see that. Brisken was next?"

"And then Carlisle."

Moorcroft's eyes narrowed. "Carlisle? What do you want with it?"

"Guess."

Moorcroft slowly closed the file again. "Carlisle has a major stake in Moorcroft Industries at the moment. You take control of them and you have a chunk of me."

"You've got it."

Moorcroft swallowed the remainder of his Scotch in one long gulp. His fingers were very tight around the glass as he carefully set it down in front of him. "I was right, wasn't I?" he asked softly. "You are gunning for me."

"That was the plan," Rafe agreed. He studied the San Diego skyline outside the window. "Ellington, Brisken, Carlisle, and then Moorcroft. Dominoes all lined up in a neat little row."

"Why are you telling me this in advance? You're giving me time to maneuver. Why do that?"

"Because I'm canceling my plans. I've changed my mind. I'm not going to topple my little row of dominoes after all. I just wanted you to know what almost happened." Rafe's mouth curved faintly. "It's about the only satisfaction I'm going to get."

"To what do I owe this unexpected generosity of spirit?" Moorcroft looked more wary than ever.

"My wife. She didn't like being the reason for the collapse of an empire the size of yours. She's a soft little creature in some ways." Rafe grinned and took a sip of Scotch. "Plenty of spirit, though. Feisty as hell. You haven't been through anything until you've been through a wedding night with a bride who wants to lecture you on business ethics."

"We're talking about Margaret Lark, I take it? You've married her?" Moorcroft looked a little bewildered.

"Day before yesterday."

"Congratulations," Moorcroft said dryly. "You're a lucky man. I guess I am, too, if the reason you're calling off the revenge bit is on account of her. Looks like she saved my tail. So she was worried enough about me to make you change your whole battle plan. Interesting."

"Don't get too excited," Rafe advised. "It wasn't you she was concerned about. It was all the other innocent people who would go down with you. There's always a lot of bloodletting in the case of an unfriendly takeover. You know that."

"She wouldn't want that on her conscience."

"No."

"She's a real lady, isn't she?"

"Yeah. She's a lady all right. You forgot that last year."

Moorcroft nodded. "I shouldn't have said some of the things I did last year."

"No," Rafe agreed, his eyes still on the view.

"You know why I said them?"

"Sure. You wanted her and you knew you'd never have her," Rafe said succinctly.

"Never in a million years. She never gave me any sign of being interested in all the time she worked for me. Totally ignored every approach I tried to make. Then you appeared on the scene and she fell right into your hands."

"Yeah, well, if it makes you feel any better, I had something going for me you didn't have."

"What's that?" Moorcroft glanced in disgust at Rafe's hand-tooled boots.

"I was the man of her dreams. Straight out of one of her books."

"Women."

"Yeah." Rafe put his glass down on the desk and smiled fleetingly. "Maggie says they're going to take over the business world one of these days and show us how to run things right."

"I can't wait." Moorcroft looked at the Ellington file and then at Rafe. He frowned. "Is this business between us really over, Cassidy?"

"Almost." Rafe slid his boots off the desk, got up and peeled off his jacket. Then he started to roll up his sleeves.

"What the hell do you think you're doing?" Moorcroft got slowly to his feet.

"Finishing it." Rafe smiled. "You get to keep your company but I can't let you get off scot-free after insulting my wife's honor. One way or another you've got to pay for that, Moorcroft. You know how it is. Code of the West and all that."

"I suppose it won't do me any good to remind you she wasn't your wife at the time?"

"Nope. Doesn't matter. She still belonged to me. She has since the day I met her, whether she knew it or not. You want to take off your jacket so it doesn't get messed up? Looks like nice material."

Moorcroft eyed him for a long moment. Then he sighed again, shrugged off his jacket and unfastened the gold links on his cuffs.

Rafe went over to the door and locked it.

When he walked out of the office ten minutes later he paused briefly to tug his Stetson low over his eyes. He smiled brilliantly at the two secretaries. "Your boss won't be taking any more appointments today, ladies."

"YOU'RE MARRIED? WHAT the hell do you mean, you're married?" Connor Lark roared at his daughter as he climbed out of the car and went around to the passenger side to open the door for Bev. "We go away for a few days to give you and Cassidy a chance to work out your differences and you up and get hitched. Couldn't you at least have waited until we got back?"

"Sorry, Dad, Rafe was in a hurry. Hello, Bev. How was Sedona?"

"Just lovely." Bev gave her a quick hug and then stood back to look at her new daughter-in-law. "Did that son of mine really marry you while we were gone?"

"It was real cheap and tacky, Bev. A Vegas wedding, no less. But it was for real." Margaret smiled warmly at the older woman but a part of her was waiting to make certain Bev approved. *You'd make him a better mistress than a wife.*

"My dear, I couldn't be more delighted," Bev said gently. "You'll make him a wonderful wife. And Rafe knew it all along. We'll have to give him credit for that, won't we? Don't worry about the cheap and tacky wedding. We'll make up for it with a lovely reception. I can't wait to start planning it."

"Well, there's no rush," Margaret assured her dryly. "The groom isn't even in town."

Connor plucked a suitcase out of the trunk. "Where the devil is he?"

"Took off this morning with hardly a goodbye kiss. Just announced at breakfast he was catching a plane to California. I haven't seen him since. Can you imagine? And after all those promises he made about not letting his business dominate his life anymore, he no sooner gets my name on a marriage certificate than he takes off. I guess the honeymoon is over."

Bev frowned. "Is that true, dear? He's gone off on business? I can't believe h 'd do such a thing."

"I can." Margaret grinned. "But in this case I'm going to let him get away with it. I think I know where he went."

"Yeah?" Connor turned his head at the sound of a familiar car coming up the long, sweeping drive. "Where was that?"

Margaret watched the Mercedes come toward them, a sense of deep satisfaction welling up within her. "He had to take care of some unfinished business in San Diego."

The Mercedes came to a halt and Rafe got out. Margaret raced toward him and threw herself into his arms. "It's about time you got here," she whispered against his chest as she hugged him fiercely.

Rafe sucked in his breath and winced slightly. "Easy, honey."

Margaret looked up in alarm. "Rafe, are you all right?"

"Never better." He was grinning again as he bent his head to kiss her soundly.

"I was afraid you wouldn't get home this evening."

"Hey, I'm a married man now. I've got responsibilities here at home." He looked at Connor and Bev and nodded a friendly greeting. "Looks like we're going to be one big happy family again tonight. Damn. I was hoping for a little privacy. This is supposed to be a honeymoon, you know."

"Don't worry, Cassidy, your Mom and I won't be staying long," Connor assured him. "We're on our way to California. Just wanted to check up on you two and make sure you hadn't throttled each other while we were out of town."

"As you can see, Maggie and I have worked out our little differences. Hang on a second."

Rafe released Margaret to open the rear door of the Mercedes. He reached inside to remove a large, flat parcel.

"What's that?" Margaret asked curiously.

"A wedding present."

Margaret quickly dragged the package into the house and ripped off the protective wrapping while everyone stood around and watched. She laughed up at Rafe with sheer delight as she stood back to admire Sean Winters's *Canyon*.

"It's beautiful, Rafe. Thank you."

"I still think it looks like a bunch of squiggly lines but I'll try to think of it as an investment in my future brother-in-law's career."

MUCH LATER THAT NIGHT Margaret snuggled up beside her husband, drew an interesting circle on his bare chest and smiled in the shadows. "You went to see Jack Moorcroft today, didn't you?"

Rafe caught her teasing fingers and kissed them. "Uh-huh."

"You told him he was off the hook? That you aren't going to ruin him?"

"That's what I told him, all right."

Margaret levered herself up on her elbow to look down at him. "Rafe, I'm so proud of you for being able to handle that situation in a mature, reasonable, civilized fashion."

"That's me," he agreed, his lips on the inside of her wrist, "a mature, reasonable, civilized man."

Margaret studied his bent head and experienced a sudden jolt of unworthy suspicion. "You did behave in a mature, reasonable, civilized way when you went to see him, didn't you, Rafe?"

"Sure." He was kissing her shoulder now, pushing her gently back down onto the pillows.

"No Code of the West stuff or anything?" she persisted as she felt herself slipping under his sensual spell. "Rafe, you didn't do anything rash while you were visiting Moorcroft, did you?"

He kissed her throat and then raised his head to look down at her with gleaming eyes. "Maggie, love, I'm a businessman, not a gunfighter or an outlaw. Your romantic imagination sometimes gets a little carried away."

"I'm not so sure about that. Where you're concerned, my romantic imagination tends to be right on target." She reached up to put her arms around his neck and draw him down to her. "Remind me in the morning to send a telegram to some friends."

"Sure. Anything you say, Maggie, love. In the meantime what do you say we go for another midnight ride?"

"That sounds wonderful," she whispered, looking up at him with all her love in her eyes.

KATHERINE INSKIP HAWTHORNE got her telegram while she was eating papaya at breakfast with her husband on Amethyst Island. Sarah Fleetwood Trace found hers waiting for her when she got back from a treasure-hunting honeymoon.

> Married a cowboy. Definitely an old-fashioned kind of guy. Code of the West, etc. A little rough around the edges but fantastic in the saddle. Can't wait for you to meet him. Suggest we all vacation on Amethyst Island this year.
>
> Love,
> Maggie

Sarah reached for the telephone at once and dialed Amethyst Island. "*Maggie?* She's let him talk her into letting herself be called Maggie?"

Katherine laughed on the other end of the line. "Obviously the woman is in love. How about that vacation here on the island?"

"Sounds like a truly brilliant idea to me," Sarah said, glancing at Gideon. "We'll all go treasure-hunting."

"It seems," said Katherine, "that we've already found our treasures."

"I think you're right."

* * * * *

THE COUGAR

Dear Reader,

I'm thrilled to have *The Cougar* reissued in *Tough Enough*. How exciting!

I love writing books about ranching, cowboys and the West. I was born in San Diego, but my parents were tumbleweeds by nature and we moved a lot—twenty-two times in the first eighteen years of my life—always settling somewhere rural. I lived in Arizona, New Mexico, Montana, Idaho and Oregon. Even as a child, as I lived in these different states, I saw different mind-sets, priorities, emphases upon particular ideals. For instance, I've always found there's a huge difference between Easterners and Westerners, and I sometimes showcase that fascinating "divide" in my work, such as in *The Last Cowboy* (available now) and *The Wrangler* (coming soon).

My knowledge of the West, which is woven into my books, comes from these many years of travel. In *The Cougar* I also tried to incorporate some of my experiences as a volunteer firefighter and EMT in Arizona. I don't believe a writer can ever write outside herself; she must come from a point within her own experiences. Please enjoy *The Cougar* and visit me at www.lindsaymckenna.com.

Sincerely,

Lindsay McKenna

To my readers

CHAPTER ONE

"THIS WASN'T a very good idea, Rachel Donovan." The words rang out briefly in the interior of the brand-new car that Rachel was driving. Huge, fat snowflakes were falling faster and faster. It was early December. Why shouldn't it be snowing in Oak Creek Canyon, which lay just south of Flagstaff near Sedona? Her fingers tightened around the steering wheel. Tiredness pulled at her. A nine-hour flight from London, and then another six hours to get to Denver, Colorado, was taking its toll on her. As a homeopathic practitioner, she was no stranger to the effects of sleep deprivation.

Rubbing her watering eyes, she decided that the Rachel of her youth, some thirty years ago, was at play this morning. Normally, she wasn't this spontaneous, but in her haste to see her sisters as soon as possible, she'd changed her travel plans. Instead of flying into Phoenix, renting a car and driving up to Sedona, she'd flown into Denver and taken a commuter flight to Flagstaff, which was only an hour away from her home, the Donovan Ranch.

Home... The word made her heart expand with warm feelings. Yes, she was coming home—for good. Her older sister, Kate, had asked Rachel and their younger sister, Jessica, to come home and help save the ranch, which was teetering on the edge of bankruptcy. A fierce kind of sweetness welled up through Rachel. She couldn't wait to be living on the ranch with her sisters once again.

Glancing at her watch, she saw it was 7:00 a.m. She knew at this time of year the highways were often icy in the world-famous canyon. There was a foot of snow on the ground already—and it was coming down at an even faster rate as she drove carefully down the twisting, two-lane asphalt highway. On one side the canyon walls towered thousands of feet above her. On the other lay a five-hundred-foot-plus drop-off into Oak Creek, which flowed at the bottom of the canyon.

How many times had she driven 89A from Sedona to Flag? Rachel had lost count. Her eyes watered again from fatigue and she took a swipe at them with the back of her hand. Kate and Jessica were expecting her home at noon. If she got down the canyon in one piece, she would be home at 9:00 a.m. and would surprise them. A smile tugged at the corners of her full mouth. Oh, how she longed to see her sisters! She'd missed them so very much after leaving to work in England as a homeopath.

The best news was that Kate was going to marry her high school sweetheart, Sam McGuire. And Jessica had found the love of her life, Dan Black, a horse wrangler who worked at the ranch. Both were going to be married seven days from now, and Rachel was going to be their maid of honor. Yes, things were finally looking up for those two. The good Lord knew, Kate and Jessica deserved to be happy. Their childhood with their alcoholic father, Kelly Donovan, had been a disaster. As each daughter turned eighteen, she had fled from the ranch. Kate had become a rebel, working for environmental causes. Jessica had moved to Canada to pursue her love of flower essences. And Rachel—well, she'd fled the farthest away—to England.

Rachel felt the car slide. Instantly, she lifted her foot off the accelerator. She was only going thirty miles an hour, but black ice was a well-known problem here in this part of Arizona. It killed a lot of people and she didn't want to be the next victim. As she drove down the narrow, steep, road, dark green Douglas firs surrounded her. Ordinarily, Rachel would be enthralled with the beauty and majesty of the landscape—this remarkable canyon reminded her of a miniature Grand Canyon in many respects. But she scarcely noticed now. In half an hour, she would be home.

Her hands tightened on the wheel as she spotted a yellow, diamond-shaped sign that read 15 mph. A sharp hairpin curve was coming up. She knew this curve well. She glanced once again at the jagged, unforgiving face of a yellow-and-white limestone cliff soaring thousands of feet above her and disappearing into the heavily falling snow. Gently she tested her brakes on the invisible, dangerous black ice. The only thing between her and the cliff that plunged into the canyon was a guardrail.

Suddenly, Rachel gasped. Was she seeing things? Without thinking, she slammed on the brakes. Directly in front of her, looming out of nowhere, was a huge black-and-gold cat. Her eyes widened enormously and a cry tore from her lips as the car swung drunkenly. The tires screeched as she tried to correct the skid. Impossible! Everything started to whirl around her. Out of the corner of her eye, she saw the black-and-gold cat, as large as a cougar, jump out of the way. Slamming violently against the cliff face, Rachel screamed. The steering wheel slipped out of her hands. A split second later, she watched in horror as the guardrail roared up at her.

The next moment there was a grinding impact. Throwing up her hands to protect her face, she felt the car become airborne. Everything seemed to suddenly move into slow motion. The car was twisting around in midair. She heard the glass crack as her head smashed against the side window. The snow, the dark shapes of the fir trees, all rushed at her. The nose of the car spiraled down—down into the jagged limestone wall well below the guardrail. Oh, no! She was going to die!

A thousand thoughts jammed through her mind in those milliseconds. What had been up on that highway? It wasn't a cougar. What *was* it? Had she hallucinated? Rachel knew better than to slam on brakes on black ice! How stupid could she be! But if she hadn't hit the brakes, she'd have struck that jaguar. Had there been a jaguar at all? Was it possible? She had to be seeing things! Now she was going to die!

Everything went black in front of Rachel. The last thing she recalled was the motion of her car as it arched down like a shot fired from a cannon, before hitting the side of the cliff. The last sound she heard was her own scream of absolute terror ringing through the air.

WARM LIQUID WAS FLOWING across Rachel's parted lips. She heard voices that seemed very far away. As she slowly became conscious, the voices grew stronger—and closer. Forcing open her eyes, she at first saw only white. Groggily, she looked closer and realized it was snow on part of the windshield. The other half of the windshield was torn away, the white flakes lazily drifting into the passenger's side of the car.

The accident came back to her as the pain in her

head and left foot throbbed in unison. Suddenly she realized she was sitting at an angle, the car twisted around the trunk of a huge Douglas fir.

Again she heard a voice. A man's voice. It was closer this time. Blinking slowly, Rachel lifted her right arm. At least *it* worked. The seat belt bit deeply into her shoulder and neck. The air bag, deflated now, had stopped her from being thrown through the windshield. A branch must have gouged out the right half of the windshield. If anyone had been sitting there, they'd be dead.

It was cold with the wind and snow blowing into the car. Shivering, Rachel closed her eyes. The image of the jaguar standing in the middle of that icy, snow-covered highway came back to her. How stupid could she have been? She knew not to slam on brakes like that. Where had the jaguar come from? Jaguars didn't exist in Arizona! Her head pounded as she tried to make sense of everything. She was in trouble. Serious trouble.

Again, a man's voice, deep and commanding, drifted into her semiconscious state. Help. She needed medical help. If only she could get to her homeopathic kit in the backseat. Arnica was what she needed for tissue trauma. Her head throbbed. She was sure she'd have a goose egg. Arnica would reduce the swelling and the pain.

The snowflakes were falling more thickly and at a faster rate now. How long had she been unconscious? Looking at her watch, Rachel groaned. It was 8:00 a.m. She'd been down here an hour? She had to get out! Rachel tried to move, but her seat belt was tightly constricting. She hung at a slight angle toward the passenger side of the car. Struggling weakly, she tried to find the seat belt latch, but her fingers were cold and numb.

"Hey! Are you all right?"

Rachel slowly lifted her head. Her vision was blurred for a moment, and when it cleared she noticed her side window was gone, smashed out, she guessed, in the crash. A man—a very tall, lean man with dark, short hair and intense blue eyes, wearing a navy blue jacket and pants—anchored himself against the car. He was looking at her, assessing her sharply. Rachel saw the patch on his jacket: EMT. And then she saw another patch: Sedona Fire Department.

"No…no…I'm not all right," she whispered, giving up on trying to find the seat belt latch.

"Okay…just hold on. Help's here. My name is Jim. We're from the Sedona Fire Department. We got a 911 call that an auto had flipped off the highway. Hold on while I get my buddies down here."

Rachel sank back, feeling relief. This man… Jim… radiated confidence. Somehow she knew she'd be okay with him. She watched through half-closed eyes as he lifted the radio to his strong-looking mouth and talked to someone far above them. The snow was thickening. The gray morning light accentuated his oval face, his strong nose and that mouth. He looked Indian. Rachel briefly wondered what kind. With his high cheekbones and dark hair, he could be Navajo, Hopi or from one of many other tribal nations.

Something about him made her feel safe. That was good. Rachel knew that he could get her out of this mess. She watched as he snapped the radio onto his belt and returned his full attention to her, trying to hide his worry.

"Helluva way to see Arizona," he joked. "The car is wrapped around this big Douglas fir here, so it and you aren't going anywhere. My buddies are bringing down a stretcher and some auto-extrication equipment. My job is to take care of you." He smiled a little as he reached in the window. "What's your name?"

"Rachel…" she whispered.

"Rachel, I'm going to do a quick exam of you. Do you hurt anywhere?"

She closed her eyes as he touched her shoulder. "Yes…my head and my foot. I—I think I've got a bump on my head."

His touch was immediately soothing to her, though he wore latex gloves. But then, so did she when she had to examine a patient. With AIDS, HIV and hepatitis B all being transmissible via blood and fluids, medical people had to protect themselves accordingly. As he moved his hands gently across her head, she could feel him searching for injury. Something in her relaxed completely beneath his ministrations. She felt his warm, moist breath, his face inches from hers as he carefully examined her scalp.

"Beautiful hair," he murmured, "but you're right— you've got a nice goose egg on the left side of your head."

One corner of her mouth turned up as she lay against the car seat. "If that's all, I'm lucky. I hate going to hospitals."

Chuckling, Jim eased a white gauze dressing against her hair and then quickly placed a bandage around her head. "Yeah, well, you'll be going to Cottonwood Hospital anyway. If nothing more than to make sure you're okay."

Groaning, Rachel barely opened her eyes. She saw that he'd unzipped his jacket and it hung open, revealing a gold bar over the left top pocket of his dark blue shirt that read J. Cunningham. *Cunningham.* Frowning, she looked up at him as he moved his hands in a gentle motion down her neck, searching for more trauma.

"Cunningham's your last name?" she asked, her voice sounding faint even to her.

"Yeah, Jim Cunningham." He glanced down at her. She was pasty, her forest-green eyes dull looking. Jim knew she was in shock. He quickly pressed his fingertips against her collarbone, noticing her pale pink angora sweater and dark gray wool slacks. Under any other circumstance, she would turn a man's head. "Why?" he teased. "Has my reputation preceded me?" He quickly felt her arms for broken bones or signs of bleeding. There were some minor cuts due to flying glass from the windshield, but otherwise, so far, so good. He tried not to show his worry.

"Of the Bar C?" she asked softly, shutting her eyes as he leaned over her and pressed firmly on her rib cage to see if she had any broken ribs. How close he was! Yet his presence was utterly comforting to Rachel.

"Yes…how did you know?" Jim eased his hands down over her hips, applying gentle pressure. If she had any hip or pelvic injuries, they would show up now. He watched her expression closely. Her eyes were closed, her thick, dark lashes standing out against her pale skin. She'd had a nosebleed, but it had ceased. Her lips parted, but she didn't answer his question. Looking down and pushing aside the deflated air bag, he saw that her left foot was caught in the wreckage. *Damn.* That wasn't a good sign. His mind whirled with possibilities. He needed to get a cuff around her upper arm and check her blood pressure. What if her foot was mangled? What if an artery was severed? She could be losing a lot of blood. She could die on them.

He had to keep her talking. Easing out of the car window, he reached into his bright orange EMT bag. Looking up, he saw his partner, Larry, coming down, along with four other firefighters bringing the stretcher and ropes as well as auto-extrication equipment.

"Well," Jim prodded, as he pushed up her sleeve and slipped the blood-pressure cuff around her upper left arm, "am I a wanted desperado?"

Rachel needed his stabilizing touch and absorbed it hungrily. Consciousness kept escaping her. For some reason she would slip away, only to be brought back by his deep, teasing voice. "Uh, no...."

"You sound like you know me. Do you?" He quickly put the stethoscope to her arm and pumped up the cuff. His gaze was focused on the needle, watching it closely as he bled off the air.

Rachel rallied. Opened her eyes slightly, she saw the worry in Jim's face. The intensity in his expression shook her. "You don't remember me, do you?" she said, trying to tease back. Her voice sounded very far away. What was going on? Why wasn't she able to remain coherent?

Damn! Jim kept his expression neutral. Her blood pressure wasn't good. Either she had a serious head injury or she was bleeding somewhere. He left the cuff on her arm and removed the stethoscope from his ears. She lay against the seat, her eyes closed, her body limp. Her breathing was slowly becoming weaker and weaker. His medical training told him she was losing a lot of blood. Where? It *had* to be that foot that was jammed in the wreckage.

He *had* to keep her talking. "I'm sorry," he apologized, "I don't remember you. I wish I did, though." And that was the truth. She was a beautiful woman. *Stunning* was a word Jim would use with her. Her dark brown hair was thick and long, like a dark cape across her proud shoulders.

"Listen, I'm going to try and get this door open." Jim made a signal to Larry to hurry even faster down the slippery incline. Studying the jagged cliff, Jim realized that if the car hadn't wrapped itself around this fir tree, it would have plunged another three hundred feet. More than likely, Rachel would be dead.

Larry hurried forward. He was a big man, over six feet tall, and built like a proverbial bull.

"Yeah, Cougar, what are the stats?" He dropped his bag and moved gingerly up to Jim.

Scowling, Jim lowered his voice so no one but his partner would hear. "She's dumping on us. I think she's hemorrhaging from her left foot, which is trapped beneath the dash of the car. Help me get this door open. I need to get a cuff on her upper leg. It'll have to act like a tourniquet. Then those extrication guys can get in here and cut that metal away so we can get her foot free to examine it."

"Right, pard."

Rachel heard another male voice, but it was Jim's voice she clung to. Her vision was growing dim. What was wrong with her? She heard the door protest and creak loudly as it was pulled opened in a series of hard, jerking motions. In moments, she heard Jim's voice very close to her ear. Forcing open her eyes, she saw that he was kneeling on the side of the car where the door was now open. She felt his hand moving down her left leg, below her knee.

"Can you feel that?" he demanded.

"Feel what?" Rachel asked.

"Or this?"

"No…nothing. I feel nothing, Jim."

Jim threw Larry a sharp look. "Hand me your blood-pressure cuff. We're going to apply a tourniquet." In the gray light of the canyon, with snowflakes twirling lazily around them, Jim saw that her left foot and ankle had been twisted and trapped in the metal upon impact. With Larry's help, he affixed the cuff around her slim calf and then inflated it enough to halt the blood flow in that extremity.

Four other firefighters arrived on scene. Larry put a warm, protective blanket across Rachel. He then got into the backseat and held her head straight while Jim carefully placed a stabilizing cervical collar around her neck, in case she had an undetected spinal injury. He was worried. She kept slipping in and out of consciousness.

As he settled into the passenger seat beside her, and the firefighters worked to remove the metal that trapped her leg, Jim tried to draw her out of her semiconscious state.

"Rachel," he called, "it's Jim. Can you hear me?"

She barely moved her lips. "Yes…"

He told her what the firefighters were going to do, and that there would be a lot of noise and not to get upset by it. All the while, he kept his hand on hers. She responded valiantly to his touch, to his voice, but Jim saw Larry shake his head doubtfully as he continued to gently hold her head and neck.

"You said you heard of me," Jim teased. He watched her lashes move upward to reveal her incredible eyes. Her pupils were wide and dilated, black with a crescent of green around them. "Well? Am I on a wanted poster somewhere?" he asked with a smile.

Jim's smile went straight to Rachel's heart. It was boyish, teasing, and yet he was so male that it made her heart beat a little harder in her chest. She tried to smile back and realized it was a poor attempt. "No... not a wanted poster. I remember you from high school. I'm Rachel Donovan. You know the Donovan Ranch?"

Stunned, Jim stared. "Rachel Donovan?" His head whirled with shock. That was right! He recalled Jessica Donovan telling him over a month ago that Rachel, the middle daughter, was moving home from England to live at the ranch.

"That's me," Rachel joked softly. She forced her eyes open a little more and held his gaze. "You used to pull my braids in junior high, but I don't think you remember that, do you?"

Jim forced a grin he didn't feel at all. "I do now." And he did. Little Rachel Donovan had been such a thin stick of a girl in junior high. She had worn her long, dark brown flowing mane of hair in braids back then, like her mother, Odula, an Eastern Cherokee medicine woman. Rachel was the spitting image of her. Jim recalled the crush he'd had on little Rachel Donovan. She'd always run from him. The only way he'd get her attention was to sneak up, tweak one of her braids and then run away himself. It was his way of saying he liked her, for at that age, Jim had been too shy to tell her. Besides, there were other problems that prevented him from openly showing his affection for her.

"You were always teasing me, Jim Cunningham," Rachel said weakly. Her mouth was dry and she was thirsty. The noise of machinery filled the car. If it hadn't been for Jim's steadying hand on her shoulder, the sound would have scared her witless.

"Hey, Cougar, we're gonna have to take the rest of this windshield out. Gotta pull the steering wheel up and away from her."

Jim nodded to Captain Cord Ramsey of the extrication team. "Okay." He rose up on his knees and took a second blanket into his hands.

"Rachel," he said as he leaned directly over her, "I'm going to place a blanket over us. The firefighters have to pull the rest of the window out. There's going to be glass everywhere, but the blanket will protect you."

Everything went dark before Rachel's eyes. Jim Cunningham had literally placed his body like a wall between her and the firefighters who were working feverishly to free her. She felt the heat of his body as he pulled the blanket over their heads. How close he was! She was overwhelmed by the care he showed toward her. It was wonderful.

When he spoke, his voice was barely an inch from her ear.

"Okay, they're going to pull that windshield any moment now. You'll hear some noise and feel the car move a bit. It's nothing to be concerned about."

"You're wonderful at what you do," Rachel whispered weakly. "You really make a person feel safe... that everything's going to be okay even if it isn't...."

Worried, Jim said, "Rachel, do you know what blood type you are?"

"AB positive."

His heart sank. He struggled to keep the disappointment out of his voice. "That's a rare blood type."

She smiled a little. "Like me, I guess."

He chuckled. "I have AB positive blood, too. How about that? Two rare birds, eh?"

Rachel heard the windshield crack. There was one brief, sharp movement. As Jim eased back and removed the blanket, she looked up at him. His face was hard and expressionless until he looked down to make sure she was all right. Then his features became very readable. She saw concern banked in his eyes.

"Listen, Jim, in the backseat there's a kit. A homeopathic kit. It's important you get to it. There's a remedy in there. It's called Arnica Montana. I know I'm bleeding. It will help stop it. Can you get it for me? Pour some pellets into my mouth?"

He frowned and looked in the backseat. There was a black physician's bag there on the seat next to Larry. "You a doctor?"

"No, a homeopath."

"I've vaguely heard about it. An alternative medicine, right?" He reached over the backseat and brought the leather case up front, resting it against his thigh as he opened it. He found a small plastic box inside along with a lot of other medical equipment. "This box?" he asked, holding it up for her to look at.

"Yes…that's the one. I'll need two pills."

Opening it, Jim located the bottle marked Arnica. He unscrewed the cap and put a couple of white pellets into her mouth.

"Thanks…." Rachel said. The sweetness of the small pellets tasted good to her. "It will help stop the shock and the bleeding."

Jim put the bag aside. Worriedly, he took another blood-pressure reading. She was no longer dumping as before. He suspected the tourniquet on her lower

leg had halted most of the b[...]
good news.

"Did I hear someone call you Cou[...]

Distracted because the extrication te[...] prying the metal away from her foot, [...] "Yeah, that's my nickname."

"H-how did you get it?" Rachel felt the powe[...] the homeopathic remedy begin to work on her immediately. "Listen, this remedy I took will probably make me look like I'm unconscious, but I'm not. It's just working to stabilize me, so don't panic, okay?"

Jim nodded and placed himself in front of Rachel to protect her again as the extrication equipment began to remove the metal from around her foot. "Okay, sweetheart, I won't panic." He watched her lashes drift down as he shielded her with his body. Her color was no longer as pasty, and that was promising. Still, her blood pressure was low. Too low.

Looking up at Larry, Jim said, "As soon as we get her out of here, have Ramsey call the hospital and see if they've got AB positive blood standing by. We're going to need it."

"Right."

Rachel savored Jim's nearness. She heard the screech of metal as it was being torn away to release her foot. She hoped her injury wasn't bad. She had a wedding to attend in a week. Her foot couldn't be broken!

"What's the frown for?" Jim asked. Her face was inches from his. He saw the soft upturn of the corners of her mouth. What a lovely mouth Rachel had. The spindly shadow of a girl he'd known was now a mature swan of indescribable beauty.

"Oh...the weddings—Katie and Jessica. I'm supto be their maid of honor. My foot…I'm worried about my foot. What if I broke it?"

"We'll know in just a little while," he soothed. Instinctively, he placed his hand on her left shoulder. The last of the metal was torn away.

"Cougar?"

"Yeah?" Jim twisted his head toward Captain Ramsey.

"She's all yours. Better come and take a look."

Rachel felt Jim leave her side. Larry's hands remained firm against her head and neck, however.

Cunningham climbed carefully around the car. The temperature was dropping, and the wind was picking up. Blizzard conditions were developing fast. Jim noted the captain's wrinkled brow as he made his way to the driver's side. Getting down on his hands and knees, squinting in the poor light, he got his first look at Rachel's foot.

He'd been right about loss of blood. He saw where an artery on the top of her foot had been sliced open. Quickly examining it, he placed a dressing there. Turning, he looked up at the captain.

"Get the hospital on the horn right away. We're definitely going to need a blood transfusion for her. AB positive." Rachel had lost a lot of blood, there was no doubt. If he hadn't put that blood-pressure cuff on her lower leg when he did, she would have bled to death right in front of him. Shaken, Jim eased to his feet.

"Okay, let's get her out of the car and onto a spine board." When he looked up to check on Rachel, he saw that she had lost consciousness again. So many memories flooded back through Jim in those moments. Good ones. Painful ones. Ones of yearning. Of unrequited love that was never fulfilled. Little Rachel Donovan. He'd had a crush on her all through school.

As Jim quickly positioned the spine board beneath Rachel with the help of the firefighters, he suddenly felt hope for the first time in a long time. Maybe, just maybe, life was giving him a second chance with Rachel. And then he laughed at himself. The hundred-year-old feud between the Cunninghams and Donovans was famous in this part of the country. Still he wondered if Rachel had ever had any feelings for him?

Right now, Jim couldn't even think about the past. His concern was for Rachel's loss of blood and her shock. The clock on the car had stopped at 7:00 a.m. That was when the accident had probably occurred. And it had taken them an hour to get here. Whether he wanted to admit it or not, her life hung in a precarious balance right now.

"Hey," Ramsey said, getting off the radio, "bad news, Cougar."

"What?" Jim eased Rachel onto the spine board and made her as comfortable as possible.

"No AB positive blood at Cottonwood."

Damn! "Try Flagstaff."

Ramsey shook his head. "None anywhere."

Placing another blanket across Rachel, Jim glanced up at his partner. "You tell Cottonwood to stand by for a blood transfusion, then," he told the captain. "I've got AB positive blood. She needs at *least* a pint or we aren't going to be able to save her."

"Roger," Ramsey grunted, and got on the radio again to the hospital.

CHAPTER TWO

THE FIRST thing Rachel was aware of was a hand gently caressing her hair. It was a nurturing touch, almost tender as it brushed across her crown. Unfamiliar noises leaked into her groggy consciousness, along with the smell of antiseptic. Where was she? Her head ached. Whoever was caressing her hair soothed the pain with each touch. Voices. There were so many unfamiliar voices all around her. Struggling to open her eyes, she heard a man's voice, very low and nearby.

"It's okay, Rachel. You're safe and you're going to be okay. Don't try so hard. Just lay back and take it easy. You've been through a lot."

Who was that? The voice was oddly familiar, and yet it wasn't. The touch of his hand on her head was magical. Rachel tried to focus on the gentle caress. Each time he followed the curve of her skull, the pain went away, only to return when he lifted his hand. Who was this man who had such a powerful touch? Rachel was no stranger to hands-on healing. Her mother, Odula, used to lay her hands on each of them when they were sick with fever or chills. And amazingly, each time, their aches and pains had disappeared.

The antiseptic smell awakened her even more—the smell of a hospital. She knew the scent well, having tended many patients at the homeopathic hospital in London. Her mind was fuzzy, so she continued to focus on the man's hand and his nearness. She felt his other hand resting on her upper arm, as if to give her an anchor in the whirling world of gold-and-white light beneath her lids.

Gathering all her strength, Rachel forced her lashes to lift. At first all she saw was a dark green curtain in front of her. And then she heard a low chuckle to her right, where the man was standing—the one who caressed her as if she were a very beloved, cherished woman. His warm touch was undeniable. Her heart opened of its own accord and Rachel felt a rush of feelings she thought had died a long time ago. Confused by the sights and sounds, she looked up, up at the man who stood protectively at her side.

Jim's mouth pulled slightly. "Welcome back to the real world, Rachel." He saw her cloudy, forest-green eyes rest on him. There was confusion in their depths. Nudging a few strands of long, dark brown hair away from her cheek, he said in a low, soothing tone, "You're at the Flagstaff Hospital. We brought you here about an hour ago. You had a wreck up on 89A coming out of Flag earlier this morning. Do you remember?"

Rachel was mesmerized by him, by his low tone, which seemed to penetrate every cell of her being like a lover's caress. He had stilled his hand, resting it against her hair. His smile was kind. She liked the tenderness burning in his eyes as he regarded her. Who was he? His face looked familiar, and yet no name would come. Her mouth felt gummy. Her foot ached. She looked to the left, at her surroundings.

"You're in E.R., the emergency room, in a cubical," Jim told her. "The doc just got done looking at you. He just stitched up your foot where you severed a small artery. You took a pint of whole blood, and he said the bump on your head is going to hurt like hell, but it's not a concussion."

Bits and pieces of memory kept striking her. The jaguar. The jaguar standing in the middle of that ice-covered highway. Rachel frowned and closed her eyes.

"The cat...it was in the middle of the road," she began, her voice scratchy. "I slammed on the brakes. I didn't want to hit it.... The last thing I remember is spinning out of control."

Jim tightened his hand slightly on her upper arm. He could see she was struggling to remember. "A cat? You mean a cougar?"

Everything was jumbled up. Rachel closed her eyes. She felt terribly weak—far weaker than she wanted to feel. "My kit...where is it?"

Jim saw a dull flush of color starting to come back to her very pale cheeks. The blood transfusion had halted her shock. He'd made sure she was covered with extra blankets and he'd remained with her in E.R. through-out the time, not wanting her to wake up alone and confused.

"Kit?"

"Yes..." She moved her lips, the words sticking in her dry mouth. "My homeopathic kit...in my car. I need it...."

He raised his brows. "Oh...your black bag. Yeah, I brought it in with me. Hold on, I'll be right back."

Rachel almost cried when he left her side. The strong, caring warmth of his hand on her arm was very stabilizing. The noise in E.R. was like a drum inside her head. She heard the plaintive cry of a baby, some-one else was groaning in pain—familiar sounds to her as a homeopath. She wished she could get up, go dispense a remedy to each of them to ease their pain and discomfort. She wasn't in England any longer, though; she was in the U.S. Suddenly she felt disoriented.

Her ears picked up the sound of a curtain being drawn aside. She opened her eyes. He was back, with her black leather physician's bag.

"Got it," he said with a smile, placing the bag close to her blanketed leg.

As he opened it, Rachel tried to think clearly. "Who are you? I feel like I know you…but I'm not remembering names too well right now."

His mouth curved in a grin as he opened the bag. "Jim Cunningham. I'm the EMT who worked with you out at the accident scene." He pulled out the white, plastic box and held it where she could see it.

"Oh…"

Chuckling, he said, "Man, have I made a good impression on you. Here you are, the prettiest woman I've seen in a long time, and you forget my name."

His teasing warmth fell across her. Rachel tried to smile, but the pain in her head wouldn't let her. There was no denying that Jim Cunningham was a very good-looking man. He was tall, around six foot two, and lean, like a lithe cougar with a kind of boneless grace that told her he was in superb physical condition. The dark blue, long-sleeved shirt and matching pants he wore couldn't hide his athletic build. The silver badge on his left pocket, the gold nameplate above it and all the patches on the shoulders of his shirt gave him a decided air of authority.

Wrinkling her nose a little, she croaked, "Don't take it personally. I'm feeling like I have cotton stuffed between my ears." She lifted her hand and found it shaky.

"Just tell me which one you want," he said gently.

"You're pretty weak yet. In another couple of hours you'll feel a lot better than you do right now."

Alarmed at her weakness, Rachel whispered, "Get me the Arnica."

"Ah, the same one you used out at the accident site. Okay." He hunted around. There were fifty black-capped, amber bottles arranged by alphabetical order in the small case. Finding Arnica, he uncapped it.

"Now what?"

"My mouth. Drop a couple of pellets in it."

Jim carefully put two pellets on her tongue. "Okay, you're set." He capped the amber bottle. "What is this stuff, anyway? The E.R. doc wanted to know if it had side effects or if it would cause any problems with pre-scription drugs."

The pellets were sugary sweet. Rachel closed her eyes. She knew the magic of homeopathy. In a few minutes, her headache would be gone. And in a few more after that, she'd start feeling more human again.

"That's okay," Jim murmured as he replaced the vial into the case, "you don't have to answer the questions right now." He glanced up. "I called your family. I talked to Kate." He put the box back into Rachel's bag and set it on a chair nearby. "They're all waiting out in the visitors' lounge. Hold on, I'll get them for you."

Rachel watched through half-closed eyes as Jim opened the green curtain and disappeared. She liked him. A lot. What wasn't there to like? she asked herself. He was warm, nurturing, charming—not to mention terribly handsome. He had matured since she'd known him in school. He'd been a tall, gangly, shy kid with acne on his face. She remembered he was half Apache and half Anglo and that they'd always had that common bond—being half-Indian.

So many memories of her past-of growing up here in Sedona, of the pain of her father's alcoholism and her mother's endless suffering with the situation-flooded back through her. They weren't pleasant memories. And many of them she wanted to forget.

Jim Cunningham... In school she'd avoided him like the plague because Old Man Cunningham and her father had huge adjoining ranches. The two men had fought endlessly over the land, the often-broken fence line and the problems that occurred when each other's cattle wandered onto the other's property. They'd hated one another. Rachel had learned to avoid the three Cunningham boys as a result.

Funny how a hit on the head pried loose some very old memories. A crooked smile pulled at Rachel's mouth. And who had saved her? None other than one of the Cunninghams. What kind of karma did she have? She almost laughed, and realized the pain in her head was lessening quickly; her thoughts were rapidly clearing. Thanks to homeopathy. And Jim Cunningham.

"Rachel!"

She opened her eyes in time to see Jessica come flying through the curtains. Her younger sister's eyes were huge, her face stricken with anxiety. Reaching out with her right hand, Rachel gave her a weak smile.

"Hi, Jess. I'm okay...really, I am...."

Then Rachel saw Kate, much taller and dressed in Levi's and a plaid wool coat, come through the curtains. Her serious features were set with worry, too.

Jessica gripped Rachel's hand. "Oh, Rachel! Jim called us, bless him! He didn't have to do that. He told us everything. You could have died out there!" She gave a sob, then quickly wiped the tears from her eyes. Leaning down, she kissed Rachel's cheek in welcome.

Kate smiled brokenly. "Helluva welcome to Sedona, isn't it?"

Grinning weakly, Rachel felt Kate's work-worn hand fall over hers. "Yes, I guess it is."

Kate frowned. "I thought you were flying into Phoenix, renting a car and driving up from there?"

Making a frustrated sound, Rachel said, "I was going to surprise you two. I got an earlier flight out of Denver directly into Flag. I was going to be at the ranch hours earlier that way." She gave Kate a long, warm look. "I really wanted to get home."

"Yeah," Kate whispered, suddenly choked up as she gripped her sister's fingers, "I guess you did."

Sniffing, Jessica wiped her eyes. "Are you okay, Rachel? What did the doctor say?"

Rachel saw the curtains part. It was Jim Cunningham. Her heart skipped a beat. She saw how drawn his face was and his eyes seemed darker than she recalled. He came and stood at the foot of the gurney where she was lying.

"Dr. Forbush said she had eight stitches in her foot for a torn artery, and a bump on the head," he told them. He held Rachel's gaze. She seemed far more alert now, and that was good. When he'd stepped into the cubicle, he'd noticed that her cheeks were flushed. Pointing to her left foot, he said, "She lost a pint of blood out there at the wreck. She got that replaced and the doc is releasing her to your care." And then he smiled teasingly down at Rachel. "That is, unless you want to spend a night here in the hospital for observation?"

Rachel grimaced. "Not on your life," she muttered defiantly. "I work in them, I don't stay in them."

Chuckling, Jim nodded. He looked at the three Donovan sisters. "I gotta get going, but the head nurse, Sue

Young, will take care of getting you out of this place."
He studied Rachel's face and felt a stirring in his heart.
"Stay out of trouble, you hear?"

"Wait!" Rachel said, her voice cracking. She saw
surprise written on his features when he turned to her
again. "Wait," she pleaded. "I want to thank you...."
Then she smiled when she saw deviltry in his eyes as
he stood there, considering her plea.

"You serious about that?"

"Sure."

"Good. Then when you get well, have lunch with
me?"

Stunned, Rachel leaned back onto the bed. She
saw Jessica's face blossom in a huge smile. And Kate
frowned. Rachel knew what her older sister was thinking. He was a Cunningham, their enemy for as long as
any of them could recall.

"Well..."

Jim raised his hand, realizing he'd overstepped his
bounds. "Hey, I was just teasing. I'll see you around.
Take care of yourself...."

"I'll be right back," Kate murmured to her sisters,
and she quickly followed after him.

Jim was headed toward the small office in the back
of E.R. where EMTs filled out their accident report
forms when he heard Kate Donovan's husky voice.

"Jim?"

Turning, he saw her moving in his direction. Step-
ping out of the E.R. traffic, he waited for her. The serious look on her face put him on guard. She was the
oldest of the three Donovan daughters and the owner of
a ranch, which was teetering precariously on the edge
of bankruptcy. He knew she had worked hard since assuming the responsibilities of the ranch after Kelly died

in an auto accident earlier in the year. Because of that, Jim also knew she had more reason to hate a Cunningham than any of the sisters. Inwardly, he tried to steel himself against anything she had to say. His father, unfortunately, had launched a lawsuit against Kate's ranch right now. There was nothing Jim could do about it, even though he'd tried to talk his father into dropping the stupid suit. Driven by the forty-year vendetta against Kelly Donovan, he'd refused to. It made no difference to him that the daughters were coming home to try and save their family ranch. The old man couldn't have cared less.

With such bad blood running between the two families, Jim was trying to mend fences where he could. His two older brothers weren't helping things, however. They derived just as much joy and pleasure out of hurting people, especially the Donovans, as their old man. Jim was considered the black sheep of the family, probably because he was the only Cunningham who wasn't into bad blood or revenge. No, he'd come home to try and fix things. And in the months since he'd been home, Jim had found himself living in hell. He found his escape when he was on duty for the fire department. But the rest of the time he was a cowboy on the family ranch, helping to hold it together and run it. Ordinarily, he'd loved the life of a rancher, but not anymore. These days his father was even more embittered toward the Donovans, and now he had Bo and Chet on his side to wage a continued war against them.

As Kate Donovan approached him, Jim understood how she felt toward him. It wasn't anything personal; it was just ancient history that was still alive and injuring all parties concerned. Even him. The darkness in her eyes, the serious set of her mouth, put him on guard.

He studied her as she halted a few feet away from him, jamming her hands into the deep pockets of the plaid wool jacket she wore.

"I want to thank you," Kate rasped, the words coming out strained.

Reeling, Jim couldn't believe his ears. He'd expected to catch hell from Kate for suggesting lunch with Rachel. He knew she had a lot of her father in her and could be mule-headed, holding grudges for a long time, too.

"You didn't have to call us," Kate continued. "You could have left that to a nurse here in E.R., I know." Then she looked up at him. "I found out from the nurse before I went in to see Rachel that you saved her life—literally."

Shrugging shyly, Jim said, "I did what I could, Kate. I'd do it for anyone." He didn't want her to think that he'd done something special for Rachel that he wouldn't do for others. In his business as an EMT, his job was to try and save lives.

"Damn, this is hard," Kate muttered, scowling and looking down at her booted feet. Lifting her head, she pinned him with a dark look. "I understand you just gave her a pint of your blood. Is that true?"

He nodded. "Rachel's blood type is a rare one." Looking around the busy hospital area, he continued, "This is a backwoods hospital, Kate. They can't always have every rare blood type on hand. Especially in the middle of Arizona, out in the wilds." He tried to ease her hard expression with his teasing reply.

Kate wasn't deterred in the least. "And your partner, Larry, who I just talked to out at the ambulance, said you'd stopped Rachel from losing even more blood by putting a tourniquet on her leg?"

"I put a blood-pressure cuff around Rachel's lower

leg to try and stop most of the bleeding, yes." Inwardly, Jim remained on guard. He never knew if Kate Donovan was going to pat him on the head or rip out his jugular. Usually it was the latter. He saw her expression go from anger to confusion and then frustration, and he almost expected her to curse him out for volunteering his own blood to help save Rachel's life. After all, it was Cunningham blood—the blood of her arch enemy. The enemy that her father had fought against all his life.

Kate pulled her hand out of her pocket and suddenly thrust it toward him. "Then," she quavered, suddenly emotional, "I owe you a debt I can't begin to pay back."

Staring at her proffered hand, Jim realized what it took for Kate to do that. He gripped her hand warmly. The tears in her eyes touched him deeply. "I'm glad it was me. I'm glad I was there, Kate. No regrets, okay?"

She shook his hand firmly and then released it. "Okay," she rasped nervously, clearing her throat. "I just wanted you to know that I know what really happened."

He gave her a slight smile. "And there's nothing to pay back here. You understand?" He wanted both families to release the revenge, the aggressive acts against one another. Kelly Donovan was dead, though Jim's father was still alive and still stirring up trouble against their closest neighbors. Kate was struggling to keep the ranch afloat, and Jim admired her more than he could ever say. But if he told her that she wouldn't believe him, because he was a Cunningham—bad blood.

Nodding, she wiped her eyes free of tears. "You sure know how to balance ledgers, don't you?"

Scrutinizing her closely, Jim said quietly, "I assume you're talking about the ledger between our two families?"

"Yes." She stared up at him. "I can't figure you out—yet."

"There's nothing to figure out, Kate."

"Yes," she growled, "there is."

His mouth curved ruefully. "I came home like you did—to try and fix things."

"Then why does your old man have that damned lawsuit against us?"

Kate's frustration paralleled his own. Opening his hands, Jim rasped, "I'm trying to get him to drop the suit, Kate. It has no merit. It's just that same old revenge crap from long ago, that's all."

She glared at him. "We are hitting rock bottom financially and you and everyone else knows it. Rachel came home to try and make money to help us pay the bills to keep our ranch afloat. If I have to hire a lawyer and pay all the court costs, that's just one more monetary hemorrhage. Can't *you* do anything to make him stop it?"

"I'm doing what I can."

She looked away, her mouth set. "It's not enough."

Wearily, Jim nodded. "Kate, I want peace between our families. Not bloodshed or lawsuits. My father has diabetes and often refuses to take his meds, so he exhibits some bizarre behavior."

"Like this stupid lawsuit?"

"Exactly." Glancing around, Jim pulled Kate into the office, which was vacant at the moment. Shutting the door, he leaned against it as he held her stormy gaze. "Let's bury the hatchet between us, okay? I did not come home to start another round of battles with you or anyone else at the Donovan Ranch."

"You left home right after high school," Kate said in a low voice. "So why did you come back now?"

"I never approved of my father's tactics against you or your family. Yes, I left when I was eighteen. I became a hotshot firefighter with the forest service. I didn't want to be a part of how my father was acting or behaving. I didn't approve of it then and I don't now. I'm doing what I can, Kate. But I've got a father who rants and raves, who's out of his head half the time. Then he stirs up my two brothers, who believe he's a tin god and would do anything he told them to do. They don't stop to think about the consequences of their actions."

Kate wrapped her arms against her body and stared at him, the silence thickening. "Since you've come back, things have gotten worse, not better."

Releasing a sigh, Jim rested against the edge of the desk. "Do you know what happens when a diabetic doesn't watch his diet or doesn't take his meds?" he asked in a calm tone.

"No," she muttered defensively. "Are you going to blame your old man's lawsuit and everything else on the fact that he's sick and won't take the drugs he's supposed to take?"

"In part, yes," Jim said. "I'm trying to get my brothers to work with me, not against me, on my father taking his medication daily. I'm trying to get our cook to make meals that balance my father's blood sugar and not spike it up so he has to be peeled off the ceiling every night when I get home."

Kate nodded. "If you think I feel sorry for you, I don't."

"I'm not telling you this to get your sympathy, Kate," he said slowly. "I'm trying to communicate with you and tell you what's going on. The more you understand, the less, I hope, you'll get angry about it."

"Your father is sick, all right," Kate rattled. "He hasn't changed one iota from when I was a kid growing up."

"I'm trying to change that, but it takes time." Jim held her defiant gaze. "If I can keep channels of communication open between us, maybe I can put out some brushfires before they explode into a wildfire. I'd like to be able to talk with you at times if I can."

Snorting, Kate let her arms fall to her sides. "You just saved Rachel's life. Your blood is in her body. I might be pigheaded, Cunningham, but I'm not stupid. I owe you for her life. If all you want in return is a little chat every once in a while, then I can deal with that."

Frustration curdled Jim's innards. He'd actually given one and a half pints of blood and he was feeling light-headed, on top of being stressed out from the rescue. But he held on to his deteriorating emotions. "I told you, Kate—no one owes me for helping to save Rachel's life."

"I just wonder what your father is going to say. This ought to make his day. Not only did you save a Donovan's neck, you gave her your blood, too. Frankly," Kate muttered, moving to the door and opening it, "I don't envy you at all when you go home tonight. You're going to have to scrape that bitter old man of yours off the ceiling but good this time."

Jim nodded. "Yeah, he'll probably think I've thrown in with the enemy." He said it in jest, but he could tell as Kate's knuckles whitened around the doorknob, she had taken the comment the wrong way.

"Bad blood," she rasped. "And it always will be."

Suddenly he felt exhausted. "I hope Rachel doesn't take it that way even if you do." There was nothing he could do to change Kate's mind about his last name,

Cunningham. As her deceased father had, she chose to associate all the wrongdoings of the past with each individual Cunningham, whether involved in it or not. And in Jim's case, he was as much the victim here as were the Donovan sisters. He'd never condoned or supported what his father had done to Kelly Donovan over the years, or how he'd tried to destroy the Donovan Ranch and then buy it up himself. But Kate didn't see it—or him—as separate from those acts of his father. She never would, Jim thought tiredly.

"Rachel's a big girl," Kate muttered defiantly. "I'm not going to brainwash her one way or another about you Cunninghams."

"Right now, Rachel needs peace and quiet," Jim answered. "She was in pretty deep shock out there. If you could give her two or three days of rest without all this agitation, it would help her a lot."

Kate nodded. "I'll make sure she gets the rest."

The office turned silent after Kate Donovan left. Sighing, Jim rubbed his brow. What a helluva morning! His thoughts moved back to Rachel. Old feelings he'd believed had died a long time ago stirred in his chest. She was so beautiful. He wondered if she had Kate's bitterness toward the Cunninghams. Jim cared more about that than he wanted to admit.

First things first. Because he'd given more than a pint of blood, he'd been taken off duty by the fire chief, and another EMT had been called in to replace him on the duty roster. Well, he'd fill out the accident report on Rachel and then go home. As he sat down at the desk and pulled out the pertinent form, Jim wondered if news of this event would precede him home. He hoped not—right now, he was too exhausted to deal with his father's ire. What he felt was a soul tiredness, though, more than just physical tiredness. He'd been home almost a year now, and as Kate had said, not much had changed.

Pen in hand, the report staring up at him, Jim tried to order his thoughts, but all he could see was Rachel's pale face and those glorious, dark green eyes of hers. What kind of woman had she grown into after she'd left Sedona? He'd heard she'd moved to England and spent most of her adult life there. Jim understood her desire to escape from Kelly Donovan's drunken, abusive behavior, just as he'd taken flight from his own father and his erratic, emotional moods. Jim's fingers tightened around the pen. Dammit, he was drawn to Rachel—right or wrong. And in Kate Donovan's eyes, he was dead wrong in desiring Rachel.

With a shake of his head, he began to fill out the form. Why the hell had he asked Rachel out to lunch? The invitation had been as much a surprise to him as it had been to the Donovan women. Kate was the one who'd reacted the most to it. Jessica was too embroiled in worry for Rachel to even hear his teasing rejoinder. And Rachel? Well, he'd seen surprise in her green eyes, and then something else.... His heart stirred again—this time with good, warm feelings. He wondered at the fleeting look in Rachel's eyes when he'd made his sudden invitation.

Would she consider going to lunch with him? Was he crazy enough to hold on to that thought? With a snort, Jim forced his attention back to his paperwork. Right now, what he had to look forward to was going back to the Bar C and hoping his father hadn't heard what had happened. If he had, Jim knew there would be a blisteringly high price to pay on his hide tonight.

CHAPTER THREE

"I HEARD you gave blood to one of those Donovan bitches."

Jim's hand tightened on the door as he stepped into the Cunningham ranch house. Frank Cunningham's gravelly voice landed like a hot branding iron on him, causing anger to surge through Jim. Slowly shutting the door, he saw his father in his wheelchair sitting next to the flagstone fireplace. The old man was glaring at him from beneath those bushy white eyebrows, his gray eyes flat and hard. Demanding.

Jim told himself that he was a grown man, that his gut shouldn't be clenching as it was now. He was over thirty years old, yet he was having a little boy's reaction to a raging father. Girding himself internally, Jim forced himself to switch to his EMT mode. Shrugging out of his heavy jacket, he placed it on a hook beside the door.

"Looks like news travels fast," he said as lightly as possible. Judging from the wild look in his father's eyes, he guessed he hadn't taken diabetes medication.

"Bad news always does, dammit!" Frank punched a finger at Jim as he sauntered between the leather couch and chair. "What are you doing, boy? Ruining our good name? How could you?"

Halting in front of him, Jim placed his hands on his hips. He was tired and drained. Ordinarily, giving blood didn't knock him down like this. It was different knowing who the accident victim was, though. He was still reeling from the fact that it was little Rachel Donovan, the girl he'd had a mad crush on so long ago.

"Have you taken your pill for your sugar problem?" Jim asked quietly.

Cursing richly, Frank Cunningham snarled, "You answer my questions, boy! Who the *hell* do you think you are, giving blood to—"

"You call her a bitch one more time and it will be the last time," Jim rasped, locking gazes with his angry father. "Rachel doesn't deserve that from you or anyone. She could have died out there early this morning."

Gripping the arms of his wheelchair with swollen, arthritic fingers, Frank glared at him. "You don't threaten me, boy."

The word *boy* grated on Jim's sensitized nerves. He reminded himself one more time that he'd come home to try and pull his family together. To try and stop all the hatred, the anger and fighting that the Cunninghams were known for across two counties. Maybe he'd been a little too idealistic. After all, no one had even invited him back. It was one thing to be called home. It was quite another to wonder every day whether he'd have a home to come back to. Frank Cunningham had thrown him out when he was eighteen and Jim had never returned, except for Christmas. Even then, the holidays became a battleground of sniping and snarling, of dealing with the manipulations of his two brothers.

"Look, Father," Jim began in a strained toned, "I'm a little out of sorts right now. I need to lie down for a while and rest. Did you take your medicine this morning at breakfast? Did Louisa give it to you?"

Snorting, Frank glared at the open fireplace, where a fire crackled and snapped. "Yes, she gave it to me," he muttered irritably.

A tired smile tugged at the corners of Jim's mouth. "Did you take it?"

"No!"

In some ways, at seventy-five, Frank was a pale ghost of his former self. Jim recalled growing up with a strapping, six-foot-five cowboy who was tougher than the drought they were presently enduring. Frank had made this ranch what it was: the largest and most prosperous in the state of Arizona. Jim was proud of his heritage, and like his father, he loved being a cowboy, sitting on a good horse, working ceaselessly during calving season and struggling through all the other demanding jobs of ranching life.

Pulling himself out of his reverie, Jim walked out to the kitchen. There on the table were two tiny blue tablets, one for diabetes and one for high blood pressure. He picked them up and got a glass of water.

He knew his father's mood was based directly on his blood sugar level. If it was too high, he was an irritable son of a bitch. If it was too low, he would go into insulin shock, keel over unconscious and fall out of his wheelchair. Jim had lost track of how many times he'd had to pull his father out of insulin shock. He could never get it through Frank's head that he might die from it. His father didn't seem to care. Frank's desire to live, Jim realized, had left when their mother died.

Jim walked back out into the living room. It was a huge, expansive room with a cathedral ceiling and the stuffed heads of elk, deer, peccary and cougar on the cedar walls. The aged hardwood floor gleamed a burnished gold color. A large Navajo rug of red, black and gray lay in the center of the room, which was filled with several dark leather couches and chairs set around a rectangular coffee table.

"Here, Dad, take it now," Jim urged gently.

"Damn stuff."

"I know."

"I *hate* taking pills! Don't like leaning on anything or anyone! That's all these are—crutches," he said, glaring down at the blue pill in his large, callused palm.

Jim patiently handed him the glass of water. Neither of his brothers would ensure that Frank took his medicine. If they even saw the pills on the kitchen table, they ignored them. Jim had once heard Bo say that it would be just that much sooner that the ranch would be given to him.

As he stood there watching his father take the second pill, Jim felt his heart wrench. Frank was so thin now. His flesh, once darkly tanned and hard as saddle leather, was washed out and almost translucent looking. Jim could see the large, prominent veins in his father's crippled hands, which shook as he handed the glass back to him.

"Thanks. Now hit the hay. You look like hell, son."

Jim smiled a little. Such gruff warmth from his father was a rare gift and he absorbed it greedily. There were moments when Frank was human and compassionate. Not many, but Jim lived for them. "Okay, Dad. If you need anything, just come and get me."

Rubbing his hand through his thick silver hair, Frank grunted. "I got work to do in the office. I'll be fine."

"Okay…."

JIM WAS SITTING ON HIS bed and had pushed off his black boots when he heard someone coming down the hardwood hall. By the sound of the heavy footsteps, he knew it was Bo. Looking up, he saw his tall, lean brother standing in the doorway. By the state of his muddied Levi's and snow-dampened sheepskin coat, Bo had been out working. Taking off his black Stetson hat, he scowled at Jim.

"What's this I hear about you giving blood to one of those Donovan girls? Is that true? I was over at the hay and feed store and that was all they were talkin' about."

With a shake of his head, Jim stretched out on top of his double bed, which was covered with a brightly colored, Pendleton wool blanket. Placing his hands behind his head, he looked up at the ceiling.

"Gossip travels faster than anything else on earth," he commented.

Bo stepped inside the room. His dark brows drew down. "It's true, then?"

"Yeah, so what if it is?"

Settling the hat back on his head, Bo glared down at him. "Don'tcha think your goody-two-shoes routine is a little out of control?"

Smarting at Bo's drawled criticisms, Jim sat up. "I know you wish I'd crawl back under a rock and disappear from this ranch, Bo, but it isn't going to happen."

Bo's full lips curved into a cutting smile. "Comin' home to save all sinners is a little presumptuous, don't you think?"

Tiredness washed across Jim, but he held on to his deteriorating patience. "Someone needs to save this place."

"So you gave blood to Rachel Donovan. Isn't that a neat trick. You think by doing that, you'll stop the war between us?"

Anger lapped at him. "Bo, get the hell out of here.

I'm beat. If you want to talk about this later, we'll do it then."

Chuckling indulgently, Bo reached for the doorknob. "Okay, little bro. I'll see you later."

Once the door shut, Jim sighed and lay back down. Closing his eyes, he let his arm fall across his face. The image of Rachel Donovan hovered beneath his eyelids. Instantly, he felt warmth flow through his tense body, washing away his irritation with his father, his anger toward his older brother. She had the most incredible dark green eyes he'd ever seen. Jim recalled being mesmerized by them as a young, painfully shy boy in junior high. He'd wanted to stare into them and see how many gold flecks he could find among the deep, forest-green depths.

Rachel had been awkward and skinny then. Now she was tall, elegant looking and incredibly beautiful. The prettiest, he felt, of the three sisters. She had Odula's face—high cheekbones, golden skin, dark brown hair that hung thick and heavy around her shoulders. Finely arched brows and large, compassionate eyes. Her nose was fine and thin; her mouth—the most delectable part of her—was full and expressive. Jim found himself wondering what it would be like to kiss that mouth.

At that thought, he removed his arm and opened his eyes. What the hell was he doing? His father would have a stroke if he suspected Jim liked Rachel Donovan. Frank Cunningham would blow his top, as usual, and spout vehemently, "That's like marrying the plague!" or something like that. Donovan blood, as far as Frank was concerned, was contaminated filth of the worst kind. Jim knew that to admit his interest in Rachel would do nothing but create the worst kind of stress in this household. His older brothers would ride roughshod over him, too. He was sure Frank would disown him—again—as he had when Jim was eighteen.

Jim closed his eyes once more and felt the tension in his body. Why the hell had he come home? Was Bo right? Was he out to "save" everyone? Right now, he was trying to juggle his part-time job as an EMT and work full-time at the ranch as a cowboy. Jim didn't want his father's money, though Bo had accused him of coming home because their father was slowly dying from diabetes. Bo thought Jim was hoping to be written back into the will. When Jim had left home, Frank had told him that the entire ranch would be given to Bo and Chet.

Hell, Jim couldn't care less about who was in the will or who got what. That didn't matter to him. What did matter was family. His family. Ever since his mother had died, the males in the family had become lost and the cohesiveness destroyed. His mother, a full-blooded Apache, had been the strong, guiding central core of their family. The backbiting, the manipulation and power games that Bo and Chet played with their father wouldn't exist, Jim felt, if she were still alive. No, ever since his mother's death when he was six years old, the family unit had begun to rot—from the inside out.

Jim felt the tension bleeding out of him as he dwelled on his family's history. He felt the grief over losing his mother at such a young, vulnerable age. She had been a big woman, built like a squash, her black, flashing eyes, her copper skin and her playful smile so much a part of her. She'd brought joy and laughter to the ranch. When she died, so had the happiness. No one had laughed much after that. His father had changed drastically. In the year following his mother's death, Jim saw what loving and losing a person did to a man. Frank had turned to alcohol and his rages became known county wide. He'd gotten into bar fights. Lawsuits. He'd fought with Kelly Donovan on almost a daily basis. Frank Cunningham had gone berserk over his wife's passing. Maybe that's why Jim was gun-shy of committing to a relationship. Or maybe Rachel Donovan had stolen his heart at such a young age that he wanted no one but her—whether he could ever have her or not.

All Jim could do back then was try to hold the rest of his suffering, grieving family together. He hadn't had time for his own grief and loss as he'd tried to help Bo and Chet. Even though he was the youngest, he was always the responsible one. The family burden had shifted to Jim whenever their father would disappear for days at a time. Frank would eventually return, unshaven and dirty, with the reek of alcohol on his breath. The weight of the world had been thrust upon Jim at a young age. Then, at eighteen, right after high school graduation, Jim had decided he had to escape. And he did—but the price had been high.

Slowly, ever so slowly, Rachel's face formed before his closed eyes again. Jim felt all his stress dissolve before the vision. She had such a peaceful look about her. Even out there at the accident site, she hadn't panicked. He admired her courage under the circumstances.

Suddenly, anger rose within him. Dammit, he *wanted* to see her again. How could he? If Frank knew, he'd hit the ceiling in a rage. Yet Jim refused to live his life knowing what his father's knee-jerk reaction would be. Still, it was hell having to come back to the ranch and take a gutful of Frank's verbal attacks. But if Jim moved to his own place in Sedona, which was what he wanted to do, who would make sure his father took his meds?

Feeling trapped, he turned on his side. He felt the fingers of sleep encroaching on his worry and his desires. The last thing he saw as he drifted off was Rachel trying to smile gamely up at him in the E.R. when she regained consciousness. He recalled how thick and silky her hair had felt when he'd touched it. And he'd seen how his touch had affected her. In those moments, he'd felt so clean and hopeful again—two things he hadn't felt in a long, long time. Somehow, someway, he was going to find a way to see her again. He *had* to.

RACHEL ABSORBED THE WARMTH of the goose-down quilt lying over her. She was in her old bed, in the room she'd had as a child. She was back at the Donovan Ranch. Gloomy midafternoon light filtered through the flowery curtains at the window. Outside, snowflakes were falling slowly, like butterflies. The winter storm of this morning had passed on through.

Her foot ached a little, so she struggled to sit up. On the bed stand was her homeopathic kit. Opening it, she found the Arnica and took another dose.

"You awake?"

Rachel heard Jessica's hopeful voice at her door before her younger sister smiled tentatively and entered the room. Jessica's gold hair was in two braids and the oversize, plaid flannel shirt she wore highlighted her flushed cheeks.

"Come on in," Rachel whispered.

Pushing a few strands of hair off her face, Jessica sat down at the bottom of the bed and faced Rachel. "I thought you might be awake."

"I slept long and hard," Rachel assured her as she

placed the kit back on the bed table. She put a couple of pillows behind her and then pushed the quilt down to her waist. The flannel nightgown she wore was covering enough in the cool room. There was no central heating in the huge, main ranch house. Only the fireplace in the living room provided heat throughout the winter. Rachel didn't mind the coolness, though.

Jessica nodded and surveyed her. "How's your foot?"

"Okay. I just took another round of Arnica."

"What does that do for it?"

Rachel smiled, enjoying her sister's company. Jessica was so open, idealistic and trusting. Nothing like Kate, who distrusted everyone, always questioning their motives. "It reduces the swelling of the soft tissue. The pain will go away in about five minutes."

"Good." Jessica rubbed her hands down her Levi's. "I was just out checking on my girls—my orchids. The temperature is staying just fine out there in the greenhouse. This is the first big snow we've had and I was a little worried about them."

Rachel nodded. "Where's Kate?"

"Oh, she and Sam and Dan are out driving the fence line. Earlier today, she got a call from Bo Cunningham who said that some of our cattle were on their property—again."

Groaning, Rachel said, "Life doesn't change at all, does it, Jess?"

Giggling, Jessica shook her head. "No, it doesn't seem to, does it? Don't you feel like you're a teenager again? We had the same problems with the Cunninghams then as we do now." She sighed and opened her hands. "I wish they wouldn't be so nasty toward us. Frank Cunningham hates us."

"He hates everything," Rachel murmured.

"So how did Jim turn out to be so nice?"

"I don't know." Rachel picked absently at the bed-cover. "He *is* nice, Jess. You should have seen him out there with me, at the accident. I was in bad shape. He was so gentle and soothing. I had such faith in him. I knew I'd be okay."

"He's been home almost a year now, and he's trying to mend a lot of fences."

"Are you saying he was nice to me because of the feud between our families?"

Jessica shook her head. "No, Jim is a nice guy. Somehow, he didn't get Frank's nasty genes like the other two boys did." She laughed. "I think he has his mother's, instead."

Rachel smiled. "I know one thing. I owe Jim my life."

"You owe him more than that," Jessica said primly as she tucked her hands in her lap. "Did he tell you he gave a pint of *his* blood to you?"

"What?" Rachel's eyes grew wide.

"Yeah, the blood transfusion. You lost a lot from the cut across your foot," she said, pointing to Rachel's foot beneath the cover. "I found out about it from the head nurse in E.R. when we came in to see how you were. Jim had called us from hospital and told us what had happened. Well," she murmured, "he was selective in what he told us. He really downplayed his part in saving you. He's so humble that way, you know? Anyway, I was asking the nurse what all had been done for you, because we don't have medical insurance and I knew Kate would be worrying about the bill. I figured I'd do some investigating for her and get the info so she wouldn't have to do it later." Clasping her hands together, she continued, "You have a rare type of blood.

They didn't have any on hand at the hospital, nor did they have any in Cottonwood. So I guess Jim volunteered his on the spot. He has the same blood type as you do." She smiled gently. "Wasn't that sweet of him? I mean, talk about a symbolic thing happening between our two families."

Rachel sat there, digesting her sister's explanation. Jim's blood was circulating in her body. It felt right. And good. "I—see...." Moistening her lips, she searched Jessica's small, open face. She loved her fiercely for her compassion and understanding. "How do you feel about that?"

"Oh, I think it's wonderful!"

"And Kate?" Tension nagged at Rachel's stomach over the thought of her older sister's reaction. Kate held grudges like their father did.

Jessica gazed up at the ceiling and then at her. "Well, you know Kate. She wasn't exactly happy about it, but like she said, you're alive and that's what counts."

"I'm glad she took the high road on this," Rachel murmured, chuckling.

Jessica nodded. "We owe Jim so much. Kate knows that and so do I. I think he's wonderful. He's trying so hard to patch things up between the two families."

"That's a tall order," Rachel said. She reached for the water pitcher on the bed stand. Pouring herself a glassful, she sipped it.

"I have faith in him," Jessica said simply. "His integrity, his morals and values are like sunshine compared to the darkness of the Cunningham ranch in general. I believe he can change his father and two brothers."

"You're being overidealistic," Rachel cautioned.

"Maybe," she said. Reaching out, she ran her hand along Rachel's blanketed shin. "We're all wondering *what* made you skid off 89A. You know that road like the back of your hand. And you're used to driving in snow and ice."

Setting the glass on the bed table, Rachel frowned. "You're probably going to think I'm crazy."

Laughing, Jessica sat up. "Me? The metaphysical brat of the three of us? Nooo, I don't think so, Rachel." Leaning forward, her eyes animated, she whispered, "So tell me what happened!"

Groaning, Rachel muttered, "I saw a jaguar standing in the middle of 89A as I rounded that last hairpin curve."

Jessica's eyes widened enormously. "A jaguar? You saw a jaguar?"

Rachel grimaced. "I told you you'd think I was crazy."

Leaping up from the bed, her sister whispered, "Oh, gosh! This is *really* important, Rachel." Typical of Jessica, when she got excited she had to move around. She quickly rounded the bed, her hands flying in the air. "It was a jaguar? You're positive?"

"I know what I saw," Rachel said a bit defensively. "I know I was tired and I had jet lag, but I've never hallucinated in my life. No, it *was* a jaguar. Not a cougar, because I've seen the cougars that live all around us up here. It was a jaguar, with a black-and-gold coat and had huge yellow eyes. It was looking right at me. I was never so startled, Jess. I slammed on the brakes. I know I shouldn't have—but I did. If I hadn't, I'd have hit that cat."

"Oh, gosh, this is *wonderful!*" Jessica cried. She clapped her hands together, coming to a sudden halt at the end of Rachel's bed.

"Really? What's so wonderful about it? If this story

ever gets out, I'll be the laughingstock of Sedona. There're no jaguars in Arizona."

Excitedly, Jessica whispered, "My friend Moyra, who is from Peru, lived near me for two years up in Canada. She helped me get my flower essence business going and tended my orchid girls with me. What a mysterious woman she was! She was very metaphysical, very spiritual. Over the two years I knew her, she told me that she was a member of a very ancient order called the Jaguar Clan. She told me that she took her training in the jungles of Peru with some very, very old teachers who possessed jaguar medicine."

Rachel opened her mouth to reply, but Jessica gripped her hand, her words tumbling out in a torrent. "No, no, just listen to me, okay? Don't interrupt. Moyra told me that members of the Jaguar Clan came from around the world. They didn't have to be born in South America to belong. I guess it has something to do with one's genes. Anyway, I saw some very strange things with Moyra over the two years she was with me."

"Strange?"

"Well," she said, "Moyra could read minds. She could also use mental telepathy. There were so many times I'd start to ask her a question and she'd answer before I got it out of my mouth! Or..." Jessica paused, her expression less animated "...when Carl, my ex-husband, was stalking me and trying to find out where I was hiding, Moyra told me that she'd guard me and make sure he never got to me. I remember four different times when she warned me he was close and protected me from being found by him."

"You mean," Rachel murmured, "she *sensed* his presence?"

"Something like that, but it was more, much more.

She had these heightened senses. And—" Jessica held her gaze "—I saw her do it one day."

"Do what?"

Jessica sighed and held up her right hand. "I *swear* I'm telling you the truth on this, Rachel. I was taking a walk in the woods, like I always did in the afternoon when I was done watering my girls in the greenhouse. It was a warm summer day and I wanted to go stick my feet in the creek about half a mile from where we lived. As I approached the creek, I froze. You won't believe this, but one minute I saw Moyra standing in the middle of the creek and in the next I saw a jaguar! Well, I just stood there in shock, my mouth dropping open. Then suddenly the jaguar turned back into Moyra. She turned around and looked right at me. I blinked. Gosh, I thought I was going crazy or something. I thought I was seeing things."

Jessica patted her sister's hand and released it. "There were two other times that I saw Moyra change into a jaguar. I don't think she meant for me to see it— it just happened."

"A woman who turns into a jaguar?" Rachel demanded.

"I know, I know," Jessica said. "It sounds crazy, but listen to this!" She sat down on the edge of the bed and faced Rachel. "I got up enough courage to ask Moyra about what I'd seen. She didn't say much, but she said that because she was a member of this clan, her spirit guide was a male jaguar. Every clan member has one. And that this spirit guide is her teacher, her protector, and she could send it out to help others or protect others if necessary." Excitedly, Jessica whispered, "Rachel, the last thing Moyra told me before I drove down here to live was that if I ever needed help, she would be there!"

Stymied, Rachel said, "That jaguar I saw was Moyra—or Moyra's spirit guardian?" Rachel had no trouble believing in spirit guardians, because Odula, their mother, had taught them from a very early age that all people had such guides from the invisible realms. They were protectors, teachers and helpers if the person allowed them to be.

"It must have been one or the other!" Jessica exclaimed in awe.

"Because," Kate Donovan said, walking through the door and taking off her damp wool coat, "about half a mile down 89A from where you crashed, there was a fuel-oil tanker that collided with a pickup truck." She halted and smiled down at Jessica, placing her coat on a chair. "What you don't know, Rachel, is that five minutes after you spun out on that corner, that pickup truck slid into that tanker carrying fuel oil. There was an explosion, and everyone died."

Stunned, Rachel looked at Jessica. "And if I hadn't spun out on that corner…"

Kate brought the chair over and sat down near her bed. "Yep, *you* would have been killed in that explosion, too."

"My God," Rachel whispered. She frowned.

Jessica gave them both a wide-eyed look. "Then that jaguar showing up saved your life. It really did!"

Kate combed her fingers through her long, dark hair, which was mussed from wearing a cowboy hat all day. "I heard you two talking as I came down the hall. So you think it was your friend's jaguar that showed up?"

Jessica nodded. "I have no question about it. Even now, about once a month, I have this dream that's not a dream about Moyra. She comes and visits me. We talk over what's happening in our lives. Stuff like that.

She's down at a place called the Village of the Clouds, and she said she's in training. She didn't say for what. She's very mysterious about that."

"So, your friend comes in the dream state and visits with you?" Rachel asked. Odula had placed great weight and importance on dreaming, especially lucid dreaming, which was a technique embraced whole-heartedly by the Eastern Cherokee people.

"Yes," Jessica said in awe. "Wow…isn't that something?" She looked up at Kate. "How did you find this out?"

"At the E.R. desk as I was signing Rachel out. Once they had you extricated from your rental car," Kate told Rachel, "Jim's ambulance had to drive up to Flagstaff to get you E.R. care because of that mess down on 89A. There was no way they could get through to the Cottonwood Hospital. There were fire trucks all over the place putting out the fire from that wreck."

Rachel studied her two sisters. Kate looked drawn and tired in her pink flannel shirt, Levi's and cowboy boots. She worked herself to the bone for this ranch. "Once upon a time, jaguars lived in the Southwest," Rachel told them.

"Yeah," Kate muttered, "until the good ol' white man killed them all off. I hear, though, they're coming back. There're jaguars living just over the border in Mexico. It wouldn't surprise me if they've already reached here." She rubbed her face. "And this Rim country where we live is ideal habitat for them." She smiled a little. "Maybe what you saw wasn't from the spirit world, after all. Maybe it was a live one. The first jaguar back in the States?"

"Oh," Jessica said with a sigh, "that would be neat, too!"

They all laughed. Rachel reached out and gripped Kate's work-worn hand. "It's so good to be home. It feels like old times, doesn't it? The three of us in one or the other's bedroom, chatting and laughing?"

"Yeah," Kate whispered, suddenly emotional as she gripped Rachel's hand. "It's nice to have you both here. Welcome home, sis."

Home. The word sent a tide of undeniable warmth through Rachel. She saw tears in Jessica's eyes and felt them in her own.

"If it wasn't for Jim Cunningham," Rachel quavered, "I wouldn't be here at all. We owe him a lot."

Kate nodded grimly. "Yes, we do."

"Tomorrow I want to see him and thank him personally," Rachel told them. "Jessica, can you find out if he's going to be at the fire department in Sedona?"

"Sure, no problem." She eased off the bed and wiped the tears from her eyes. "He's the sweetest guy."

Kate snorted. "He's a Cunningham. What's the old saying? A tiger can't change his stripes?"

Rachel grinned at her older sister's sour reaction. "Who knows, Kate? Jim may not be a tiger at all. He may be a jaguar in disguise."

"You know his nickname and his Apache name are both Cougar," Jessica said excitedly.

"Close enough for me," Rachel said with a smile.

CHAPTER FOUR

"HEY, Cunningham, you got a visitor!"

Jim lifted his head as his name was shouted through the cavernous area where the fire trucks and ambulance sat waiting for another call. The bay doors were open and bright winter sunlight poured inside the ambulance where Jim sat, repacking some of the shelves with necessary items.

Who could it be? Probably one of his brothers wanting to borrow some money from him as usual. With a grunt he eased out of the ambulance and swung around the corner.

His eyes widened and he came to an abrupt halt. Rachel Donovan! Swallowing his surprise, he stood watching as she slowly walked toward him. Noontime sunlight cascaded down, burnishing her long dark hair with hints of red and gold. She wore conservative, light gray woolen slacks and a camel-colored overcoat.

Struck by her beauty, her quiet presence as she met and held his gaze, he watched her lips lift into a smile. Heat sheeted through him as he stood there. Like a greedy beggar, he absorbed her warm gaze. Her green eyes sparkled with such life that he felt his breath momentarily hitch. This wasn't the woman he'd met at the car accident. Not in the least. Amazed that she seemed perfectly fine three days after nearly losing her life, Jim managed a shy grin of welcome.

"Hey, you look pretty good," he exclaimed, meeting her halfway across the bay.

Rachel felt heat sting her cheeks. She was blushing again! Her old childhood response always seemed to show up at the most embarrassing times. She studied the man before her; he was dressed in his usual dark blue pants and shirt, the patches for the fire department adorning the sleeves. When he offered his hand to her, she was struck by the symbolic gesture. A Donovan and a Cunningham meeting not in anger, but in friendship. As far as she knew it was a first, and Rachel welcomed it.

As she slid her hand into his big square one she felt the calluses and strength of it. Yet she could feel by his grip that he was carefully monitoring that strength. But what Rachel noticed most of all was the incredible warmth and joy in his eyes. It stunned her. He was a Cunningham, she, a Donovan. Nearly a century-old feud stood between them, and a lot of bad blood.

"I should hope I look better," Rachel replied with a low, husky laugh. "I'm not a homeopath for nothing."

Jim forced himself to release Rachel's long, thin fingers. She had the hands of a doctor, a surgeon, maybe. There was such a fluid grace about her as she moved. Suddenly he remembered that she could have bled to death the other day if they hadn't arrived on scene to help her when they had, and he was shaken deeply once again.

"I'm just finishing up my shift." He glanced at his watch. "I have to do some repacking in the ambulance. Come on back and keep me company?"

She touched her cheek, knowing the heat in it was obvious. "I didn't want to bother you—"

"You're not a bother, believe me," he confided sincerely as he slid his hand beneath her elbow and guided her between the gargantuan fire trucks to the boxy ambulance that sat at the rear.

As Rachel allowed him to guide her, she saw a number of men and women firefighters, most of them watching television in the room off the main hangar. Yet she hardly noticed them. So many emotions were flowing through her as Jim cupped her elbow. What she recalled of him from junior high was a painfully shy teenager who couldn't look anyone directly in the eye. Of course, she understood that; she hadn't exactly been the homecoming queen type herself. Two shadows thrown together by life circumstance, Rachel thought, musing about their recent meeting.

Once they reached the back of the ambulance, Jim urged her to climb in. "You can sit in the hot seat," he joked, and pointed to the right of the gurney, where the next patient would lie.

Rachel carefully climbed in. She sat down and looked around. "Is this the one I was in?"

Jim smiled a little and opened up a box of rolled bandages. He counted out six and then stepped up into the ambulance. "Yes, it was," he said, sliding the plastic door on one of the shelves to one side to arrange the bandages. "We call her Ginger."

"I like that. You named your truck."

"Actually, my partner, Larry, named her." Jim made a motion toward the front of the ambulance. "All the fire trucks are ladies and they all have names, too." He studied Rachel as he crouched by one of the panels. "You look like your accident never happened. How are you feeling?"

With a slight laugh, she said, "Well, let's put it this way—my two sisters, Kate and Jessica, are getting married this Saturday out at the ranch. I'm their maid of honor. I could *not* stay sick." She pointed to her foot, which sported a white dressing across the top. "I had to get well fast or they'd have disowned me for not showing up for their weddings."

"You look terrific," Jim murmured. "Like nothing ever happened."

She waved her hands and laughed. "*That* was thanks to you and homeopathy. When I got back to the ranch, I had Jessica bath the wound with tincture of Calendula three times a day." She patted her injured foot. "It really speeded up the healing."

"And that stuff you took? What did you call it? Arnica? What did it do for you?"

She was pleased he remembered the remedy. "Arnica reduces the swelling and trauma to injured soft tissue."

He slid the last door shut, his inventory completed. "That's a remedy we could sure use a lot of around here. We scrape so many people up off the highway that it would really help."

Rachel watched as he climbed out of the ambulance. There was no wasted motion about Jim Cunningham. He was lithe, like the cougar he was named after. And she liked the sense of steadiness and calmness that emanated from him like a beacon. His Apache blood was obvious in the color of his skin, his dark, cut hair and high cheekbones. What she liked most were his wide, intelligent eyes and his mouth, which was usually crooked in a partial smile. Jim was such an opposite to the warring Cunningham clan he'd been born into. He was like his mother, who had been known for her calm, quiet demeanor. Rachel knew little more about her, except that she'd been always full of laughter, with a twinkle in her eye.

"We're done here," Jim said genially, holding out his hand to her. He told himself he was enjoying Rachel too much. He wondered if she was married, but he didn't see a wedding ring on her left hand as he took it into his own. She stepped carefully out of the ambulance to the concrete floor beside him. "And I'm done with my shift." He glanced at his watch. "Noon, exactly." And then he took a huge risk. "If I recall, up at the Flag hospital I offered you lunch. I know a great little establishment called the Muse Restaurant. Best mocha lattes in town. How about it?" His heart pumped hard once, underscoring just how badly he wanted Rachel to say yes.

Jim saw her forest-green eyes sparkle with gold as he asked her the question. Did that mean yes or no? He hoped it meant yes and found himself holding his breath, waiting for her answer. As he studied her upturned face, he felt her undeniable warmth and compassion. There was a gentleness around her, a Zen-like quality that reminded him of a quiet pool of water—serene yet very deep and mysterious.

"Actually," Rachel said with a laugh, "I came here to invite *you* to lunch. It was to be a surprise. A way of thanking you for saving my neck."

A powerful sensation moved through Jim, catching him off guard. It was a delicious feeling.

"That's a great idea," he murmured, meaning it. "But I asked first, so you're my guest for lunch. Come on, we'll take my truck. It's parked just outside. I'll bring you back here afterward."

Rachel couldn't resist smiling. He looked boyish as the seriousness in his face, the wrinkle in his brow disappeared in that magical moment. Happiness filled her, making her feel as if she were walking on air. Once again Jim cupped his hand on her elbow to guide her out of the station. She liked the fact that he matched his stride to hers. Normally she was a fast walker, but the injury to her foot had slowed her down.

Jim's truck was a white Dodge Ram with a shiny chrome bumper. It was a big, powerful truck, and there was plenty of Arizona—red mud which stuck to everything—on the lower half of it, probably from driving down the three-mile dirt road to the Cunningham ranch. He opened the door for her and she carefully climbed in.

Rachel was impressed with how clean and neat the interior was, unlike many men's pickups. As she hooked the seat belt, she imagined the orderliness came from him working in the medical field and understanding the necessity of cleanliness. She watched as Jim climbed in, his face wonderfully free of tension. He ran his fingers through his short, dark hair and then strapped himself in.

"Have you thought about the repercussions of being seen out in public with me?" he drawled as he slipped the key into the ignition. The pickup purred to life, the engine making a deep growling sound.

Wrinkling her nose, Rachel said, "You mean the gossip that will spread because a Cunningham and a Donovan broke bread together?"

Grinning, he nodded and eased the truck out of the parking spot next to the redbrick building. "Exactly."

"I was over at Fay Seward's, the saddle maker's, yesterday, and she was telling me all kinds of gossip she'd heard about us."

Moving out into the traffic, slow moving because of the recent snow, Jim chuckled. "I'll bet."

Rachel looked out the window. The temperature

was in the low thirties, the sky bright blue and filled with nonstop sunlight. She put her dark glasses on and simply enjoyed being near Jim as he drove from the tourist area of Sedona into what was known as West Sedona. "I really missed this place," she whispered.

The crimson rocks of Sedona created some of the most spectacular scenery he'd ever seen. Red sandstone and white limestone alike were capped with a foot of new, sparkling snow from the storm several days before. With the dark green mantle of forest across the top of the Rim, which rose abruptly to tower several thousand feet above Sedona, this was a place for an artist and photographer, he mused.

Glancing over at her, he asked, "Why did you stay away so long?"

Shrugging, Rachel met his inquiring gaze. "Isn't it obvious? Or is it only to me?"

Gripping the steering wheel a little more tightly, he became serious. "We both left when we were kids. Probably for similar reasons. I went into the forest service and became a firefighter. Where did you go? I heard you moved overseas?"

Pain moved through Rachel. She saw an equal amount in Jim's eyes. It surprised her in one way, because the men she had known never allowed much emotion to show. "I moved to England," she said.

"And Jessica went to Canada and Kate became a tumbleweed here in the States."

"Yes."

Jim could feel her vulnerability over the issue. "Sorry, I didn't mean to get so personal." He had no right, but Rachel just seemed to allow him to be himself, and it was much too easy to become intimate with her. Maybe it was because she was in the medical field; she had a doctor's compassion, but more so.

With a wave of her hand, she murmured, "No harm done. I knew when I moved home to try and help save our ranch that there were a lot of buried wounds that needed to be aired and cleaned out and dressed."

"I like your analogy. Yeah, we all have old wounds, don't we?" He pulled into a shopping center with a huge fountain that had been shut off for the winter. Pointing up the walk, he said, "The Muse—a literary café. All the writers and would-be writers come here and hang out. Since you're so intelligent, I thought you might enjoy being with your own kind."

Smiling, Rachel released the seat belt. "How did you know I'm writing a book?"

Jim opened his door. "Are you?"

With a laugh, she said, "Yes, I am." Before she could open her own door, Jim was there to do it. He offered his hand and she willingly took it because the distance to the ground was great and she had no desire to put extra stress on the stitches still in her foot.

"Thank you," she said huskily. How close he was! How very male he was. Rachel found herself wanting to sway those few inches and lean against his tall, strong frame. Jim's shoulders were broad, proudly thrown back. His bearing was dignified and filled with incredible self-confidence.

Unwilling to release her, Jim guided Rachel up the wet concrete steps. "So what are you writing on?" The slight breeze lifted strands of her dark hair from her shoulders, reminding him how thick and silky it was. His fingers itched to thread through those strands once again.

"A book on homeopathy and first aid. I'm almost

finished. I already have a publisher for it, here in the States. It will be simultaneously published by an English firm, too."

He opened the door to the restaurant for her. "How about that? I know a famous person."

With a shake of her head, Rachel entered the warm restaurant, which smelled of baking bread. Inhaling the delicious scent, she waited for Jim to catch up with her. "Mmm, homemade bread. Doesn't it smell wonderful?"

He nodded. "Jamie and his partner, Adrian, make everything fresh here on the premises. No canned anything." He guided her around the corner to a table near the window. Each table, covered in white linen, was decorated with fresh, colorful flowers in a vase. The music was soft and New Age. In each corner stood towering green plants. Jim liked the place because it was alive with plants and flowers.

Rachel relinquished her coat to Jim. He placed it on one of several hooks in the corner. The place was packed with noontime clientele. In winter and spring, Sedona was busy with tourists from around the world who wanted to escape harsh winters at home. The snowfall earlier in the week was rare. Sedona got snow perhaps two to four times each winter. And usually, within a day or two, it had melted and been replaced with forty-degree weather in the daytime, thirty-degree temperatures at night.

Sitting down, Jim recognized some of the locals. He saw them watching with undisguised interest. The looks on their face said it all: a Cunningham and Donovan sitting together—peacefully—what a miracle! Frowning, Jim picked up the menu and then looked over at Rachel, who was studying hers.

"They've got great food here. Anything you pick will be good."

Rachel tried to pay attention to the menu. She liked the fact that Jim sat at her elbow and not across from her. It was so easy to like him, to want to get to know him better. She had a million questions to ask him, but knew she had to remain circumspect.

After ordering their lunch, and having steaming bowls of fragrant mocha latte placed in front of them, Rachel began to relax. The atmosphere of the Muse was low-key. Even though there wasn't an empty table, the noise level was low, and she appreciated that. Setting the huge bowl of latte down after taking a sip, she pressed the pink linen napkin briefly to her lips. Settling the napkin back in her lap, she met and held Jim's warm, interested gaze. He wasn't model handsome. His face had lines in it, marks of character from the thirty-some years of his life. His thick, dark brows moved up a bit in inquiry as she studied him.

"I know what you're thinking," he teased. "I'll bet you're remembering this acne-covered teenager from junior high school, aren't you?"

She folded her hands in front of her. "No, not really. I do remember you being terribly shy, though."

"So were you," he said, sipping his own latte. Jim liked the flush that suddenly covered her cheeks. There was such painfully obvious vulnerability to Rachel. How had she been able to keep it? Life usually had a way of knocking the stuffing out of most people, and everyone he knew hid behind a protective mask or wall as a result. Rachel didn't, he sensed. Maybe that was a testament to her obvious confidence.

"I was a wallflower," Rachel conceded with a nervous laugh. "Although I did attend several clubs after school."

"Drama and photography, if my memory serves me."

Her brows rose. "That's right! Boy, what a memory *you* have." She was flabbergasted that Jim would remember such a thing. If he remembered that, what else did he recall? And why would he retain such insignificant details of her life, anyway? Her heart beat a little harder for a moment.

With a shy shrug, Jim sipped more of his latte. "If the truth be told, I had a terrible crush on you back then. But you didn't know it. I was too shy to say anything, much less look you in the eyes." He chuckled over the memory.

Gawking, Rachel tried to recover. "A crush? On me?"

"Ridiculous, huh?"

She saw the pain in his eyes and realized he was waiting for her to make fun of him for such an admittance. Rachel would never do that to anyone. Especially Jim.

"No!" she whispered, touched. "I didn't know...."

"Are you sorry you didn't know?" Damn, why had he asked that? His stomach clenched. Why was it so important that Rachel like him as much as he had always liked her? His hands tightened momentarily around his bowl of latte.

"Never mind," he said, trying to tease her, "you don't have to answer that on the grounds it may incriminate you—or embarrass me."

Rachel felt his tension and saw the worry in his eyes. A scene flashed inside her head of a little boy cowering, as if waiting to get struck. Sliding her fingers around her warm bowl of latte, she said, "I wish I had known, Jim. That's a beautiful compliment. Thank you."

Unable to look at her, he nervously took a couple of sips of his own. Wiping his mouth with the napkin, he muttered, "The past is the past."

Rachel smiled gently. "Our past follows us like a good friend. I'm sure you know that by now." Looking around, she saw several people staring openly at them with undisguised interest. "Like right now," she mused, "I see several locals watching us like bugs under a microscope." She met and held his gaze. Her lips curved in a grin. "Tell me our pasts aren't present!"

Glancing around, Jim realized Rachel was right. "Well, by tonight your name will be tarnished but good."

"What? Because I'm having lunch with the man who saved my life? I'd say that I'm in the best company in the world, with no apology. Wouldn't you?"

He felt heat in his neck and then in his face. Jim couldn't recall the last time he'd blushed. Rachel's gently spoken words echoed through him like a bell being rung on a very clear day. It was as if she'd reached out and touched him. Her ability to share her feelings openly was affecting him deeply. Taking in a deep breath, he held her warm green gaze, which suddenly glimmered with tears. Tears! The soft parting of her lips was his undoing. Embarrassed, he reached into his back pocket and produced a clean handkerchief.

"Here," he said gruffly, and placed it in her hand.

Dabbing her eyes, Rachel sniffed. "Don't belittle what you did for me, Jim. I sure won't." She handed it back to him. He could barely meet her eyes, obviously embarrassed by her show of tears and gratitude. "You and I are in the same business in one way," she continued. "We work with sick and injured people. The only difference is your EMT work is immediate, mine is more long-term and certainly not as dramatic."

He refolded the handkerchief and stuffed it back into his rear pocket. "I'm not trying to make little of what we did out there for you, Rachel. It wasn't just me that saved your life. My partner, Larry, and four other fire-fighters were all working as a team to save you."

"Yes, but it was your experience that made you put that blood-pressure cuff on my leg, inflate it and stop the hemorrhaging from my foot."

He couldn't deny that. "Anyone would have figured that out."

"Maybe," Rachel hedged as she saw him begin to withdraw from her. Why wouldn't Jim take due credit for saving her life? The man had great humility. He never said "I," but rather "we" or "the team," and she found that a remarkable trait rarely seen in males.

Lowering her voice, she added, "And I understand from talking to Kate and Jessica, that you gave me a pint of your blood to stabilize me. Is that so?"

Trying to steel himself against whatever she felt about having his blood in her body, Jim lifted his head. When he met and held her tender gaze, something old and hurting broke loose in his heart. He recalled that look before. Rachel probably had forgotten the incident, but he never had. He had just been coming out of the main doors to go home for the day when he saw that a dog had been hit by a car out in front of the high school. Rachel had flown down the steps of the building, crying out in alarm as the dog was hurled several feet onto the lawn.

Falling to her knees, she had held the injured animal. Jim had joined her, along with a few other concerned students. Even then, Rachel had been a healer. She had torn off a piece of her skirt and pressed it against the dog's wounded shoulder to stop the bleeding. Jim had dropped his books and gone to help her. The dog had had a broken leg as well.

Jim remembered sinking to his knees directly opposite her and asking what he could do to help. The look Rachel was giving him now was the same one he'd seen on her face then. There was such clear compassion, pain and love in her eyes that he recalled freezing momentarily because the energy of it had knocked the breath out of him. Rachel had worn her heart on her sleeve back then, just as she did now. She made no excuses for how she felt and was bravely willing to share her vulnerability.

Shaken, he rasped, "Yeah, I was the only one around with your blood type." He opened his hands and looked at them. "I don't know how you feel about that, but I caught hell from my old man and my brothers about it." He glanced up at her. "But I'm not sorry I did it, Rachel."

Without thinking, Rachel slid her hand into his. Hers was slightly damp, while his was dry and strong and nurturing. She saw surprise come to his eyes and felt him tense for a moment, then relax.

As his fingers closed over Rachel's, Jim knew tongues would wag for sure now about them holding hands. But hell, nothing had ever felt so right to him. Ever.

"I'm grateful for what you did, Jim," Rachel quavered. "I wouldn't be sitting here now if you hadn't been there to help. I don't know how to repay you. I really don't. If there's a way—"

His fingers tightened around hers. "I'm going hiking

in a couple of weeks, near Boynton Canyon. Come with me?" The words flew out of his mouth. What the hell was he doing? Jim couldn't help himself, nor did he want to. He saw Rachel's eyes grow tender and her fingers tightened around his.

"Yes, I'd love to do that."

"Even though," he muttered, "we'll be the gossip of Sedona?"

She laughed a little breathlessly. "If I cared, really cared about that, I wouldn't be sitting here with you right now, would I?"

A load shifted off his shoulders. Rachel was free in a way that Kate Donovan was not, and the discovery was powerful and galvanizing. Jim very reluctantly released her hand. "Okay, two weeks. I'm free on Saturday. I'll pack us a winter picnic lunch to boot."

"Fair enough," Rachel murmured, thrilled over the prospect of the hike. "But I have one more favor to ask of you first, Jim."

"Name it and it's yours," he promised thickly.

Rachel placed her elbows on the table and lowered her voice. "It's a big favor, Jim, and you don't have to do it if it's asking too much of you."

Scowling, he saw the sudden worry and seriousness on her face. "What is it?"

Moistening her lips, Rachel picked up her purse from the floor and opened it. Taking out a thick, white envelope, she handed it to him. "Read it, please."

Mystified, Jim eased the envelope open. It was a wedding invitation—to Kate's and Jessica's double wedding, which would be held on Saturday. He could feel the tension in Rachel. His head spun with questions and few answers. Putting the envelope aside, he held her steady gaze.

"You're serious about this…invitation?"

"Very."

"Look," he began uneasily, holding up his hands, "Kate isn't real comfortable with me being around. I understand why and—"

"Kate was the one who suggested it."

Jim stared at her. "What?"

Rachel looked down at the tablecloth for a moment. "Jim," she began unsteadily, her voice strained, "I've heard why you came back here, back to Sedona. You want to try and straighten out a lot of family troubles between yourself, your father and two brothers. Kate didn't trust you at first because of the past, the feud between our families…actually, between our fathers, not us for the most part." She looked up and held his dark, shadowed gaze. "Kate doesn't trust a whole lot of people. Her life experiences make her a little more paranoid than me or Jessica, but that's okay, too. Yesterday she brought this invitation to me and told me to give it to you. She said that because you'd saved my life, she and Jessica wanted you there. That this was a celebration of life—and love—and that you deserved to be with us."

He saw the earnestness in Rachel's eyes. "How do you feel about it? Having the enemy in your midst?"

"You were never my enemy, Jim. None of you were. Kelly had his battles with your father. Not with me, not with my sisters. Your brothers are another thing. They aren't invited." Her voice grew husky. "I *want* you to be there. I like Kate's changing attitude toward you. It's a start in healing this wound that festers among us. I know you'll probably feel uncomfortable, but by showing up, it's a start, even if only symbolically, don't you think? A positive one?"

In that moment, Jim wished they were anywhere but out in a public place. The tears in Rachel's eyes made them shine and sparkle like dark emeralds. He wanted to whisper her name, slide his hands through that thick mass of hair, angle her head just a little and kiss her until she melted into his being, into his heart. Despite her background, Rachel was so fresh, so alive, so brave about being herself and sharing her feelings, that it allowed him the same privilege within himself.

He wanted to take her hand and hold it, but he couldn't. He saw the locals watching them like proverbial hawks now. Jim didn't wish gossip upon Rachel or any of the Donovan sisters. God knew, they had suffered enough of it through the years.

One corner of his mouth tugged upward. "I'll be there," he promised her huskily.

CHAPTER FIVE

"WHERE you goin' all duded up?" Bo Cunningham drawled as he leaned languidly against the open door to Jim's bedroom.

Jim glanced over at his brother. Bo was tall and lean, much like their father. His dark good looks had always brought him a lot of attention from women. In high school, Bo had been keenly competitive with Jim. Whatever Jim undertook, Bo did too. The rivalry hadn't stopped and there was always tension, like a razor, between them.

"Going to a wedding," he said.

He knotted his tie and snugged it into place against his throat. In all his years of traveling around the U.S. as a Hotshot, he'd never had much call for wearing a suit. But after having lunch with Rachel, he'd gone to Flagstaff and bought one. Jim had known that when his two brothers saw him in a suit, they'd be sure to make fun of him. Uniform of the day around the Bar C was jeans, a long-sleeved shirt and a cowboy hat. He would wear his dark brown Stetson to the wedding, however. The color of his hat would nearly match the raw umber tone of his suit. A new white shirt and dark green tie completed his ensemble.

Bo's full lips curled a little. "I usually know of most weddin's takin' place around here. Only one I know of today is the Donovan sisters."

Inwardly, Jim tried to steel himself against the inevitable. "That's the one," he murmured, picking up
his brush and moving it one last time across his short,
dark hair. It was nearly 1:00 p.m. and the wedding was
scheduled for 2:00. He had to hurry.

"You workin' at bein' a traitor to this family?"

Bo's chilling question made him freeze. Slowly
turning, he saw that his brother was no longer leaning
against his bedroom door, but standing tensely. The
stormy look on his face was what Jim expected.

Picking up his hat, Jim stepped toward him. "Save
your garbage for somebody who believes it, Bo." Then
he moved past him and down the hall. Since Jim had
come home, Bo had acted like a little bantam rooster,
crowing and strutting because their father was planning in leaving Bo and Chet the ranch—and not Jim.
Frank Cunningham had disowned his youngest son the
day he'd left home years before. As Jim walked into the
main living area, he realized he'd never regretted that
decision. What he did regret was Bo trying at every
turn to get their father to throw him off the property
now.

As Jim settled his hat on his head, he saw his father
positioned near the heavy cedar door that he had to
walk through to get to his pickup. The look on his father's face wasn't pleasant, and Jim realized that Bo,
an inveterate gossip, had already told him everything.

"Where you goin', son?"

Jim halted in front of his father's wheelchair. As he
studied his father's eyes, he realized the old man was
angry and upset, but not out of control. He must have
remembered his meds today. For that, Jim breathed an
inner sigh of relief.

"I'm going to a wedding," he said quietly. "Kate and

Jessica Donovan are getting married. It's a double wedding."

His father's brows dipped ominously. "Who invited you?"

"Kate did." Jim felt his gut twist. He could see his father's rage begin to mount, from the flash of light in his bloodshot eyes to the way he set his mouth into that thin, hard line.

"You could've turned down the invitation."

"I didn't want to." Jim felt his adrenaline start to pump. He couldn't help feeling threatened and scared— sort of like the little boy who used to cower in front of his larger-than-life father. When Frank Cunningham went around shouting and yelling, his booming voice sounded like thunder itself. Jim knew that by coming back to the ranch he would go through a lot of the conditioned patterns he had when he was a child and that he had to work through and dissolve them. He was a man now, not a little boy. He struggled to remain mature in his reactions with his father and not melt into a quivering mass of fear like he had when he was young.

"You had a choice," Frank growled.

"Yes." Jim sighed. "I did."

"You're doin' this on purpose. Bo said you were."

Jim looked to his right. He saw Bo amble slowly out of the hallway, a gleeful look in his eyes. His brother *wanted* this confrontation. Bo took every opportunity to make things tense between Jim and his father in hopes that Jim would be banned forever from the ranch and their lives. Jim knew Bo was worried that Frank would change his will and give Jim his share of the ranch. The joke was Jim would never take it. Not on the terms that Frank would extract from him. No, he wouldn't play those dark family games anymore. Girding himself against his father's well-known temper, Jim looked down into his angry eyes.

"What I do, Father, is my business. I'm not going to this wedding to hurt you in any way. But if that's what they want you to believe, and you want to believe it, then I can't change your mind."

"They're *Donovans!*" Frank roared as he gripped the arms of his wheelchair, his knuckles turning white. His breathing became harsh and swift. "Damn you, Jim! You just don't get it, do you, boy? They're our enemies!"

Jim's eyes narrowed. "No, they're not our enemies! You and I have had this argument before. I'm not going to have it again. They're decent people. I'm not treating them any differently than I'd treat you or a stranger on the street."

"Damn you to hell," Frank snarled, suddenly leaning back and glaring up at him. "If I wasn't imprisoned in this damned chair, I'd take a strap to you! I'd stop you from going over there!"

"Come on, Pa," Bo coaxed, sauntering over and patting him sympathetically on the shoulder. "Jim's a turncoat. He's showin' his true colors, that's all. Come on, lemme take you to town. We'll go over to the bar and have a drink of whiskey and drown our troubles together over this."

Glaring at Bo, Jim snapped, "He's diabetic! You know he can't drink liquor."

Bo grinned smugly. "You're forcing him to drink. It's not my fault."

Breathing hard, Jim looked down at his father, a pleading expression in his eyes. Before Frank became diabetic, he'd been a hard drinker. Jim was sure he was an alcoholic, but he never said so. Now Jim centered his anger on Bo. His brother knew a drink would make his father's blood sugar leap off the scale, that it could damage him in many ways and potentially shorten his life. Jim knew that Bo hated his father, but he never showed it, never confronted him on anything. Instead, Bo used passive-aggressive ways of getting what he wanted. This wasn't the first time his brother had poured Frank a drink or two. And Bo didn't really care what it did to his father's health. His only interest was getting control of the ranch once Frank died.

Even his father knew alcohol wasn't good for his condition. But Jim wasn't about to launch into the reasons why he shouldn't drink. Placing his hand on the doorknob, he rasped, "You're grown men. You're responsible for whatever you decide to do."

THE WEDDING WAS TAKING place at the main ranch house. The sky was sunny and a deep, almost startling blue. As Jim drove up and parked his pickup on the graveled driveway, he counted more than thirty other vehicles. Glancing at his watch, he saw that it was 2:10 p.m. He was late, dammit. With his stomach still in knots from his confrontation with his father, he gathered up the wedding gifts and hurried to the porch of the ranch house. There were garlands of evergreen with pine cones, scattered with silver, red and gold glitter, framing the door, showing Jim that the place had been decorated with a woman's touch.

Gently opening the door, he saw Jessica and Kate standing with their respective mates near the huge red-pink-and-white flagstone fireplace. Rachel was there, too. Reverend Thomas O'Malley was presiding and sonorously reading from his text. Walking as quietly as he could, Jim felt the stares of a number of people in the gathered group as he placed the wrapped gifts on a table at the back of the huge room.

Taking off his hat, he remained at the rear of the crowd that had formed a U around the two beautiful brides and their obviously nervous grooms. Looking up, he saw similar pine boughs and cones hung across each of the thick timbers that supported the ceiling of the main room. The place was light and pretty compared to the darkness of his father's home. Light and dark. Jim shut his eyes for a moment and tried to get a hold on his tangled, jumbled emotions.

When he opened his eyes, he moved a few feet to the left to get a better look at the wedding party. His heart opened up fiercely as he felt the draw of Rachel's natural beauty.

Both brides wore white. Kate had on a long, traditional wedding gown of what looked to Jim like satin, and a gossamer veil on her hair. Tiny pearl buttons decorated each of her wrists and the scoop neck of her dress. Kate had never looked prettier, with her face flushed, her eyes sparkling, her entire attention focused on Sam McGuire, who stood tall and dark at her side. In their expressions, Jim could see their love for one another, and it eased some of his own internal pain.

Jessica wore a tailored white wool suit, decorated with a corsage of several orchids. In her hair was a ringlet of orchids woven with greenery, making her look like a fairy. Jim smiled a little. Jessica had always reminded him of some ethereal being, someone not quite of this earth, but made more from the stuff of heaven. He eyed Dan Black, dressed in a dark blue suit and tie, standing close beside his wife-to-be. Jim noticed the fierce love in Black's eyes for Jessica. And he saw tears running down Jessica's cheeks as she began to repeat her vows to Dan.

The incredible love between the two couples soothed whatever demons were left in him. Jim listened to Kate's voice quaver as she spoke the words to Sam. McGuire, whose face usually was rock hard and expressionless, was surprisingly readable. The look of tenderness, of open, adoring love for Kate, was there to be seen by everyone at the gathering. Jim's heart ached. He wished he would someday feel that way about a woman. And then his gaze settled on Rachel.

The ache in his heart softened, then went away as he hungrily gazed at her. He felt like a thief, stealing glances at a woman he had no right to even look at twice. How she looked today was a far cry from how she'd looked out at the accident site. She was radiant in a pale pink, long-sleeved dress that brushed her thin ankles. A circlet of orchids similar to Jessica's rested in her dark, thick hair, which had been arranged in a pretty French braid, and she carried a small bouquet of orchids and greenery in her hands. She wore no make-up, which Jim applauded. Rachel didn't need any, he thought, struck once again by her exquisite beauty.

Her lips were softly parted. Tears shone in two paths across her high cheekbones as the men now began to speak their vows to Kate and Jessica. Everything about Rachel was soft and vulnerable, Jim realized. She didn't try to hide behind a wall like Kate did. She was open, like Jessica. But even more so, in a way Jim couldn't yet define. And then something electric and magical happened. Rachel, as if sensing his presence, his gaze burning upon her, lifted her head a little and turned to look toward him. Their eyes met.

In that split second, Jim felt as if a lightning bolt

had slammed through him. Rachel's forest-green eyes were velvet and glistening with tears. He saw the sweet curve of her full lips move upward in silent welcome. Suddenly awkward, Jim felt heat crawling up his neck and into his face. Barely nodding in her direction, he tried to return her smile. He saw relief in her face, too. Relief that he'd come? Was it personal or symbolic of the fragile union being forged between their families? he wondered. Jim wished that it was personal. He felt shaken inside as Rachel returned her attention to her sisters, but he felt good, too.

The dark mass of knots in his belly miraculously dissolved beneath Rachel's one, welcoming look. There was such a cleanness to her and he found himself wanting her in every possible way. Yet as soon as that desire was born, a sharp stab of fear followed. She was a Donovan. He was a Cunningham. Did he dare follow his heart? If he did, Jim knew that the hell in his life would quadruple accordingly. His father would be outraged. Bo would use it as another lever to get him to look unworthy to Frank. Jim had come home to try and change the poisonous condition of their heritage. What was more important—trying to change his family or wanting to know Rachel much, much better?

THERE WAS A WHOOP and holler when both grooms kissed their brides, and the party was in full swing shortly after. Jim recognized everyone at the festive gathering. He joined in the camaraderie, the joy around him palpable. The next order of business was tossing the bridal bouquets. Jim saw Rachel stand at the rear of the excited group of about thirty women, and noticed she wasn't really trying to jockey for a position to possibly catch one of those beautiful orchid bouquets. Why not?

Both Kate and Jessica threw their bouquets at the same time. There were shrieks, shouts and a sudden rush forward as all the women except Rachel tried to catch them. Ruby Forester, a waitress in her early forties who worked at the Muse Restaurant, caught Jessica's. Kate's bouquet was caught by Lannie Young, who worked at the hardware store in Cottonwood. Both women beamed in triumph and held up their bouquets.

Remaining at the rear of the crowd, Jim saw two wedding cakes being rolled out of the kitchen and into the center of the huge living room. From time to time he saw Rachel look up, as if searching for him in the crowd of nearly sixty people. She was kept busy up front as the cakes were cut, and then sparkling, nonalcoholic grape juice was passed around in champagne glasses.

After the toast, someone went over to the grand piano in the corner, and began to play a happy tune. The crowd parted so that a dance floor was spontaneously created. A number of people urged Kate and Sam out on the floor, and Jim saw Jessica drag Dan out there, too. Jim felt sorry for the new husbands, who obviously weren't first-rate dancers. But that didn't matter. The infectious joy of the moment filled all of them and soon both brides and grooms were dancing and whirling on the hardwood oak floor, which gleamed beneath them.

Finishing off the last of his grape juice, Jim saw a number of people with camcorders filming the event. Kate and Jessica would have a wonderful memento of one of the happiest days of their lives. He felt good about that. It was time the Donovans had a little luck, a little happiness.

After the song was finished, everyone broke into applause. The room rang with laughter, clapping and

shouts of joy. The woman at the piano began another
song and soon the dance floor was crowded with other
well-wishers. Yes, this was turning into quite a party.
Jim grinned and shook a number of people's hands,
saying hello to them as he slowly made his way toward
the kitchen. He wanted to find Rachel now that her
duties as the maid of honor were pretty much over.

The kitchen was a beehive of activity, he discovered
as he placed his used glass near the sink. At least seven
women were bustling around placing hors d'oeuvres
on platters, preparing them to be taken out to serve to
the happy crowd in the living room. He spotted Rachel
in the thick of things. Through the babble he heard
her low, husky voice giving out directions. Her cheeks
were flushed a bright pink and she had rolled up the
sleeves on her dress to her elbows. The circlet of orchids looked fetching in her hair. The small pearl earrings in her ears, and the single-strand pearl necklace
around her throat made her even prettier in his eyes, if
that were possible.

Finally, the women paraded out, carrying huge silver
platters piled high with all types of food—from meat to
fruit to vegetables with dip. Jim stepped to one side and
allowed the group to troop by. Suddenly it was quiet in
the kitchen. He looked up to see Rachel leaning against
the counter, giving him an amused look.

He grinned a little and moved toward her. The pink
dress had a mandarin collar and showed off her long,
graceful neck to advantage. The dress itself had an
empire waistline and made her look deliciously desirable.

"I got here a little late," he said. "I'm sorry."

Pushing a strand of dark hair off her brow, Rachel
felt her heart pick up in beat. How handsome and dan-

gerous Jim looked in his new suit. "I'm just glad you came," she whispered, noting the genuine apology in his eyes.

"I am, too." He forced himself not to reach out and touch her—or kiss her. Right now, Rachel looked so damned inviting that he had to fight himself. "Doesn't look like your foot is bothering you at all."

"No, complete recovery, thanks to you and a little homeopathic magic." She felt giddy. Like a teenager. Rachel tried to warn herself that she shouldn't feel like this toward any man again. The last time she'd felt even close to this kind of feeling for a man, things hadn't ended well between them. Trying to put those memories aside, Rachel lifted her hands and said, "You clean up pretty good, too, I see."

Shyly, Jim touched the lapel of his suit. "Yeah, first suit I've had since…I don't remember when."

"Well," Rachel said huskily, "you look very handsome in it."

Her compliment warmed him as if she had kissed him. Jim found himself wanting to kiss her, to capture that perfect mouth of hers that looked like orchid petals, and feel her melt hotly beneath his exploration. He looked deep into her forest-green eyes and saw gold flecks of happiness in them. "I hope by coming in late I didn't upset anything or anyone?"

She eased away from the counter and wiped her hands on a dish towel, suddenly nervous because he was so close to her. Did Jim realize the power he had over her? She didn't think so. He seemed shy and awkward around her, nothing like the in-charge medic she'd seen at her accident. No, that man had been confident and gentle with her, knowing exactly what to do and when. Here, he seemed tentative and unsure. Rachel laughed at herself as she fluttered nervously around the kitchen, realizing she felt the same way.

"I have to get back out there," she said a little breathlessly. "I need to separate the gifts. They'll be opening them next."

"Need some help?"

Hesitating in the doorway, Rachel laughed a little. "Well, sure.... Come on."

Jim and Rachel took up positions behind the linen-draped tables as the music and dancing continued unabated. He felt better doing something. Occasionally, their hands would touch as they closed over the same brightly wrapped gift, and she would jerk hers away as if burned. Jim didn't know how to interpret her reaction. He was, after all, a dreaded Cunningham. And more than once he'd seen a small knot of people talking, quizzically studying him and then talking some more. Gossip was the lifeblood of any small town, and Sedona was no exception. He sighed. Word of a Cunningham attending the Donovan weddings was sure to be the chief topic at the local barbershop come Monday morning.

Worse, he would have to face his father and brothers tonight at the dinner table. His stomach clenched. Trying to push all that aside, he concentrated on the good feelings Rachel brought up in him. Being the maid of honor, she had to make sure everything ran smoothly. It was her responsibility to see that Kate and Jessica's wedding went off without a hitch. And it looked like everything was going wonderfully. The hors d'oeuvres were placed on another group of tables near the fireplace, where flames were snapping and crackling. Paper plates, pink napkins and plenty of coffee, soda and sparkling grape juice would keep the guests well fed in the hours to come.

It was nearly 5:00 p.m. by the time the crowd began to dissipate little by little. Jim didn't want to go home. He had taken off his coat, rolled up his shirtsleeves and was helping wash dishes out in the kitchen, along with several women. Someone had to do the cleanup. Kate and Sam had gone to Flagstaff an hour earlier, planning to stay at a friend's cabin up in the pine country. Jessica and Dan had retired to their house on the Donovan spread, not wanting to leave the ranch.

Jim had his hands in soapy water when Rachel reappeared. He grinned at her as she came through the doorway. She'd changed from her pink dress into a pair of dark tan wool slacks, a long-sleeved white blouse and a bright, colorful vest of purple, pink and red. Her hair was still up in the French braid, but the circlet of orchids had disappeared. The pearl choker and earrings were gone, too.

She smiled at him as she came up and took over drying dishes from one of the older women. "I can see the look on your face, Mr. Cunningham."

"Oh?" he teased, placing another platter beneath the warm, running water to rinse it off.

"The look on your face says, 'Gosh, you changed out of that pretty dress for these togs.'"

"You're a pretty good mind reader." And she was. Jim wondered if his expression was really that revealing. Or was it Rachel's finely honed observation skills that helped her see through him? Either way, it was disconcerting.

"Thank you," she said lightly, taking the platter from him. Their fingers touched. A soft warmth flowed up her hand, making her heart beat a little harder.

"I'm sorry I didn't get to dance with you," Rachel said in a low voice. There were several other women in the kitchen and she didn't want them to overhear.

Jim had asked her to dance earlier, but she had reluctantly chosen kitchen duties over his invitation. He'd tried not to take her refusal personally—but he had. The Cunningham-Donovan feud still stood between them. He understood that Rachel didn't want to be seen in the arms of her vaunted enemy at such a public function.

"That's okay. You were busy." Jim scrubbed a particularly dirty skillet intently. Just the fact that Rachel was next to him and they were working together like a team made his heart sing.

"I wished I hadn't been," Rachel said, meaning it. She saw surprise flare in his eyes and then, just as quickly, he suppressed his reaction.

"You know how town gossip is," Jim began, rinsing off the iron skillet. "You just got home and you don't need gossip about being caught in the arms of a Cunningham haunting your every step." He handed her the skillet and met her grave gaze.

Pursing her lips, Rachel closed her fingers over his as she took the skillet. She felt a fierce longing build in her. She saw the bleakness in Jim's eyes, and heard the past overwhelming the present feelings between them. She wanted to touch him, and found herself inventing small ways of doing just that. The light in his eyes changed as her fingertips brushed his. For an instant, she saw raw, hungry desire in his eyes. Or had she? It had happened so fast, Rachel wondered if she was making it up.

"That had nothing to do with it, Jim," she said, briskly drying the skillet. "Kate told me you'd come home to try and mend some family problems. She told me how much you've done to try and make that happen. I find it admirable." Grimacing, she set the skillet aside and watched him begin to scrub a huge platter. "I really admire you." And she did.

Jim lifted his chin and glanced across his shoulder at her. There was pleasure in his eyes. Shrugging her shoulders, Rachel said, "I don't know if you'll be successful or not. You have three men who want to keep the vendetta alive between us. And I'm *sure,*" she continued huskily, holding his gaze, "that you caught hell today for coming over here."

Chuckling a little, Jim nodded and began to rinse the platter beneath the faucet. "Just a little. But I don't regret it, Rachel. Not one bit."

She stood there assessing the amount of discomfort she heard in his voice. She was a trained homeopath, taught to pay attention to voice tone, facial expressions and body language, and sense on many level what was really being felt over what was being verbally said. Jim was obviously trying to make light of a situation that, in her gut, she knew was a huge roadblock for him.

"Did your father get upset?"

Obviously uncomfortable, Jim handed her the rinsed platter. "A little," he hedged.

"Probably a lot. Has Bo changed since I saw him in school? He used to be real good at manipulating people and situations to his own advantage."

Jim pulled the plug and let the soapy water run out of the sink. "He hasn't changed much," he admitted, sadness in his voice.

"And Chet? Is he still a six-year-old boy in a man's body? And still behaving like one?"

Grinning, Jim nodded. "You're pretty good at pegging people."

Drying the platter, Rachel said, "It comes from being a homeopath for so many years. We're trained to observe, watch and listen on many levels simultaneously."

Jim rinsed off his soapy hands and took the towel she handed him. "Thanks. Well, I'm impressed." He saw her brows lower in thought. "So, what's your prescription for my family, Doctor?"

She smiled a little and put the platter on the table behind them. The other women had left, their duties done, and she and Jim were alone—at last. Rachel leaned against the counter, with no more than a few feet separating them. "When you have three people who want a poisonous situation to continue, who don't want to change, mature or break certain habit patterns, I'd say you're in over your head."

Unable to argue, he hung the cloth up on a nail on the side of the cabinet next to the sink. Slowly rolling his sleeves down, Jim studied her. "I won't disagree with your assessment."

Her heart ached for him. In that moment, Rachel saw a vulnerable little boy with too much responsibility heaped upon his shoulders at too young an age. His mother had died when he was six, as she recalled, leaving three little boys robbed of her nurturing love. Frank Cunningham had lost it after his wife died. Rachel remembered that story. He'd gone on a drinking binge that lasted a week, until he finally got into a fight at a local bar and they threw him in the county jail to cool down. In the meantime, Bo, Chet and Jim had had to run the ranch without their grief-stricken father. Three very young boys had been saddled with traumatic responsibilities well beyond their years or understanding. Rachel felt her heart breaking for all of them.

"Hey," she whispered, "everyone's leaving. I'd love

to have some help moving the furniture back into place in the living room. It's going to quiet down now. Do you have time to help me or do you have to go somewhere?"

Jim felt his heart pound hard at the warmth in her voice, the need in her eyes—for his company. Her invitation was genuine. A hunger flowed through him. He ached to kiss Rachel. To steal the goodness of her for himself. Right now he felt impoverished, overwhelmed by the situation with his family, and he knew that by staying, he was only going to make things worse for himself when he did go home. His father expected him for dinner at 6:00 p.m. It was 5:30 now.

As Jim stood there, he felt Rachel's soft hand, so tentative, on his arm. Lifting his head, he held her compassionate gaze. "Yeah, I can stick around to help you. Let me make a phone call first."

Smiling softly, Rachel said, "Good."

CHAPTER SIX

JIM ENJOYED the quiet of the evening with Rachel. The fire was warm and cast dancing yellow light out into the living room, where they sat on the sofa together, coffee in hand. It had taken them several hours to get everything back in order and in place. Rachel had fixed them some sandwiches a little while ago—a reward for all their hard work. Now she sat on one end of the sofa, her long legs tucked beneath her, her shoes on the floor, a soft, relaxed look on her face.

Jim sat at the other end, the cup between his square hands. Everything seemed perfect to him—the quiet, the snowflakes gently falling outside, the beauty of a woman he was drawn to more and more by the hour, the snap and crackle of the fire, the intimacy of the dimly lit room. Yes, he was happy, he realized—in a way he'd never been before.

Rachel studied Jim's pensive features, profiled against the dark. He had a strong face, yet his sense of humor was wonderful. The kind of face that shouted of his responsible nature. Her stomach still hurt, they had laughed so much while working together. Really, Rachel admitted to herself, he was terribly desirable to her in every way. Rarely had she seen such a gentle nature in a man. Maybe it was because he was an EMT and dealt with people in crisis all the time. He was a far cry from her father, who had always been full of rage.

Maybe her new relationship with Jim was a good sign of her health—she was reaching out to a man of peace, not violence.

Pulling herself from her reverie, she said, "Did I ever tell you what made me slam on my brakes up there in the canyon?"

Jim turned and placed his arm across the back of the couch. "No. I think you said it was a cat."

Rachel rolled her eyes. "It wasn't a cougar. When I got home from E.R., I asked Jessica to bring me an encyclopedia. I lay there in bed with books surrounding me. I looked under *L* for leopard, and that wasn't what I saw. When I looked under *J* for jaguar..." She gave him a bemused look. "That was what I saw out there, Jim, in the middle of an ice-covered highway that morning—a jaguar." She saw the surprise flare in his eyes. "I thought I was hallucinating, of course, but then something very unusual—strange—happened."

"Oh?" Jim replied with a smile. He liked the way her mouth curved into a self-deprecating line. Rachel had no problem poking fun at herself—she was confident enough to do so. As she moved her hand to punctuate her story, he marveled at her effortless grace. She was like a ballet dancer. He wanted to say that she had the grace of a jungle cat—a boneless, rhythmic way of moving that simply entranced him.

"Jessica and Kate came in about an hour later to check on me, and when I showed them the picture in the encyclopedia, well, Jessica went bonkers!" Rachel chuckled. "She began babbling a mile a minute-you know how Jess can get when she's excited—and she told me the following story, which I've been meaning to share with you."

Interested, Jim placed his empty coffee cup on the

table. The peacefulness that surrounded Rachel was something he'd craved. Any excuse to remain in her company just a few minutes longer he'd take without apology. "Let's hear it. I like stories. I recall Mom always had a story for me at bedtime," he said wistfully, remembering those special times.

Sipping her coffee thoughtfully, Rachel decided to give Jim all the details Jessica had filled her in on since the day she'd come home from the hospital. "A while back, Morgan Trayhern and his wife, Laura, visited with us. They were trying to put the pieces of their lives back together after being kidnapped by drug lords from South America. An Army Special Forces officer by the name of Mike Houston was asked to come and stay with them and be their 'guard dog' while they were here with us. Dr. Ann Parsons, an M.D. and psychiatrist who worked for Morgan's company, Perseus, also stayed here." Rachel gestured to the north. "They each stayed in one of the houses here at the ranch.

"Jessica made good friends with Mike and Ann while we were here for the week following Kelly's funeral. At the time, I was too busy helping Kate to really get to know them, although we shared a couple of meals with them and I helped Morgan and Laura move into the cabin up in the canyon, where they stayed." She frowned slightly. "One of the things Jessica said was that she confided in Mike. She asked how he, one man, could possibly protect anyone from sneaking up on Morgan and Laura if they wanted to, the ranch was so large. I guess Mike laughed and said that he had a little help. Jessica pressed him on that point, and he said that his mother's people, the Quechua Indians, had certain people within their nation who had a special kind of medicine. 'Medicine,' as you know, means a skill or talent. He said he was born with jaguar medicine."

Laughing, Rachel placed her cup on the coffee table. The intent look in Jim's eyes told her he was fascinated with her story. He wasn't making fun of her or sitting there with disbelief written across his face, so she continued. "Well, this little piece of information really spurred Jessica on to ask more questions. You know how she is." Rachel smiled fondly. "As 'fate' would have it, Jessica's good friend, Moyra, who lived up in Vancouver, was also a member of a Jaguar Clan down in Peru. And, of course, Mike was stationed in Peru as a trainer for Peruvian soldiers who went after the drug lords and stopped cocaine shipments from coming north to the U.S. Jessica couldn't let this little development go, so she really nagged Mike to give her more information.

"Mike told her that he was a member of the Jaguar Clan. He teasingly said that down there, in Peru, they called him the Jaguar god. Of course, this really excited Jessica, who is into paranormal things big-time." Again, Rachel laughed softly. "She told Mike that Moyra had *hinted* that members of the Jaguar Clan possessed certain special 'powers.' Did he? Mike tried to tease her and deflect her, but she just kept coming back and pushing him for answers. Finally, one night, just before she left to go home to Canada, Mike told her that people born with Jaguar Clan blood could do certain things most other people could not. They could heal, for one thing. And when they touched someone they cared about or loved, that person could be saved—regardless of how sick or wounded he or she was. Mike admitted that he'd gotten his nickname out in the jungles fighting cocaine soldiers and drug lords. He told her that one time, one of his men got hit by a bullet and was bleeding to death. Mike placed his hand over the wound and, miraculously, it stopped bleeding. The man lived. Mike's legend grew. They said he could bring the dying back to life."

Fascinated, Jim rested his elbows on his knees and watched her shadowed features. "Interesting," he murmured.

"I thought so. But here's the really interesting part, Jim." She moved to where he was sitting, keeping barely a foot between them. Opening her hands, she whispered. "Jessica also told me more than once that Moyra had a jaguar spirit guardian. Jessica is very clairvoyant and she can 'see' things most of us can't. She told me that when Carl, her ex-husband, was stalking her, Moyra would know he was nearby. One afternoon, Jessica was taking a walk in the woods when she came to a creek and saw Moyra." Rachel shook her head. "This is going to sound really off-the-wall, Jim."

He grinned a little. "Hey, remember my mother was Apache. I was raised with a pretty spiritually based system of beliefs."

Rachel nodded. "Well, Jessica swears she saw Moyra standing in the middle of the creek, and then the next moment she saw a jaguar there instead!"

"Moyra turned into a jaguar?"

Rachel shrugged. "Jessica swears she wasn't seeing things. She watched this jaguar trot off across the meadow and into the woods. Jessica was so stunned and shocked that she ran back to the cabin, scared to death! When Moyra came in a couple hours later, Jessica confronted her on it. Moyra laughed, shrugged it off and said that shape-shifting was as natural as breathing to her clan. And wasn't it more important that she and her jaguar guardian be out, protecting Jessica from Carl?"

With a shake of his head, Jim studied Rachel in the firelight. How beautiful she looked! He wanted to kiss her, feel her ripe, soft lips beneath his mouth. Never had he wanted anything more than that, but he placed steely control over that desire. He liked the intimacy that was being established between them. If he was to kiss her, it might destroy that. Instead, he asked, "How does this story dovetail into your seeing that jaguar?"

Rachel laughed a little, embarrassed. "Well, what you didn't tell me was that there was a terrible accident a mile below where I'd crashed!"

He nodded. "That's right, there was. I didn't want to upset you."

Rachel reached out and laid her hand on his arm. She felt his muscle tense beneath her touch. Tingles flowed up her fingers and she absorbed the warmth of his flesh. Reluctantly, she withdrew her hand. The shadows played against his strong face, and she felt the heat of his gaze upon her, making her feel desired. Heat pooled within her, warm and evocative.

Clearing her throat, she went on. "Jessica was the one who put it all together. She thinks that the jaguar was protecting me from becoming a part of that awful wreck down the road. We calculated later that if I hadn't spun out where I did, I could easily have been involved in that fiery wreck where everyone was burned to death." Rachel placed her arms around herself. "I know it sounds crazy, but Jessica thinks the jaguar showed up to stop me from dying."

"You almost did, anyway," Jim said, scowling.

She relaxed her arms and opened her hands. "I never told you this, Jim. I guess I was afraid to—afraid you'd laugh at me. But I did share it with my sisters. Until you arrived, I kept seeing this jaguar. I saw it circle my car. I thought I was seeing things, of course." She frowned. "Did *you* see any tracks around the car?"

"I wasn't really paying attention," he said apologetically. "All my focus was on you, the stability of the car, and if there were any gas leaks."

Nodding, Rachel said, "Of course…"

"Well…" Jim sighed. "I don't disbelieve you, Rachel."

She studied him in the growing silence. "I thought you might think I was hallucinating. I *had* lost a lot of blood."

"My mother's people have a deep belief in shape-shifters—people who can turn from human into animal, reptile or insect form, and then change back into a human one again. I remember her sitting me on her knee and telling me stories about those special medicine people."

"Jessica thinks it was Moyra who came in the form of a jaguar to protect me until you could arrive on scene." She laughed a little, embarrassed over her explanation.

Jim smiled thoughtfully. "I think because we're part Indian and raised to know that there is an unseen, invisible world of spirits around us, that it's not really that crazy an explanation. Do you?"

Somberly, Rachel shook her head. "Thanks for not laughing at me about this, Jim. There's no question you helped save my life." She held his dark stare. "If it wasn't for you, I wouldn't be sitting here right now." She eased her hand over his. "I wish there was some way I could truly pay you back for what you did."

His fingers curled around her slender ones, as his

heart pounded fiercely in his chest. "You're doing it right now," he rasped, holding her soft, glistening gaze. The fact that Rachel could be so damned open and vulnerable shook Jim. He'd met so few people capable of such honest emotions. Most people, including himself, hid behind protective walls. Like Kate Donovan did, although she was changing, most likely softened because of her love for Sam McGuire.

Rachel liked the tender smile on his mouth. "Now that the weddings are over, I have a big job ahead of me," she admitted in a low voice. "My sisters are counting on me to bring in some desperately needed money to keep the ranch afloat." Looking up, she stared out the window. A few snowflakes twirled by. "If we don't get good snowfall this winter, and spring rains, we're doomed, Jim. There's just no money to keep buying the hay we need to feed the cattle because of the continued drought."

"It's bad for every rancher," he agreed. "How are you going to make money?"

She leaned back on the couch and closed her eyes, feeling content despite her worry. The natural intimacy she felt with Jim was soothing. "I'm going to go into Sedona on Monday to find an office to rent. I'm going to set up my practice as a homeopath."

"If you need patients, I'll be the first to make an appointment."

She opened her eyes and looked at him. He was serious. "I don't see anything wrong with you."

Grinning a little, he said, "Actually, it will be for my father, who has diabetes. Since meeting you, I did a little research on what homeopathy is and how it works. My father refuses to take his meds most of the time, unless I hand them to him morning and night."

"Can't your two brothers help out?" She saw his scowl, the banked anger in his eyes. Automatically, Rachel closed her fingers over his. She enjoyed his closeness, craved it, telling herself that it was all right. Part of her, however, was scared to death.

"Bo and Chet aren't responsible in that way," he muttered, sitting up suddenly. He knew he had to get home. He could almost feel his father's upset that he was still at the Donovan Ranch. Moving his shoulders as if to get rid of the invisible loads he carried, he turned toward Rachel. Their knees met and touched. He released her hand and slid his arm to the back of the couch behind her. The concern in her eyes for his father was genuine. It was refreshing to see that she could still feel compassion for his father, in spite of the feud.

"Your father's diabetes can worsen to a dangerous level if he doesn't consistently take his meds."

"I know that," Jim said wearily.

"You're carrying a lot of loads for your family, aren't you?"

Rachel's quietly spoken words eased some of the pain he felt at the entire situation. "Yes…"

"It's very hard to change three people's minds about life, Jim," she said gently.

One corner of his mouth lifted in a grimace. "I know it sounds impossible, but I have to try."

Feeling his pain and keeping herself from reacting to it the way she wanted to was one of the hardest things Rachel had ever done. In that moment, she saw the exhaustion mirrored in Jim's face, the grief in his darkened eyes.

"You go through hell over there, don't you?"

He shrugged. "Sometimes."

Rachel sat up. "You'll catch a lot of hell being over here for the wedding."

"Yes," he muttered, slowly standing up, unwinding his long, lean frame. It was time to go, because if he didn't, he was going to do the unpardonable: he was going to kiss Rachel senseless. The powerful intimacy that had sprung up between them was throbbing and alive. Jim could feel his control disintegrating moment by moment. If he didn't leave—

Rachel stood up and slipped her shoes back on her feet. "I'll walk you to the door," she said gently. Just the way Jim moved, she could tell he wasn't looking forward to going home. Her heart bled for him. She knew how angry and spiteful Old Man Cunningham could be. As Jim picked up his suit coat and shrugged it across his broad shoulders, Rachel opened the door for him, noticing how boyish he looked despite the suit he wore. He'd taken off the tie a long time ago, his open collar revealing dark hair on his chest.

They stood in the foyer together, a few inches apart. Rachel felt the power of desire flow through her as she looked up into his burning, searching gaze. Automatically, she placed her hand against his chest and leaned upward. In all her life she had never been so bold or honest about her feelings. Maybe it was because she was home, and that gave her a dose of security and confidence she wouldn't have elsewhere. Whatever it was, Rachel followed her heart and pressed her lips to the hard line of his mouth.

She had expected nothing in return from Jim. The kiss was one to assuage the pain she saw banked in his eyes—the worry for his father and the war that was ongoing in his family. Somehow, she wanted to soothe and heal Jim. He had, after all, unselfishly saved her life, giving his blood so that she might live. She told her frightened heart that this was her reason for kissing him.

As Rachel's soft lips touched his mouth, something wild and primal exploded within Jim. He reached out and captured her against him. For an instant, as if in shock, she stiffened. And then, just as quickly, she melted against him like a stream flowing gently against hard rock. Her kiss was unexpected. Beautiful. Necessary. He opened his mouth and melded her lips more fully against his. Framing her face with his hands, he breathed her sweet breath deep into his lungs. The knots in his gut, the worry over what was waiting for him when he got home tonight, miraculously dissolved. She tasted of sweet, honeyed coffee, of the spicy perfume she'd put on earlier for the wedding. Her mouth was pliant, giving and taking. He ran his tongue across her lower lip and felt her tremble like a leaf in a storm beneath his tentative exploration.

How long had it been since he'd had a woman he wanted to love? Too long, his lonely heart cried out. Too long. His craving for her warmth, compassion and care overrode his normal control mechanisms. Hungrily, Jim captured Rachel more fully against him. Her arms slid around his shoulders and he felt good and strong and needed once again. Just caressing the soft firmness of her cheek, his fingers trailing across her temple into the softness of her hairline, made him hot and burning all over. He felt her quiver as he grazed the outside curve of her breast, felt her melting even more into his arms, into his searching mouth as it slid wetly across her giving lips. He was a starving thief and he needed her. Every part and cell of her. His pulse pounded through him, the pain in his lower body building to an excruciating level.

Rachel spun mindlessly, enjoying the texture of his searching mouth as it skimmed and cajoled, his hands framing her face, his hard body pressing her against the door. She felt him trembling, felt his arousal against her lower body, and a sweet, hot ache filled her. It would be so easy to surrender to Jim in all ways. So easy! Her heart, however, was reminding her of the last time she'd given herself away. Fear began to encroach upon her joy. Fear ate away at the hot yearning of her body, her burning need for Jim.

"No…"

Jim heard Rachel whisper the word. Easing away from her lips, which were now wet and soft from his onslaught, he opened his eyes and looked down at her. Though her eyes were barely opened, he saw the need in them. And the fear. Why? Had he hurt her? Instantly, he pulled back. The tears in her eyes stunned him. He *had* hurt her! *Damn!* He felt her hands pressing against his chest, pushing him away. She swayed unsteadily and he cupped her shoulders. Breathing erratically, he held her gently. She lifted her hand to touch her glistening lips. A deep flush covered her cheeks and she refused to looked up at him.

Angry with himself for placing his own selfish needs before hers, he rasped, "I'm sorry, Rachel…."

Still spinning from the power of his kiss, Rachel couldn't find the right words to reply. Her heart had opened and she'd felt the power of her feelings toward Jim. Stunned in the aftermath of his unexpected response, she whispered, "No…." and then she couldn't say anything else. Rocking between the past and the present, she closed her eyes and leaned against the door.

"I shouldn't have done it," Jim said thickly. "I took advantage.... I'm sorry, Rachel...." Then he opened the door and disappeared into the dark, cold night.

Rachel was unable to protest Jim's sudden departure. She could only press her hand against her wildly beating heart and try to catch her breath. One kiss! Just one kiss had made her knees feel like jelly! Her heart had opened up like a flower, greedy for love, and she was left speechless in the wake of his branding kiss. When had *any* man ever made her feel like that? At the sound of the engine of a pickup in the distance, her eyes flew open. She forced herself to go out to the front porch. Wanting to shout at Jim, Rachel realized it was too late. He was already on the road leading away from the ranch, away from her.

She stood on the porch, the light surrounding her, the chill making her wrap her arms around herself. A few snowflakes twirled lazily down out of an ebony sky as she watched Jim drive up and out of the valley, the headlights stabbing the darkness. What had she done? Was she crazy? Sighing raggedly, she turned on her heel and went back into the ranch house.

As she quietly shut the huge oak door, she felt trembly inside. Her mouth throbbed with the stamp of Jim's kiss and she could still taste him on her lips. Moving slowly to the couch, she sat down before she fell down, her knees still weak in the aftermath of that explosive, unexpected joining. Hiding her face in her hands, Rachel wondered what was wrong with her. She couldn't risk getting involved again. She couldn't stand the possible loss; she remembered how badly things had ended the last time—all the fears that had kept her from happiness before threatened to ruin her relationship again. But Jim was so compelling she ached to have him, explore him and know him on every level. He was so unlike the rest of his family. He was a decent human being, a man struggling to do the right thing not only for himself, but for his misguided, dysfunctional family. With a sigh, she raised her head and stared into the bright flames of the fire. Remembering the hurt in his eyes when she'd stopped the kiss, she knew he didn't know why she'd called things to a halt. He probably thought it had to do with him, but it hadn't. Somehow, Rachel knew she had to see him, to tell him the truth, so that Jim didn't take the guilt that wasn't his.

Worriedly, Rachel sat there, knowing that he would be driving home to a nasty situation. Earlier, she'd seen the anguish in his eyes over his family. Taking a pillow, she pressed it against her torso, her arms wrapped around it. How she ached to have Jim against her once again! Yet a niggling voice reminded her that he had a dangerous job as an EMT. He went out on calls with the firefighters. Anything could happen to him, and he could die, just like… Rachel shut off the flow of her thoughts. Oh, why did she have such an overactive imagination? She sighed, wishing she had handled things better between her and Jim. He probably felt bad enough about her pushing him away in the middle of their wonderful, melting kiss. Now he was going to be facing a very angry father because he had been here, on Donovan property. Closing her eyes, Rachel released another ragged sigh, wanting somehow to protect Jim. But there was nothing she could do for him right now. Absolutely nothing.

"JUST WHERE THE HELL have you been?" Frank Cunningham snarled, wheeling his chair into the living room as Jim entered the ranch house at 9:00 p.m.

Trying to quell his ragged emotions, Jim quietly shut the door. He turned and faced his father. The hatred in Frank's eyes slapped at him. Jim stood in silence, his hands at his side, waiting for the tirade he knew was coming. Glancing over at the kitchen entrance, he saw Bo and Chet standing on alert. Bo had a smirk on his face and Chet looked drunker than hell. Inhaling deeply, Jim could smell the odor of whiskey in the air. What had they been doing? Plying their father with liquor all night? Feeding his fury? Playing on his self-righteous belief that Jim had transgressed and committed an unpardonable sin by spending time at the Donovans? Placing a hold on his building anger toward his two manipulative brothers, Jim calmly met his father's furious look.

"You knew where I was. I called you at five-thirty and told you I wouldn't be home for dinner."

Frank glared up at him. His long, weather-beaten fingers opened and closed like claws around the arms of the chair he was imprisoned in. "Damn you, Jim. You know better! I've begged you not to consort with those Donovan girls."

Jim shrugged tensely out of his coat. "They aren't girls, father. They're grown women. Adults." He saw Bo grin a little as he leaned against the door, a glass of liquor in his long fingers. "And you know drinking whiskey isn't good for your diabetes."

"You don't care!" Frank retorted explosively. "I drank because you went over there!"

"That's crap," Jim snarled back. "I'm not responsible for what you do. I'm responsible for myself. You're not going to push that kind of blame on me. Guilt might have worked when we were kids growing up, Father, but it doesn't cut it now." His nostrils quivered as he tried to withhold his anger. He saw his father's face grow stormy and tried to shield himself against what would come next. A part of him was so tired of trying to make things better around here. He'd been home nearly a year, and nothing had changed except that he was the scapegoat for the three of them now—just as he had been as a kid growing up after their mother's death.

"Word games!" Frank declared. He wiped the back of his mouth with a trembling hand. "You aren't one of us. You are deliberately going over to the Donovan place and consorting with them to get at me!"

Jim raised his gaze to Bo. "Who told you that, Father? Did Bo?"

Bo's grin disappeared. He stood up straight, tense.

Frank waved his hand in a cutting motion. "Bo and Chet are my eyes and ears, since I can't get around like I used to. You're sweet on Rachel Donovan, aren't you?"

Bo and Chet were both smiling now. Anger shredded Jim's composure as he held his father's accusing gaze.

"My private life is none of your—or their—business." He turned and walked down the hall toward his bedroom.

"You go out with her," Frank thundered down the hall, "and I'll disown you! Only this time for good, damn you!"

Jim shut the door to his bedroom, his only refuge. In disgust, he hung up his suit coat and looped the tie over the hangar. Breathing hard, he realized his hands were shaking—with fury. It was obvious that Bo and Chet had plied their father with whiskey, nursing all his anger and making him even more furious. Sitting down on the edge of his old brass bed, which creaked with his sudden weight, Jim slipped off his cowboy boots. Beginning at noon tomorrow, he was on duty for the next forty-eight hours. At least he'd be out of here and away from his father's simmering, scalding anger, his constant snipping and glares over his youngest son's latest transgression.

Undressing, Jim went to the bathroom across the hall and took a long, hot shower. He could hear the three men talking in the living room. Without even bothering to try and listen, Jim was sure it was about him. He wanted to say to hell with them, but it wasn't that easy. As he soaped down beneath the hot, massaging streams of water, his heart, his mind, revolved back to Rachel, to the kiss she'd initiated with him. He hadn't expected it. So why had she suddenly pushed him away? He didn't want to think it was because his last name was Cunningham. That would hurt more than anything else. Yet if he tried to see her when he got off duty, his family would damn him because she was a Donovan.

Scrubbing his hair, he wondered how serious Frank was about disowning him. The first time his father had spoken those words to him, when he was eighteen, Jim had felt as if a huge, black hole had opened up and swallowed him. He'd taken his father's words seriously and he'd left for over a decade, attempting to remake his life. Frank had asked him to come home for Christmas—and that was all.

Snorting softly, Jim shut off the shower. He opened the door, grabbed a soft yellow towel and stepped out. He knew Frank would follow through on his threat to kick out of his life—again. This time Jim was really worried, because neither Bo nor Chet would make sure Frank took his meds for his diabetic condition. If Jim wasn't around on a daily basis to see to that, his father's health would seriously decline in a very short time. He didn't want his father to die. But he didn't want to lose Rachel, either.

Rubbing his face, he drew in a ragged breath. Yes, he liked her—one helluva lot. Too much. How did a man stop his heart from feeling? From wanting? Rachel fit every part of him and he knew it. He sensed it. Could he give her up so that his father could live? What the hell was he going to do?

CHAPTER SEVEN

"DAMMIT all to hell," Chet shouted as he entered the ranch house. He jerked off his Stetson and slammed the door behind him. Dressed in a sheepskin coat, red muffler and thick, protective leather gloves, he headed toward his father, who had just wheeled into the living room.

Jim was rubbing his hands in the warmth of the huge, open fireplace at one end of the living room when Chet stormed in. His older brother had a glazed look in his eyes, a two-day beard on his cheeks and an agitated expression on his face.

"Pa, that dammed cougar has killed another of our cows up in the north pasture!" Chet growled, throwing his coat and gloves on the leather couch. "Half of her is missing. She was pregnant, too."

Frank frowned, stopped his wheelchair near the fireplace where Jim was standing. "We've lost a cow every two weeks for the last four months this way," he said, running his long, large-knuckled hands through his thick white hair.

As Jim turned to warm his back, Chet joined them at the fireplace, opening his own cold hands toward the flames. Chet's eyes were red and Jim could smell liquor on his breath. His brother was drinking like Frank used to drink before contracting diabetes, he realized with concern. Jim sighed. The last three days, since he'd come back from the Donovan wedding party, things had been tense around the house. He was glad his forty-eight hours of duty had begun shortly thereafter, keeping him on call for two days with the ambulance and allowing him to eat and sleep at the fire station down at Sedona. Luckily, things had been quiet, and he'd been able to settle down from the last major confrontation with his father.

"Have you seen the spoor, Chet?" Jim asked.

"Well, shore I have!" he said, wiping his running nose with the back of his flannel sleeve. "Got spoor all over the place. There's about a foot of snow up there. The tracks are good this time."

"We need to get a hunting party together," Frank growled at them. "I'm tired of losing a beef every other week to this cat."

"Humph, we're losin' two of 'em, Pa. That cat's smart—picks on two for one."

"You were always good at hunting cougar," Frank said, looking up at Jim. "Why don't you drive up there and see what you can find out? Arrange a hunting party?"

Jim was relieved to have something to do outside the house. Usually he rode fence line, did repairs and helped out wherever he could with ranching duties. His father had ten wranglers who did most of the hard work, but Jim always looked for ways to stay out of the house when he was home between his bouts of duty at the fire station.

"Okay. How's the road back into that north pasture, Chet?"

"Pretty solid," he answered, rubbing his hands briskly. "The temps was around twenty degrees out there midday. Colder than hell. No snow, but cold. We need the snow for the water or we're going to have drought again," he muttered, his brows moving downward.

"I'll get out of my uniform and go check on it," Jim told his father.

With a brisk nod, Frank added, "You find that son of a bitch, you shoot it on sight, you hear me? I don't want any of that hearts and flower stuff you try to pull."

Jim ignored the cutting jab as he walked down the darkened hall to his bedroom. Moving his shoulders, he felt the tension in them ease a little. In his bedroom, he quickly shed his firefighter's uniform and climbed into a pair of thermal underwear, a well-worn set of Levi's, a dark blue flannel shirt and thick socks. As he sat on the bed, pulling on his cowboy boots, his mind—and if he were honest, his heart—drifted back to Rachel and that sweet, sweet kiss he'd shared with her. It had been three days since then.

He'd wanted to call her, but he hadn't. He was a coward. The way she'd pulled away from him, the fear in her eyes, had told him she didn't like what they'd shared. He felt rebuffed and hurt. Anyone would. She was a beautiful, desirable woman, and Jim was sure that now that she was home for good, every available male in Sedona would soon be tripping over themselves to ask her out. Shrugging into his sheepskin coat, he picked up the black Stetson that hung on one of the bedposts, and settled it on his head.

As he walked out into the living room, he saw Chet and his father talking. In another corner of the room was a huge, fifteen-foot-tall Christmas tree. It would be another lonely Christmas for the four of them. As he headed out the door, gloves in hand, he thought about Christmas over at the Donovan Ranch. In years past, they'd invited in the homeless and fed them a turkey dinner with all the trimmings. Odula, their mother, had coordinated such plans with the agencies around the county, and her bigheartedness was still remembered. Now her daughters were carrying on in her footsteps. Rachel had mentioned that her sisters would be coming back on Christmas Eve to help in the kitchen and to make that celebration happen once again.

Settling into the Dodge pickup, Jim looked around. The sky was a heavy, gunmetal gray, hanging low over the Rim country. It looked like it might snow. He hoped it would. Arizona high country desperately needed a huge snow this winter to fill the reservoirs so that the city of Phoenix would have enough water for the coming year. Hell, they needed groundwater to fill the aquifer below Sedona or they would lose thousands of head of cattle this spring. His father would have to sell some of his herd off cheap—probably at a loss—so that the cattle wouldn't die of starvation out on the desert range.

Driving over a cattle guard, Jim noticed the white snow lying like a clean blanket across the red, sandy desert and clay soil. He enjoyed his time out here alone. Off to his left, he saw a couple of wranglers on horseback in another pasture, moving a number of cows. His thoughts wandered as he drove and soon Rachel's soft face danced before his mind's eyes. His hands tightened momentarily on the wheel. More than anything, Jim wanted to see Rachel again. He could use Christmas as an excuse to drop over and see her, apologize in person for kissing her unexpectedly. Though he knew he'd been out of line, his mouth tingled in memory of her lips skimming his. She'd been warm, soft and hungry. So why had she suddenly pushed away? Was it him? Was it the fact that he was a Cunningham? Jim thought so.

Ten miles down the winding, snow-smattered road, Jim saw the carcass in the distance. Braking, he eased up next to the partially eaten cow. The wind was blowing in fierce gusts down off the Rim and he pulled his hat down a little more tightly as he stepped out and walked around the front of the truck.

As he leaned down, he saw that the cow's throat was mangled, and he scowled, realizing the cat had killed the cow by grabbing her throat and suffocating her. There was evidence of a struggle, but little blood in the snow around her. Putting his hand on her, he found that she was frozen solid. The kill had to have occurred last night.

Easing up to his full height, he moved carefully around the carcass and found the spoor. Leaning down, his eyes narrowing, he studied them intently. The tracks moved north, back up the two-thousand-foot-high limestone and sandstone cliff above him. Somewhere up there the cat made his home.

Studying the carcass once again, Jim realized that though the cat had gutted her and eaten his fill, almost ninety percent of the animal was left intact and unmolested. That gave him an idea. Getting to his feet, he went back to the pickup, opened the door and picked up the mike on his radio to call the foreman, Randy Parker.

"Get a couple of the boys out here," Jim ordered when Randy answered, "to pick up this cow carcass. Put it in the back of a pickup and bring it to the homestead. When it gets there, let me know."

"Sure thing," Randy answered promptly.

Satisfied, Jim replaced the mike on the console. He

smiled a little to himself. Yes, his plan would work—
he hoped. Soon enough, he'd know if it was going to.

RACHEL WAS IN THE KITCHEN, up to her wrists in mashed
potatoes, when she heard a heavy knock at the front
door. Expecting no one, she frowned. "I'm coming!"
she called out, quickly rinsing her hands, grabbing a
towel and running through the living room. It was December 23, and she had been working for three days
solid preparing all the dishes for the homeless people's
Christmas feast. Her sisters would be home tomorrow,
to help with warming and serving the meal for thirty
people the following day.

When she opened the door, her eyes widened enormously. "Jim!"

He stood there, hat in hand, a sheepish look on his
face. "Hi, Rachel."

Stunned, she felt color race up her throat and into her
face. How handsome he looked. His face was flushed,
too, but more than likely it was from being outdoors in
this freezing cold weather. "Hi…." she whispered. The
memory of his meltingly hot kiss, which was never far
from her heart or mind, burned through her. She saw
his eyes narrow on her and she felt like he was looking
through her.

"Come in, it's cold out there," she said apologetically,
moving to one side.

"Uh…in a minute." He pointed to his truck, parked
near the porch. "Listen, we had a cow killed last night
by a cat. Ninety percent of it is still good meat. It's
frozen and clean. I had some of our hands bring it down
in a pickup. I brought it here, thinking that you might
be able to use the meat for your meal for the homeless
on Christmas Day."

His thoughtfulness touched her. "That's wonderful! I mean, I'm sorry a cougar killed your cow...but what a great idea."

Grinning a little, and relieved that she wasn't going to slam the door in his face, he nervously moved his felt hat between his gloved fingers. "Good. Look, I know you have a slaughter-freezing-and-packing area in that building over there. I'm not the world's best at carving and cutting, but with a couple of sharp knives, I can get the steaks, the roasts and things like that, in a couple of hours for you."

Rachel smiled a little. "Since we don't have any other hands around, I'd have to ask you to do it." She looked at him intently. "Are you *sure* you want to do that? It's an awful lot of work."

Shrugging, Jim said, "Want the truth?"

She saw the wry lift of one corner of his mouth. Joy surged through her. She was happy to see Jim again, thrilled that her display the other night hadn't chased him away permanently. "Always the truth," she answered softly.

Looking down at his muddy boots for a moment, Jim rasped, "I was looking for a way to get out of the house. My old man is on the warpath again and I didn't want to be under the same roof." He took a deep breath and then met and held her compassionate gaze. "More important, I wanted to come over here and apologize to you in person, and I had to find an excuse to do it."

Fierce heat flowed through Rachel. She saw the uncertainty in Jim's eyes and heard the sorrow in his voice. Pressing her hand against her heart, which pounded with happiness at his appearance, she stepped out onto the porch. The wind was cold and sharp.

"No," she whispered unsteadily, "you don't need to

apologize for anything, Jim. It's me. I mean…when we kissed. It wasn't your fault." She looked away, her voice becoming low. "It was me…my past…."

Stymied, Jim knew this wasn't the time or place to question her response. Still, relief flooded through him. "I thought I'd overstepped my bounds with you," he said. "I wanted to come over and apologize."

Reaching out, Rachel gripped his lower arm, finding the thick sheepskin of his coat soft and warm. "I've got some ghosts from my past that still haunt me, Jim."

The desire to step forward and simply gather her slender form against him was nearly his undoing. His arm tingled where she'd briefly touched him. But when he saw her nervousness, he held himself in check understood it. Managing a lopsided, boyish smile, he said, "Fair enough. Ghosts I can handle."

"I wish I could," Rachel said, rolling her eyes. "I'm not doing so well at it."

Settling his hat back on his head, he turned and pointed toward a building near the barn. "How about I get started on this carcass? I'll wrap the meat in butcher paper and put it in your freezer."

She nodded. "Fine. I'm up to my elbows in about thirty gallons of mashed potatoes right now, or I'd come over to help you."

He held up his hand. "Tell you what." Looking at the watch on his dark-haired wrist, he said, "How about if I get done in time for dinner, I take you out to a restaurant? You're probably tired of cooking at this point and you deserve a break."

Thrilled, Rachel smiled. "I'd love that, Jim. What a wonderful idea! And I can fill you in on my new office, which I rented today!"

He saw the flush of happiness on her face. It made

him feel good, and he smiled shyly. "Okay," he rasped, "it's a date. It's going to take me about four hours to carve up that beef." By then, it would be 7:00 p.m.

"That's about how much time I'll need to finish up in the kitchen." Rachel turned. "I've got sweet potatoes baking right now. Fifty of them! And then I've got to mash them up, mix in the brown sugar, top them with marshmallows and let them bake a little more."

"You're making me hungry!" he teased with a grin. How young Rachel looked at that moment. Not like a thirty-year-old homeopath, but like the girl with thick, long braids he remembered from junior high. Her eyes danced with gold flecks and he absorbed her happiness into his heart. The fact that Rachel would go to dinner with him made him feel like he was walking on air. "I'll come over here when I'm done?"

Rachel nodded. "Yes, and I'm sure you'll want to shower before we go."

"I'm going to have to." Now he was sorry he hadn't brought a change of clothes.

"Sam McGuire didn't take all his shirts with him on his honeymoon. I'll bet he'd let you borrow a clean one," she hinted with a broadening smile.

"I'm not going to fight a good idea," Jim said. He turned and made his way off the porch. He didn't even feel the cold wind and snow as he headed back to his truck. Rachel was going to have dinner with him. Never had he expected that. The words, the invitation, had just slipped spontaneously out of his mouth. Suddenly, all the weight he carried on his shoulders disappeared. By 7:00 p.m. he was going to be with Rachel in an intimate, quiet place. Never had he looked forward to anything more than that. And Jim didn't give a damn what the locals might think.

Jim took Rachel to the Sun and Moon Restaurant.
He liked this place because it was quiet, the service
was unobtrusive and the huge, black-and-white leather
booths surrounded them like a mother's embrace. They
sat in a corner booth; no one could see them and the
sense of privacy made him relax.

Rachel sat next to him, less than twelve inches
away, in a simple burgundy velvet dress that hung to
her ankles. It sported a scoop neck and formfitting long
sleeves, and she wore a simple amethyst pendant and
matching earrings. Her hair, thick and slightly curly,
hung well below her shoulders, framing her face and
accenting her full lips and glorious, forest-green eyes.

Jim had taken a hot shower and borrowed one of
Sam's white, long-sleeved work shirts. Jim had wanted
to shave but couldn't, so knew he had a dark shadow on
his face. Rachel didn't seem to care about that, however.

After the waitress gave them glasses of water and
cups of mocha latte, she left so they could look over
the menu.

"That burgundy dress looks good on you," Jim said,
complimenting Rachel.

She touched the sleeve of her nubby velvet dress.
"Thanks. It's warm and I feel very feminine in this. I
bought it over in England many years ago. It's like a
good friend. I can't bear to part with it." She liked the
burning look in his eyes—it made her feel desirable.
But she was scared, too, though. Jim was being every
bit the gentleman. She hungered for his quiet, steady
male energy. His quick wit always engaged her more
serious side and he never failed to make her laugh.

"I'm glad we have this time with each other," he told
her as he laid the menu aside. "I'd like to hear about

your years over in England. What you did. What it was like to live in a foreign country."

She smiled a little and sipped the frothy mocha latte, which was topped with whipped cream and cinnamon sprinkles. "First I want to hear how we came by this gift of beef you brought us." She set her cup aside.

Jim opened his hands. "It's the strangest thing, Rachel. For the last four months, about once every two weeks, a cat's been coming down off the Rim and killing one of the cows. My father's upset about it and he wants me to put together a hunting party and kill it."

"This isn't the first time we've had a cougar kill stock," Rachel said.

"That's true." He frowned and glanced at her. Even in the shadows, nothing could mar Rachel's beauty. He saw Odula's face in hers, those wide-set eyes, the broadness of her cheekbones. "But I'm not sure it's a cougar."

"What?"

Shaking his head, Jim muttered, "I saw the spoor for myself earlier today. We finally got enough snow up there so we had some good imprints of the cat's paws." He held up his hand. "I know cougar." Smiling slightly, he said, "My friends call me Cougar. I got that name when I was a teenager because I tracked down one of the largest cougars in the state. He had been killing off our stock for nearly a year before my father let me track him for days on end up in the Rim country." Scowling, he continued, "I didn't like killing him. In fact, after I did it, I swore I'd never kill another one. He was a magnificent animal."

"I saw the other night that you wear a leather thong around your neck," Rachel noted, gesturing toward the open collar of his shirt, which revealed not only the thong, but strands of the dark hair of his upper chest.

Jim pulled up the thong, revealing a huge cougar claw set in a sterling silver cap and a small medicine bag. "Yeah, my father had me take one of the claws to a Navajo silversmith. He said I should wear it. My mother's uncle, who used to come and visit us as kids, was a full-blood Apache medicine man. He told me that the spirit of that cougar now lived in me."

"Makes sense."

"Maybe to those of us who are part Indian," he agreed.

Rachel smiled and gazed at the fearsome claw. It was a good inch in length. She shivered as she thought of the power of such a cougar. "How old were you when you hunted that cougar?"

"Fifteen. And I was scared." Jim chuckled as he closed his hands around the latte. "Scared spitless, actually. My father sent me out alone with a 30.06 rifle, my horse and five days' worth of food. He told me to find the cougar and kill it."

"Your father had a lot of faith in you."

"Back then," Jim said wistfully. "Maybe too much." He gave her a wry look. "If I had a fifteen-year-old kid, I wouldn't be sending him out into the Rim country by himself. I'd want to be there with him, to protect him."

"Maybe your father knew you could handle the situation?"

Shrugging painfully, Jim sipped the latte. "Maybe." He wanted to get off the topic of his sordid past. "That spoor I saw today?"

"Yes?"

"I'm sure it wasn't a cougar's."

Rachel stared at him, her cup halfway to her lips. "What then?"

"I don't know *what* it is, but I know it's not what my father thinks. I took some photos of the spoor, measured it and faxed copies of everything to a friend of mine who works for the Fish and Game Department. He'll make some inquiries and maybe I can find out what it really is."

Setting the cup down, Rachel stared at him. "This is going to sound silly, but I had a dream the other night after we…kissed…."

"At least it wasn't a nightmare."

She smiled a little nervously. "No…it wasn't, Jim. It never would be." She saw the strain in his features diminish a little.

"What about this dream you had?"

"Being part Indian, you know how we put great stock in our dreams?"

"Sure," he murmured. "My uncle Bradford taught all of us boys the power of dreams and dreaming." Jim held her gaze. Reaching out, he slipped his hand over hers, to soothe her nervousness. "So, tell me about this dream you had."

Rachel sighed. His hand was warm and strong. "My mother, Odula, was a great dreamer. Like your uncle, she taught us that dreaming was very important. That our dreams were symbols trying to talk to us. Of course," she whispered, amused, "the big trick was figuring out what the dream symbology meant."

"No kidding." Jim chortled. He liked the fact that Rachel was allowing him to hold her hand. He didn't care who saw them. And he didn't care what gossip got back to his father. For the first time, Jim felt hopeful that his father wouldn't disown him again. Frank

Cunningham was too old, too frail and in poor health. Jim was hoping that time had healed some of the old wounds between them and that his father would accept that Rachel was a very necessary part of his life.

"Well," Rachel said tentatively, "I was riding up in the Rim country on horseback. I was alone. I was looking for something—someone...I'm not sure. It was a winter day, and it was cold and I was freezing. I was in this red sandstone canyon. As we rode to the end of it, it turned out to be a box canyon. I was really disappointed and I felt fear. A lot of fear. I was looking around for something. My horse was nervous, too. Then I heard this noise. My horse jumped sideways, dumping me in the snow. When I got to my feet, the horse was galloping off into the distance. I felt this incredible power surround me, like invisible arms embracing me. I looked up..." she held his intense gaze "...and you won't believe what I saw."

"Try me. I'm open to anything."

"That same jaguar that caused me to wreck the car, Jim." Leaning back, Rachel felt his fingers tighten slightly around her hand. "The jaguar was there, no more than twenty feet away from me. Only this time, I realized a lot more. I knew the jaguar was a she, not a he. And I saw that she was in front of a cave, which she had made into a lair. She was just standing there and looking at me. I was scared, but I didn't feel like she was going to attack me or anything."

"Interesting," Jim murmured. "Then what happened?" Noting the awe in Rachel's eyes as she spoke, he knew her story was more than just a dream; he sensed it.

"I felt as if I were in some sort of silent communication with her. I *felt* it here, in my heart. I know how strange that sounds, but I sensed no danger while I was with her. I could feel her thoughts, her emotions. It was weird."

"Sort of like…" he searched for the right words "…mental telepathy?"

"Why, yes!" Rachel stared at him. "Have you been dreaming about this jaguar, too?"

He grinned a little and shook his head. "No, but when I finally met and confronted that big male cougar, we stared at one another for a long moment before I fired the gun and killed him. I *felt* him. I felt his thoughts and emotions. It was strange. Unsettling. After I shot him, I sank to my knees and I cried. I felt terrible about killing him. I knew I'd done something very wrong. Looking back on it, if I had it to do all over again, I wouldn't have killed him. I'd have let him escape."

"But then your father, who's famous for his hunting parties, would have gotten a bunch of men together and hunted him down and treed him with dogs." Rachel shook her head. "No, Jim, you gave him an honorable death compared to what your father would have done. He'd have wounded the cat, and then, when the cougar dropped from the tree, he'd have let his hounds tear him apart." Grimly, she saw the pain in Jim's eyes and she tightened her fingers around his hand. "Mom always said that if we prayed for the spirit of the animal, and asked for it to be released over the rainbow bridge, that made things right."

He snorted softly. "I did that. I went over to the cougar, held him in my skinny arms and cried my heart out. He was a magnificent animal, Rachel. He knew I was going to kill him and he just stood there looking at me with those big yellow eyes. I swear to this day that I felt embraced by this powerful sense of love from him. I *felt* it."

"Interesting," she murmured, "because in my dream about this jaguar, I felt embraced by her love, too."

"Was that the end of your dream?"

"No," she said. "I saw the jaguar begin to change."

"Change?"

Rachel pulled her hand from his. She didn't want to, but she saw the waitress was taking an order at the next table and knew she'd soon come to take theirs. "Change as in shape-shifting. You told me last time we spoke that you knew something about that."

"A little. My uncle, the Apache medicine man, said that he was a shape-shifter. He said that he could change from a man into a hawk and fly anywhere he wanted, that he could see things all over the world."

"The Navajo have their skin-walkers," Rachel said in agreement, "sorcerers who change into coyotes and stalk the poor Navajo who are caught out after dark."

"That's the nasty side of shape-shifting," Jim said. "My uncle was a good man, and he said he used this power and ability to help heal people."

"My mother told us many stories of shape-shifters among her people, too. But this jaguar, Jim, changed into a woman!" Her voice lowered with awe. "She was an incredibly beautiful woman. Her skin was a golden color. She had long black hair and these incredible green eyes. You know how when leaves come out on a tree in early spring they're that pale green color?"

He nodded. "Sure."

"Her eyes were like that. And what's even more strange, she wore Army camouflage pants, black military boots, an olive-green, sleeveless T-shirt. Across her shoulders were bandoliers of ammunition. I kid you not! Isn't that a wild dream?"

He agreed. "Did she say anything to you?"

"Not verbally, no. She stood there and I could see her black boots shifting and changing back into the feet of the jaguar. She was almost like an apparition. I was so stunned by her powerful presence that I just stood there, too, my mouth hanging open." Rachel laughed. "I felt her looking *through* me. I felt as if she were looking for someone. But it wasn't me. I could feel her probing me mentally. This woman was very powerful, Jim. I'm sure she was a medicine woman. Maybe from South America. Then I saw her change back into the jaguar. And she was gone!" She snapped her fingers. "Just like that. Into thin air."

"What happened next?"

"I woke up." Rachel sighed. "I got up, made myself some hot tea and sat out in the living room next to the fireplace, trying to feel my way through the dream. You had kissed me hours before. I was wondering if my dream was somehow linked to that, to you."

Shrugging, Jim murmured, "I don't know. Maybe my friend at the Fish and Game Department will shed some light on that spoor print. Maybe it's from a jaguar." He gauged her steadily. "Maybe what you saw on the highway that day was real, and not a hallucination."

Rachel gave a little laugh. "It looked pretty physical and real to me. *If* it is a jaguar, what are you going to do?"

Grimly, Jim said, "Number one, I'm not going to kill it. Number two, I'll enlist the help of the Fish and Game Department to track the cat, locate its lair and then lay a trap to harmlessly capture it. Then they can take the cat out of the area, like they do the black bears that get too close to civilization."

Rachel felt happiness over his decision. "That's wonderful. If it is a jaguar, it would be a crying shame to shoot her."

He couldn't agree more. The waitress came to their table then, and once they gave her their orders, Jim folded his hands in front of him and caught Rachel's sparkling gaze. Gathering up his courage, he asked, "Could you use another hand on Christmas Day to help feed the homeless? Things are pretty tense around home. I'll spend Christmas morning with my father and brothers, but around noon, I want to be elsewhere."

"You don't have to work at the fire department?" Rachel's heart picked up in beat. More than anything, she'd love to have Jim's company. Kate would have Sam at her side, and Jessica would be working with Dan. It would be wonderful to have Jim with her. She knew Kate was settling her differences with Jim, so it wouldn't cause a lot of tension among them. Never had Rachel wanted anything more than to spend Christmas with Jim.

"I have the next three days off," he said. He saw hope burning brightly in Rachel's eyes. The genuine happiness in her expression made him feel strong and very sure of himself. "So, you can stand for me to be underfoot for part of Christmas Day?"

Clapping her hands enthusiastically, Rachel whispered, "Oh, yes. I'd love to have you with us!"

Moving the cup of latte in his hands, Jim nodded. "Good," he rasped. He didn't add that he'd catch hell for this decision. His father would explode in a rage. Bo and Chet would both ride him mercilessly about it. Well, Jim didn't care. All his life, he'd try to follow his heart and not his head. His heart had led him into wildfire fighting for nearly ten years. And then it had led him home, into a cauldron of boiling strife with his family. Now it whispered that with Rachel was where he longed to be.

As he saw the gold flecks in her eyes, he wanted to kiss her again—only this time he wanted to kiss her senseless and lose himself completely in her. She was a woman of the earth, no question. He was glad they shared a Native American background. They spoke the same language about the invisible realms, the world of spirit and the unseen. Jim never believed in accidents; he felt that everything, no matter what it was, had a purpose, a reason for happening. And the best thing in his life was occurring right now.

A powerful emotion moved through him, rocking him to the core. Could it be love? Studying Rachel as she delicately sipped her latte, her slender fingers wrapped around the cup, he smiled to himself. There was no doubt he loved her. The real question was did she love him? Could she? Or would she never be able to because she was a Donovan and he a Cunningham? Would Rachel always push him away because of all the old baggage and scars between their two families?

Jim had no answers. Only questions that ate at him, gnawed away at the burgeoning love he felt toward Rachel. He knew he had to take it a day at a time with her. He had to let her adjust to her new life here in Sedona. He had to use that Apache patience of his and slow down. Let her set the pace so she would be comfortable with him. Only then, Jim hoped, over time, she would grow to love him, and want him in her life as much as he wanted her.

CHAPTER EIGHT

RACHEL tried to appear unaffected by the fact that Jim Cunningham was in the kitchen of their home on Christmas Day. Both Kate and Jessica kept grinning hugely with those Cheshire-like smiles they always gave her when they knew something she didn't. Jim had arrived promptly at noon and set to work in the kitchen with the two men while the Donovan sisters served the sumptuous meal to thirty homeless people in their huge living room.

Christmas music played softly in the background and there was a roaring blaze in the fireplace. The tall timbers were wreathed in fresh pine boughs, and the noise of people laughing, talking and sharing filled the air. Rachel had never felt so happy as she passed from one table to another with coffeepot in hand, refilling cups. Among the people who had come were several families with children. Kate and Sam had gone to stores in Flagstaff and asked for donations of presents for the children. They'd spent part of their honeymoon collecting the gifts and then wrapping them.

Each child had a gift beside his or her plate. Each family would receive a sizable portion of Jim's beef to take back to the shelter where they were living. Jessica and Dan had worked with the various county agencies to see that those who had nowhere to go would have a roof over their head for the winter. Yes, this was what

Christmas was *really* all about. And it was a tradition
their generous, loving mother had started. It brought
tears to Rachel's eyes to know that Odula's spirit still
flowed strongly through them. Like their mother, the
three daughters felt this was the way to gift humanity
during this very special season.

The delight on the children's faces always touched
Rachel deeply. For some odd reason, whenever she
looked at a tiny baby in the arms of its mother, she
thought of Jim. She felt a warm feeling in her lower
body, and the errant, surprising thought of what it might
be like to have Jim's baby flowed deliciously through
her. With that thought, Rachel almost stumbled and
fell on a rug that had been rolled to one side. She felt
her face suffuse with heat. When she went back to the
kitchen to refill her coffee urn, she avoided the look that
Jim gave her as he busily carved up one of the many
turkeys. Dan was spooning up mash potatoes, gravy
and stuffing onto each plate that was passed down the
line. Sam added cranberries, Waldorf salad and candied
yams topped with browned marshmallows.

Rachel wished for some quiet time alone with
Jim. When he'd arrived, they were already in full
swing with the start of the dinner. The kiss they'd
shared, the intimacy of their last meal together,
all came back to her. She found herself wanting to
kiss him again. And again. Oh, how she wished her
past would disappear! If she could somehow move
it aside.... There was no question she desired Jim.
And she knew she wanted to pursue some kind of relationship with him. But fear was stopping her. And
it was giving him mixed signals. Sighing, Rachel
looked forward to the evening, when things would
quiet down and they would at last be alone. She had

her own house at the ranch, and she could invite Jim over for coffee later and they could talk.

"HECK OF A DAY," JIM SAID, sipping coffee at Rachel's kitchen table. Her house, which had been built many years ago by Kelly Donovan, was smaller than the other two he'd built for his daughters, but it was intimate and Jim liked that. Although Rachel had only recently moved into it, he could see her feminine touches to the pale pink kitchen. There were some pots on the windowsill above the sink where she had planted some parsley, chives and basil. The table was covered with a creamy lace cloth—from England, she'd told him.

"Wasn't it though?" Rachel moved from the stove, bringing her coffee with her. She felt nervous and ruffled as she looked at Jim. How handsome he was in his dark brown slacks, white cowboy shirt and bolo tie made of a cougar's head with a turquoise inset for the eye. His sleeves were rolled up from all the kitchen duty, the dark hair on his arms bringing out the deep gold color of his weathered skin.

"When you came in at noon, you looked pretty stressed out," Rachel said, sitting down. Their elbows nearly touched at the oval table. She liked sitting close to him.

With a shrug, Jim nodded. "Family squabble just before I left," he muttered.

"Your father didn't want you to come over here, right?" She saw the shadowy pain in his eyes as he avoided her direct look.

"Yeah, you could say that." Jim sipped his coffee grimly.

"And you have dark shadows under your eyes."

He grinned a little and looked at her. "You don't miss much, do you?"

"I'm trained to observe," Rachel teased. Placing her hands around the fine, bone china cup, she lost her smile. "Why do you stay at your father's house if it's so hard on you?"

Pain serrated Jim. His brows dipped. "I don't know anymore," he rasped. "I thought I could help make a difference, turn the family around, but no one wants to change. They want me to change into one of them and I'm not going to do it."

"In homeopathy, it's known as an obstacle to cure," Rachel said. "They don't want to change their dysfunctional way of living because it suits their purposes to stay that way." She gave Jim a tender look. "You wanted to be healthy, not dysfunctional, so you left as soon as you could and you stayed away until just recently. I've treated thousands of people over the years and I know from experience that if they don't want to leave the job, the spouse or the family that is causing them to remain sick or unhealthy, there's little I, a homeopathic remedy or anything else can do about it."

"Sort of like the old saying you can lead a horse to water but you can't make her drink?"

"Yes," Rachel replied with a sigh, trying to give him a smile. Jim looked exhausted. She had seen that look before when a person was tired to the bones with a struggle they were losing, not winning. She opened her hands tentatively. "So, what are your options? Could you move out and maybe see your father, whom you're worried about, from time to time?"

Rearing back on two legs of the chair, Jim gazed over at her. The lamp above the table softly lit Rachel's features. He was hungry for her compassion, her understanding of the circumstances that had him caught like a vise. He valued her insights, which were wise and deep. "I've been thinking about that," he admitted reluctantly. "Only, who will make sure my father takes his meds twice daily?"

"How long has your father had diabetes?"

"Ten years."

"And how did he survive that long without you being there to make sure he took his meds?"

Wryly, he studied her in the ensuing silence. "Touché."

"Could you find a house to rent in Sedona?"

"Maybe," he said. "I'll just have to see how it goes."

"What was the fight about before you left to come to our ranch?"

His mouth quirked. "Chet's all up in arms about this cat that killed the beef. He's whipping up Bo and my father into forming a hunting party tomorrow to go track the cat, tree it and kill it. I argued not to do that, to call the Fish and Game Department and work with them to trap the cat and take it somewhere else, into a less-populated area."

Rachel felt sudden fear grip her heart. "And what did they decide?"

Easing the chair down on all four legs, Jim muttered, "They're going out tomorrow morning to hunt the cat down and kill it."

She gasped. "No!"

"I'm with you on this." Again, he studied her. "After hearing your dream, and talking more to Jessica today, I'm convinced it's a jaguar up there on the Rim, not a cougar, Rachel. Jessica's sure that it's a shape-shifter. She's worried that it's Moyra, her friend, coming to check on her, on the family." Shrugging, he eased out of the chair and stood up, coffee cup in hand. "I don't know if I believe her or not, but it really doesn't matter. I don't care if it's a cougar or a jaguar—I don't want to see it treed and killed." Leaning his hip against the counter, he asked, "Want to come with me tomorrow to track the cat? I've got the day off. I called Bob Granby, my friend from the Fish and Game Department, and told him I was going to ride out early tomorrow, get a jump on my brothers' plan, and try to find the cat first. I'll be carrying a walkie-talkie with me. Bob promised that if I could locate the cat, he'd meet us, establish jurisdiction and make my family stop the hunt. Then we could lay out bait to lure the cat into a humane device."

Her heartbeat soared. "Yes, I'd love to go with you." Then she laughed a little. "I haven't thrown a leg over a horse in a long time, but that's okay. You know, Sam and Dan are good trackers, too. They could help."

Jim shook his head. "No. If my brothers saw them, they'd probably open fire on them. Besides, this is on Cunningham land and they don't want them trespassing. I can't risk a confrontation, Rachel."

"What about me? What if they see me with you?"

"That's a little different. They don't get riled with a woman. They will with a man, though. Some of the Old West ethics are still alive and well in them." He smiled briefly.

"Just tell me your plans," she said, "and I'll come with you."

"If you can pack us a lunch and dinner, I hope to be able to track the cat and locate it by no later than tomorrow afternoon. We'll have a two-hour head start on their hunting party. If we could use Donovan horses, that would keep what I'm doing a secret."

Rachel felt her stomach knot a little. "What will your

brothers do if they find out you've beat them to the punch on this?"

"Scream bloody blue murder, but that's all." Jim chuckled. "They've had enough tangles with the law of late. Neither of them wants to see the inside of a county jail again for a long time. Once they know I'm working for the Fish and Game Department, they'll slink off."

Sighing, Rachel nodded. "Okay, I'll let Kate know. I'm sure Sam will make sure we've got two excellent trail and hunting horses. I'll pack our food."

Jim nodded, then looked at his watch. It was nearly midnight. "I need to get going," he said reluctantly, not wanting to leave. Setting the coffee cup on the table, he reached into his back pocket and brought out a small, wrapped gift. "It's not much, but I wanted to give you something for Christmas."

Touched, Rachel took the gift, thrilling as their fingers met. "Why, thank you! I didn't expect anything...." She removed the bright red ribbon and the gold foil wrapping.

Jim felt nervous. Settling his hands on his hips, he watched the joy cross Rachel's face. Her eyes, her beautiful forest-green eyes, sparkled. It made him feel good. Better than he'd felt all day. Would Rachel like his gift? He hadn't had much time to find something in Sedona that he thought she might want. He hoped she'd like it at least.

Rachel gasped as the paper fell away. Inside were two combs for her hair. They were made of tortoiseshell, and each one had twelve tiny, rounded beads of turquoise across the top. Sliding her fingers over them, she saw they were obviously well crafted.

"These are beautiful," she whispered, as she gazed

up at his shadowed, worried features. "I've never seen anything like them...."

Shyly, Jim murmured, "I have a Navajo silversmith friend, and I went over to his house yesterday. You have such beautiful hair," he continued, gesturing toward her head. "And I knew he was working on a new design with hair combs." He smiled a little as he saw that she truly did treasure his gift. "When I saw these, I knew they belonged to you."

Without a word, Rachel got up and threw her arms around his neck, pressing herself to him. "Thank you," she quavered near his ear. She felt Jim tense for a moment, as if surprised, and then his arms flowed around her, holding her tightly, his hand sliding up her spine. Heat flared in her and she lifted her face from his shoulder to look up at him. His eyes were hooded and burning—with desire. Breathless and scared, Rachel felt the old fear coming up. She didn't care. She was in the arms of a man who was strong and good and caring. Although his gift was small, it was thoughtful and it touched her like little else could.

Closing her eyes, Rachel knew he was going to kiss her. Nothing had ever seemed so right! As her lips parted, she felt the powerful stamp of his mouth settle firmly upon hers and she surrendered completely to him, to his strong, caring arms and to the heat that exploded violently within her. His lips were cajoling and skimmed hers teasingly at first. She felt his moist breath against her cheek. The taste of coffee was present on his lips. His beard scraped her softer skin, sending wild tingles through her. His fingers moved upward, following the line of her torso, barely brushing the curvature of her firm breasts.

More heat built within her and she felt an ache between her thighs. How long had it been since she'd made love? Far too long. Her body screamed out for Jim's continued touch, for his hands to cup her breasts more fully, to touch and tease them. Instead, he slid his hand across her shoulders, up the slender expanse of her neck to frame her face. He angled her jaw slightly so that he could have more contact with her mouth. His tongue trailed a languid pattern of fire across her lower lip. She quivered violently. He groaned. Their breath mingled, hot, wild and swift. Her heart pounded in her breast as his mouth settled firmly over hers. She lost herself in the power of him as a man, in the cajoling tenderness he bestowed upon her, the give and take of his mouth upon hers and the sweet, hot wetness that was created between them.

Slowly, ever so slowly, Jim eased away from her mouth. Rachel wanted to cry out that she wanted more of him, of his touch. The dark gleam in his eyes showed the primal side of him, and she shivered out of need, wondering what it would be like to go all the way with Jim. She felt his barely leashed control, felt it in the tremble of his hands along the sides of her face as he continued to hungrily press her into himself in those fragile moments strung between them.

"If I don't go now," he told her thickly, "I won't leave...." The pain in his lower body attested to his need of Rachel. She was soft, supple and warm in his arms. He saw the drowsy look in her eyes, how much his capturing kiss had affected her. Gently, he ran his hands across her crown and down the long, thick strands of her hair. She swayed unsteadily, and he held her carefully in his arms. It was too soon, his mind shrilled at him. Rachel had to have time to get to know him. And vice versa. He'd learned patience a long time ago when it came to relationships. And more than anything, Jim wanted his relationship with Rachel to develop naturally, and not become a pressure to her. When he saw the question in her gaze, he knew he'd made the right decision. Despite the desire burning in her eyes, he also saw fear banked in their depths. She was afraid of something. Him? Her past? Maybe a man she had known in England. That thought shattered him more than any other. Yes, he had to back off and find out more about her and what she wanted out of life— and if he figured in her dream at all.

Easing away, he smiled a little. "We're going to be getting up at the crack of dawn to leave. We need to get some sleep." What Jim really wanted was to sleep with Rachel in his arms. But he didn't say that.

"Yes…" Rachel whispered, her voice faint and husky. She wanted Jim to stay, and the words were almost torn from her. But it wouldn't be fair to him—or her. If she was lucky, maybe tomorrow, as they tracked the cat, she could share her fears, her hopes and dreams with him.

THE SNORT OF THE HORSES, the jets of white steam coming from their nostrils, were quickly absorbed by the thick pine forest that surrounded them as Rachel rode beside Jim. They had been in the saddle for nearly three hours and the temperature hovered in the low thirties up on the Rim. Bundled up, Rachel had never felt happier. And she knew why. It was because she was with Jim. They had spoken little since he'd started tracking. The spoor was still visible, thanks to the snow that hadn't yet melted off the Rim. Down below on the desert floor, the drifts had already disappeared.

Jim rode slightly ahead on a big black Arabian geld-

ing. There was a rifle in the leather case along the right
side of his saddle, beneath his leg. Rachel knew he
didn't want to use it, but if the cat attacked, they had
to defend themselves. It was a last resort. His black
Stetson was drawn low across his brow as he leaned
over the horse, looking for spoor. There weren't many,
and Rachel was amazed at how well he could track on
seemingly nothing. Occasionally he'd point out a tiny
broken twig on a bush, a place where the snow had
melted, a part of an imprint left in the pine needles—
rocks that she wouldn't have seen without Jim's exper-
tise.

Unable to get their heated kiss out of her head,
Rachel waited for the right time to talk to him. Right
now, he needed silence in order to concentrate. They
were two hours ahead of his family's hunting party. Bo
and Chet weren't great at tracking, and Jim hoped his
brothers would lose the trail, anyway.

He held up his hand. "Let's stop here for a bite to
eat." He twisted around in the saddle, resting his hand
on the rump of his gelding. Rachel was beautiful in
her dark brown Stetson. She had a red wool muffler
wrapped around her neck, and she wore a sheepskin
jacket, Levi's, boots and thick, protective gloves. He
was glad she'd dressed warmly, even though the temperature was rising and he was sure it would get over
thirty-two degrees in the bright sunshine. Dismount-
ing, he dropped the reins on the gelding, knowing that a
ground-tied horse, once the reins were dropped, would
not move.

Coming around, he held out his hands to Rachel,
placing them around her waist and lifting her off the
little gray Arabian mare she rode. He saw surprise and
then pleasure in her eyes as she settled her own hands

trustingly on his upper arms while he gently placed her feet on the ground. It would have been so easy to lean down and take her ripe, parted lips, so easy… Tearing himself out of that mode, Jim released her.

"What have you brought for us to eat?" He took the horses and tied them to a nearby tree. The trail had led them into a huge, jagged canyon of red-and-white rock. Noticing a limestone cave halfway up on one wall, he realized it was a perfect place for a cat to have a lair.

Rachel felt giddy. Jim's unexpected touch was exhilarating to her. Taking off her gloves, she opened up one of the bulging saddlebags. "I know this isn't going to be a surprise to you. Turkey sandwiches?"

Chuckling, Jim grinned and came and stood next to her. "We'll sit over there," he said. There were some black lava rocks free of snow that had dried in the sunlight. "I like turkey."

"I hope so." Rachel laughed softly. She purposely kept her voice low. When tracking, making noise wasn't a good idea.

"Come on," he urged, taking the sandwich wrapped in tinfoil. "Let's rest a bit. Your legs have to be killing you."

Rachel was happy to sit with her back against his on the smooth, rounded surface of the lava boulder. It was a perfect spot, the sunlight lancing down through the fir, spotlighting them with warmth. She removed her hat and muffler and opened up her coat because it was getting warmer. Picking up her sandwich, she found herself starved. Between bites, she said, "My legs feel pretty good. I'm surprised."

"By tonight," he warned wryly, "your legs will be seriously bowed."

She chortled. "That's when I take Arnica for sore muscles."

He grinned and ate with a contentment he'd rarely felt. The turkey tasted good. Rachel had used a seven-grain, homemade brown bread. Slathered with a lot of mayonnaise and a little salt on the turkey, the sandwich tasted wonderful. Savoring the silence of the forest, the warmth of the sun, the feel of her resting against his back and left shoulder, he smiled.

"This is the good life."

Rachel nodded. "I love the peace of the forest. As a kid, I loved coming up on the Rim with my horse and just hanging out. When I was in junior high and high school, I was in the photography club, so I used to shoot a lot of what I thought were 'artistic' shots up here." She laughed and shook her head. "The club advisor, a teacher, was more than kind about my fledgling efforts."

Smiling, Jim said, "I almost joined the photography club because you were in it."

Her brows arched and she twisted around and caught his amused gaze. "You're kidding me!"

"No," he said, holding up his hand. "Honest, I had a crush on you for six years. Did you know that?"

Even though he'd already confessed his boyhood crush, his words still stunned her. Maneuvering around so that she sat next to him, their elbows touching, she finished off her sandwich and leaned down to wipe her fingers in the snow and pine needles to clean them off. "I still can't believe you had a crush on me."

"Why is that so hard to believe? I thought you were the prettiest girl I'd ever seen." And then his smile softened. "You still are, Rachel."

Her heart thumped at the sincerity she heard in Jim's

voice, and the serious look she saw on his face. "Oh," she said in a whisper, "I never knew back then, Jim...."

Chuckling, he took a second sandwich and unwrapped it. "Well, who was going to look at a pimply faced teenager? I wasn't the star running back of the football team like Sam was. I was shy. Not exactly good-looking. More the nerd than the sports-hero type." He chuckled again. "You always had suitors who wanted your attention."

"Well," she began helplessly, "I didn't know..."

He caught and held her gaze. "Let's face it," he said heavily, "back then, as kids, we wouldn't have stood a chance anyway. You were a hated Donovan. If my father had seen me get interested in you, all hell would've broken loose."

Glumly, Rachel agreed. "He'd have probably beaten you within an inch of your life. Come to think of it, so would my dad."

"Yeah, two rogue stallions against one scrawny teenage kid with acne isn't exactly good odds, is it?"

Laughing a little, Rachel offered him some of the corn chips she'd bagged up for them. Munching on the salty treat, she murmured, "No, that's not good odds. Maybe it's just as well I didn't know, then...."

The silence enveloped them for a full five minutes before either spoke again. Rachel wiped the last of the salt and grease from the chips off on her Levi's. There was something lulling and healing about being in a forest. It made what she wanted to share with Jim a little easier to undertake. Folding her hands against her knees, she drew them up against her.

"When I moved to England, a long time ago, Jim, I went over there to get the very best training possible to become a homeopath. I had no desire to live at the ranch. I knew my mother wanted all of us girls to come home, but none of us could stomach Kelly's drinking habits." She shook her head and glanced at Jim. His eyes were dark and understanding. "I loved my mother so much, but I just couldn't bring myself to come back home after I graduated from four years' training at Sheffield College. I went on to become a member of the Royal Society of Homeopaths and worked with several M.D.s at a clinic in London. I really loved my work, and how homeopathy, which was a natural medicine, could cure terrible illnesses and chronic diseases.

"I was very good at what I did, and eventually, the administrator at Sheffield College asked me to come back and teach. They offered me not only a teaching position, but said I could write a book on the topic and keep practicing through clinic work at their facility."

"It sounds like a dream come true for you," Jim said.

"Well, it was even more than that," she said ruefully, leaning down and picking up a damp, brown pine needle. Stroking it slowly with her fingertip, she continued, "I met Dr. Anthony Armstrong at the clinic. He was an M.D. Over time, we fell in love." She frowned. "Because of my past, my father, I was really leery of marriage. I didn't want to get trapped like my mother had been. Tony was a wonderful homeopath and healer. We had so much in common. But I kept balking at setting a wedding date. This went on for five years." Rachel shook her head. "I guess you could say I was gun-shy."

Jim's heart sank. "You had good reason to be," he answered honestly. "Living with Kelly was enough to make all three of you women gun-shy of marriage and of men in general." And it was. Jim had feared Kelly himself. Nearly anyone with any sense had. The man had been unstable. He'd blow up and rage at the slightest indiscretion, over things that didn't warrant such a violent reaction. As much as Jim tried to imagine what it had been like for Rachel and her sisters, he could not. What he did see, however, was the damage that it had done to each of them, and he realized for the first time how deeply wounded Rachel had been by it as well.

"I was scared, Jim," she said finally, the words forced out from between her set lips. "Tony was a wonderful friend. We loved homeopathy. We loved helping people get well at the clinic. We had so much in common," she said again.

"But did you love him?"

Rachel closed her eyes. Her lips compressed. "Do you always ask the right question?" She opened her eyes and studied Jim's grave face. His ability to see straight through her, to her core, was unsettling but wonderful. Rachel had never met a man who could see that deep inside her. And she knew her secret vulnerabilities were safe with Jim.

"Not always," Jim murmured, one corner of his mouth lifting slightly, "but I try, and that's what counts." Seeing the fear and grief in Rachel's eyes, he asked gently, "So what happened? Did you eventually marry him?"

Allowing the pine needle to drop, she whispered, "No…I was too scared, Jim. Tony and I—well, we were good friends. I gradually realized I really didn't love him—not like he loved me. Maybe, in my late twenties, I was still gun-shy and wasn't sure about love, or what it was really supposed to be. I had a lot of phone conversations with my mother about that. I just wasn't sure what love was."

Seeing the devastation on Rachel's face, hearing the

apology in her husky voice, he bit back the question that whirled in his head: *And now? Do you know what love is? Do you know that what we have is love?* "Time heals old wounds," he soothed. "I've seen it for myself with my father. When I left at age eighteen, I hated him. It took me ten years to realize a lot of things, and growing up, maturing, really helped."

"Doesn't it?" Rachel laughed softly as she lifted her head and looked up at the bright blue sky. The sunlight filtered delicately down among the fir boughs, dancing over the snow patches and pine needles.

"That's why I came home. Blood is thicker than water. I thought I could help, but I haven't been able to do a damned thing." Ruefully, he held her tender gaze. "The only good thing that's happened out of it is meeting you again."

Her throat tightened with sudden emotion and she felt tears sting the backs of her eyes. Her voice was off-key when she spoke. "When I became conscious in that wreck and saw you, your face, I knew I was going to be okay. I didn't know how, but I knew that. You had such confidence and I could feel your care. You made me feel safe, Jim, in a way I've never felt safe in my life." She tried to smile, but failed. Opening her hands, Rachel pushed on, because if she didn't get the words out, the fear would stop her from ever trying again.

"I know we haven't known each other long, but I feel so good around you. I like your touch, your kindness, the way you treat others. There's nothing not to like about you." She laughed shyly. Unable to meet his gaze because she was afraid of what she might see, she went on. "I'm so afraid to reach out...to—to like you...because of my past. I hurt Tony terribly. I kept the poor guy hanging on for five years thinking that I could remake myself, or let go of my paranoia about marriage, my fear of being trapped by it. I thought it would go away with time, but that didn't happen. I felt horrible about it. That poor man waited in hope for five years for me to get my act together—and I never did." Sorrowfully, Rachel turned and met Jim's gaze. It took the last of her courage to do that because he deserved no less than honesty from her.

"Now I've met you. And what I feel here—" she touched her heart with her hand "—is so strong and good and clean that I wake up every morning happy, so happy that I'm afraid it's all a dream and will end. That's stupid, I know. I know better than that. It's not a dream...."

Gently, Jim turned and captured her hands in his. "Maybe it's a dream that's been there all along, but due to life and circumstances, you couldn't dream it—until now?"

Just the tenderness of his low voice made her vision blur with tears. Rachel hung her head. She felt Jim's hands tighten a little around hers. "I'm so scared, Jim... of myself, of how I feel about you...of the fact that your family would come unglued if—if I let myself go and allow the feelings I have for you to grow. I'm scared of myself. I wonder if I'll freeze again like I did with Tony. I don't want to hurt anyone. I don't want to make you suffer like I did him."

"Listen to me," Jim commanded gruffly as he placed his finger beneath Rachel's chin, making her look up at him. Tears beaded her thick, dark lashes and there was such misery in her forest-green eyes. "Tony was a big boy. He knew the score. You weren't teenagers. You were adults. And so are we, Rachel." Jim slid his hand across the smooth slope of her cheek. "I know you're scared. Now I know why. That's information that can help us make decisions with each other." He brushed several strands of dark hair away from her delicate ear. "I couldn't give a damn that my last name is Cunningham and yours is Donovan. The feud our fathers and grandfathers waged with one another stops here, with us. We aren't going to fight anymore. It's this generation that has to begin the healing. I know you know that. So does Kate and Jessica. My family doesn't—not yet. And maybe they never will. But I can't live my life for them. I have to live my life the way I think it should go."

Rachel closed her eyes as he stroked her cheek. His hand was roughened from hard work, from the outdoors, and she relished his closeness, his warmth.

"I guess," Jim rasped in a low voice, "I never got over my crush on you, Rachel." He saw her eyes open. "What I felt as an awkward, gawky teenager, I feel right now. When I saw it was you trapped in that car, I almost lost it. I almost panicked. I was so afraid that you were going to die. I didn't want you to leave me." He shook his head and placed his hand over hers again. "When you needed that rare blood type, and I had the same type, I knew something special was going down. I knew it here, in my heart. I was glad to give my blood to you. For me, with my Apache upbringing, I saw it symbolically, as if the blood from our two families was now one, in you." He gazed into her green eyes and hoped she understood the depth of what he was trying to share with her.

"In a way, we're already joined. And I want to pursue what we have, Rachel—if you want to. I'm not here to push you or shove you. You need to tell me if I have a chance with you."

CHAPTER NINE

BEFORE Rachel could answer, both horses suddenly snorted and started violently. Jim and Rachel jumped to their feet and turned toward the fir tree, where the horses were firmly tied and standing frozen, their attention drawn deeper into the canyon.

Rachel's eyes widened enormously and her heart thudded hard in her chest. There, no more than a hundred feet away on the wall of the canyon next to the cave, stood a huge, stocky jaguar. The cat switched its tail, watching them.

Jim moved in front of her, as if to protect her. She could feel the fine tension in his body, and she gasped. The jaguar was real! Though the cat was a hundred feet above them and unable to leap toward them, her emotions were screaming in fear.

"Don't move," Jim rasped. His eyes narrowed as he slowly turned and fully faced the jaguar. For some reason, he sensed it was a female, just as in Rachel's dream. The cat was positively huge! He'd seen photos and films of jaguars, but never one in the wild. They were a lot stockier than the lithe cougar and weighed a helluva lot more. The cat's gold-and-black fur looked magnificent against the white limestone cliff. Between her jaws was a limp jackrabbit she'd obviously brought back to her lair to enjoy.

The snort of the horses echoed warningly down the

canyon walls and Jim automatically put his arm out, as if to stop Rachel from any forward movement. He felt her hand on the back of his shoulder.

Rachel was mesmerized by the stark beauty of the jaguar as the cat lowered her broad, massive head and gently placed the dead rabbit at her feet. Looking down at them as if she were queen of all she surveyed and they mere subjects within her domain.

"She's beautiful!" Rachel whispered excitedly. "Look at her!"

Jim barely nodded. He was concerned she would attack. Fortunately, both horses were trained for hunting and were able to stand their ground rather than tear at their reins to get away—which any horse in its right mind would have done under the present circumstances. He estimated how long it would take to reach his gelding, unsnap the leather scabbard, pull out the rifle, load it and aim it. The odds weren't in his favor.

"She's not going to harm us," Rachel whispered. Moving closer to Jim, their bodies nearly touching as she dug her fingers into his broad shoulder. "This is so odd, Jim. I feel like she's trying to communicate with us. Look at her!"

He couldn't deny what Rachel had voiced. The cat lazily switched her tail, but showed no sign of alarm at being so near to them. Instead, she eased to the ground, the rabbit between her massive front paws. Sniffing the morsel, she raised her head and viewed them again.

"Listen to me, Rachel," Jim said in a very low voice, keeping his eyes on the jaguar. "I want you to slowly back away from me. Mount your horse and, as quietly as you can, *walk* it out of the canyon. Once you get down the hill, take the walkie-talkie you have in the saddlebag and make a call to Bob. Tell him we've located the cat and it's a jaguar. The walkie-talkie won't work up here in the fir trees. You need an open area. It might take you fifteen minutes to ride down this slope to the meadow below. Call him and then wait for him down there. I know he's on 89A waiting for us. He can drive through the Cunningham ranch. Tell him to go to the northernmost pasture. We'll meet him there."

"What are you going to do?"

"Stay here."

Alarmed, Rachel asked, "Why? Why not come with me?"

"Because if she wants to charge someone, I'd rather it be me, not you." He reached behind him and his hand found her jean-clad thigh. Patting her gently, he said, "Go on. I'll come down the hill fifteen minutes from now. I just want to give you a head start. The cat isn't going to follow you if she has me here. Besides, she's eating her lunch right now. If she's starving, that rabbit will put a dent in her appetite and she'll be far less likely to think of us as a meal."

Rachel understood his logic. "Okay, I'll do it." Her heart still pounded, but it wasn't fear she felt in the jaguar's presence, just a thrilling excitement.

He nodded slowly. "I'll see you in about twenty minutes down below in that meadow?"

Compressing her lips, Rachel reached out and squeezed his hand. "Yes," she said. "*You* be careful."

He smiled tensely. "I don't get any sense she's going to attack us."

"Me neither." Rachel released his shoulder. "She's so beautiful, Jim! And she's the one I saw standing in the middle of 89A. I'd swear it because I remember that black crescent on her forehead. I thought it looked odd, out of place there. It's impossible that two jaguars would have that same identical marking, isn't it?"

"Yeah, they're all marked slightly different," he agreed. "Sort of like fingerprints, you know?" He felt safe enough to turn his head slightly. Rachel's eyes were huge and full of awe as she gazed up on the cliff wall at the cat. Her cheeks were deeply flushed with excitement. Hell, he was excited, too.

"I think this is wonderful!" she gushed in a low voice. "The jaguars are back in Arizona!"

Chuckling a little, Jim said, "Well, *some* people will be thrilled with this discovery and others won't be. Like my family. Now we know who's been eating a beef every two weeks."

Frowning, Rachel sighed. "Thank goodness the Fish and Game Department will capture her and take her someplace where she won't get killed by man."

"I talked to Bob this morning. He said jaguars were not only protected in South and Central America, but that they would be federally protected here if they ever migrated far enough north to cross the border."

"Well," Rachel said, "she certainly has. It's nice to know she can't be shot by your brothers, though they'd probably do it anyway if they had the chance, I'm sorry to say."

Glumly, Jim agreed. "No argument there. Better get going."

She patted his shoulder. "This whole day has been an incredible gift. I'll see you in about twenty minutes." Then she slowly backed away from him.

Jim tensed when the jaguar snapped up her head as Rachel began to move. Would the cat attack? Run away? He watched, awed by the beauty and throbbing power that seemed to emanate from the animal. She

agnificent beast—so proud and queenly in the
ay she lifted her head to observe them. As Rachel
mounted her horse and walked it out of the canyon, the
cat flicked its tail once and then resumed eating her
kill.

Recalling the time he'd hunted and trapped the
mountain lion up here on the Rim, Jim realized this
was a far cry from that traumatic event. Glancing down
at his watch, he decided to give Rachel twenty minutes
before he mounted up to go back down the slope and
join her in the meadow. If the truth be known, he savored this time with the jaguar. He felt privileged and
excited. This time he didn't have to kill, as he had with
the mountain lion. The memory caused shame to creep
through him as he stood there observing the jaguar.
After he'd killed the cougar, his father had slapped him
on the back, congratulating him heartily. Jim had felt
like crying. He'd killed something wild and beautiful
and had seen no sense to it.

His Apache mother had given each of her sons an
Apache name when they were born. Even though it
wasn't on his birth certificate, she'd called him Cougar.
He remembered how she had extolled his cougar medicine, and how she made him realize how important it
was. Even though he'd only been six years old when
she died, her passionate remarks had made a lasting
impression on him.

The past unfolded gently before him as he stood
there. His mother had always called him Cougar because Jim was a white man's name, she'd told him teasingly. In her eyes and heart, he was like the cougar, and
he knew he would learn how to become one because
the cougar was the guardian spirit that had come into
this life with him. Jim recalled the special ceremony

his mother's people had had for him when he was five years old. Since she was Chiricahua, they'd traveled back to that reservation and her people had honored him. The old, crippled medicine man had given him a leather thong with a small beaded pouch attached to it. Inside the pouch was his "medicine."

To this day, Jim wore that medicine bag around his neck. The beading had long ago fallen off and he'd had to change the leather thong yearly. Whether it was crazy or not, Jim had worn that medicine bag from the day it had been placed on him during that ceremony. The medicine man had told him that the fur of a cougar was in the bag, that it was his protector, teacher and guardian. Sighing, Jim looked down at the rapidly melting midday snow. Maybe that was why that mountain lion never charged him when he came upon him that fateful day so long ago. The cat had simply looked at him through wise, yellow eyes and waited. It was as if he knew Jim had to kill him, so he stood there, magnificent and proud, awaiting his fate.

Suddenly Jim felt as if the claw he wore next to his small medicine bag was burning in his chest. Without thinking, Jim rubbed that area of his chest. He wondered if this jaguar sensed his cougar medicine. He knew that the great cats were related to one another. Was that why she chose not to charge him? His Anglo side said that was foolish, but his Apache blood said that he was correct in this assumption. The jaguar saw him as one of them. She would not kill one of her own kind. And then a crazy smile tugged at a corner of Jim's mouth. Rachel must have jaguar medicine, for it was this cat that had saved her from a fiery death at the accident that occurred less than a mile down the road. It was this cat that had leaped into the middle of the highway to stop her.

With a shake of his head, he knew life was more mystical than practical at times. He recalled the dream Rachel had had of the jaguar turning into a warrior woman. Gazing up at the animal, he smiled. There was no question he was being given a second chance. This time he wasn't going to kill. He was going to trap her and have her taken to an area where no Anglo's rifle could rip into her beautiful gold-and-black fur.

Remembering Rachel, he glanced at his watch. To his surprise, fifteen minutes had already flown by! Jim wished he could slow down time and remain here, just watching the jaguar, who had finished her meal and was licking one paw with her long, pink tongue.

RACHEL HAD JUST REACHED the snow-covered meadow when to her horror she saw two cowboys emerge from the other end of it. Halting her horse, she realized it was Bo and Chet Cunningham and they had spotted her. Hands tightening on the reins, Rachel was torn by indecision. Should she try and outrun them? Her horse danced nervously beneath her, which wasn't like the animal at all. When she saw the rifles they carried on their saddles and the grim looks on their unshaven faces, she felt leery and decided to stand her ground. When the two men saw her, they spurred their mounts forward, the horses slipping and sliding as they thundered across the small meadow.

"Who the hell are you?" Bo demanded, jerking hard on the reins when he reached her. His horse grunted, opened its mouth to escape the pain of the bit and slid down on its hindquarters momentarily.

Rachel's horse leaped sideways. Steadying the

animal, she glared at Bo. The larger of the two brothers, he looked formidable in his black Stetson, sheepskin coat and red bandanna. Danger prickled at Rachel and she put a hand on her horse's neck to keep him calm.

"I'm Rachel Donovan. Your brother—"

"A Donovan!" Chet snarled, pulling up on the other side of her horse.

Suddenly Rachel and her lightweight Arabian were trapped by two beefy thirteen-hundred-pound quarter horses. Bo's eyes turned merciless. "What the hell you doin' on our property, bitch?" he growled. His hand shot out.

Giving a small cry of surprise, Rachel felt his fingers tangle in her long, thick hair. Her scalp radiated with pain as he gave her a yank, nearly unseating her from the saddle. She pulled back on the reins so her mare wouldn't leap forward.

"Oww!" she cried. "Let me go!"

Breathing savagely, Bo wrapped his fingers a little tighter in her hair. "You bossy bitch. What the hell you doin' on Cunningham property? You're not welcomed over here."

She could smell whiskey on his breath as he leaned over, his face inches from hers. Hanging at an angle, with only her legs keeping her aboard her nervous horse, Rachel tried to think. As the pain in her scalp intensified, the feral quality in Bo's eyes sent a sheet of fear through her.

"Let's get 'er down," Chet snapped. "Let's teach her a lesson she won't forget, Bo. A little rape oughta keep her in line, wouldn't ya say?"

Rachel cried out in terror. Without thinking, she raised her hand to slap Bo's away. Knocking her arm away, Bo cursed and balled his right hand into a fist.

Before she could protect herself, she saw his fist swing forward. Suddenly the side of her head exploded in stars, light and pain.

She was falling. Semiconscious, she felt the horse bolt from beneath her. Landing on her back, she hit the ground hard, and her breath was torn from her. She saw Chet leap from his horse, his face twisted into a savage grin of confidence as he approached her. She struggled to sit up but he straddled her with his long, powerful legs, slamming her back down into the red mud and snow. She felt his hands like vises on her wrists, pulling them above her head. Screaming and kicking out, she tried to buck him off her body, but he had her securely pinned. Grinning triumphantly at her, he placed his hand on the open throat of her shirt and gave a savage yank. The material ripped with a sickening sound.

"No!" Rachel shrieked. "Get off me!" She managed to get one hand free and she struck at Chet. She heard Bo laugh as the blow landed on the side of Chet's head.

"Ride 'er strong, brother. Hold on, I'll dismount and come and help you."

Panic turned to overwhelming terror. Sobbing, Rachel fought on, pummeling Chet's face repeatedly until he lifted his arms to protect himself.

At the same time, she heard Bo give a warning scream.

"Look out! A cougar! There's that cougar comin'!"

As Chet slammed Rachel down to the ground again, her head snapped back. Blood flowed from her nose and as she tried to move, she felt darkness claiming her. Chet dragged himself off her and ran for his horse, which danced nervously next to where she lay in the snow.

Bo cursed and jerked his horse around as the large cat hurtled toward them.

"Son of a bitch!" he yelled to Chet, and he made a grab for his rifle. His horse shied sideways once it caught sight of the charging cat coming directly at him.

Chet gave a cry as he remounted, his horse bucking violently beneath him as he clung to the saddle horn. The animal was wild with fear and trying to run.

Rachel rolled onto her stomach, dazed. The jaguar was charging directly down upon them. For a moment, she thought she was seeing things, but there was no way she could deny the reality of the huge cat's remarkable agility and speed, the massive power in her thick, short body as she made ground-covering strides right at them.

Snow and mud flew in sheets around the cat as she ran. Then suddenly the jaguar growled, and Rachel cried out as the sound reverberated through her entire being.

"Kill it!" Chet screeched, trying to stop his horse. He yanked savagely on one rein, causing his horse to begin to circle. *"Kill it!"* he howled again.

Bo pulled his horse to a standstill and made a grab for his rifle. But before he could clear the weapon from the scabbard, the jaguar leaped directly at him.

Rachel saw the cat's thick back legs flex as she leaped, saw the primal intent in her gold eyes rimmed in black. Everything seemed to move in slow motion. Rachel heard herself gasp and she raised her arms to protect herself from Bo's horse, which was dancing sideways next to her in order to escape the charge. Mud and snow flew everywhere, pelting Rachel as she watched the cat arch gracefully through the air directly at Bo, her huge claws bared like knives pulled from sheaths.

Bo gave a cry of surprise as the jaguar landed on the side of his horse. His mount reared and went over backward, carrying rider and cat with him. As Rachel rolled out of the way and jumped to her feet, she heard another shout. It was Jim's voice!

Staggering dazedly, Rachel looked toward where Jim was flying down the snow-covered slope at a hard gallop, his face stony with anger. The snarl of the jaguar behind her snagged Rachel's failing attention. Her knees weakened as she turned. To her horror, she saw the jaguar take one vicious swipe at the downed horse and rider. Bo cried out and the horse screamed, its legs flailing wildly as it tried to avoid another attack by the infuriated jaguar.

Within seconds, the jaguar leaped away, taking off toward the timberline at a dead run. Though Bo was on the ground his horse had managed to get to its feet and run away, back toward the ranch. Chet had gotten his horse under control finally, but his hands were shaking so badly he couldn't get his rifle out of its sheath.

Bo leaped to his feet with a curse. He glared as Jim slid his horse to a stop and dismounted. "Get that damn cougar before he gets away!" Bo shouted, pointing toward the forest where the cat had disappeared once again.

Ignoring his brother, Jim ran up to Rachel. When he saw the blood flowing down across her lips and chin, the bruise marks along her throat, her shirt torn and hanging open, rage tunneled up through him. He reached out to steady her and she sagged into his arms with a small, helpless cry. Gripping her hard, he eased her to the ground. Breathing raggedly he glanced up at

Bo, who was looking down at his left leg, where one of his leather chaps had been ripped away. The meadow looked like a battlefield. Blood was all over the place.

"Are you all right, Rachel?" Jim asked urgently, touching her head and examining her.

"Y-yes...." Rachel whispered faintly.

"What happened? Did the jaguar—"

"No," she rattled, her voice cracking. "Bo hit me. They saw me, trapped me between their horses. Your brother jerked me by my hair. When he went for my throat to haul me off my horse, I tried to shove his arm away. That's when Bo hit me." Blinking, Rachel held Jim's darkening gaze. "Chet tried to rape me. Bo was coming to help him until the jaguar charged...." Gripping his hand, she rasped, "Jim, that jaguar came out of nowhere. She protected me. I—I...they were going to rape me.... They thought I was alone. They didn't give me a chance to explain why I was on their property. Bo and Chet just attacked."

"Don't move," Jim rasped.

Rachel watched dazedly as Jim leaped to his feet. The attack of the jaguar had left her shaking. Terror still pounded through her and she didn't want Jim to leave. In four strides, he approached Bo, grabbing him by the collar of his sheepskin coat.

"What the hell do you think you were doing?" Jim snarled, yanking Bo so hard that his neck snapped back. He saw his brother's face go stormy.

"Get your hands off me!"

"Not a chance," Jim breathed savagely. Then he doubled his fist and hit Bo with every ounce of strength he had. Fury pumped through him as he felt Bo's nose crack beneath the power of his assault. His brother crumpled like a rag doll.

Chet yelled at him to stop, but kept his fractious horse at a distance. "You can't hit him!" he shrieked.

Jim hunkered over Bo, who sat up, holding his badly bleeding nose. "You stay down or next time it'll be your jaw," he warned thickly. Bo remained on the ground.

Straightening up, Jim glared at Chet. "Get the hell out of here," he ordered.

"But—"

"*Now!*" Jim thundered, his voice echoing around the small meadow. Jabbing his finger at Chet, he snarled, "You tell Father that this cat is under federal protection. The Fish and Game Department is going to come in and trap it and take it to another area. If either of you think you're going to kill that jaguar, I'll make sure it doesn't happen. You got that?"

Chet glared at him, trying to hold his dancing horse in place. "Jaguar? You're crazy! That was a cougar. We saw it with our own eyes!"

Blinking in confusion, Jim looked over at Rachel. When he saw her sitting in the snow, packing some of it against the right side of her swollen face and bleeding nose, he wanted to kill Bo for hurting her. Leaning down, he grabbed his brother by his black hair. "You sick son of a bitch," he snarled in his face. "You had no *right* to do that to Rachel—to any woman!" He saw Bo's face tighten in pain as he gripped his hair hard. "How does it feel?" Jim rasped. "Hurts, doesn't it? You ever think about that before you beat up on someone, Bo?"

"Let go of me!"

"You bastard." Jim shoved him back into the snow. "Now you lay there and don't you move!" He turned and strode back to Rachel. Leaning down, his hands on her shoulders, he met her tear-filled eyes.

"Hang on," he whispered unsteadily, "I'm calling for help."

"Just get Bob Granby. I didn't make the call yet, Jim...."

Nodding, he went over to his horse and opened one of his saddlebags. His gaze nailed Bo, who was sitting up, nursing his bloody nose and sulking. Pulling out a small first-aid kit, he went back to Rachel.

"Get my homeopathic first-aid kit," she begged. "I can stop the bleeding and the swelling with it."

He went to her horse and got the small plastic kit. Kneeling beside her, his hand still shaking with rage, he opened the kit for her. "I'm sorry," he rasped, meaning it. As she opened one of the vials and poured several white pellets into her hand, he felt a desire to kill Bo and Chet for what they'd done to her. Rachel's cheek was swollen and he knew she'd have a black eye soon. Worse, her nose looked puffy, too, and he wondered if it was broken. Setting the kits down, he waited until she put the pellets in her mouth.

"Let me see if your nose is broken," he urged as he placed one hand behind her head. It was so easy, so natural between them. The tension he'd seen in her, the wariness in her eyes fled the moment he touched her. A fierce love for her swept through him. As gently as possible, he examined her fine, thin nose.

"Good," he whispered huskily, trying to smile down at her. "I don't think it's broken."

Rachel shut her eyes. With Jim close, she felt safe. "Did you see what happened?" she quavered.

"Yeah, I saw all of it," he told her grimly. Placing a dressing against her nose, he showed her how to hold it in place. "Stay here. I want to make that call to Bob and a second one to the sheriff."

Eyes widening, Rachel looked up at the grim set of his face. "The sheriff?"

"Damn straight. Bo's going up on assault charges. He's not going to hit you and get away with it," he growled as he rose to his feet.

Rachel closed her eyes once again. Her head, cheek and nose were throbbing. Within minutes, the homeopathic remedy stopped the bleeding and took away most of the pain in her cheekbone area. As she sat there in the wet snow, she began to shiver and realized shock was setting in. Lying down, she closed her eyes and tried to concentrate on taking slow, deep breaths to ward it off. The snort and stomp of nervous horses snagged her consciousness. She heard Jim's low, taut voice on the walkie-talkie, Chet's high, nervous voice as he talked to Bo in the background.

What had happened? Chet said a cougar had charged them. Yet Rachel had seen the female jaguar. And how had Jim known she was in trouble? He'd come off that mountain at a dangerous rate of speed. It was all so crazy and confusing, she thought, feeling blackness rim her vision. She hoped the homeopathic remedy would pull her out of the shock soon. It should. All she had to do was lie quietly for a few minutes and let it help her body heal itself from the trauma.

More than anything, Rachel wanted to be home. The violence in Bo's eyes had scared her as nothing else ever had. She knew that if the jaguar had not charged him, if Jim hadn't arrived when he did, they would have raped her—simply because she was a Donovan. The thought sickened her. Jim was right—the sheriff must be called. She had no problem laying charges against Bo and Chet. If she had her way, it would be the last time Bo ever cocked his fist at a woman. The last time.

Judging from the murderous look in Jim's eyes, he was ready to beat his older brother to a pulp. Rachel had seen the savagery in Jim's face, but she knew he wasn't like his two older brothers. He'd hit Bo just enough to disable him so he couldn't hurt either of them in the meantime. Unlike his brothers, Jim had shown remarkable restraint.

A fierce love welled up through Rachel as she lay there in the cooling snow. Though she felt very cold and emotionally fragile at the moment, the heat of the sun upon her felt good. No one had ever hurt her like this in her life. The shock had gone deep within her psyche. The last thing Rachel expected was to be physically attacked. Now all she wanted to do was get Bob Granby up here with the humane trap. And then she wanted to go home—and heal. More than anything, Rachel needed Jim right now, his arms around her, making a safe place for her in a world gone suddenly mad.

CHAPTER TEN

RACHEL's head ached as she sat on the edge of the gurney in the emergency room at the Flagstaff Hospital. If it weren't for Jim's presence and soothing stability through a host of X-rays and numerous examinations by doctor and nurses who came into her cubical from time to time, her frayed nerves would be completely shot. Luckily, Jim knew everyone in the E.R., making it easier for her to tolerate the busy, hectic place.

Rachel closed her eyes and held the ice pack against her badly swollen cheek. She'd found out moments earlier that her cheekbone had sustained a hairline fracture. At least her nose wasn't broken, she thought with a slight smile. Jim's hand rarely left hers. She could tell he was trying to hide his anger and upset from her. Bob Granby from the Fish and Game Department had come out and met them on the Cunningham land about the same time a deputy sheriff, Scott Maitland, had rolled up. Chet and Bo were taken into custody and transported to the Flagstaff jail, awaiting charges.

Rachel was about to speak when the green curtains surrounding her cubical parted. She felt Jim's hand tighten slightly around hers as Deputy Scott Maitland approached the gurney. She knew Maitland was going to ask for a statement. Her head ached so badly that all she wanted to do was crawl off alone to a quiet place and just rest.

Maitland tipped his gray Stetson in her direction. "Ms. Donovan?"

Rachel sat up a little and tried to smile, but wasn't successful. "Yes?"

Apologetically, Maitland looked over at Jim and reached out to shake his hand. "Sorry about this, Jim."

"Thanks, Scott." He looked worriedly at Rachel. "She's in a lot of pain right now and some shock. Can you take her statement later?"

Maitland shook his head. He held a clipboard in his large hands. "I'm afraid not. Your father already has his attorney, Stuart Applebaum, up at the jail demanding bail information for your brothers. We can't do anything until I take your statements."

Rachel removed the ice pack and tried to focus on the very tall, broad-shouldered deputy. The Maitlands owned the third largest cattle ranch in Arizona. The spread was run by two brothers and two sisters and Scott was the second oldest, about twenty-eight years old. The history of the Maitland dynasty was a long and honorable one that Rachel, who was a history buff, knew well. For her senior thesis, she'd written up the history of cattle ranching for Arizona. She knew from her research that Cathan Maitland had come from Ireland during the Potato Famine in the mid-1800s and claimed acreage up around Flagstaff. He'd then married a woman Comanche warrior, whose raiding parties used to keep the area up in arms, as did the Apache attacks.

As Rachel looked up into Scott's clear gray eyes, she saw some of that Comanche heritage in him, from his thick, short black hair to his high cheekbones and golden skin. He had a kind face, not a stern one, so she relaxed a little, grateful for his gentle demeanor as he walked over and stood in front of her. His mouth was pulled into an apologetic line.

"Looks like you're going to be a raccoon pretty soon," he teased.

Rachel touched her right eye, which she knew was bruised and darkening. "You're right," she said huskily.

"I'll try and make this as painless and fast as possible," he told her. "I think the docs have pretty much wrapped you up and are ready to sign you out of here so you can go home and rest." His eyes sparkled. "I'll see if I can beat their discharge time for you."

"Thanks," Rachel whispered, and placed the ice pack back on her cheek very gently.

"Just tell me in your own words what happened," Maitland urged, "and I'll fill out this report."

Rachel tried to be as clear and specific as possible as she told the story. When she said that she had seen the jaguar, Scott's eyes widened.

"A jaguar?"

"Yes," Rachel murmured. She looked at Jim, who continued to hold her hand as she leaned against his strong, unyielding frame. "Jim saw it, too."

"I did, Scott. A big, beautiful female jaguar."

"I'll be damned," he said, writing it down.

"Why are you acting so surprised?" Jim inquired.

"Well, your brothers swear they were attacked by a cougar." Maitland studied Rachel. "And you're saying you saw a jaguar come running down that hill and attack Bo?"

"I'm positive it was a jaguar," Rachel said.

"Scott, let me break in here and tell you something Rachel doesn't know yet. When she left to head down to the meadow, that female jaguar just sat at the opening to her lair, cleaning off her paws after finishing her jackrabbit. And then suddenly she jumped up, leaped off that ledge and ran right by me." Jim scratched his head. "She stopped about a hundred feet away from me, growled, looked down the mountain and then back at me. As crazy as this sounds, I got the impression I had to hurry—that something was wrong." Grimly, his eyes flashing, he added, "I leaped into the saddle and rode hell-bent-for-leather down that mountain. That jaguar was right in front of me, never more than a hundred yards away. She was running full bore. So were we. When I came out of the woods, I saw my brothers had Rachel down on the ground. That was when the jaguar really sped up. She was like a blur of motion as she ran right for Bo."

"I saw the jaguar leap," Rachel told Scott in a low voice. "I heard her growl and saw her jump. I saw her slash out with her claws at Bo." She frowned. "You saw Bo's chaps, didn't you?"

"Yeah." Scott chuckled. "No way around that. That cat slashed the hell out of them and that's thick cowhide leather." He scratched his jaw in thought. "The only disagreement we've got here is that two witnesses say it was a cougar and you both say it was a jaguar."

"Does it really matter?" Rachel asked grimly.

"No, I guess it doesn't. The fact that Bo assaulted you and Chet threatened you with rape is the real point of this report."

Shivering, Rachel closed her eyes. She felt Jim place his arm around her and draw her against him more tightly. Right now she felt cold and tired, and all she wanted was rest and quiet, not this interrogation.

"Let's try and get this done as soon as possible," Jim

urged his friend. "She's getting paler by the moment and I want to get her home so she can rest."

"Sure," Maitland murmured.

RACHEL NEVER THOUGHT that being home—her new home on her family ranch—would ever feel so good. But it did. Kate and Jessica had come over as soon as Jim had driven into the homestead. They'd fussed over her like two broody hens. Kate got the fire going in the fireplace out in the living room and Jessica made her some chamomile tea to soothe her jangled nerves. Jim had gotten her two high-potency homeopathic remedies, one for her fracture and the other for her swollen cheek and black eye. She drank the tea and took the remedies. Five minutes later, she was so tired due to the healing effects of the remedies that she dropped off asleep on her bed, covered by the colorful afghan knit by her mother many years before.

Jim moved quietly down the carpeted hall to Rachel's bedroom. The door was open and Kate and Jessica had just left. He'd told them he was going to stay with Rachel for a while just to make sure she was all right. The truth was he didn't want to leave her at all. Torn between going home and facing his infuriated father and remaining with her, he stood poised at the door.

Rachel lay on her right side, her hands beneath the pillow where her dark hair lay like a halo around her head. The colorful afghan wasn't large enough to cover her fully and he was concerned about the coolness in the house. The only heat supply was from the fireplace, and it would take a while to warm the small adobe home. Moving quietly, he went to the other side of the old brass bed, pulled up a dark pink, cotton goose-down bedspread and gently eased it over her. Snugging it gently over her shoulders, he smiled down at Rachel as she slept.

Her golden skin looked washed out, almost pasty. Reaching down, he grazed her left cheek, which was soft and firm beneath his touch. Her lips were slightly parted. She looked so vulnerable. Rage flowed through him as he straightened. His right hand still throbbed and he was sure he'd probably fractured one of his fingers in the process of slugging Bo. Flexing his fingers, Jim felt satisfaction thrum through him. At least Bo was suffering just a little from hurting Rachel. If Jim had his way, his brother was going to suffer a lot more. This was one time that neither his father's lawyer nor his money would dissuade Rachel from putting both his brothers up on charges that would stick. With their past criminal record, they were looking at federal prison time.

Jim needed to get home and he knew it. Leaning over, he cupped her shoulder and placed a light kiss on her unmarred brow.

"Sleep, princess," he whispered. *I love you.* And he did. A lump formed in his throat as he left the bedroom and walked quietly down the hall. Shrugging into his sheepskin coat and settling the black Stetson on his head, he left her house. Outside, the sun was hanging low in the west, the day nearly spent. What a hell of a day it had been. As he drove his pickup down the muddy red road, Jim's thoughts revolved around his love for Rachel. He knew it was too soon to share it with her. Time was needed to cultivate a relationship with her. If he'd had any doubt about his feelings for her, he'd lost them all out there in that meadow.

Working his mouth, Jim drove down 89A toward Sedona. Just before town was the turnoff for the Bar C.

His hands tightened on the steering wheel as he wound down Oak Creek Canyon. The world-famous beauty of the tall Douglas firs, the red and white cliffs rising thousands of feet on both sides of the slash of asphalt, did not move him today as they normally did.

Would Rachel allow him to remain in her life after what had happened? Would his Cunningham blood taint her so that she retreated from him, from the love he held for her? He sighed. There would be a trial. And Jim was going to testify with Rachel against his brothers. Everything was so tenuous. So unsure. He felt fear. Fear of losing Rachel before he'd ever had her, before she could know his love for her.

Jim tried to gather his strewn emotions, knowing all hell would break lose once he stepped into the main ranch house when he got home. His father, because he was wheelchair bound, relied on one of them to drive him wherever he wanted to go. Jim was sure Frank was seething with anger and worry over Bo and Chet. But his father ought to be concerned about Rachel, and what they had done to her—and what they would have done had it not been for that jaguar attacking.

Shaking his head as he drove slowly down the dirt road toward home, Jim wondered about the discrepancy in the police report. How could Bo and Chet have seen a cougar when it was a jaguar? What the hell was going on here? No matter, the fish and game expert would see the tracks, would capture the jaguar in a special cage, and that would be proof enough. His brothers were well known for their lies. This was just one more.

"WHAT THE HELL IS GOING on?" Frank roared as Jim stepped through the door into the living room. He angrily wheeled his chair forward, his face livid.

Quietly shutting the door, Jim took off his hat and coat and hung them on hooks beside it. "Bo and Chet are up on assault charges," he said quietly as he turned and faced his father.

"Applebaum tells me Rachel Donovan is pressing charges. Is that true?"

Allowing his hands to rest tensely on his hips, Jim nodded. "Yes, and she's not going to withdraw them, either. And even if she did," he said in a level tone, holding his father's dark gaze, "I would keep my charges against them, anyway."

"How could you? Dammit!" Frank snarled, balling up his fist and striking the chair arm. "How can you do this to your own family? Blood's thicker than water, Jim. You *know* that! When there's a storm, the family goes through it together. We're supposed to help and protect one another, not—"

"Dammit, Father," he breathed savagely, "Bo hit Rachel. She's got a fractured cheekbone. Not that you care." His nostrils flared and his voice lowered to a growl. "You don't care because she's a Donovan. And you couldn't care less what happens to anyone with that last name." Punching his finger toward his father, he continued, "I happen to love her. And I don't know if she loves me. This situation isn't going to help at all. But whatever happens, I'll tell you one thing—they aren't getting away with it this time. All your money, your influence peddling and the political strings you pull aren't going to make the charges against them go away. Chet and Bo were going to rape her. Did you know that? Is that something you condone?" He straightened, fury in his voice. "Knowing you, you'd condone it because her last name was Donovan."

Stunned, Frank looked up at him. "They said nothing about rape. Applebaum said Bo threw a punch her way because she lashed out at him."

"Yeah, well, it connected, Father. Big-time." Jim pushed his fingers angrily through his short hair and moved over to the fireplace. He felt his father's glare follow him. Jim's stomach was in knots. He was breathing hard. A burning sensation in the middle of his chest told him just how much he wanted to cry with pure rage over this whole fiasco.

Frank slowly turned his wheelchair around. Scowling at Jim. "What's this you said about loving this woman?"

"Her name is Rachel Donovan, Father. And yes, I love her."

"She love you?" he asked, his voice suddenly weary and old sounding.

Jim pushed his shoulders back to release the terrible tension in them. "I don't know. It's too soon. And too damn much has happened. I'll be lucky if she doesn't tar and feather me with the same brush as Bo and Chet."

"My own son…falling in love with a Donovan…. My God, how could you do this to me, Jim? How?"

Looking into his father's eyes, Jim saw tears in them. That shook him. He'd never seen his father cry——ever. "You know," Jim rasped, "I would hope the tears I see in your eyes are for what Rachel suffered at their hands and not the fact that I love her."

Frank's mouth tightened. "Get out of here. Get out and don't ever come back. You're a turncoat, Jim. I'm ashamed of you. My youngest boy, a boy I'd hoped would someday run the Bar C with his brothers…." He shook his head. His voice cracked with raw emotion. "Just when I need you the most, you turn traitor on me.

And you're willing to sell your brothers out, too. How could you? Your own family!"

Fighting back tears, Jim held his father's accusing gaze as a lump formed in his throat. He wanted to scream at the unfairness of it all. Suddenly, he didn't care anymore. "I've spent nearly a year here, trying to straighten out things between you, me, and my brothers," he said thickly, "and it backfired on me. I got warned more times than not that I can't fix three people who'd like to stay the way they are." He headed slowly to his coat and hat. "You can't see anything because you're blinded by hate, Father. The word *Donovan* makes you like a rabid dog. Well," he said, jerking his coat off the hook, "I won't be part and parcel of what you, Bo or Chet want to do. I don't give a damn about this ranch, either, if it means others will suffer in order to claim it." He shrugged on his coat. "You're willing to do anything to get revenge for transgressions that died with Kelly."

His heart hurt in his chest and his voice wobbled dangerously as he jerked open the door. Settling his hat on his head, he rasped unevenly, "I'll be moving out. In the next week, I'll come over and pick up my stuff. I'll be seeing you in court."

"RACHEL, YOU LOOK SO SAD," Jessica said with a sigh. She touched her sister's shoulder as she headed for the store in Rachel's kitchen. "The homeopathy sure helped get rid of that shiner you had and there's hardly any swelling left on your cheek. But nothing has cheered you up yet." She smiled brightly and poured some tea for both of them. Sunlight lanced through the curtains, flooding the cheery kitchen.

Thanking Jessica for the tea, Rachel squeezed a bit of fresh lemon into it. "I'm okay…really, I am."

Jessica sat down across from her and frowned. "It's been four days now since it happened. You just mope around. Something's wrong. I can feel it around you."

The tart, sweet tea tasted good to Rachel. Gently setting the china cup down on the saucer, she stared at it and said softly, "I wonder why Jim hasn't come by?"

"Ahh," Jessica said with a burgeoning smile, "that's it, isn't it? Why, I didn't know you were sweet on him, Rachel."

Looking up at her youngest sister, Rachel whispered, "I guess what happened out there in the meadow did something to me—ripped something away so I could see or feel more…." Lamely, she opened her hands. "I know he probably thinks I think less of him because of what his two brothers did to me."

"Hmm," Jessica murmured, "I don't sense that." She laughed, pressing her hand to the front of the green plaid, flannel, long-sleeved shirt.

"Your intuition?" Rachel valued Jessica's clairvoyant abilities.

"Maybe Jim hasn't come around because he's busy. You know, with two brothers in jail, someone has to run the Bar C, and he's got a part-time job as an EMT with the Sedona Fire Department. I imagine between the two, it has kept him hopping."

"Always the idealist."

Chortling, Jessica asked, "Do you like the alternative?"

"No," Rachel admitted sadly, sipping her tea. "I think Jim's avoiding me."

"I don't."

There was a knock on the front door. Jessica grinned

and quickly stood up, her long blond braids swinging. "Are you expecting anyone?"

"No," Rachel said.

"I'll get it. You stay here."

Rachel was about to protest that she wasn't an invalid—and that Kate and Jessica were doting too much over her—when she heard a man's low, husky voice. *Jim.* Instantly, her heart began to beat hard in her chest and she nearly spilled the contents of her cup as she set it askew on the saucer.

"Look who's here!" Jessica announced breathlessly as she hurried back into the kitchen, her eyes shining with laughter.

Jim took off the baseball cap he wore when he was on EMT duty. He saw Rachel stand, her fingertips resting tentatively on the table, her cheeks flushed a dull red. Would she rebuff him? Tell him to leave? He was unsure as he held her widening eyes.

"Hi," he said with a broken smile. "I just thought I'd drop over and see how you were coming along."

Jessica patted his arm in a motherly fashion. "Believe me, you're just what the doctor ordered, Jim. Listen, I gotta go! Dan is helping me repot several of my orchid girls over in the greenhouse and he needs my guidance." She flashed them both a smile, raised her hand and was gone, like the little whirlwind she was.

When Jim heard the front door close, he met and held Rachel's assessing, forest green gaze. "I wasn't sure if I should drop over unannounced or not," he began, the cap in his right hand.

"I—I'm glad to see you," she said. "Would you like to have some tea? Jessica just made some a little while ago." The look on his face tore at her. She saw dark smudges beneath his bloodshot eyes and a strain around his mouth. He looked as if he hadn't slept well at all.

"Uh…tea sounds great," and he replied, maneuvering around to the chair and pulling it out. He placed his dark blue cap on the table and said, "I can't stay long." He patted the pager on his belt. "I'm on duty."

Nervously, Rachel went over to the kitchen cabinet and pulled out another cup and saucer. Jim was here. Here! How could she tell him how much she missed his presence in her life? Compressing her lips, she poured him some tea and placed it in front of him.

"Kate brought over some fresh doughnuts that Sam picked up from the bakery this morning. You look a little pasty. Maybe some food might help?"

Jim looked up. "That sounds good," he said. "I'll take a couple if you have them handy." He studied the woman before him. Rachel's hair was combed and hung well below her shoulders, glinting with red-gold highlights. She wore a pale yellow, long-sleeved blouse, tan slacks and dark brown loafers. In his eyes, she'd never looked more beautiful. Her black eye was gone and he saw only the slightest swelling along her right cheekbone. She almost looked as if nothing had happened. But it had.

Thanking her for the chocolate-covered doughnuts, he watched as she sat down next to him after pouring herself more hot tea. He gauged the guarded look on her features.

"How are you surviving?" he asked, munching on a doughnut. For the first time in four days, he found himself hungry. Ravenous, in fact—but even more, he was starved for her company, her voice, her presence.

"Oh, fine…fine…." Rachel waved her hands in a nervous gesture. "But you don't look too good." She avoided his eyes. "I've been worried about you, Jim. About you having to go over to your father's home and live there and take the heat from him about your brothers." She gestured toward his face. "You look like you haven't been sleeping well, either."

With a grimace, he wiped his mouth with a napkin. "A lot's changed since we last were together," he admitted slowly.

"Is your father okay?"

He heard the genuine worry in Rachel's voice. Her insight, her care of others was one of the many things he loved fiercely about her. Putting the cup aside, he laid his arms on the table and held her gaze.

"He had a stroke four days ago."

"Oh, no!" Rachel cried.

Scowling, Jim rasped, "Yeah...."

"And what's his prognosis?"

He shook his head and avoided her eyes. "The docs up in Flag say he's going to make it. His whole right side is paralyzed, though, and he can't talk anymore."

Squeezing her eyes shut, Rachel whispered, "Oh, Jim, I'm so sorry. This is awful." She opened her eyes. "Why didn't you call and tell me about it?"

Shrugging painfully, he put the doughnuts aside. "Honestly?"

"Always," she whispered, reaching out and slipping her fingers into his hand.

"I was afraid after what happened that you wouldn't want to be around me anymore...because of my brothers. You know, the Cunningham name and all...."

Rachel felt her heart break. Tears gathered in her eyes. "Oh, Jim, no! Never...not ever would I let how I feel toward you change just because of your last name." She reached out and took his other hand. "Is there any-

thing we can do to help you? Or your father?" She knew
Frank Cunningham would be an invalid now, confined
to bed unless he went through therapy. And even then,
Frank would be bound to a wheelchair for the rest of
his life. She saw tears glimmer in Jim's eyes and then
he forced them away. His hands felt strong and good
on hers.

Without a word, she released his hands, stood up and
came around the table. Moving behind him, she slid
her arms around him and pressed her uninjured cheek
against his and just held him. She felt so much tension
in him, and as she squeezed him gently, he released a
ragged sigh. His hands slid across her lower arms, and
she closed her eyes.

"I feel so awful for all of you," she whispered brokenly. "I'm sorry all this happened."

The firmness of her flesh made him need her even
more. Without a word, Jim eased out of her arms and
stood up. Putting the chair aside, he faced Rachel. Tears
ran down her cheeks. She was crying for his father, for
him and for the whole, ugly situation. Her generosity,
her compassion, shook him as nothing else ever could.

"What I need," he said unsteadily as he held out his
hand toward Rachel, "is you…just you…."

CHAPTER ELEVEN

As RACHEL pressed herself to Jim, his arms went around her like steel bands. The air rushed out of her lungs, and she felt his shaven cheek against her own. A shudder went through him as he buried his face in her thick, dark hair. Clinging to her like a man who was dying and could be saved only by her. Her heart opened and she sniffled, the tears coming more and more quickly.

"I'm sorry, so sorry," she sobbed. "I didn't mean to cause this kind of trouble…and your father—"

"Hush," Jim whispered thickly, framing her face with his hands. He was mindful of her fractured right cheekbone, and he barely touched that area of her face. He looked deeply into her dark, pain-filled eyes. Tears beaded on her dark lashes. Her mouth was a tortured line. "This isn't your fault. None of it, princess."

He winced inwardly as he realized he'd allowed his endearment for her slip out. Rachel blinked once, as if assimilating the word. She gulped, her hands caressing the back of his neck and shoulders.

"There's been so much misery between our families," she whispered unsteadily. "I was hoping…oh, how I was hoping things would settle down now that Kelly was gone."

Caressing her uninjured cheek, Jim wiped the tears away with his fingers. "We aren't going to pay the price that those two decided to pay one another, Rachel. We aren't. You and I—" he looked deeply into her eyes, his voice low and fervent "—can have a better life. A happier one if we want it. We can make better decisions than they ever have. We should learn from them, not duplicate their actions."

Closing her eyes, she felt a fine quiver go through her. "Not like Chet and Bo," she admitted painfully.

He nodded grimly. "We're nothing like those two. They have to find their own way now. Father is mute. He'll never speak again. He'll never be able to wield the power or call in the chips like he did before his stroke." Caressing her hair, Jim added wearily, "Chet and Bo will go to prison for at least a couple of years. I've talked to the district attorney for Coconino County, and he said that, based upon the evidence and our testimony and their past jail records, the judge won't be lenient. He shouldn't be."

Numbly, Rachel rested her brow against his chin. She felt the caress of his fingers through her hair and relaxed as he gently massaged her tense neck and shoulders. "It's all so stupid," she said. "They could have done so many other things with their lives—good things."

"They made their bed," Jim told her harshly, flattening his hands against her supple back, "now let them lie in it."

Surrendering to his strength, Rachel flowed against him. She heard Jim groan in utter pleasure. Breathing in his masculine scent, she reveled in his warm, tender embrace. As the moments flowed by, she closed her eyes and simply absorbed his gentle and protective nature.

Pressing a kiss to her hair, Jim finally eased Rachel away just enough to look into her languid eyes. There was a sweet, spicy fragrance to her hair and he inhaled it deeply. Rachel was life. *His* life. He saw the gold flecks in the forest-green depths of her eyes, and he fought the urge to lean down and take her delicious, parted lips. Instead, he asked wryly, "We never got to finish our conversation up on the Rim, do you realize that?"

Heat burned in Rachel's cheeks as she stood in his arms, her hands on his hard biceps. "You're right…we didn't."

"What do you think? Am I worth the risk? I know you are."

Shyly, Rachel searched his serious features. "Yesterday," she whispered, "I thought a lot about you…how long I've known you, and how I hadn't realized you had a crush on me back then."

"My crush on you," Jim told her, moving a strand of hair away from her flushed cheek, "never ended."

Swallowing hard, Rachel nodded. "I began to understand that."

"I'm scared. Are you?"

"Very," Rachel admitted in a strained voice, her fingers digging a little more firmly into his arms. "When Bo knocked me off the horse, I thought I was going to die, Jim. I could see the hatred in both your brothers' eyes and I knew…" She swallowed painfully. Her eyes misted and her voice softened. "I knew I loved you and I didn't have the courage to tell you I did. And I was sorry because I thought I'd never see you again." A sob stuck in her throat, and she felt hot tears spilling down her cheeks again.

Jim held her hard against him and gently rocked her back and forth. "It's okay, princess. I know you love me." He laughed a little shakily. "What a crazy time this is." He kissed her hair and then carefully cupped her face. "I love you, Rachel Donovan. And ten thousand stampeding horses aren't going to stop me from seeing you whenever I can."

His mouth was warm and strong as it settled against her tear-bathed lips. Rachel moaned, but it was a moan of surrender, of need of him. She tasted the sweet tartness of the lemon and sugar on his lips, the scent of juniper around him as he deepened his exploration of her. Her breath became ragged and her heart pounded. The power of his mouth, the searching heat of him surrounded her, drugged her, and she bent like a willow in his arms.

Just then, his beeper went off.

"Damn," he growled, tearing his mouth from hers. Apologetically, he eased Rachel into the nearest chair. "I'm sorry," he said, looking down at the pager. "Larry and I are on duty. It's probably an EMT call."

"The phone's in the living room," Rachel whispered, dizzy from his unexpected, tender kiss. Touching her tingling lower lip, she felt euphoria sweep through her. Just the sound of his steady, low voice as he talked on the phone, was comforting to her. He loved her. The admission was sweet, filled with promise. And filled with terror. But as she sat there remembering the taste and touch of Jim, Rachel realized her terror hadn't won. It was still there, but not as overwhelming as before. Maybe the fact that she had almost died made her realize how good life was with Jim in it.

Jim walked back into the kitchen, his brow knitted.

"I've got to go. There's been a multiple accident about a mile down 89A from here."

Rachel nodded and stood up. Her knees felt weak. Before she could speak, he slid his arm around her, drew her against him and captured her parted lips with his mouth. It was a hot, searching, almost desperate kiss. Before she could respond, he released her and rasped, "I get off tomorrow at noon. I'll bring lunch."

Then he was gone. Rachel swayed. Touching her lips gently, she felt a stab of fear—only this time she was worried over Jim and the accident scene. She remembered his promise of lunch tomorrow and the thought blanketed her, filling her with warmth. Never had she felt this way before. Her heart throbbed with a joy she'd never known. Love. She was in love with Jim Cunningham.

A little in shock over the realization, Rachel sat down before she fell down. She heard a knock at the front door, and then Kate's voice rang through the house.

"Rachel?"

"In here," she called. "Come on in."

Kate took off her cowboy hat and ran her fingers through her dark, tangled hair. She grinned as she came into the kitchen.

"I just saw Jim leaving in a hurry. He on call?"

"Yes. There's been a bad accident a mile down from our ranch on 89A. Are Dan and Sam here?"

"Yep," she said with a sigh, going over to the kitchen counter and pouring herself a cup of tea. "It's really nice," she murmured, "that you're home now. I like having an excuse to escape from vetting horses and cattle and to come over here and see you."

Smiling up at her older sister, Rachel patted the chair next to her own. "Isn't it great? Come, sit down. You're working too hard, Kate." Rachel knew her sister was up well before daybreak every day, and rarely did she and Sam hit the sack until around midnight. She didn't know how Kate did it. Perhaps she had Kelly's drive and passion for the ranch more than any of the sisters.

Flopping down on the chair, Kate sipped her tea. "Mmm, this hits the spot on a cold day." She crossed her legs. Her cowboy boots were scuffed and dusty. "Did you hear the latest? Sam and I just came in from Sedona."

"No." Rachel rolled her eyes. "I hate town gossip. You know that."

"Mmm, you'll be interested in this," Kate said. She took another gulp of the steaming tea and sat up. Tapping the table with her finger, she said, "We heard from Deputy Scott Maitland that Bo and Chet are probably going away to do federal prison time."

Rachel nodded. "Yes, Jim just told me the same thing."

"They deserve it," she growled. "If I'd been there, I'd probably have blown their heads off with my rifle, and then I'd never live outside of prison bars again."

Rachel grimaced. "Thank goodness you weren't there, then. You've seen enough of that place."

Kate made a face. "No kidding."

"Did you hear that Jim's father had a stroke? He's up at the Flag hospital recovering."

Shocked, Kate sat up. "No. What happened?"

"I'm not sure. Maybe it was the shock of Bo and Chet being in jail."

"Or you pressing charges," Kate muttered angrily.

"I'm surprised that Old Man Cunningham didn't keel over of a stroke a decade ago. He's always blowing his top over some little thing."

"Two of your sons going to prison isn't little," Rachel said softly. "The ranch, from what Jim said, is in his brothers' names."

"Is Old Man Cunningham paralyzed?"

"Yes. He's pretty bad," Rachel murmured worriedly.

"Well," Kate said, pushing several strands of hair away from her flushed cheek, "that means Jim is going to have to assume the running of the Bar C."

Surprised, Rachel bolted upright. She stared at Kate. "What?"

"Sure," she said, leaning back in the chair and sipping her tea, "someone's got to run it now that the old man can't. Chet and Bo are probably looking at five years in the pen. Maybe they'll get off in two and a half for good behavior. If Jim doesn't quit his job as an EMT and return to the ranch, it will fall apart. Who will be there to pay the bills? Give the wranglers their checks? Or manage the place?" With a shake of her head, Kate said, "Boy, what goes around comes around, doesn't it? Cunningham was trying to put us out of business and look what's happened to him." She brightened a little. "Come to think of it, that trumped-up lawsuit he's got against us will die on the vine, too." Smiling grimly, she got up and poured herself another cup of tea. "This disaster might be a blessing in disguise. If we can get his lawyer off our backs, we won't have to spend money filing—money we don't have."

Rachel nodded and watched her sister sit back down. She wondered about everything Kate had told her.

Would Jim really settle down to ranching life on his father's spread? For the first time, she saw hope for a future with Jim.

THE NOONTIME SUN STREAMED into Rachel's small but cozy kitchen as Jim sat sharing the lunch he'd promised with her. He'd stopped at a deli in town and gotten tuna sandwiches, sweet pickles and two thick slices of chocolate cake. Ever since he'd arrived, he'd been longing to take her in his arms again, to finish what they'd only started yesterday. But he could still see a slight swelling along her right cheekbone where it had been fractured. As badly as he wanted to make love to her, he would wait until she was healed. The way she carefully ate told him that moving her jaw caused her pain. Instead, he decided to tell her his news. "I quit my job at the fire department."

"To run the ranch?" Rachel asked, carefully chewing her sandwich and studying the man before her. Jim wore his dark blue uniform, leaving his baseball cap on the side of the table as he ate. He looked exhausted, and Rachel knew it was due to worrying over his father's condition. She was glad he'd come by, though—how she had looked forward to seeing him again!

"Yes," he said, sipping the hot coffee. "I talked to the hospital and they're beginning recovery therapy for my father. He's got all kinds of medical insurance, so it won't be a problem that way, thank God."

Rachel raised her brows. "It's a good thing he has insurance. We have none. Can't afford it."

"Like about one-third of all Americans," Jim agreed somberly.

"When will you bring him home?"

"In about a week, from the looks of it."

"How do you feel about running the Bar C?" she asked tentatively.

"Odd, I guess." He exchanged a warm look with her. "When I left after high school, I figured I'd never be back. When I did come home, Father told me Bo and Chet would take over the ranch after he died."

"How did you feel about that?"

"I didn't care."

"And now?"

He grinned a little. "I still don't." Reaching out, he captured her hand briefly. "I've got my priorities straight. I want a life with the woman who stole my heart when I was a teenager."

She smiled softly at the tenderness that burned in his eyes. "I still can't believe you loved me all those years, Jim. You never said a thing."

"I was a shy kid," he said with a laugh. "And I had the curse of my father's Donovan-hating on top of it. That was the best reason not to approach you."

Rachel nodded and reluctantly released his hand. "I know," she whispered sadly. Holding his gaze, she asked, "Have you ever wondered what our lives might have been like if our fathers hadn't been carrying on that stupid feud?"

"Yeah," he said fondly, finishing off his second sandwich. Being around Rachel made him famished. "We'd probably have married at eighteen, had a brood of kids and been happy as hell."

Rachel couldn't deny the possible scenario. "And now? What do you want out of life, Jim?"

Somberly, he picked up her hand as she laid her own half-eaten sandwich aside. "You. Just you, princess."

Coloring, she smiled. "That's a beautiful endearment."

"Good, because as an awkward, shy teenager, I used to fantasize that you were a princess from a foreign country—so beautiful and yet untouchable."

Her voice grew strained with tears. "What a positive way to look at it, at the situation." Rachel gently pressed the back of his hand to her left cheek. The coals of desire burned in his eyes and she ached to love Jim. He'd made it clear earlier that, because her cheekbone was fractured, they should wait, and she'd agreed. To even try and kiss him was painful. Waiting was tough, but not impossible for Rachel. She understood on a deeper level that they needed the time to reacquaint themselves with one another, without all the family fireworks and dramatics going on around them.

He eased his hand from hers. "I brought something with me that I've been saving for a long, long time." He grinned sheepishly and dug into the left pocket of his dark blue shirt. "Now," he cautioned her lightly, "you have to keep this in perspective, okay?"

Rachel smiled with him. Jim suddenly was boyish, looking years younger. His eyes sparkled mischievously as he pulled something wrapped in a tissue from his pocket. "Well, sure. What is it, Jim?"

Chuckling, he laid the lump of tissue on the table between them. "I had such a crush on you that I saved my money and I went to Mr. Foglesong's jewelry store and bought you this. I kept dreaming that someday you'd look at me, or give me a smile, and we would meet, and at the right moment, I could give you this." He gestured toward it. "Go ahead, it's yours. A few years late, but it's yours, anyway."

Jim saw Rachel's cheeks flush with pleasure as she carefully unwrapped the tissue on the table. He heard her audible gasp and saw her dark green eyes widen beautifully.

"Now, it's nothing expensive," he warned as she picked up a ring encrusted with colorful gems on a silver band. "It's base metal covered with electroplated silver. The stones are nothing more than cut glass."

Touched beyond words, Rachel gently held the ring encircled with sparkling, colorful "diamonds." "Back then, every girl wore her boyfriend's ring around her neck on a chain."

He laughed. "Yeah, going steady."

"And you were going to give this to me?" She held it up in a slash of sunlight that crossed the table where they sat. The ring sparkled like a rainbow.

"I wanted to," Jim told her ruefully. "I saved my money and bought it the first year I saw you in junior high."

The realization that Jim had kept this ring through six years of school and never once had she even said hello to him or smiled at him broke her heart. No, he was a Cunningham, and Rachel, like her sisters, had avoided anyone with that name like the plague. She felt deep sadness move through her as she slipped the ring on the fourth finger of her right hand. It fit perfectly. Tears burned in her eyes as she held out her hand for him to inspect.

"How does it look?" she quavered.

Words choked in Jim's throat as he slid his hands around hers. "Nice. But what I'm looking at is beautiful."

Sniffing, Rachel wiped the tears from her eyes with

trembling fingers. "This is so sad, Jim. You carried this ring for six years in school hoping I'd say hello to you, or at least look you in the eye. Every time I saw a Cunningham coming, I'd turn the other way and leave. I'm so sorry! I didn't know…. I really didn't know…."

"Hush, princess, it doesn't matter. You came home and so did I, and look what happened." His mouth curved into a gentle smile as he held her tear-filled eyes. "We have a chance to start over, Rachel. That's how I see it." Gripping her hand more firmly, he continued, "Life isn't exactly going to be a lot of fun this next six weeks, but after that, things should settle out a little."

"I know," she agreed. Six weeks. The trial would be coming up in a month and then Chet and Bo would get from the judge what they deserved. It would take six weeks for her fractured cheekbone to heal. And then… Her heart took off at a gallop. Then she could make love to Jim. The thought was hot, melting and full of promise. She ached to have him, love him and join with him in that beautiful oneness.

"I'm sure my brothers will be going to prison," Jim said in a low voice. "And my father is going to take up a lot of my time. I'll have to get used to running the ranch. I was thinking of asking Sam for some help and guidance. He was the manager of the Bar C for a while, and he knows the inner workings of it. He can kind of shadow me until I get into the full swing of things."

Rachel nodded. "I know Sam would do anything to help out. We all will, Jim."

"Do you know how good that is to hear?" he rasped. "No more fighting between the Donovans and the

Cunninghams. Now we'll have peace. Isn't that something?"

It was. Rachel sat there in awe over the realization. "I never thought of it in those terms before, but you're right." She gave a little laugh. "Just think, the next time your cattle stray onto our land or vice versa, no nasty phone calls. Just a call saying, 'hey, your cows are straying again.'" She laughed. "Do you know how *good* that will be?"

"The range war between us is over," he said, patting her hand and admiring the ring on her finger once again. It was a child's innocent love that had bought that present for her, but Jim felt his heart swell with pride that Rachel had put it on, nevertheless.

"There's something I want to tell you," he said. "When I left here the other day after Bo and Chet assaulted you, I went home and had it out with my father." He frowned. "It probably contributed to him having a stroke, but I can't be sorry for what I told him." He held Rachel's soft green eyes. "I told him I was in love with you."

"Oh, dear, Jim."

"He needed to hear it from me," he rasped. "He didn't like it, but that's life."

"And he accused you of being a traitor?"

"Yes," Jim replied, amazed by her insight. But then, he shouldn't be surprised. She had always been a deep and caring person. "He said I was being a traitor to the family."

"What else? I can see it in your eyes."

Ordinarily, Jim would feel uncomfortable revealing so much of himself, but with Rachel, he felt not only safe in showing those depths within him, but he wanted to. "My father disowned—for the second time."

"No...." Rachel pressed her hand against her heart as she felt and heard the pain in his voice, saw it clearly in his face and eyes. "And then he had that stroke?"

"He had one of the wranglers drive him up to the Flag jail. From what I hear from Scott Maitland, who was there when my father entered into the jail facility, he got into a hell of a fight with the sheriff of Coconino Country, Slade Cameron. That's when he had the stroke. They called 911 and he was taken right over to the hospital from there. Scott told me at the hospital, after I arrived, that my father was demanding that Cameron let my brothers go on bail. The judge had refused them bail, too, and Cameron was backing the judge's decision to the hilt."

Inwardly, Rachel shivered. She knew why the judge had not given them bail. The Cunningham brothers had a notorious history of taking revenge on people who pressed charges against them. That was why they had gotten away without punishment until now—they'd threatened their victims until they dropped the charges. But not this time. Rachel would have kept pressing charges even if they had gotten bail.

"So his anger blew a blood vessel in his brain," Jim told her quietly. "I'm surprised it hadn't happen before this, to tell you the truth."

She nodded and got up. Leaning against the counter, she studied him in the gathering warmth and silence. "How are you feeling about all this?"

Shrugging, Jim eased out of the chair and came to her side. He slid his arm around her shoulders and guided her into the living room. "Guilty. I can't help but feel that way, but I wasn't going to live a lie with my father, either. He had to know I loved you and that I was going to testify in your defense at Chet's and Bo's trial."

She moved with him to the purple-pink-and-cream-colored couch near the fireplace. Sitting down, she leaned against him, contented as never before. "And even though he's disowned you a second time, you're going to stay and run the ranch?"

Jim absorbed the feel of her slender form. How natural, how good it felt to have Rachel in his arms. Outside the picture window, he saw snowflakes twirling down again. The fire crackled pleasantly, and he'd never felt happier—or sadder. "Yes. This disowning thing is a game with my father. I know he meant it, but now it doesn't matter."

Rachel rested her head against his strong, capable shoulder. "And you really want to run the Bar C?"

"Sure." He grinned down at her. "Once a cowboy, always a cowboy."

"An EMT cowboy. And a firefighter."

"All those things," Jim agreed.

"And when Bo and Chet get out of prison, what will you do? Hand the ranch over to them to run?"

Sobering, Jim nodded. He moved his fingers languidly down her shoulder and upper arm. "Yes," he said grimly, "I will."

"He'll never be able to run it," Rachel said worriedly.

"Bo and Chet are the owners, technically. I know they aren't going to want me around when they get out."

"And your father? What will you do? Continue to live there?"

Gently, he turned Rachel around so that she faced

him. "When the time's right, I'm going to propose to you. And if you say yes, you'll live over on the Bar C with me. We have several other homes. I'll put my father in one of them and we'll live at the main ranch house. Even though he disowned me, he's going to need me now. And I'm hoping we can mend fences, at least for the sake of his health. When Bo and Chet get out, you and I will leave."

Rachel thrilled to the idea of being Jim's wife. His partner for life. All her previous fears were gone and she knew that was because she was certain of her love for Jim. Heat burned in her cheeks and she held his hopeful gaze. "Kate wants us to live here. In this house, Jim. She already told me we were welcome here in case we got 'serious' about one another."

Grinning, he caressed her hair and followed the sweep of it down her shoulder. "Kate saw us getting together?"

"Kate's not a dumb post."

Chuckling, Jim nodded. "No, I'd never accuse her of being that, ever."

Sliding her hand up his cheek, Rachel felt the sandpaper quality of his skin beneath her palm. She saw Jim's eyes go dark with longing—for her. It was such a delicious feeling to be wanted by him. "Then you wouldn't mind living here and working on the Donovan Ranch instead when the time came?"

"No," he whispered, leaning over and placing a very light kiss on the tip of her nose, "why should I? I'll have you. That's all I'll ever need, princess. Where I live with you doesn't matter at all. It never did."

Sliding into his waiting arms, Rachel closed her eyes and rested her head against Jim's shoulder. A broken sigh escaped her. The next six weeks were going to be a special hell for all of them on many levels. The trial would tear them all apart, she knew. And Jim would be away from her more than with her because he would have to be at the Bar C learning how to manage the huge ranch. And she, well, she had just rented an office in Sedona and there was a lot of pressure on her to get patients and start making money and contributing to paying off that huge debt against the ranch.

"I can hardly wait," Rachel quavered, "for these next six weeks to be done and gone."

Holding her tightly, Jim ran his hand along the line of her graceful back. Pressing a kiss to her hair, he murmured fervently, "I know, princess. Believe me, I know…"

CHAPTER TWELVE

THE MID-FEBRUARY sunlight was strong and bright as Rachel sat on her horse, her leg occasionally touching Jim's as the gelding moved to nibble the green grass shoots that surrounded them. The patches of snow here and there on the red clay soil of the Cunningham pasture was strong evidence of the fact that the steady snowfall would break some of the drought conditions that had held everyone captive.

"The cattle are going to eat well," Jim commented as he moved his hat up on his brow and gazed at Rachel. She looked beautiful in Levi's, a long-sleeved white blouse, leather vest and black Stetson cowboy hat. Her hair was caught up in a single braid that lay down the middle of her back.

Nodding, she leaned down and stroked the neck of her black Arabian mare. "For once."

They sat on their horses on a hill that overlooked both Donovan and Cunningham ranch land, a barbed wire fence marking the division line. Down below, on the Donovan side, Kate and Sam were working to repair the fence so that their cattle wouldn't wander over onto Cunningham property. At least, Jim thought, this time there was going to be teamwork between the two families, and not angry words followed by violence.

"How's your father?" Rachel asked. Jim's face took

on a pained expression. Frank Cunningham had never recovered after the stroke as the doctors had hoped. He was now bedridden, with twenty-four-hour nursing care at the ranch house. Jim divided his duties between managing the huge ranch and trying to help his father, who had given up on living. She knew it was just a matter of time. Frank hadn't been doing well since he'd found out that his two sons were going to prison. Bo got a year and Chet two years.

"Father's little better today," he said, wiping the sweat off his brow. "That's why I came out with the line crew."

"It does you good to get out of that office you've been living in."

Grinning a little, he held Rachel's dancing, lively gaze. "I was going stir-crazy in there, if you want the truth." Jim knew that ever since the trial, which had taken place two weeks earlier, Rachel had been upset and strained. For the first time, he was seeing her more relaxed. Now she had a thriving office filled with patients who wanted natural medicine, like homeopathy, instead of drugs. To say she was a little busy was an understatement. Income from her growing business was helping to pay off some bills on the Donovan Ranch.

"What's the chances of you coming over for dinner tonight?" Rachel asked, her heart beating a little harder. The ache to be with Jim, to share more time with him, never left her. The last six weeks had been a hell for them. They needed a break. She needed him. The stolen kisses, the hot, lingering touches, weren't enough for her anymore.

Frowning, Jim said, "How about a picnic tomorrow? I wanted to go back up on the Rim and explore where they captured that jaguar and took her away." Reaching over, he closed his hand over hers. "Want to come along?"

"I'll provide the lunch?" Rachel asked, thrilling at his strong, steady grip on her hand. The burning hunger in his eyes matched her own feelings. How she hungered to have a few moments alone with Jim! The demands in their lives had kept them apart and she wanted to change that.

"You bet," he murmured with a smile.

"Have you heard from Bob Granby in the Fish and Game Department about how the jaguar is getting along in her new haunt?"

Jim shifted in the saddle, the leather creaking pleasantly beneath him. "Matter of fact, I did. She's been taken over to the White Mountain area and is getting along fine there. He said two more jaguars have been spotted in the mountains north of Tucson, so they are migrating north for sure."

"I love how things in nature, if they are disturbed, will come back into harmony over time."

Reluctantly releasing Rachel's hand, Jim nodded. "I like the harmony we're establishing right now between the two ranches."

"It will last only a year," she commented sadly.

He studied her. "Not if you agree to marry me, Rachel."

Her heart thudded. She stared at Jim. "What?"

He grinned a little. "Well? Will you?"

She saw that boyish grin on his face, his eyes tender with love—for her. Lips parting, she tried to find the words to go along with her feelings.

"Is your stunned look a no or a yes?" he teased,

his grin widening. Over the last six weeks, they had grown incredibly close. Nothing had ever felt so right or so good to Jim. He prayed silently that Rachel wanted marriage as much as he did.

Touching her flaming cheeks, Rachel said, "Let me think about it? I'll give you an answer tomorrow at lunch, okay?"

Nodding, he picked up the reins from the neck of the quarter horse he rode. A part of him felt terror that she'd say no. Another part whispered that Rachel truly needed the time. But that was something he could give her. Leaning over, he curved his hand behind her neck and drew her to him.

"What we have," he told her, his face inches from hers, "is good and beautiful, princess. I'll wait as long as you want me to." He smiled a little, recalling that she had made the other man in her life wait five years and even then she couldn't marry him. Things were different this time around and Jim knew it. Over the last six weeks, he'd watched Rachel's fear dissolve more and more. The fact that he'd loved her since he was a teenager, he was sure, had something to do with it. Leaning over a little more, he crushed her lips to his and tasted sunlight, the clean, fresh air on them. It was so easy to kiss Rachel. And how wonderful it would be to love her fully. Her cheek was healed now, and he didn't have to worry about possibly hurting her when he kissed her hard and swiftly. And he knew she wanted him, too, noting her warm, hot response to his mouth skimming hers.

Easing away, Jim reluctantly released her. There was a delicious cloudiness in Rachel's eyes, and he read it as longing—for him. "I'll meet you at the north pasture at ten tomorrow morning?" he asked huskily.

Rachel felt dizzy with heat, with an aching longing for Jim. Every time he stole a kiss unexpectedly from her, she wanted him just that much more. Touching her lips, she nodded. He look so handsome and confident, sitting astride his bay gelding with that dangerous look glittering in his eyes, one corner of his mouth pulled into a slight, confident smile.

"Yes—tomorrow...."

RACHEL FOUND KATE OUT in the barn, feeding the brood-mares for the evening. She helped her older sister finish off the feeding by giving the pregnant Arabian mares a ration of oats. When they were done, Rachel sat down on a bale of hay at one end of the barn. Kate walked up, took off her hat and, wiping her brow with the back of her hand, joined her.

"Thanks for the help."

Rachel nodded. "I need to share something with you, Kate, and I wanted you to hear it from me and not sec-ondhand."

She saw Kate's face go on guard. Rachel smiled a little. "It's good news, Kate."

"Whew. Okay, what is it?" she asked, running her fingers through her hair. "I could use good news."

Wasn't that the truth? Rachel smiled tentatively. "Jim asked me to marry him today." She watched Kate's ex-pression carefully. "I've already told Jessica and Dan. Now I want to tell you and Sam. I'd like to know how you feel about the possibility." Her gut clenched a little as she waited for Kate to speak.

"Jim's a good man," Kate said finally, in a low voice.

She picked at some of the alfalfa hay between her legs where she straddled the bale. Her brows knitted as she chose her words. "I didn't like him before. But that's because his last name is Cunningham." Looking up, she smiled apologetically. "I'm the last one who should be holding a grudge. The more I saw of Jim in different circumstances, the more I realized that he was genuine. He's not like the others in his family. And he's trying to straighten things out between the two families."

"If I tell him yes," Rachel whispered, a catch in her voice, "that means I'll be living over there for a while, at least until Bo and Chet come back to claim the ranch."

"And then," Kate said, straightening and moving her shoulders a little, "you can come home and have your house back if you want."

"Then you don't mind if I tell Jim yes?"

Kate gave her a silly grin. Leaning over, she hugged Rachel tightly for a moment. "You love each other! Why should I stand in the way? Jim's a good person. He means to do right by others. He can't help it if he's got rattlesnakes for brothers."

Grinning, Rachel gripped Kate's long, callused hand. "Thanks, Kate. Your blessing means everything to me. I—I didn't want to come back here and not be welcomed."

Tears formed in Kate's eyes and she wiped them away self-consciously. "Listen, I've committed enough mistakes for the whole family. You've both forgiven me. Why can't I do the same for you and Jim? So, when's the big day?"

"I don't know—yet. Jim and I are going to ride up

on the Rim tomorrow morning where we found the jaguar's den. I'm packing a lunch."

Rising, Kate said, "Great! I'm sure you'll know a lot more when you come down." Holding her hand out to Rachel, she sighed. "Isn't it wonderful? We've all come home from various parts of the world and we're getting our ranch back on its feet. Together."

Rachel released Kate's hand and walked slowly down the aisle with her. She slipped her arm around her sister's slender waist. "Dreams do come true," she agreed. "I hated leaving here when I did. I cried so much that first year I was gone. I was so homesick for Mama, for this wonderful land…."

Sighing, Kate wrapped her arm around Rachel's waist. The gloom of the barn cast long shadows down the aisle as they slowly walked together. "All three of us were. At least we had the guts to come back and work to save our ranch."

"And we're finally coming out from under the bank's thumb!" Rachel laughed, feeling almost giddy about their good fortune. Kate and Sam had sold off half the Herefords for a good price. With the bank loan paid off, they now had a clear shot at keeping the ranch once and for all.

Kate looked down at her, smiling. "Want another piece of good news?"

"Sure? Gosh, two in a row, Katie. I don't know if I can handle it or not!"

She laughed huskily. Patting her abdomen, she said, "I'm pregnant."

Stunned, Rachel released her and turned, her mouth dropping open. "What?"

Coloring prettily, Kate kept her hand across her abdomen. "I just found out this afternoon. Doc Kalden-baugh said I was two and a half months along. Isn't that wonderful?"

"And Sam? Does he know about it?" Rachel asked, feeling thrilled. She saw the shyness in Kate's face and the joy in it, too.

"Sure, he was with me."

"Oh!" Rachel cried, throwing her arms around Kate and hugging her. "This is so wonderful! I'm gonna be an aunt!"

Kate laughed self-consciously. "Hey, I'm going to need all the help I can get. This mothering role isn't one I know a whole lot about."

Tears trickled down Rachel's cheeks. "Don't worry," she whispered, choking up, "Jessica and I will love being aunts and helping you out. I think among the three of us, we can do the job, don't you?"

Kate grinned mischievously. "You mean Jessica hasn't told you yet?"

"Told me what?"

"She's expecting, too."

Stunned, Rachel stared. "What? When did this all happen? Where was I?"

Chuckling, Kate said, "We both went to Doc Kalden-baugh today. Seems Jessica is expecting twins. They run in Dan Black's family, you know."

Rachel pressed her hands to her cheeks, dumb-founded. She saw Kate's eyes sparkle with laughter over her reaction.

"So, little sis, you and Jim had better get busy, eh? I'm assuming you want children?"

"More than anything," Rachel said, her voice soft and in awe. "You're *both* pregnant!"

"Yes," Kate gave her a satisfied smile. She turned and shut the barn doors for the night with Rachel's help. "Sam is going to hire a couple more wranglers now that we have some money. Then I can ease off on some of the work I've been doing. He wants me to take it easy." She laughed as she brought the latch down on the door. "I can't exactly see me knitting and crocheting in the house all day, can you?"

Rachel shook her head. "No, but Sam's right—you do need to ease off on some of that hard, physical labor you do on the ranch. I'm sure Jessica could use some help in her flower essence business. You like the greenhouse."

"I was thinking I would help her," Kate said. Patting Rachel on the shoulder, she said, "I'll let Jessica know I told you the big news. When you see Jim tomorrow, and say yes, tell him from me that I'm glad he's going to be a part of our family."

Rachel nodded and gripped her sister's hand for a moment. Kate's blessing made things right. "I will," she whispered. "And thanks for understanding."

"Around here," Kate said, looking up at the bright coverlet of stars in the black night above them, "everything is heart centered, Rachel. I like living out of my heart again. This ranch is our heart, our soul. I'm looking forward to having kids running around again. I'm really looking forward to seeing life and discoveries through their eyes. You know?"

Rachel did know. She lifted her hand. "Good night, Kate. That baby you're carrying will be one of the most loved children on the face of this earth." And it would be. As Rachel made her way through the darkness, broken by patches of light from the sulfur lamps placed here and there around the ranch, she smiled softly. They had suffered so much—each of them—and now life was giving them gifts in return for their courage. Her heart expanded and she longed to see Jim. Rachel could hardly wait for morning to arrive.

"ISN'T THAT WONDERFUL NEWS?" Rachel asked as she sat on the red-and-white-checkered blanket. Jim had spread the picnic blanket out at the mouth to the canyon, beneath an alligator juniper that was probably well over two hundred years old. Above them was the empty lair where the jaguar had once lived.

He munched thoughtfully on an apple. Lying on his side, his cowboy hat hung on a low tree limb, he nodded. "Twins. Wow. Jessica and Dan are going to be busy."

Chuckling, Rachel put the last of the chocolate cake and the half-empty bottle of sparkling grape juice back into the saddlebags. "No kidding."

"You like the idea of being an aunt?" Jim asked, slowly easing into a sitting position. He watched as Rachel put the items away. No matter what she did, there was always grace about her movements. Today she wore her hair loose and free, with dark strands cascading across her pale pink cowboy shirt.

"I love the idea."

He caught her hand. "What do you think about having children?"

His hand was warm and dry as she met and held his tender gaze. "I've always wanted them. And you?"

"They're a natural part of life—and love," he said slowly as he pulled a small box from his pocket. Placing the gray velvet box in the palm of her hand, he whispered, "Open it, Rachel…."

Heart pounding, she smiled tremulously. Rachel knew it was a wedding ring. She loved the idea of him asking to marry her here, in this special canyon the jaguar had come home to. In many ways, the Donovan women were like that jaguar—chased away by a man. And they, too, had finally returned home.

Her fingers trembled as she opened the tiny brass latch. Inside was a gold band. Instead of a diamond, however, there were eight channel-cut stones the same height as the surface of the ring so they wouldn't snag or catch on anything. Each stone was a different color, and as Rachel removed the ring, they sparkled wildly in the sunlight.

"This is so beautiful, Jim," she whispered. Tears stung her eyes as she held it up to him. "It's like this ring." She held up her hand, showing him the "going steady" ring he'd bought so long ago and that she'd faithfully worn since he'd gotten up the courage to give it to her.

Touched, Jim nodded. "Do you like it?"

"Like it?" Rachel stroked the new ring. "I love it…."

"I had it made by a jeweler in Sedona. He's well known for one-of-a-kind pieces. I drew him a picture of the other ring and he said he could do it. Instead of cut glass, though, each of those are gemstones. There's a small emerald, topaz, pink tourmaline, ruby, white moonstone and opal set in it."

Amazed at the simple beauty of the wedding ring, Rachel sighed. "Oh, Jim, this is beyond anything I could imagine."

Wryly, he said, "Can you imagine being my wife?"

Lifting her chin, Rachel met and held his very serious gaze. "Yes, I can."

Satisfaction soared through him. "Let's see if it fits." He took the ring and slid it onto her finger. The fit was perfect. Holding her hand, he added huskily, "You name the date, okay?"

Sniffing, she wiped the tears from her cheeks with her fingers. "My mother's birthday was March 21. I'd love to get married on that day and honor her spirit, honor what she's given the three of us. Is that too soon?"

Grinning, Jim brought her into the circle of his arms. "Too soon?" He pressed a kiss to her hair as she settled against his tall, hard frame. "I was thinking, like, tomorrow?"

Rachel laughed giddily. "Jim! You don't mean that, do you?"

He leaned down and held Rachel in his arms, taking her mouth gently. She was soft and warm and giving. As her hand slid around his neck, a hot, trembling need poured through him. He skimmed her lips with his and felt her quiver in response. She tasted of sweet cherries and chocolate from the cake she'd just eaten. Running his hands through her thick, unbound hair, he was reminded of the strength that Rachel possessed.

Drawing her onto the blanket, he met her eyes, dazed with joy and need. "I want to love you," he rasped, threading his fingers through her hair as it fell against the blanket like a dark halo. Sunlight filtering through the juniper above them dappled the ground with gold. The breeze was warm and pine scented. Everything was perfect with Rachel beside him. Nothing had ever felt so right to Jim as this moment.

"Yes…" Rachel whispered as she moved her hands to his light blue chambray shirt. She began to unsnap the pearl buttons one at a time until the shirt fell away, exposing his darkly haired chest. Closing her eyes, Rachel spread her hands out across his torso, the thick, wiry hair beneath her palms sending tingles up her limbs. There was such strength to Jim, she realized, as she continued to languidly explore his deep, well-formed body. At the same time, she felt his fingers undoing the buttons on her blouse. Each touch was featherlight, evocative and teasing. Her nipples hardened in anticipation as he moved the material aside, easing it off her shoulders. The sunlight felt warm against her exposed skin as the last of her lingerie was shed.

The first, skimming touch of his work-roughened fingers along her collarbone made her inhale sharply. Opening her eyes, she drowned in his stormy ones. They had always called him Cougar and she could see and feel his desire stalking her now. As he spread his hand outward to follow the curve of her breast, her lashes fluttered closed. Hot, wild tingling sped through her and she moaned as his fingers cupped her flesh.

Moments later, she felt his lips capture one hardened nipple and a cry of pleasure escaped her lips. Instinctively, she arched against him. His naked chest met hers. A galvanizing fire sizzled through her as he suckled her. The heat burned down her to her lower abdomen, an ache building so fiercely between her thighs that she moaned as his hand moved to release the snap on her Levi's. Never had Rachel felt so wanted and desired as now. As he lifted his head, he smiled down at her. His gaze burned through her, straight to her heart, to her soul. This was the man she wanted forever, she realized dazedly.

As he slipped out of his Levi's, after pulling hers from her legs, Rachel felt shaky with need. Her mind wasn't functioning; she was solely captive to her emotions, to the love she felt for Jim as he eased her back down on the blanket. As his strong, sun-darkened body met and flowed against hers, she released a ragged little sigh. Automatically, she pressed herself wantonly against him. His hand ranged down across her hip to her thigh. As she met his mouth, and he plundered her depths hotly, she slid her hand up and over his chest. Their breathing was hot and shallow. Their hearts pounded in fury and need.

The moment his hand slid between her thighs, silently asking her to open to him, she felt his tongue move into her mouth. Where did rapture begin and end? Rachel wasn't sure as his tongue stroked hers at the same time his fingers sought and found the moist opening to her womanhood. Sharp jolts of heat moved up through her. The cry in her throat turned to a moan of utter need. In moments, she felt him move across her, felt his knee guide her thighs open to receive all of him, and she clung to his capturing, cajoling mouth.

She throbbed with desire. She couldn't wait any longer. Thrusting her hips upward, she met him fearlessly, with equal passion. The moment he plunged into her, she gave a startled cry, but it was one of utter pleasure, not pain. His other hand settled beneath her hips and he moved rhythmically with her. The ache dissolved into hot honey within her. This warmth of the sunlight on her flesh, his mouth seeking and molding, their breath wild and chaotic, all blended into an

incredible collage of movement, sound, taste and pleasure. A white-hot explosion occurred deep within her,
and Rachel threw back her head with a cry and arched
hard against him. Through the haze of sensations she
heard him growl like the cougar he really was. His
hands were hard on her shoulders as he thrust repeatedly into her, heightening her pleasure as the volcanic
release flowed wildly through her. In those moments,
the world spun around them. There was only Jim, his
powerful embrace, his heart thundering against hers as
they clung to one another in that beautiful moment of
creation between them.

LANGUIDLY, RACHEL RELAXED in his arms in the aftermath. Barely opening her eyes, she smiled tremulously
up at him. His face glistened with perspiration; his eyes
were banked with desire and love for her alone. Stretch-
ing fully, Rachel lay against his muscular length, his
arms around her, holding her close to him.

"I love you," Jim rasped as he kissed her hair, her
temple and her flushed cheek. "I always have, sweet
woman of mine." And she was his. In every way. Never
had Jim felt more powerful, more sure of himself as a
man, as now. She was like sweet, hot honey in his arms,
her body lithe, warm and trembling. How alive Rachel
was! Not only was there such compassion in her, he was
lucky to be able to share her passion as well. Moving
several damp strands of hair from her brow, he drowned
in her forest-green eyes, which danced with gold flecks.
Her lips were parted, glistening and well kissed. She
had a mouth he wanted to kiss forever.

His words fell softly against her ears. Rachel sighed
and closed her eyes, resting her brow against his jaw.

Somewhere in the background, she heard the call of a raven far above the canyon where they lay. She felt the dappled sunlight dancing across her sated form. The breeze was like invisible hands drying and softly caressing her. More than anything, she absorbed Jim's love, the protectiveness he naturally accorded her as she lay in his arms. This was a man whose heart, whose morals and values were worth everything to her—and then some. It didn't matter that his last name was Cunningham. By them loving one another, Rachel thought dazedly, still lost in the memory of their lovemaking, a hundred-year-old feud no longer existed between their families.

Moving her hand in a weak motion across his damp chest, she smiled softly. "I love you so much, darling." She looked up into his eyes. "I'm looking forward to spending the rest of my life showing you just how much."

Tenderly, he caught and held her lips beneath his. It was a soft kiss meant to seal her words between them. He felt as if his heart would explode with happiness. Did anyone deserve to feel this happy? He thought not as he wrapped her tightly against him. Chuckling a little, he told her, "Well, maybe as of today, we'll start a new family dynasty. A blend of Cunningham and Donovan blood."

The thought of having Jim's baby made her feel fulfilled as never before. Rachel laughed a little. "You can't have a feud this way, can you?"

"No," he answered, sighing. So much worry and strain sloughed off of him in that moment as he moved his large hand across her rounded abdomen. Rachel had wide hips and he knew she'd carry a baby easily within

her. Their children. The thought brought him a sense
of serenity he'd never known before this moment.

As Jim looked down at Rachel, he cupped her cheek
and whispered, "I'll love you forever, princess. You and
as many children we bring into the world because of
the love we hold for one another."

* * * * *

MURDER AT
LAST CHANCE RANCH

Dear Reader,

I love writing about murder, love and second chances.
Some people get it right the first time. Some have to
go through their share of trouble before they get their
happy ending.

Murder at Last Chance Ranch, set in my home state of
Montana, is about finding that happy ending against
all odds.

I'm so glad this story was chosen to be part of this book.
I hope you enjoy it.

B.J. Daniels

To Parker, the man who gave me my happy ending.

CHAPTER ONE

TEDDI MACLANE reined in her horse as she spotted the old blue pickup parked in front of the ranch house. She'd warned Vance not to come around again. What was it going to take to put that man behind her?

Swinging down from the saddle, she fought the urge to charge straight up to the house and confront him. But the sun had set. It would be dark soon and she wanted to take care of her horse before she saw Vance.

She knew she was just giving herself time to calm down. The last time she'd had a run-in with him was still fresh in her mind. At least this time it wouldn't be in front of the entire town.

Cursing the man under her breath, she unsaddled her horse, imagining Vance sprawled in her rocker on the porch, his boots resting on the railing and that smirk on his face, the one that said he'd brought trouble with him. As usual. Vance Sheridan was her second worst mistake, one that she had more than lived to regret.

Her horse and tack put away, she walked toward the house, fighting to rope in her temper. She kicked a dirt clod with the toe of her boot as she rounded the corner of the house, shoving back her Western hat, ready for a fight.

Vance wasn't on the porch.

She shot a look toward his pickup; half expecting to find him slumped behind the wheel sleeping off an afternoon at the Roundup Bar.

But the pickup was empty.

She felt her anger simmer to a boil as she mounted the steps and saw that her front door was partially ajar. Vance had gone too far this time. She'd have his sorry behind thrown in jail. Or not, she thought, reminding herself who was sheriff.

No, she would take care of this herself. She'd been running this ranch by herself since her father died. She should be able to get rid of a no-good skunk like Vance Sheridan without any help. Especially since the man didn't have the sense God gave a goose. Vance hadn't even turned on a light, which meant he was probably asleep on her couch and had been for some time.

She stormed into the dark living room, fighting mad and caught a boot toe. Before she knew what was happening, she went sprawling face-first onto the wood floor.

Stunned, she sat up, suddenly aware that the floor was wet, her hands sticky with something dark. She caught a whiff of a smell she knew and felt her heart take off at a gallop. As she glanced toward the open doorway, she saw what she'd tripped over.

Crab-crawling back to the wall she struggled to her feet and fumbling, found the light switch. The overhead lights flashed on.

Vance Sheridan lay sprawled on the floor in a pool of blood. Beside him was her .45. And as she gazed down at her hands, she saw that she was now covered with his blood.

But she knew as bad as things looked, they were about to get worse as she staggered to the phone and called Sheriff Jake Rawlins—the last man on earth she wanted to see—especially with her soon-to-be ex-husband dead on her living room floor.

CHAPTER TWO

TEDDI MACLANE was sitting on the porch in the dark when Sheriff Jake Rawlins pulled into the ranch yard. The patrol car's headlights swept across the front of the ranch house illuminating her huddled form in the rocker.

He parked off to one side of Vance Sheridan's pickup, got out and, turning on his flashlight, trailed the beam across the yard and up the steps.

In the distance he heard the call of a coyote from the dense pines etched black against the midnight-blue sky. Only a sliver of moon and a few stars hovered over the ranch in the chilly silence that followed.

Teddi didn't glance up as he crossed the porch and stopped in front of her, his flashlight beam pointed at the porch floor. In the diffused light he could see that she was shivering, her hands clenched together around her knees. It wasn't until she looked up that he saw how pale she was, how scared.

It was so out of character for Teddi that his first instinct was to gather her in his arms.

For just an instant he forgot this was the woman who'd broken his heart. The memory roped in any inclination he had to comfort her. That and the fact that he was the sheriff and from what he could see, Teddi MacLane was his number-one suspect.

Their eyes locked. Something flickered in all that blue. Regret? Or was it only fear? He tried not to read anything into it. Just as he tried not to imagine how different things would have been if she hadn't run off with Vance Sheridan.

Jake had gotten over the shock. But he was still dealing with the hurt and anger. Seeing her now made him realize he needed to keep working on both.

"Took you long enough to get here," she said, going on the offensive. That was Teddi—always coming out fightin'.

Not that she had the right. If anyone should be angry here it was him—not the other way around. She'd made her choice. And lived with it—for a few months anyway.

Jake had heard that she'd kicked Vance out and filed for divorce, but that didn't mean she still hadn't loved the damned fool cowboy. Nor did it mean she hadn't killed him, Jake thought, hoping with all his heart this didn't turn out to be a crime of passion.

With Teddi, he'd never known what to expect. It was why he'd fallen in love with her. But it was probably also why he'd let her get away.

"I was on the other side of the county," he said, trying to hide his irritation as he pulled out his notebook and pen. "Why don't you tell me what happened here."

"I have no idea what happened. I came back from a horseback ride to find his pickup in my yard and him dead on my living room floor."

"You touch anything?"

She gave him a withering look and held up her

blood-encrusted hands. "I *fell* over him. Does that answer your question?"

He gave her a long hard look, then made a few notes before he asked, "You see or hear anyone leave as you were returning?"

She shook her head and he thought he saw tears. She had to know how bad this looked for her given that she'd threatened to kill Vance last week in front of a dozen witnesses—himself included.

"Anything you want to tell me before I take a look at the body?" he asked.

Her defiant gaze came up to meet his. "Why don't you just ask me straight out, Jake, if I killed him?"

"Did you?"

"*No.*"

"If Vance came out here to threaten you…" He knew he was offering her a way out while at the same time praying she didn't take it.

"It wasn't self-defense," she said irritably. "I didn't shoot him. I wanted to. But I didn't."

He nodded, not convinced. At one time, he'd thought he knew her but he was no longer sure about that. He could feel the distance between them, wide as the Montana wilderness.

"There is one thing you should know," she said and seemed to hesitate.

"Whoever shot him used my gun so there's a good chance my prints will be on the murder weapon."

Great. That explained the fear. "Where did you keep the gun?"

"Where it always is. On top of the cabinet by the door."

"Loaded?"

"Wouldn't be much good if it wasn't."

"What about Vance? Did he know where it was?"

"I'm sure he did," she said, her gaze locking with his. "I believe I took it down the day I asked Vance to leave."

"You threatened him with it?" Jake asked with a groan.

"I believe it was more like a promise."

"Anyone else know about the gun?"

"Everyone knew. Even you as I recall."

He watched her hug her knees tighter to her chest to hide the fact that she was trembling.

"Stay here," he said, then softening, he took off his jacket and laid it over her shoulders.

She stiffened at his touch, but drew the jacket around her. "Thanks."

He nodded and stepped toward the door, his boot soles echoing across the porch. The door was ajar, a sliver of light spilling out onto the worn boards.

With a gloved finger, he pushed the door all the way open. Vance Sheridan lay on his back on the floor, with what appeared to be three distinct bullet holes in his chest.

Past the body, Jake could see where Teddi had fallen and slid through the blood pool. There were tracks to the wall, a smear on the light switch plate and more blood nearby on the phone.

He carefully stepped around the body. The .45 was lying a few feet away where it had apparently been dropped. Too far away to have been a suicide. Not that

Vance would have shot himself once let alone three times.

If Teddi had killed Vance, would she have just left the gun lying on the floor next to the body? She would have been upset and anyone who watched TV knew the slugs could be traced back to the gun, so maybe she would have.

Jake turned at a sound behind him. Teddi was standing in the doorway, his coat draped over her shoulders. He should have known she wouldn't do what he'd told her to. She'd quit listening to him a long time ago.

She still looked pale but her back was steel-rod straight, that angry defiant look on her face. He was glad to see that she wasn't going to fall apart on him. But then he would have expected nothing less from her.

Behind her, the flashing lights of the coroner's van appeared on the road along with the lonely wail of the siren.

"You do realize that whoever killed him is hoping I take the fall, don't you?" she asked.

It definitely looked that way. That is, if you believed that Teddi hadn't killed her almost ex-husband, which was exactly what Jake wanted to believe.

But if someone was framing her, she'd certainly done a good job of making it easy for them after threatening to kill Vance in front of a bunch of witnesses. He kept this thought to himself though.

He didn't need to tell Teddi that she was in a world of trouble. Unless he could find a person with a better motive and opportunity than hers, she could be facing murder charges.

"Was Vance living here?" he asked.

She mugged a face at him. "Don't tell me you didn't hear that I'd thrown him out and filed for divorce."

"I'm just doing my job. I have to ask." *Yeah, you keep telling yourself that.*

"It must have made your day when you heard," she said, her voice breaking.

"I never wanted to see you unhappy."

She smiled at that, her gaze challenging. He'd had his chance to marry her, but he'd dragged his feet and this is what it had gotten him. Gotten them both.

He looked down at his notebook. "Did you invite Vance out to the ranch, maybe to discuss something?"

"There was nothing to discuss," she said. "He knew better than to come out here. I'd told him if I caught him out here, I'd shoot him."

He looked up from his notebook.

"Oh for cryin' out loud," she snapped. "It's just an expression."

"What was Vance doing here?"

"I have no idea."

"Any idea who might have wanted him dead?"

"Besides most anyone who knew him?"

He felt himself getting even more irritated with her. He'd thought it would be good for them to date other people, to make sure before their relationship went any farther. After all, they'd been dating since they were in high school. She was the one who'd decided to get married out of the blue. And to Vance Sheridan. Like it was *his* fault it hadn't worked out.

"What about the door? Was it locked?"

She gave him another impatient look. "Who do you

know in this part of Montana who locks his doors? Anyway, if someone needs something I own bad enough, I'd prefer they not break a window to get it."

"So your front door wasn't locked?" he repeated, pen poised over his notebook.

"What do you think?"

"Dang it, Teddi. Just answer the darned question."

"What's the point? You're just looking for something that will get me sent to prison. It's what I deserve, right? I was stupid enough to marry Vance."

He looked off the end of the porch to the mountains and the tall silky green pines for a moment before turning back to her. The night air was cool, the breeze stirred the loose hair at her temple. She had a smudge of dirt on one cheek and smelled of horse leather. She couldn't have looked more beautiful.

"I'm trying to find out who killed Vance but I need your help," he said. "I know you're not telling me everything."

She got that stubborn look on her face that he knew too well. "I don't know who killed him. I didn't invite him out here."

He knew she was holding something back. But getting it out of her was another matter. "When was the last time you saw him?"

"Last week. Wednesday." Her eyes were on him again. "You should recall. You were at the Roundup when I threatened to kill him."

"That's the last time you saw him?"

She nodded.

The coroner's van pulled up in the ranch yard, the whine of the siren dying away into the night.

"I'm going to need you to come down to the office and make a statement," he said. "We'll also be checking for any gunpowder residue."

"Fine. Just get him out of my house."

"You can't stay here tonight, Teddi. This is a crime scene."

"I'm not leaving the ranch and unless you plan to arrest me—"

Jake groaned. "You can stay in the bunkhouse. I'll have a deputy camp out nearby to protect the crime scene."

TEDDI MOVED DOWN THE porch as the coroner and two assistants got out of his van. Like a lot of coroners in the small towns across Montana, A. J. Hanover was also the local doctor.

He climbed the steps, tipping his hat to her, brows furrowed. She didn't doubt that word had traveled like wildfire through the county about Vance's murder. She'd bet the cowboys at the Roundup Bar and Grill were taking bets as to whether or not she killed him.

Anyone who knew Vance knew she had motive.

She stayed out of the way as the sheriff went to his patrol car for his camera. She tried not to watch what was happening inside her house, ignoring the occasional flash as photos were taken. Each time, she was reminded of the scene she'd tripped over. Vance dead. She could believe that someone would want to kill him. It was harder for her to accept her lack of reaction to his death—other than fear that Jake believed she'd killed him.

Standing in the cool darkness of the porch, she

looked up at the stars. Dozens had come out. She used to try to count them when she was a girl. A sliver of moon hung just over the mountains. The scene looked surreal as if she hadn't stood on this very spot and looked out at this landscape all her life.

But she'd never had a dead body lying in her living room before.

"Cause of death appears to be a gunshot to the heart," she heard the coroner tell the sheriff. "The gunpowder and burns on his shirt would indicate he was shot at close range."

"You think he knew his killer?" Jake asked quietly.

She didn't need to hear the answer. She'd seen enough to know how much trouble she was in—especially with Sheriff Jake Rawlins investigating the murder.

What had Vance been doing here? Waiting for her? No, he would know she'd gone for a horseback ride. She was a creature of habit and even Vance knew that much about her. Was it possible he had planned to meet someone at her house, knowing she would be gone?

Another patrol car came up the road. Two deputies she knew got out, tipped their hats to her and went inside. Jake came out but said nothing. She watched him walk down to her barn. Of course he would check out her story. The sheriff no longer trusted her.

A few minutes later, the coroner and deputies brought out the body, clad in a black bag on a stretcher. She saw Jake come back from the barn and studied his expression as he climbed the porch stairs. He'd found her horse and tack. It would still be damp from her long ride earlier. At least this, he would believe.

Unfortunately it didn't give her an alibi. She could have come back earlier than she said and killed Vance, then called the sheriff. She could even have staged falling over him. But what fool would use her own gun and leave it on the floor next to the body?

Someone smart, she thought. Someone much smarter than her.

JAKE HAD BROUGHT TEDDI back from town after getting her sworn statement and checking her clothing and skin for gunpowder residue. Small amounts had been found, but could be accounted for when she fell over the body.

Teddi hadn't said anything on the drive out to the ranch or when they'd arrived. She'd gone straight to the bunkhouse, leaving him with the deputy and the crime scene.

He couldn't do much until tomorrow, but he was too restless to go home. He turned at the sound of a vehicle coming up the ranch road way too fast. With a groan, he recognized the rig.

"Where is she?" Molly Price demanded after coming to a dust-boiling stop in the front yard.

Jake could have reminded her that this was a crime scene, but he knew he would be wasting his breath. "She's staying in the bunkhouse."

"Don't even try to stop me from seeing her," she said as she got out of her pickup.

He wouldn't dream of it. Especially since he knew Teddi needed her best friend right now.

"If you think she killed Vance you're even dumber than I thought."

Jake knew only too well what Molly thought. She wasn't one to hold back her feelings. She and Teddi had that in common. But he hadn't needed Molly to tell him what a fool he'd been to let Teddi go.

"The evidence will decide who killed Vance," he said, hating how pompous he sounded.

Molly snorted and said something under her breath he was glad he didn't catch as she headed for the bunkhouse.

TEDDI WAS RELIEVED TO open the door and find Molly on the steps.

"This stinks," Molly said and hugged her.

That pretty much covered it, Teddi thought as Molly stepped back from the hug to study her.

"You all right?"

Teddi nodded.

"I heard you found Vance."

Amazing how quickly news traveled in small-town Montana.

"He was killed with my gun," Teddi said as they stepped inside to sit down.

Molly groaned. "The one you kept by the door. Everyone knew about that gun, including Vance."

"But I'm not sure he knew it was loaded," Teddi said. "When I threatened him with it, he didn't take it very seriously."

Molly laughed. "That was Vance. Not real bright."

"I was the one who wasn't real bright marrying him. What was I thinking?"

"You were thinking it would make Jake Rawlins come to his senses."

Teddi looked at her friend. "That's the craziest thing I've ever heard."

"Isn't it though."

"I've made so many mistakes," Teddi said with a sigh.

"It's not your fault. It's that Jake Rawlins. If he was half a man—" Molly stopped abruptly as Teddi burst into laughter. "What's so funny?"

"That you're sitting here blaming Jake."

"He *let* you marry Vance."

"As if he could have stopped me." Teddi shook her head. "I'm the one who hurt Jake, not the other way around."

"Jake didn't even put up a decent fight for you," Molly declared with a snort. "I could kick his backside from here to North Dakota."

Teddi laughed again. "I'm so glad you're here. I am a little surprised though that Jake let you through."

"Like he could stop me, either."

Jake could have stopped her but he hadn't. Had he known how much she needed her best friend?

"You're still in love with him, aren't you?"

Teddi didn't answer. She didn't need to. She couldn't hide her true heart from her friend. "I hurt him."

"Jake hurt you. He's the one who should have asked you to marry him. He had his chance. He blew it."

"He wasn't ready to get married." She got up and walked to the window. The lights were on in the house, Jake's patrol car parked outside alongside the deputy's. That little voice in her head whispered the words she'd feared, words that made her chest ache so badly she could barely breathe.

Jake hadn't loved her enough. Not enough to marry her. Not enough to keep her from marrying Vance. Just plain not enough.

The thought pierced her heart like the tip of a blade.

Molly rose and joined her at the window. "Feet of clay," she muttered as Jake came out of the ranch house. "He hates himself for losing you, you know. That's what makes him so irascible."

Teddi smiled, loving her friend for trying to make her feel better. But Teddi knew Jake. His pride would never let him forgive her. She'd destroyed any chance they had. She'd done it as intentionally as whoever had shot Vance three times in the chest at close range.

CHAPTER THREE

VANCE SHERIDAN had been staying at a run-down motel on the edge of town since he and Teddi had split up.

As Jake drove out to the motel the next morning, he recalled the day he'd heard about the breakup and impending divorce. Teddi was right, as much as he hated to admit it, he'd been glad. He'd wanted her marriage to fail. He'd wanted her to realize how wrong she'd been to marry Vance. It gave him little satisfaction to know how petty and bitter he'd been. How petty and bitter he could still be.

The owner of the motel was waiting for him in front of unit number eight. "Not much to see," Carl Brainerd said as he unlocked the room.

Brainerd was right. Vance didn't have much to show for his twenty-nine years on earth let alone his six-month marriage to Teddi.

All of his belongings apparently fit into two large suitcases. Both were lying open on the floor next to his bed in the corner of the motel room.

Jake looked through both suitcases, checked the bathroom medicine cabinet for anything of interest and then dug through dirty take-out containers and empty beer cans piled on the nightstands.

He found the receipt under the cardboard of an

empty six-pack of beer. Apparently Vance had purchased a dozen red roses the morning he died.

Had Vance thought he could get Teddi back with a
dozen roses? Jake scoffed at the idea. For starters, she
would have preferred a surprise moonlight horseback
ride or an impromptu picnic by the creek. At least the
woman Jake thought he'd known would have.

He tried to remember if he'd seen any flowers at the
murder scene. But then he hadn't been looking for any.

He found another receipt in the cluttered motel room.
This one was from a jewelry store and also from the
morning of Vance Sheridan's death.

Jake started with the flower shop. Mabel Harper remembered selling Vance the dozen roses.

"He stood over there and wrote something on a card,
put it in one of the envelopes then said he'd be taking
the flowers with him. And no, I didn't see what he
wrote."

"How did he pay for the roses?" A dozen roses
weren't cheap and word around town was that Vance
was broke, it was one reason he was trying to get Teddi
to take him back.

"Credit card," Mabel said one eyebrow arching up.

"Who's name was on the card?"

"Vance Sheridan. But I suspected something was
wrong even though the card went through so I called
Teddi."

Jake knew what was coming.

"Teddi had no idea Mr. Sheridan had gotten a card
using her good credit—and had it billed to her."

"Let me guess," Jake said. "Teddi threw a fit."

Mabel nodded. "I don't blame her a bit for shooting the man."

"We don't know who shot him," Jake said with an inward groan. "The murder is still under investigation."

"Still, I think it was in her right to shoot him."

He figured Mabel wasn't alone in believing that Teddi killed Vance. As he left, he wondered if Teddi had realized right away that the marriage was a mistake but just hadn't been able to admit it.

At the jewelry store, he got the same story. Vance had bought a pair of diamond earrings, paid with the same credit card, which apparently Teddi hadn't been able to cancel yet. The clerk had called Teddi with the same results.

It angered him that Vance thought he could get Teddi back with diamond earrings. Didn't the man know that Teddi would have preferred a new Western hat or a pair of fancy boots? Obviously not.

Upon inquiry, Jake learned that Vance had left the jewelry store and gone across the street to the Roundup Bar and Grill. It wasn't surprising to hear that Vance had been drinking before he was killed.

Jake walked over to the Roundup. Several of the regulars Vance drank with were sitting at the bar.

"Were any of you here yesterday when Vance came in?"

One of the guys, Al Knox, nodded.

"Can you tell me how long he was here?"

Knox shrugged. "He had a few beers then left after the second phone call."

"Phone call?"

The men exchanged glances.

"Teddi called him. I could hear her yelling. Vance was laughing. Seems he'd used her credit card to buy a few things and she found out."

Jake could feel the evidence against Teddi piling up like a snowbank in winter.

"And the second call?"

"She called back. Couldn't hear her that time."

"How do you know the second call was from Teddi?"

Al shrugged again. "Vance said it was her when he hung up. Said she needed to see him. Planned to settle up with him. Vance was pretty happy since he was into Leroy Barrows for quite a lot of money from a poker game the night before."

Was this what Teddi had been holding back? Or was there even more incriminating evidence he was going to find?

As he drove out toward her ranch, he couldn't help but be angry with her for not telling him about the credit card and the call to Vance at the Roundup. And where were the roses and diamond earrings Vance had bought her?

Since they weren't found in Vance's truck or his motel room, Teddi must still have them. The diamond earrings would incriminate her since Vance had bought them that morning. If Teddi had the earrings, then she had seen Vance yesterday—the day he died.

It would mean she'd lied about that, he thought with a curse. And probably lied about killing Vance as well.

Teddi came out of the bunkhouse as he parked and got out of his rig. She wore jeans, boots and a pale blue Western shirt with silver snaps. Her blond hair was pulled up into a ponytail, her Western straw hat pulled low to block the sun. Or to hide her expressive blue eyes from him?

"Sheriff," she said by way of greeting.

"Mrs. Sheridan."

She bristled, just as he knew she would. "I hope we can keep this short. I have a ranch to run." Teddi had been single-handedly running the ranch since her father had died and was as independent as any woman he'd ever known.

As much as he'd loved her, he'd never felt as if she'd needed him. Another reason he hadn't married her when he'd had the chance?

"You won't have a ranch to worry about much longer if you don't start telling me the truth," he said unable to hide his anger. "Why didn't you tell me Vance used a credit card yesterday morning that was billed to you? Also that you threatened to kill him when you heard?"

"It seemed repetitious since I've threatened that so many times, don't you think?" she asked sarcastically. "Have you come out here to arrest me?"

"Why didn't you tell me that you called Vance at the bar yesterday?"

She shrugged. "I didn't think it was important."

"I have a witness who says you invited Vance out to the ranch."

"That's not true."

"You didn't call him back after the first call and say you would settle with him?"

She laughed. "What do you think?" she asked cocking her head to one side to grin at him. "Like I would have given him a dime. Over his dead body."

"That's exactly what worries me. You didn't get him out here?"

"I just told you I didn't," she snapped.

He glanced toward the house where the yellow crime scene tape was still barring the front door. "I need to know what happened to the gifts he gave you."

When she didn't answer, he shifted his gaze back to her and saw the high color in her cheeks, the shine of anger and pain in her eyes, and realized what a damned fool he was.

While he'd been taking satisfaction in the fact that he knew Teddi better than her husband, he'd completely missed it.

"He didn't give *you* the gifts." Jake swore under his breath. He wouldn't have blamed Teddi for killing Vance at that moment. "Do you have any idea who—"

"No," she said turning away. "I didn't care. I just didn't want to be footing the bill for him to romance some other woman."

Did she really not care? Jake had been a sheriff long enough to know that for a woman to shoot a man three times at close range she *cared*. She cared way too much.

To make matters worse, it appeared Vance had known his killer well enough to let the person get very close—and with a loaded gun. All the evidence pointed to a woman—and a crime of passion. All the evidence pointed to Teddi.

TEDDI HAD KNOWN JAKE would find out. Her face flamed with embarrassment as she watched him drive away. It wasn't bad enough that she'd married a penniless rodeo cowboy but she'd wed a no-account cheating one who was going to get her sent to prison for his murder.

And to think she'd actually thought marrying Vance was the safe thing to do. She'd known he could never break her heart. He could hurt her. He'd proven that. But as for heartbreak, well Vance hadn't had what it took—unlike Jake.

She grabbed her purse and keys. It was high time she did something to help herself. As it stood, her life was in Jake Rawlins's hands. The one man who she feared would love to see her go to prison.

"Who was Vance seeing?" Teddi asked a few minutes later as she slid onto a stool at the Roundup Bar.

Molly glanced up from cutting slices of lemon and grimaced. "Honey, you don't want to do this."

"No, I don't. But someone was angry enough at Vance to kill him. I'm putting my money on some woman he wronged."

Molly nodded solemnly. "I just know what I hear."

The curse of a bar owner.

Her friend seemed to brace herself as if Teddi wasn't going to like it. "Lana Morgan."

Teddi didn't think she was capable of feeling anything but numb after everything that had happened. But she was wrong. The name hit her like a punch in the stomach. Lana Morgan. "Ouch."

"You want me to go with you?"

"No," she said sliding off the bar stool. "My humiliation doesn't need an audience, but thanks for the offer."

"With the way Lana feels about you, you might want a backup," Molly said. "I can still throw a nasty left hook."

Teddi laughed, remembering how it had always been

Teddi and Molly against Lana and her group of popular girls in high school.

"It could get ugly," Molly said.

Teddi couldn't imagine things getting any uglier than they already were as she drove out to Lana's place, an old farmhouse, just down the road from her own.

She parked when she saw Lana's SUV parked out front. Bracing herself for what she knew wouldn't be pretty, she got out. She'd known Lana since grade school. They'd competed against each other for grades, rodeo prizes, scholarships and boys. One of those boys had been Jake.

Teddi hadn't taken a step away from her car when she heard a vehicle pull up and turned as a patrol car roared up. Sheriff Jake Rawlins scowled at her from behind the wheel.

"What do you think you're doing?" he demanded.

"Visiting a sick friend," she shot back. The woman had to be sick if she thought going after Vance was going to hurt Teddi.

Jake pulled off his hat and raked a hand through his thick hair. "If I was smart, I'd throw you in jail for your own protection."

"I didn't know it was against the law to visit my not-quite-ex-husband's girlfriend," she said, standing her ground.

"This is a *murder* investigation, Teddi."

"I'm more than aware of that," she snapped back.

They both turned at the sound of a door opening. "I wish someone had told me there was going to be a party," Lana said from the porch. "I would have dressed up." She wore jeans and an oversize man's shirt—one of Vance's that Teddi had bought him, Teddi noted.

"Teddi was just leaving," Jake said.

"Sorry," Teddi said, "but I need to talk to Lana. So unless you plan to arrest me…"

Lana had stepped to the edge of the porch and was watching with obvious amusement. "You two going to fight over me? This ought to be good."

"You are only hurting your case by being here, don't you know that?" Jake whispered.

"I'm not sitting back and going to prison for a crime I didn't commit, Sheriff," she hissed back. "Arrest me or leave me alone."

The radio in his patrol car squawked. He cursed under his breath and reached to answer the call. He listened for an instant before turning to Teddi. "I'll be back. Don't kill anyone while I'm gone." With that, he drove off, his tires throwing up a cloud of dust.

"You really have a way with men," Lana commented. "What do you want?"

Teddi walked over to the porch. "I came about Vance."

"What about him?" Lana asked with a smirk.

"For starters," she said as she stepped past the woman onto the porch and through the doorway into the living room, "where are the gifts he gave you?"

"Hey!" Lana hollered behind her. "Get out of my house."

Teddi sniffed the air, expecting the strong sweet fragrance of a dozen roses. She turned, frowning, to look at Lana who stood in the doorway. "You were so mad at him you didn't even *keep* the roses? You must have been *furious* enough to kill him."

"I don't know what you're—"

But Teddi didn't catch the rest of it. She pushed past, descending the porch steps and making a beeline to the trash container waiting on the curb.

"I'm calling the sheriff!" Lana yelled after her as Teddi lifted the lid.

Bloodred rose petals and broken stems were crushed into the trash. Teddi turned to look back at Lana Morgan, who stood on the porch with her cell phone in her hand and a stricken look on her face.

"Don't bother to call Jake," Teddi said as she looked up to see a familiar patrol car headed their way again. "Here he comes now."

"I TOLD YOU, I DON'T KNOW anything about any diamond earrings," Lana said irritably.

Once Jake had seen the destroyed roses, Teddi had demanded to know what Lana had done with the other gift and with just the mention of diamond earrings, it had become clear from Lana's angry reaction that she hadn't been the recipient.

Jake had insisted Teddi leave and he took the now-furious Lana inside to question her. "If Vance didn't give you the other gift and he didn't give them to Teddi…"

"I could care less what happened to them," Lana said, scowling at him.

"Apparently, he gave them to someone else. And no, I wouldn't know who that would be."

Jake thought he saw a slight change in her expression. "A name come to mind?"

Lana wet her lips. "I saw him talking to a woman one night outside the Roundup. It was too dark to see who and they were both gone when I drove back past."

She realized she'd given herself away. "I was curious, all right?"

Or she was already starting to get suspicious of Vance. And angry like she was now.

"You ask him about it?" Jake knew she had.

"He said he couldn't remember, then said it was probably Molly. He said she was giving him a hard time about Teddi."

Molly? Jake didn't like the sound of that, especially given how protective Molly was of Teddi.

"Why don't you tell me about the roses?" he said.

"What's to tell? Vance said he was going back to his wife—that Teddi was taking him back."

Jake noticed the discrepancy. Teddi was taking him back? Al Knox had said she was settling with him. "He told you this where?"

"I ran into him as he was leaving the bar."

Checking up on Vance again? Jake wondered.

"He told me Teddi had called and was taking him back."

"And the roses?" Jake asked.

"Apparently they were a consolation prize." She met his gaze. "I never did like taking second place."

Jake couldn't have missed her meaning. He'd made the mistake of taking Lana out after Teddi had married Vance. He'd known Teddi would hear about it. When he hadn't called Lana again, he'd gotten a sample of her anger.

So how mad would she have been if she'd found out that she wasn't even second, or even maybe third or fourth? And what if she'd known about the earrings? Found out that while she got roses, some other woman was getting diamonds?

Of course there was always the chance that Vance decided to give the earrings to Teddi as a peace offering, only someone killed him and took the diamond earrings before Teddi returned to the ranch house. A long shot at best.

What if Lana had followed Vance?

"You must have been pretty mad at Vance."

"If you think you can use me to get Teddi off, think again. I wouldn't have wasted a bullet on Vance. Let alone three."

"Who told you he'd been shot three times?" Jake asked.

Lana laughed. "Everyone in town knows. They also know who killed him. Teddi MacLane."

"Where were you yesterday afternoon?" he asked.

"Here. Alone."

"Did anyone see you? Anyone call who can verify that?"

She shook her head. "I didn't know I was going to need an alibi."

He recalled seeing the empty quart container of chocolate-mint ice cream in the trash as well several empty boxes of chocolates and dozens of used tissues mixed in with the demolished roses.

He had a pretty good idea of how Lana had spent her

afternoon. But had she sat here wallowing in self-pity until she was so angry she could kill Vance? Her place was only a short distance from Teddi's ranch. She could even have gone there by horseback.

"I'd like to see the clothing you were wearing yesterday," he said.

"Sorry, I threw it in the wash this morning. I didn't know you'd be interested."

Right. "I don't have to tell you not to leave town, do I?" he asked.

She rolled her eyes. "I'm not going *anywhere.*"

"Vance was seeing someone else," Teddi told Molly as they talked quietly at the end of the bar. The place was pretty quiet this afternoon. Some of the regulars were at the other end of the bar and a young couple was playing pool while a country-western song played on the jukebox.

Why did every country-western song remind her of Jake?

"I have no idea who else it might have been, seriously," Molly said. "It was no secret he was seeing Lana. But if there was someone else, he sure didn't let on, which is strange. He liked to brag to the guys."

Teddi just bet he did. Vance was as subtle as a bulldozer. So why keep this other woman a secret?

Hap Ryerson's pickup wasn't parked outside the Roundup Bar and Grill, something that surprised the sheriff as he drove on down the road to find Hap at home.

Hap Ryerson was a rancher's son who'd never done

much ranching. After his father had turned over the place to him, Hap had sold off most of the land, leased the rest and become a regular at the Roundup Bar—something that hadn't pleased Hap's wife, Sarah.

And at the Roundup, Hap was considered Vance Sheridan's closest drinking buddy.

As Jake parked and went to the door, he thought about two weeks ago when he had to come out here on a domestic disturbance call. Hap had a bad habit of getting drunk and coming home looking for trouble. Unfortunately, his wife, Sarah, would never press charges.

When Hap opened the door to Jake's knock, he didn't look any happier to see him this time than last.

"What brings you out this way, Sheriff?" Hap asked, blocking the doorway.

Jake pulled off his hat. "Mind if I come in, Hap? I'd like to ask you a few questions."

Hap was big and blond. He'd been a lady-killer in high school when he'd been a star on the football team. "About what?"

Sarah Ryerson appeared in the hallway behind Hap. She was as dark haired as Hap was blond. The two had been high school sweethearts.

"I need to talk to you about Vance Sheridan's murder," Jake said and caught Sarah's worried expression since Hap still hadn't moved. "I could come back with a warrant if you like."

"Can't imagine how I can help you but come on in," Hap said with obvious reluctance.

"Hello, Sarah," Jake said.

"Sheriff. If the two of you will excuse me, I have to

see to my baking in the kitchen." She scurried off, but not before Jake had seen the black eye she'd tried to hide under a ton of makeup.

Hap led him into the living room. Jake caught a whiff of what smelled like brownies baking in the kitchen. He would have loved to have arrested Hap on domestic abuse, but Sarah had insisted the single call was a mistake. No way would she have pressed charges. And there hadn't been another call since. Jake knew if he asked her about her eye, she would lie. He'd seen enough of these kinds of cases to know that wives often covered for their husbands; just as they covered up their injuries.

"When was the last time you saw Vance?" Jake asked, taking out his notebook and pen.

"The day he died," Hap said. "I was sitting right next to him at the bar when he got the calls. Teddi called yelling at him, then must have calmed down some because she called right back."

"You're sure it was Teddi who called the second time?"

"Vance ought to know his own wife's voice, don't you think? Why would he lie?"

Probably for the same reason Vance would cheat on Teddi. The man was a fool.

"Tell me what you heard of the phone call."

Hap shrugged. "I had to go to the john but when I came back Vance was all smiles. Said Teddi had finally come around. She was going to settle up with him and that he was going out to get what he deserved."

Pretty much what Al Knox had told Jake.

"Were you at the card game the night before?" Jake asked. "I heard Vance lost to Leroy Barrows."

Hap nodded. "Vance planned to pay Leroy when he settled with Teddi."

"Vance couldn't have expected to get much given that he and Teddi were only married six months."

Hap shrugged. "All I know is that Vance needed that money. He was into Leroy pretty deep."

Motive. Leroy had to know that he'd never see that money. Jake felt like he'd gotten his first possible break in the case.

JAKE FOUND TEDDI sitting on the bunkhouse steps, staring up at the clouds.

Without a word he sat down beside her. The afternoon was warm. A faint breeze carried the sweet earthy scent of pine down from the mountains around them.

"I was scared of marriage," he said.

She glanced over him.

"I realized what a fool I'd been the moment I heard about you and Vance, but by then…"

"It was too late," she finished for him. "I'd run off and married Vance."

"I'm sorry."

"Me too," she said quietly next to him and went back to staring up at the clouds.

He studied her. Her face was lit from the sun and an inner light that never seemed to dim. Just the sight of her filled him with so much regret he ached.

He cleared his throat. "If you're worried about going to prison for Vance's murder…"

She brushed that off with a wave of her hand. "I

know you'd never let me go to prison for a crime I didn't commit."

He chuckled at that.

She glanced over at him, her blue eyes large and liquid. "You're just not that kind of man."

What kind of man was he that he'd let this woman slip through his fingers? He could hear the crickets chirping in the nearby bushes, feel the sun warm his face, smell the rich scent of freshly cut hay.

He rose to his feet. "I'll find Vance's killer."

She smiled up at him. "I never doubted it."

He grinned, knowing that was a lie. He left her sitting there. As the sun dipped behind the mountains, an owl hooted from its roost by the barn. It was the loneliest sound he'd ever heard.

CHAPTER FOUR

JAKE GOT the call as he was heading back to town.

"Thought you'd want to know right away. Your victim had gunpowder burns on his hands."

"Which would indicate that he shot himself?"

"Or that he struggled with his killer for the gun."

Jake rubbed a hand over his face and swore under his breath. He'd been under the assumption that Vance was killed by a woman. But Vance was big and strong. It would have taken a man to wrestle the gun away from Vance and pump three shots into him.

Unfortunately, Leroy Barrows, the man Vance owed money to, was a slight man. He couldn't have put up much of a fight against Vance Sheridan.

"Which means I've been going at this all wrong," Jake said to himself as he hung up.

Vance had used a credit card billed to Teddi to buy diamond earrings. If Teddi hadn't called him and offered to settle, then Vance would know after the first phone call at the bar that she'd canceled the card.

He needed money. Was it possible he had planned to give Teddi the diamond earrings as a peace offering but realizing that wasn't going to work, wouldn't he try to turn them into cash?

It seemed like a reasonable assumption.

There wasn't a pawnshop in town, but there were

two shops in the next largest town. Jake stopped by the jewelry store to borrow a pair of earrings comparable to the ones Vance had purchased.

No luck at the first pawnshop and Jake was beginning to question his theory when the owner of the second pawn shop recognized the diamond earrings.

"They weren't pawned," the elderly owner informed him. "Sold them outright. You'd think they were blood diamonds the way she wanted to get rid of them," he said with a chuckle that told Jake the pawnshop owner had gotten a deal on them.

"*She?*"

"A pretty little thing. Long dark hair, big brown eyes. Cute as she could be. I just assumed she wanted the money so she could leave the guy who gave her the shiner," the pawnbroker said.

Jake swore under his breath. He could see where the pawnshop owner might jump to that assumption but the sheriff knew that wasn't the case.

Sarah Ryerson had gotten rid of the diamond earrings to protect her husband.

TEDDI WAS TOO RESTLESS to sit still. Earlier, she'd come home and done chores, feeling frustrated and helpless. She had no idea who else Vance might have been seeing.

But it kept her mind off thinking about Jake and what he'd said when he'd come out to see her.

Grabbing her hat, she headed for the barn. The only thing that would settle her down was a ride.

She had just started to saddle her horse when she

heard a vehicle pull into the ranch yard. Had Jake come back?

She put down the saddle and started toward the door of the barn.

But before she could reach it, the doorway filled with the dark silhouette of a man. This man was stockier, thicker at the middle. Not Jake.

She stopped, sensing something wrong.

"Hap?" Teddi said as Hap Ryerson stepped into the light.

She knew the man although she didn't think they'd spoken more than a dozen words to each other over the years. He'd been two years ahead of her in school, popular, a football star and dated the prettiest most popular girl—Sarah Collins. Sarah and Lana Morgan had been best friends.

Since then, Teddi knew that Hap had become a regular at the Roundup Bar and even more recently, he'd become Vance's best buddy.

Molly didn't have much regard for Hap and from what Teddi had heard through the grapevine, neither did anyone else in town. Pine Creek was a working community and Hap didn't work.

"Something I can help you with?" she asked trying to imagine what Hap was doing here. Something in the way he was just standing though put her on guard.

"If this is about Vance…" she said, feeling her unease grow as Hap stepped deeper into the barn.

But it wasn't until Hap moved closer and she saw the expression on his face that her fear spiked and she knew she was in terrible trouble.

HAP RYERSON'S PICKUP wasn't at the Roundup Bar. Nor was it parked in front of the house as Jake got out of his patrol car.

All the color drained from Sarah Ryerson's face as she opened the door to him. Her black eye was now turning yellow at one corner under her makeup.

"Sheriff," she said but didn't invite him in.

"We need to talk about Vance Sheridan."

Sarah Ryerson seemed to shrink before his eyes. She glanced around as if after someone might hear. "Come in."

The house was cool and dim. She dropped in a chair across from him, her head down. "You have the wrong idea."

"Why don't you straighten me out then."

"We weren't having an affair."

"But Hap thought you were."

She nodded miserably. "It's all my fault. I was flattered by the attention and Hap—" She waved a hand through the air.

And Hap was at the bar all the time, coming home drunk and mean. Jake got that part.

"Vance gave you diamond earrings."

"They were just a present. He knew I wasn't happy and he thought…" She looked up at Jake, tears in her eyes. "He was kind to me. It wasn't as if he expected anything in return."

Jake wondered if the woman was really that naive. "Hap found out?"

"He doesn't know about the earrings, I got rid of them, but he came home early from the Roundup and saw Vance driving off."

"That's when he gave you the black eye."

She touched the corner of her eye, ducking her head again. "Hap was sorry."

They always were. Until the next time. "Where is your husband now?"

"He said he was going by the Roundup to have a drink."

Jake called the Roundup Bar as soon as he reached his car. "Have you seen Hap Ryerson?" he asked when Molly answered.

"He was in earlier, throwing down drinks like there was no tomorrow. I was about to cut him off when he just up and left."

"Any idea where he went?"

"Nope, but he was upset about something. He left a full beer on the bar. That's not like Hap," Molly said.

Jake hung up and called Teddi's number. The phone rang four times before voice mail picked up. He left a message. "Call me when you get this. It's important."

Where was she? And more to the point, where was Hap?

Jake turned his patrol car toward the Last Chance Ranch, hoping to hell he was wrong.

"HAP, WHAT'S GOING ON?" Teddi asked, even though it was pretty clear. She could see the fury in his expression and smell the alcohol on him.

"This mess…" he said, slurring his words.

She backed up, banging into the stall door, her mind racing for a way out of this.

"…it's all your fault," Hap said.

Did he think she'd killed Vance?

"If you'd been the kind of wife Vance needed he would have left my Sarah alone."

Sarah? Teddi could have argued that Vance's behavior had nothing to do with her, but she could tell that wasn't what Hap wanted to hear right now.

She considered her chances of trying to get past Hap in the narrow aisle between the stalls and thought better of it.

"Sarah loves you," she said, grasping at straws. "She wasn't interested in Vance." But even as she said it, she knew the kind of charming web that Vance could weave. Any woman could find herself susceptible to Vance—at least for a while.

"If you hadn't married Vance Sheridan none of this would have happened," Hap said. "Vance would have gone back on the rodeo circuit. He would have left town."

He had no idea how much she'd wished she'd done just that. Unfortunately, Vance wouldn't have left town, though. He had nowhere to go.

"Hap, that's not true. Vance was washed up in rodeo," she said. "He'd burned too many bridges." She'd found this all out, of course, *after* she'd married him.

"It doesn't matter," Hap slurred. "Nothing matters." He grabbed a shovel from the front of the last stall where she'd been working earlier.

Her pulse jumped as he lifted the shovel and moved clumsily toward her. He had her trapped and even full of alcohol she knew he wasn't going to miss with something the size of a shovel blade.

"Hap, you don't want to do this." She stepped back as he closed the distance between them. "This is crazy."

The pitchfork she'd used earlier was stuck in a bale of hay behind her and to her right. She edged away from Hap and toward the pitchfork, hoping she could reach it before Hap got within shovel-swinging distance.

"Vance told me you were taking him back, but I knew better," Hap said as he stumbled toward her, the shovel handle clutched in his meaty fists. "I knew you. You weren't taking him back. Nor were you settling with him. Vance was lying. Lying to me. His best friend. I knew then that he was going to Sarah."

Teddi kept backing up, slowly so he wouldn't realize where she was headed. Just a little farther.

"I'd suspected it. Sarah got all sparkly-eyed around Vance. I knew that look." Meanness closed over his features like a mask. "I followed him after he left my house but he must have spotted me because he turned toward your ranch."

Vance had known she wouldn't be home because she always went for a long horseback ride when she was upset. And he had sure as the devil upset her earlier that day and he knew it since she'd called him at the bar, furious.

She stumbled into the hay bale.

Hap was still coming toward her, mumbling about Vance denying everything. She knew Vance would have tried to bluff his way out of it when confronted. He would have gone into the house, pretending he thought she was in there waiting for him.

"It was self-defense," Teddi said making Hap stop. He blinked at her as if he'd been lost in memory. "He pulled the gun down and threatened you, right?"

"I took the gun away from him. I was so angry…"
His gaze focused on her again.

Even Hap, as loaded as he was, knew that shooting
a man three times at point-blank range would be a hard
self-defense argument before a jury. Especially given
Hap's size.

"Think of Sarah," Teddi said. "Think what this will
do to her." She said the words more to herself than to
Hap. Once she grabbed the pitchfork behind her, there
would be no turning back.

"*Sarah*?" Hap let out a laugh. "She would have left
me, run off with him. *She's* the one who called Vance
that second time at the bar. I could tell by the way he
talked to her. I knew." He raised the shovel, now within
striking distance. "I thought once Vance was dead we
could go back to the way it was." He shook his head.
"You should have kept your husband at home."

As Teddi dodged to one side, she reached behind her,
grabbed the pitchfork and swung around with all her
strength. The shovel deflected her strike. A loud clatter
filled the air. Her arms chattered with the vibration.

She slipped to one side as Hap raised the shovel
again and swung.

JAKE'S HEART DROPPED WHEN he saw Hap's pickup parked
in front of Teddi's house.

He roared up into the yard, leaping out of the patrol
car and running toward the house. But he quickly found
out she wasn't inside.

As he raced back outside, he heard the scream and
tore off across the yard toward the barn.

His gun was out of the holster as he burst into the barn. "Drop it, Hap!" he yelled. "Drop it or I'll shoot."

Hap froze for just an instant, the scene branded in Jake's mind forever. Teddi caught in the corner against a stack of hay bales. Hap with a pitchfork stuck in him holding a shovel as if about to take a swing at a slow pitch.

"Drop the shovel and turn around!" Jake ordered. "Don't make me shoot you."

Hap didn't turn. The muscles in his back bunched as he swung through with the shovel. Jake aimed and fired two quick shots, both centered at heart level.

Teddi threw herself to one side as the shovel hit the wall with a clang and Hap Ryerson stumbled forward, driving the tines of the pitchfork the rest of the way through him.

Jake didn't remember covering the ground to Teddi any more than he recalled grabbing her up into his arms or her burying her face in his neck as he dropped to the floor with her, rocking her and saying all the things that he thought he'd waited too long to say.

Something had happened in that instant when he'd seen Teddi trapped at the back of the barn and Hap Ryerson standing over her with the shovel. Jake had realized how much he needed Teddi in his life, the past be damned. And he realized that Teddi needed him.

For just an instant, Jake Rawlins had seen the future *without* Teddi MacLane in his life.

"Marry me," he'd said as he carried her outside into the evening light. A few stars had popped out overhead in the vast clear deepening blue.

She had her arms around his neck, her eyes wide and shimmering. When he looked into those eyes he saw the two of them at their fiftieth anniversary surrounded by their children and grandchildren and great grandchildren. "Marry me, Teddi MacLane. I can't live another day without you."

He was afraid she'd say no. Their eyes locked for a long moment then she touched her lips to his and mouthed yes against his mouth.

The kiss was pure bliss. He hugged her to him, thanking his lucky stars that he'd been given a second chance.

* * * * *

REQUEST YOUR FREE BOOKS!

2 FREE NOVELS
FROM THE SUSPENSE COLLECTION
PLUS 2 FREE GIFTS!

YES! Please send me 2 FREE novels from the Suspense Collection and my 2 FREE gifts (gifts are worth about $10). After receiving them, if I don't wish to receive any more books, I can return the shipping statement marked "cancel." If I don't cancel, I will receive 4 brand-new novels every month and be billed just $5.99 per book in the U.S. or $6.49 per book in Canada. That's a saving of at least 25% off the cover price. It's quite a bargain! Shipping and handling is just 50¢ per book in the U.S. and 75¢ per book in Canada.* I understand that accepting the 2 free books and gifts places me under no obligation to buy anything. I can always return a shipment and cancel at any time. Even if I never buy another book, the two free books and gifts are mine to keep forever.

191/391 MDN FEME

Name _____ (PLEASE PRINT) _____

Address _____ Apt. # _____

City _____ State/Prov. _____ Zip/Postal Code _____

Signature (if under 18, a parent or guardian must sign)

Mail to the **Reader Service:**
IN U.S.A.: P.O. Box 1867, Buffalo, NY 14240-1867
IN CANADA: P.O. Box 609, Fort Erie, Ontario L2A 5X3

Not valid for current subscribers to the Suspense Collection
or the Romance/Suspense Collection.

Want to try two free books from another line?
Call 1-800-873-8635 or visit www.ReaderService.com.

* Terms and prices subject to change without notice. Prices do not include applicable taxes. Sales tax applicable in N.Y. Canadian residents will be charged applicable taxes. Offer not valid in Quebec. This offer is limited to one order per household. All orders subject to credit approval. Credit or debit balances in a customer's account(s) may be offset by any other outstanding balance owed by or to the customer. Please allow 4 to 6 weeks for delivery. Offer available while quantities last.

Your Privacy—The Reader Service is committed to protecting your privacy. Our Privacy Policy is available online at www.ReaderService.com or upon request from the Reader Service.

We make a portion of our mailing list available to reputable third parties that offer products we believe may interest you. If you prefer that we not exchange your name with third parties, or if you wish to clarify or modify your communication preferences, please visit us at www.ReaderService.com/consumerschoice or write to us at Reader Service Preference Service, P.O. Box 9062, Buffalo, NY 14269. Include your complete name and address.

SUS11